Darque Legends:
Death of Life
Book Two

Derrien Relyea

I am the Dragon, berserk indeed,
of Dragon Blood and Dragon Seed.
This is my story, so am I told,
to pass along these Legends bold.

The Return of the Dragon, the Return of the True King, and the Death of Life. Known as the Triad Prophesies, Corbyn the Fay has sought their realization throughout the ages.

The arrival of Darque the Dragon was eagerly anticipated. 'And there will be a girl child born to the Race of Man, of Dragon Blood and Dragon Seed, with flaming red hair and piercing blue eyes, who will take up the Sword and lead the Races from near extinction into a New Beginning.'

Gabriel, born and raised in obscurity, will become the most hunted man in all Kadoor. 'And through the Warriors of the Dragon Clan, the True King shall return to claim his rightful throne.'

Synahmarr, the long missing niece of the Last Dragon Matriarch, is alive! 'As a Phoenix rises from the ashes, so must the lost one rise, to avert the death of life.'

In this long awaited sequel to The Black War Begins, Darque Aalanna Grifynn is now Battle Commander of the Dragon Clan, home of the Warrior Brotherhood. At just eighteen winters, she ranks the most elite fighting force in all Kadoor. Taking her field promotion when Grifynn is forced Past the Veil afore her eyes, she and her LifeBond partner and lifemate, Gunnarr the Mighty Blue, High Prince of the Highland Dragons, lead her Warriors to victory against the Hoard in the most horrific fighting since the Last Holocaust. The Warriors are the only hope of the Resistance. With so few left, Darque must embrace her destiny or Kadoor will fall to the Evil One.

From near thirty winters past, through the Battle for the Dragon Clan and beyond, a convergence is rushing toward the mysterious Keep of St Swiftyn's. With the Sorcerer, King Shytin, and the Fates hounding their every move, can Darque rebuild the Brotherhood, find the True King, and prevent the death of life? Against incredible odds, does she have time?

Other Novels by Derrien Relyea
- Darque Legends: The Black War Begins (book one)
- Darque Legends: Death of Life (book two)

Coming Soon
- Darque Legends: Search for the Wyrdritch (book three)

In the works
- Darque Ages: The High Races Counsel (a prequel series) (working title)

You can read some of the epic poetry which inspired the Darque Legends series, online at:

http://thedragonwarrior.com

Table of Contents

Acknowledgments — *viii*

Afore The Return Of The Highlands

The True King Prophesy — 3
Double Vision — 5
The Word Sayer — 17
An Angry Child — 31
Divide and Strengthen — 41
Lost and Found — 57
Trouble on the Trip — 65
Abysmal Gorge — 71
The Ties That Bind — 113
The Dragon Lives — 123

The First Winter Of The Black War

The Black War Begins — 133
Memories of Regret — 155
The Power of a Name — 167
Goldenrod — 181

Beyond The Battle For The Dragon Clan

Telling the Tale — 189
The End of an Era — 205
Islyth in Charge — 217
The People in Retreat — 223
Trouble in Triple — 231
The Ranking of the Princes — 251
No One Left to Hear — 259
The Falcon is a Brat — 267
Priority Shift — 281
Mez Me! or, What History? — 303
Unwelcome Guests — 313
The Battle of Ice Mist Falls — 333
A New Ally — 355

A Most Unusual Duty Station 373
Recognition 383
Beware the Bastard Fay 393
Vital Information 411
A Vision Fulfilled 419
One Warrior Down 425
The First Born 435
This Could Get Ugly 441
Attack at the Keep 449
From the Bog to Darkling 457
Convergence 465

Author's Bio 469

This book is dedicated to the memory of

Roberta Jean "Bobbie" Relyea

Daughter, Mother, Grandmother, Dane, an amazing woman, a friend to many, a lifelong warrior, and the inspiration for Aalanna

(After reading the first half of *The Black War Begins*)
Mom: "Derrien, this is really good!"
Me (rather surprised and somewhat puzzled): "Thank you."
Mom: "Do you have any more? Are you working on another?"
Me: "Oh yessum! I've actually been working on several more."
Mom (with an odd look on her face that haunts me still): "Promise me you'll keep writing, get those books published. I want everyone to see what I see in you. Promise me."

Of course, I promised. And less than four months later, she was gone.

I love you, Mom. Not a day goes by that I don't think about you, wishing you were here with me. I'll keep writing. I'll keep publishing. I've got this.

Acknowledgments

This was a difficult journey for me, as so many major life changes occurred during the writing of this book. There are far too many people who are supportive of my efforts to name individually, but I send out my heartfelt thanks to you all. I would however, like to give special credit to Zemira, Pete, Uriel, my awesome artist Lisa Dixon, my brother Regan, and my niece Tirza, along with Ariel Frailich (http://ginsengpress.com), who continues to be my knight in shining armor, without whom I'd be totally lost. Sending you love and kudos and hoping you hang in there with me through the many stories I have yet to write.

Long Live Darque and the Dragon Clan!

Afore The Return Of The Highlands

The True King Prophesy

NINE WINTERS AFORE THE BATTLE FOR THE DRAGON CLAN

THE DRAGON'S DEN OF DREKINN VILLAGE

~~~~~CASTLE OF THE WARRIOR BROTHERHOOD~~~~~

"And 'twill come to pass that through the Warriors of the Dragon Clan, the True King shall return to claim his rightful throne." Staring at the plaster ceiling of their tiny bedroom, Darque repeated the prophesy for her little sister, Storrm. The younger of the Battle Commander's daughters had trouble with them earlier, and Darque had been working with her most of the evening to help her memorize their latest assignments. When their mother mysteriously disappeared soon after Storrm's birth, they became inseparable, the elder taking the mother's role, since their father's duties had him off and about most of the time. Darque would not allow her little sister to fall behind in their lessons, determined they'd advance through Training and enter the Brotherhood together.

"Darque, how by the 7th Egg do you remember all the prophesies? I can't keep up."

Exasperated, she replied curtly, "I'm only a winter your elder, and you are already seven, you can keep up. And I don't know how I remember them, I just do. And I don't know them all, just the ones given to the Clan." She furrowed her brow as she tried to think, her voice lower, her tone perplexed. "Besides, I have a feeling I'm forgetting one. A very important one."

Wrinkling her nose to emphasize her displeasure, Storrm whined, "I'm tired."

"We can sleep after you memorize this prophesy."

"Do I have to?"
~~~~~

Her voice rising with her equally rising and notorious temper, she replied, "Yes, Storrm, you have to. Now say it again."

She took a deep breath. "And it came to pass…"

Darque rebuked her quickly, "No. 'And 'twill come to pass'. Totally different meaning."

Storrm sighed and began o'er, "And 'twill, and 'twill come to pass…"

Gently urging her on, Darque cued for the next line. "That through the Warriors of the Dragon Clan…"

"That through the Warriors of the Dragon Clan… um… the True King shall… uh…"

Storrm was obviously struggling, so Darque cued her again. "The True King shall return to claim…"

"His rightful throne!" She finished triumphantly, her eyes bright, her smile wide.

Locking gazes, Darque stated, "Good. Now say it again." All business, no quarter did she give.

Storrm sighed dramatically and then started once more. "And 'twill come to pass…"

CHAPTER ONE

Double Vision

LATE SPRING/EARLY SUMMER

THIRTY WINTERS AFORE THE BATTLE FOR THE DRAGON CLAN

~~~~~WYNDSYR FOREST OUTSIDE OF KING'S GATE VILLAGE~~~~~

The Healer of the Forest stepped nimbly o'er the branches as she returned from the river to her humble cabin. They'd stayed where they'd fallen o'er the past winter as 'twas no bother, and she preferred the path covered anyway. Artemis was not overly tall nor especially short, and her muscle was lean even now at near thirty winters, still being considered a young adult. For the average lifespan of a human since the Last Holocaust was o'er a hundred winters, with most of them productive. Her clothing was draped loosely about her body, the coarsely woven fabric allowing the cool air to caress her skin. Her bare feet made not a sound; the creatures of the forest ignored her presence and continued in their cacophony of voices as she moved amongst them like a mouse rustling through the leaves.

Despite what some thought, she was meticulous in her hygiene and smelled like fresh mountain clover. When the sun rose fully, one would see her thick multi-colored hair, which would have hung gracefully but for the hacked lengths. 'Twas an odd mix of short stiffened clumps going in all different directions along with erratic braided strands, some falling past her shoulders. From a distance 'twould appear as if she were the mythical Medusa herself, with the beads and various bits of feathers and shells braided in here and there. Her skin was painted with tribal patterns beneath the customary clothing of the ones who came to her, so as not to frighten them unduly. But she would only compromise so far, and her hair was not as outlandish as 'twould have been at home with the Daggogh.
~~~~~

She stopped briefly when she caught sight of a loose feather atop one of the branches, setting down the bucket of fresh water. Reaching for the brilliant red treasure with one hand and fingering her hair with the other, she sighed. Mayhap she'd take it with her but not braid it in now, for she was in a hurry. Besides, the dark liner surrounding her lashes, the deep purples and blues upon her lids, along with the swirling patterns painted upon her temples, cheeks, and down her chin, gave the impression she needed to maintain when the villagers came seeking her special knowledge and skills, needing not this new adornment. They feared the 'Painted One' and that not only kept their respect, it helped her maintain her privacy. No one knew of her people, so they had no reference for her appearance. Still, although they might view some paint, some patterns, some hair adornments, she was not willing to allow them to see the intricate tattoos upon her upper thighs, arms, and trunk, for these bespoke ancestral secrets as well as her tribal position and hunting prowess. These she kept carefully hidden.

Tucking the feather into her bodice, she retrieved the bucket and returned to the cabin. She filled the small bowl upon the table and peered down at the moaning girl on the bed. Gently mopping her sweat streaked face, dipping the rag into the bowl, wringing it, and laying it back again upon her fevered brow, she recognized the girl was no longer aware of her surroundings and had little fight left. Artemis loosed the leather ties wrapped around her wrists and tightly secured to the bed posts, which she'd used to hold onto through the worst of the contractions. Surprised at the strength of the girl's clenched teeth upon the leather strip, she tugged carefully to remove it, and then cradled her into an upright position to take a sip of water. But she'd lost consciousness again and Artemis laid her back down. Her skills had certainly been tested with this one.

The young woman's screams had filled the prior afternoon, weakening with time. Low moans of pain and fatigue carried on throughout the long night. Artemis was a gifted Healer from a long line of Healers. She'd known 'twould be a difficult birthing and one that had to be carefully witnessed and registered. But there was no witness now. He'd left afore the previous dawn to give report to the King. If the girl lived, she'd be lucky. Or mayhap not, since this birth would most likely render her unable to ever have another child. She'd already lost much of her Life Source and Artemis was concerned for the babes without their mother. Twins were not easy to carry and birth in the best of circumstances, but the Healer was the one who always saw the worst. 'Twas just the beginning of this battle. Caring for any infant without the birth mother's milk was complicated. Artemis had a feeling there was some kind of link 'tween mother and babe, but she couldn't prove that. She only knew what she experienced, that frequently babes raised on another's milk had early health issues and sometimes lifelong problems. Midwives lost more newborns under a wet nurse than they did when their birth mother suckled them herself, but Artemis was no ordinary midwife. She had yet to lose any child she'd birthed alive. She was determined not to lose this one.

Her rock and log cabin sat in the deep of Wyndsyr Forest far outside of King's Gate Village and was visited by those of wealth and power seeking her midwifery, as well as certain other 'specialized services'. Artemis had more than she could, or would, ever use in the way of jewels, coin, and bartered items. No one came for her knowledge without expecting to pay well. She smiled. She was paid very well indeed by those who could afford to do so, but she also bartered intangibles such as knowledge, which to her way of life meant far more than gems and precious metals.

When the girl was brought to her by the King's bodyguard, she'd still been unconscious. In the beginning 'twas good, for not knowing her whereabouts upon waking or seeing how she'd gotten here, she'd been too fearful and depressed to attempt to run away. Afore long she was too ill to try, for unbeknownst even to the Healer initially, by giving her twins the Fates bespoke she would never leave.

King Bryard had actually been courting this girl all but openly, and she'd been a virgin when he took her. She was pretty enough, and one could say a lot of good things about the handsome and usually kind ruler, but 'twas also truth he was as randy as the Warriors of the Dragon Clan. Even so, his demeanor had been of growing desperation these last few winters, while the stunningly beautiful Queen Koryl had continued to be all but barren. She'd only become pregnant a handful of times since they'd shared vows, and she'd miscarried every one. Artemis knew how that had occurred, but 'twas part of her trade to keep silent. 'Twas also part of what kept her alive. The Queen's hand maiden, who happened to be the mate of her own tribe kin, Larken the Court Jongleur, had visited her cabin many times, since the Queen was a woman who enjoyed her freedoms and lavish lifestyle as well as having a near insatiable appetite for sex. Even though she wouldn't have to suffer a babe at her own breast, she would have to suffer the pregnancy, and 'twould ruin her tiny waistline. But despite the fact there had to be some bastard kin to the King out there already, Bryard had become desperate to have an official successor, and his royal consort soon saw the writing on the walls. There ensued a race to the finish, with the prize as heir apparent.

'Twas a shock to all when the girl conceived with the first sexual encounter of her life, but 'twas not the worst of it. Not a moon after, the Queen also conceived, and once confirmed, she'd swept the castle clean of his concubines. She was especially eager to rid herself of this one. With this girl sharing Bryard's affections as well as his bed, the child she carried would be the only one left to challenge her own child's succession. If she had a son, she wanted him to take the crown. The only way to do that, was to eliminate the competition. And eliminate she did. All mysteriously Passed the Veil with the exception of this one, although she thought she'd succeeded in that endeavor as well. Exchanging the powder the Queen used on the others (her knowledge of the Black Arts growing) for that which he'd obtained from Artemis, and allowing his Queen to believe the girl was as lifeless as he'd found those who hadn't taken flight earlier, the King risked much to save his pregnant mistress. Arranging to have her delivered to the Painted One, King Bryard made specific orders for the witness to observe the entire pregnancy, including the actual delivery, and report back to him on every detail. The first son birthed would take his crown, no matter the matriarch. 'Twas his ruling. Of course, the Healer had kept secrets afore and she had no difficulty with keeping undisclosed the future twins. Especially since she'd had a vague premonition growing stronger as the pregnancy advanced.

Immediately after seeing the live birth and receiving the official documents, the witness rode out to make his report. The girl was able to take a half day's respite afore the contractions began again, this time with a vengeance. The second babe would show by this sun's rise or she'd have to take it. Despite all her skill and experience, she'd been unable to turn the baby to allow a natural birth, and time had not helped. All her midwives' tricks had failed. As the early morning radiance began to stream through the small window, 'twas more than obvious the girl was losing the fight. The Healer finally had to choose. The girl or the babe? 'Twould have been a more difficult decision if not for the sire of this little one. Sighing, she knew the girl had not the strength left to hold onto this side of the Veil any longer, and 'twould be a mercy. She hadn't wanted to induce her demise for she'd not harm the babe, but she'd finally fallen comatose and didn't awaken even when the cold steel of the blade slit her belly, opening her womb to allow the breached boy his freedom at last.

"Your mother wanted you named Mikkal, if another son. You're a strapping big boy, and Mikkal 'tis," she said resolutely above his agitated cries. The girl's screams from marks past were now just a memory, the last of her depleted Life Source soaking into the rumpled bedding. Deftly, Artemis cut the cord and tied it off. Then bundling the newborn in a sheet, she laid him at his mother's swollen breast. No sense in wasting what the first one had suckled into existence. With a babe propped on each side of the lifeless girl, for a time all that could be heard was their hungry mewling. The Healer sat down and closed her weary eyes for a bit, taking advantage of the reprieve. There'd be much to do once the milk was gone; her true labors were just beginning. The King would arrive by next day she'd wager. And according to Matana, the Queen's delivery would be premature, surely due to her ingestion of a particular concoction used for that purpose. She smirked as she considered the agony that mixture would produce. And although the end result would be assured delivery without harm, she'd made certain 'twould have a delayed and prolonged affect. Koryl's child birthing would still follow after Gabriel had entered this world. She shouldn't have to be able to prove that birth order, either. The guard never left her cabin from the moment he'd transported the pregnant girl, to the moment the baby had been placed into his leather gloved hands, for just this purpose. Witness to the King, his Crown Prince was born. But if things didn't go well at the castle, these babes would have to go into hiding. Artemis had no delusions when it came to the character of the Queen, for she knew her true roots. 'Twas why she'd never told either the guard or the girl that she expected twins and the girl, having had no prior experience, knew not to suspect. 'Twas only after the first had arrived and the guard left on his duty that she'd enlightened the panic-stricken young woman, another had yet to be birthed.

She looked about the cabin. Waiting for Larken to arrive from the castle with confirmation of Koryl's delivery, she speculated about the many possible results stemming from the events of this day. The best would be to have the twins raised at Evanntyr, or even fostered to a caring and most likely needy family, to be provided with a decent education while learning the ways of life, including farming, fighting, hard work, estate management, and how to rule. But 'twould be a miniscule possibility that scenario would occur. Thinking o'er the worst, 'tween the two boys 'twas Gabriel who would be hounded, who would have to prove his worth, who would have to fight for his crown. Koryl was evil and had already proven she'd kill for her own son to take the throne. She'd have no qualms with pushing one tiny infant Past the Veil.

Artemis understood all too well what she had to do. She wasn't able to protect the First Born, as any child living with her now would be suspect and therefore in danger. She needed to divert attention while spiriting him to a safe place to live and grow. Mikkal of course, would provide that diversion but she felt certain that given her plan, his life would be protected for the next few winters at least.

'Twould ultimately require her witness to secure Gabriel's succession, for the Queen probably hadn't hesitated to kill the guard who even now should have made his report. To take the throne Gabriel had to live, first and foremost. Raised in secret, ignorant of his twin, his true identity concealed even to himself, he'd become the most hunted man in the known world if evidence of his birthright should leak, and there could be no succession for a dead man. 'Twas why she'd devised the plan in which her tribe kin had participated. And thankfully, the deception of Matana's pregnancy had gone undetected. Larken and his wife were masters of disguise as well as accomplished actors, and 'twas simply a matter of making Matana appear to go through an uncomplicated pregnancy. Artemis would do anything to protect the twins.

Hoping for the best, but preparing for the worst, she hurriedly cleaned the little cabin, waiting for her friend to return with news.

~~~~~~~~~~
~~~~~~~~~~

Larken arrived shortly thereafter, his skin tanned by the sun instead of stained by paint. He was tall with well toned muscle, but wasn't a brawny man. Still, if one were aware of his skills, one would walk a wide berth. Although Larken now appeared as any other inhabitant of King's Gate, blending in with ease, it hadn't always been so. He'd allowed his hair to grow long, keeping it pulled back with a leather strip in a single tail instead of his customary adornments and choppy cut, and he was envious of Artemis. But this was the way of the men of the village and he was required to hide his true origins, as well as his friendship with the Healer, in order to fade into obscurity, even while his position of Jongleur had him in the forefront of the castle residents. Given his expertise at disguise, he could be anywhere at any time. But the fading of the stains, the lack of the colorful and mesmerizing swirls and patterns that once covered his entire body, made him and his mate feel next to naked. However, they'd learned to ignore this sensation during the long winters ensconced within the castle 'for the greater good of their people'. With Artemis they had a mission to fulfill, reporting on the activities of this foreign tribe. For long ago the Daggogh had been warned by the one now known as Grifynn, the Battle Commander of the Dragon Clan, that one day their very existence would be threatened. The Evil One would return and they needed to be prepared. There was a time when this man lived at Evanntyr with his sister, a great Healer in her own right, and the teacher of the original Healers of the Daggogh. But that was long afore Larken's birth, their names changed multiple times. However, their teachings and warnings were never forgotten, and since that time the Healer of the Forest had always been one of the Daggogh, maintaining a presence the villagers could not detect was handed down from Healer to Healer, giving them the illusion of extreme longevity, and heightened the others' respect through fear of the possibility of Magical reprisal.

<center>~~~~~~~~~~</center>

"'Tis the worst case scenario, Artemis. The Queen has done what you feared. The guard was imprisoned in the dungeons soon after returning and the First Born was secretly declared a usurper, for which penalty is death. She yet suffers in labor, though should be very soon if not by the time I return, and if son she has, he will be declared the Crown Prince. Nevertheless, she still seeks the execution of the First Born." The nondescript young man looked at her sadly. "Your life is in as much danger now, as are the babes'," he concluded.

"True, I knew 'twould be thus, although I'd hoped not. I've known of these events for many winters and although the road ahead is rocky, I See it has some length. My own demise is hazy but not eminent, and therefore neither will the babes Pass too soon. But we must hurry and we must be clever," she reminded her friend.

Dismayed, Larken asked, "Then you do intend to use the one to shield the other?"

"To protect the First Born, yes," Artemis replied, without hesitation or remorse.

Somewhat shocked, he responded, "You will not kill him?"

Artemis made a rude noise clearly indicating her rejection of that notion, while flipping one hand o'er her shoulder. "No, I've prepared for this. But Mikkal must also be kept in the dark about his parentage, and that he is a twin. However, by keeping him here we'll both be in even more danger soon, our very existence scrutinized. As you surely must understand, I'll be able to use our peril to divert attention away from Gabriel."

Larken shook his head and continued to pursue the answer to his question. "But how do you justify such?"

Misunderstanding still, she replied, "He'll be my Claim Son for now, another babe I assisted into this world who lost his mother. Nothing like staying as close to the truth as possible as 'tis much more difficult to be caught in the web of deceit."

He tried once again to clarify his question. "No, no, Artemis, I care not to be familiar with the details of your plan, although I have my ideas. I meant, how do you justify the exploitation of one to protect the other?"

The Healer stared longingly out the small window for a time, as if envisioning another place, then took a deep breath and began. "Gabriel entered this world in light and with peace. Mikkal struggled and kicked and took everything, including the life of his own mother. 'Tis his destiny to continue to do so the entire span of his days. I have Seen this." Artemis turned and looked directly at Larken, and with urgency she continued, "I can provide the evidence for I've already managed to find a stillborn for Bryard to see. He will not know the First Born yet lives and neither shall Gabriel know of his twin. 'Tis the only way to keep them both safe. I'll conceal Mikkal in the forest with the Kahyah at guard, and the King will not know of the twin birthing. I'll raise the boy 'til he is of age, and he will mayhap then, learn the truth. If there be rumors, 'twill be thought Mikkal the true Crown Prince, but no one will know that Gabriel lives and is in hiding. No one."

Larken was much relieved. "Yes, my friend. We shall persevere. We've played our parts well and Matana has been a'bed for the past fortnight, secluded in preparation for 'childbirth'. Everyone believes she's pregnant, right along with the girl and the Queen. No one will question Gabriel's arrival. She's already lactating with the assist of your herbs, and a little more assist from me..." at which time he actually blushed afore he continued. "And once the babe is at her breast, her body will adjust to him. We shall provide the best home we can, and he'll learn all he needs to know at court. But 'twill come a time when he must be sent to the tribe. I'm leery of the gossip that may begin once he shows resemblance to Bryard, and if Mikkal and he should happen to meet, well, 'twill be best to keep them separate. However, I believe the True King shall rise when the time is right, and the true usurper shall be exposed as per the prophesy. The evidence of Gabriel's birth is safe even now. I took care of that afore I left the castle, and I even used the precaution of blood wax in the seal. Koryl will never find the documents. 'Tween that and your own knowledge, there will be no question as to the proof of birth order. As I see it, 'twill only be difficult proving Gabriel's identity as the First Born, once grown."

Again, Artemis stared out the window as if listening to a voice speaking from a great distance, afore she replied. "Do not worry so, for the One True Liege has already provided the solution. There will be no difficulty confirming his identity once 'tis revealed he yet lives." And then with some puzzlement as she recalled the Vision from her youth, repeating softly as if in a dream, the words she'd never understood, "With the one's Passing, the other is proven." Hesitating momentarily, she shook her head to help bring her back to the present. "I've Seen something within the haze of tomorrows that speaks to this as truth." Near whispering, she continued, "When I was but a child, I Saw Evanntyr. I was crying with grief and running as fast as my legs could carry me, toward the Northern Tower. Looking up, I saw two massive Dragons in the air and two Warriors of the Clan upon the wall, in two separate battles. 'Twas great turmoil, love and despair combined, emanating from these warring pairs. As I watched in horror, one Warrior and one Dragon Passed the Veil. I knew not what was happening, I was too young, but 'twas as if my heart was ripped from my chest with their loss." A moment passed and Larken could think of nothing to comfort her. He waited patiently 'til she spoke again. "'Tis more. I believe the Dragon I Saw was the Mighty Maahayyel, the Last Dragon Matriarch herself."

Larken's eyes widened as he could barely catch his breath with these revelations. "But, Artemis, how could that fight occur? I doubt not your word, but no Warrior has ever broken his Oath. What could bring the two of them to stand against each other? Yet, prophesies often intertwine with one leading to another, and although I don't like the idea of knowing such may transpire, 'tis the loss of Maahayyel which concerns me most. Such would devastate the Highlands. Her Passing would surely culminate in their final extinction." Larken could say no more, he was speechless. Closing his mouth in bewilderment he stared at Artemis, challenging her to put forth into words what they both feared.

Just as bewildered, she locked gazes with him and stated, "Yea, Larken, 'twould herald the death of life."

CHAPTER TWO

The Word Sayer

THIRTEEN WINTERS AFTER THE BIRTH OF THE TRUE KING

~~~~~IN THE WILDS OF THE RAZOR'S EDGE~~~~~

Although he was the elder 'tween them, Gheryh's tense Night Beast allowed himself to be silenced with a look, dropping his heated gaze to the thick rug of leaves at their feet, distracting himself to regain his composure. The huge Kahyah laid his long tufted ears back against his heavy mane, the black tipped bronze of his coat making him difficult to see in the shadows. The stimulation of the hunt prevented him from holding back a low chuff deep in his chest, heard only by his Handler. The Daggogh had bred and partnered with the giant creatures since the time of the Last Holocaust, using the remaining big cats, wolves, and other predators, in an effort to prevent their extinction. In the process, they developed an entirely different breed to partner with, both as guards and to help them put food at their fires in the harsh environment, in order to prevent their own extinction. She couldn't fault her hunting partner for his eagerness.

Unbeknownst to all but Gheryh, the Night Beasts were not only intelligent, they were sentient. But without the physical ability to speak the Human language known as Common Tongue, and without the use of the Link, they were forced to await the Word Sayer of their prophesies, who would be their connection with the People. There was no doubt in Ryygg's mind that Gheryh, the eldest of the Danoh of the Daggogh, was the answer to their prophesy, but she knew not yet, her true destiny.

As a child, not realizing she was different from the others, she'd sit and talk with the Beasts for marks, even though no one believed 'twas more than a vivid imagination. This behavior was ignored, for Gyrrak was indulgent. As she grew 'twas obvious the Kahyah trusted her, and whatever skill or task she wanted or required of them, 'twas easily taught. In the past they'd needed much to prevent them from breaking free of the tenuous hold upon which the Daggogh had relied. Still, if one of them should break their alliance, the fearsome animals could easily take down their Handler. But Gheryh had never been afraid of such happening. She'd heard the stories of horrible maulings that forced one slowly and painfully Past the Veil but there'd been no deaths of this kind for several generations, and those that had occurred were justifiable. Of course, being the eldest of the Danoh's children and therefore first in line of succession to lead the biggest and fiercest tribe of the Daggogh, she'd been in training to be a Handler almost since birth. Still covered in the blood of her mother's womb, she'd been placed upon the ritual stone. The highly polished, table like surface of petrified wood had once been an ancient living thing, which now stood permanently rooted in the middle of their sacred ground. The Night Beasts then turned out to decide her fate. Should they listen to the rumbling of their stomachs after a hard hunt, having just returned without being allowed to eat prior to the ceremony, or would they choose her as worthy to become a Handler? The great slavering Beasts trod all around the grounds, sniffing and pawing, pushing up the dirt and leaf litter with their noses, working their way methodically from the Human fence of the People to the very heart of the area where stood the sacred stone. Belly height to the shaggy animals, its great exposed roots sprouted forth from the base and laid 'cross the grounds outwardly like the rays of the sun, becoming ever smaller 'til they finally vanished into the dirt. The newborn girl lay quietly upon the stains of the blood of past ceremonies, silently awaiting their decision.

Her lack of fear was most unusual and the tribe held their collective breath as the Kahyah finally found her, sniffing and nosing around to see if there was anything underneath the soft, warm, and bloody being. Then one of them pushed past the pack leader and nipped the infant, bringing forth a chirp of protest, and the eldest turned upon the offender with a vengeance. The entire pack shredded the wretched delinquent and they'd each taken a part in the feast that followed, leaving the infant alone and seemingly forgotten. 'Twas up to the mother to walk through the feeding pack and retrieve her babe, which she'd attempted to do, but just as she was midway to the stone the pack leader leapt up to block her path with his body, standing with his thick mane bristling along his neck and shoulders, his great teeth bared, and a throaty, deep reverberating growl her only warning. Gheryh had been claimed by the pack.

Her father was fascinated, never having witnessed this level of acceptance from the Night Beasts afore. He'd been spectator to many such ceremonies and 'twas always possible the child would become the meal of the day. The Pack and the People had a kind of symbiotic relationship and if this powerful connection was not inherited, 'twas better to end it early. Life in the mountains was hard and there was no room for anyone who could not pull his own weight. As to the ritual, there was something about their Life Source which only the Night Beasts could sense. The ceremony had been performed since they'd bred the Beasts, for every child of a Handler as well as the children of the Danoh and Danah, and even though the infant mortality rate had declined dramatically through the many lifespans since, he believed they'd never chosen wrongly. The Handlers and noble families of the Daggogh were growing purer and stronger with this form of selective breeding, but never afore had the Kahyah chosen one of the Daggogh as their own. Gyrrak allowed the Beasts to 'keep' his daughter, while his mate Tyrran backed out of the grounds angrily, but holding her tongue. She dared not question her mate in front of the others. There'd be time at their own fire later.

In moments, a female Beast who'd recently whelped a new litter, pushed past her Handler and into the grounds. As the bitch stepped gracefully toward the stone, the thick, silver tipped fur of her coat glittered in the sunlight filtering through the mighty tree branches above. She wasted little time to establish permission from the pack leader, groveling, whining and rolling, allowing the big male to restrain her by her neck with his massive teeth afore he finally released her, giving her free access. All eyes were upon the spectacle, everyone was present by this time, and not a sound could be heard. She sniffed the infant, then nosed her hairless body, generating the chirp of protest once again, producing a warning growl from the big male. The female cringed slightly and then stepped up upon the surface. Moving the infant about to suit her, she laid carefully down on her side, wrapping her warm furry body around the newborn. Gently, using her nose and rough tongue, avoiding breaking the tender skin of the little one with her sharp teeth, she guided the hungry baby to her teat to suckle. Gheryh's first milk was not of her mother. She'd suckled first of the Night Beasts.

~~~~~~~~~~~

Gheryh's thoughts returned to the hunt as her sharp eyes noted the scrub brush at the edge of the trail afore them, and she crouched down and fingered the freshly broken twig. The leaves were damp. She touched her finger to her tongue and smiled. They were close. Their persistence would soon pay off. As she stood up with anticipation, controlling her excitement so as not to foul the moment, her thoughts flashed back once again to a few dawns earlier when she'd so stood at the fire of the Danoh.

~~~~~~~~~~~

Gheryh was the picture of patience, waiting quietly in front of her father who stared at the fire pit in the middle of the hut while Tyrran stirred the coals. She laid on a few new logs and watched them take the flame as she pushed the hanging pot away from the now blazing fire, carefully positioning it so as not to burn the contents. Gheryh knew better than to speak first. Tall, lean, and strong, at fifteen winters she was one of the fastest runners and best bowmen in the tribe. Her hair was a rich dark brown where you could see it under the dye, shells, feathers, beads, and raw jewels. Her eyes were emerald green and her skin was painted and tattooed, but not as much as 'twould be in a few more winters as she proved herself in the field. If you looked closely you'd realize she wasn't wearing much, if you could call all that painted skin 'bare', but the essentials were covered with leathers and furs. A pair of sandals consisting of a flexible sole with thin straps that held them upon her feet and criss-crossed up to her thighs, protected her during the hunt as well as providing a place to hang a few weapons and survival supplies. She wore wrist braces on both arms, with forearm cuffs to protect her during the use of her bow, her thumb ring on her hand at all times with extras in the pouch at her hip, although she could shoot without them, with either hand. The People were exceptional archers, extremely fast and accurate with a recurve bow of their own creation, and held frequent games in which they would display their expertise with trick shots. But their preferred weapons were the Star Wings and bolo nets. Both of these were thrown, and their skill equated to food at their fire. Gheryh and Ryygg never lacked for food and often shared their bounty with their elders when they were home.

His voice startled her out of the quiet of her reverie. "You behave as if the blood of the witch women coursed through your veins."

As she'd assumed he was going to discuss her upcoming mission, she was puzzled for a moment afore answering. Gheryh tried to remember the stories told her by her many aunts and uncles when she was very young, but nothing about witch women could she recall. "I know not these women," she replied with a furrowed brow.

"They were known as the Rashei," he began. "Among other things, they had an uncanny ability with animals. They seemed to understand them and 'twas said they spoke with them. But animals do not speak in words. They 'speak' in emotion; needs, wants, and desires."

Trepidation filled her as the direction the conversation was taking became clear. She'd never actually discussed it afore, but there were some of the People who'd watched her with the Kahyah, staring at her strangely. Apparently someone had taken their concerns to the Danoh. She'd always been afraid her actions would be misconstrued and now she only hoped 'twould not prevent her from continuing as Liaison. She loved her position in the tribe but although she'd miss it, she would not give up what she was beginning to feel was her destiny. If she must, she and Ryygg would leave the village. They already lived alone at home, were always alone in their working travels, and had been so since her first trip upon her thirteenth winter. She chose her words carefully, trying to explain what she took for granted. "Father, when I speak with them, I hear words, I understand what they say. I've always understood them. 'Tis as we speak now. I don't know how, or even when I discovered we were actually talking in the same manner in which I conversed with my own, but 'tis the language of the Daggogh I hear, through the voice of the Kahyah. I speak to them, and they speak to me."

Gyrrak was startled. He hadn't truly expected her to reply in such a manner. He tried to comprehend what he'd always considered his daughter's harmless, though eccentric, behavior. But with the importance of the mission upon which he was about to send her, he had to know if 'twas a danger for the People, and for their guest. If so, he'd be forced to make her stop. But could he? Was her behavior a sickness? Thinking back through her life, 'twas easy to recall how she'd always been close to the Night Beasts, she'd suckled first of them, she'd lived most of her life with them, she'd always seemed to be talking with them. But she was a Handler in training, her proximity to the Beasts was easily o'er looked, and he'd never believed she was actually... had he done her and the People a disservice by not correcting this earlier? He loved her much, but he was Danoh. He tried to clarify what she'd said, to see if he'd been mistaken. Narrowing his eyes in uncertainty, he stated firmly, "Animals do not speak, you play with them. For certain 'tis not the telepathy of the Link, and 'tis not language."

Frustration took o'er. "No, 'tis not telepathy. Nevertheless, 'tis language! Although 'tis only the Kahyah, I hear no others. But I understand them clearly and I can speak their language as well as they understanding the language of the People. You believe in the witch women. You believe they could communicate with animals. Why is it so difficult to believe your own blood?"

Shaking his head he calmly replied, "The Rashei did not speak thus with animals. What you are telling me has never been done afore." He stared deeply into her eyes, measuring her fortitude, her commitment to what she'd just declared. "Can you prove this claim?"

Her passion melted to resignation. "I see no way to do so. You, everyone, would simply think I had them trained if I told them to do something to make you believe they understood. And you would have to take my word for what they replied. Trust me, from my earliest memories I've tried to think of an appropriate test to prove to you, to anyone, their ability to speak. However, I am unable, therefore I've kept silent."

Gyrrak sat back in his chair and pondered her words. Finally, he said, "'Tis certainly a dilemma, and you are, and have been, wise in what you're thinking, for 'tis truth, 'twould be unbelievable."

"But you believe me, don't you?"

Again he hesitated, and Gheryh could hear her own heart pounding in her ears. "I am confused, but you've never lied. I believe that you believe."

The half victory she considered as no victory. Sadly, she asked, "What is your decision?"

In an unexpected show of support, Gyrrak replied, "I think for now, you should not be quite so open in your exchanges. We shall attempt to find a test of the knowledge you have, and 'til then I want you to report to me what is said and done. If they're intelligent enough to learn our language, and you can truly interpret, they could be even more important to us than one could imagine."

Near leaping o'er the hearth in joy, she hugged him. "Thank you, father!"

He could not contain his slight smile, but he quickly regained his composure and caught her eye once more. "You are my daughter. But you are a Hunter/Handler, and Liaison as well. Do not test my faith in you. Do not fail your Danoh."

She was so relieved, she blurted forth much more than she'd intended. "I will not. And father? They don't only understand our language, they think, as do the People. They are aware." Slapping her hand o'er her mouth in an effort to stuff the words back in, she stared wide eyed as Gyrrak sat in silence and gazed at the fire for several very long moments. Gheryh held her breath, daring not to move a muscle. Had she revealed too much? She should've left well enough alone. Now he'd probably find someone else to go. He'd strip her of her position; she'd be humiliated. After what seemed to be a lifetime he appeared to have come to a decision. He cleared his throat. For so long, she'd wanted to tell him. She'd blurted forth, and 'twas poor timing. Would he have accepted the truth if she'd waited?

Gyrrak thoughtfully observed his beautiful, and very stressed daughter. Tyrran had never liked how close their eldest was to the Night Beasts, and had given him much trouble after her birthing ceremony. Was his daughter the one he'd been told of in his youth? The Word Sayer of the Kahyah? He'd never said anything to anyone, not even his own mate, about the Vision he'd had while in the company of the last Healer of the Forest, the mother of Artemis. Under her guidance, and using a special potion known only to their Healers, 'twas an amazing journey that opened his senses to an otherworld. He took a deep breath. "We shall keep this knowledge 'tween us. Agreed?"

His daughter bowed her head and half kneeled with both hands crossed o'er her chest, stating in a broken voice now filled with tears of relief instead of sadness, "Yes, father."

Gyrrak stood up and walked around the girl as she also stood, signaling the change in mood and subject matter, now speaking as the leader of a great nation. "As to the mission, I am sending you after our most honored guest, but he remains unaware of his station in life. What he knows now is what we shall accept 'til he learns otherwise. This must be his breakthrough, and you will not make it for him. I am telling you to avoid leading him to his discovery. 'Twill be made in good time, when he is ready to accept the burden. In the interim, he is in great danger and he needs not for us to add weight to his load. He has much to learn, including the ways of the People. You are expected to return with him and keep the People anonymous to outsiders, as our safety is in our secrecy. You will go with a small party, I don't want to attract attention if there be eyes watching. For your knowledge only, you will lose them as soon as possible, and will return without them. Run deep, run silent, bring our guest home unharmed. I want no followers. The Hunters I send with you are expecting to be 'lost' but they know not when and they will not abandon you. They will continue to the rendezvous and will cover your return. And Gheryh? I want to field test this communication 'tween you and the Kahyah. Have them exchange information 'tween each other, and you will report when you return home."

Gheryh had difficulty hiding her shock. Expecting a full hunting party to protect them on the entire journey, she respected how much trust he was putting in her ability to complete this mission as stated. The life of the most important man on all Kadoor was to be placed in her hands. Alone.

<center>~~~~~~~~~~</center>

Gheryh's thoughts returned to their hunt once more. Ryygg was surveying the area, his extraordinary senses processing every bit of information with acute efficiency. 'Twas noteworthy that they'd lost the Hunters within a few marks of leaving the village, but Gheryh was very capable and she knew intimately every league 'tween King's Gate and their homeland. She was also unwilling to allow any others to find her favorite campsites, and knowing their path, 'twas easy to avoid them. Her hand strayed to Ryygg's thick mane. His black and gold eyes next to invisible in the shadows, he saw far more than the Human eyes of the People, but he held his Handler in high esteem. He was present when Gheryh was accepted into the Pack, and 'twas his sire who'd saved her life that day so long ago, upholding the Law against his own get, Ryygg's youngest brother, for the attempted slaying of the girl child. Her scent was as pure as he'd ever known, his sire had agreed. Then his impatient sibling rashly allowed his hunger to get the better of him, and pushing all aside, he'd almost taken the infant Beyond. The arrival of this child was the herald of a new age for the Kahyah and long they'd awaited her, the one bespoken by prophesy. She was the key to their new relationship with the People, the turning of their lives, for she was the Word Sayer. At the Acceptance, Ryygg personally pledged his life to hers in order to protect the one who would one day bring his Kind true freedom.

Gheryh pulled the Star Wing from the pouch at her shoulder and in the blink of an eye, let loose the deadly weapon. The wickedly sharp point found its target, lodging deeply in the neck of the great hoofed ellka, dropping it within a few staggering steps. Her weapon was made from the wings of the Rochas, descendants of the cockroach of ancient times. The size of large rats, the edges of their hard shell wings were sharp enough to sever a finger. Shaped like an elongated teardrop, they were coveted as eating and cooking utensils, and tools for use in tanning and for skinning, as well as for producing their throwing weapons such as the Star Wings, Fans, and Darts. Short spears and lances were also made from the wings of the Rocha. Though of small proportion, the meat was considered a delicacy by the People.

As Gheryh field dressed the carcass, Ryygg kept watch for predators. She tossed him the entrails as she went about her chore and he caught them midair, gulping them down rapidly. He didn't want to pass up the tasty treats, always wary of being attacked, but they were barely a mouthful for the huge Beast and quickly consumed. 'Twas his primary duty to keep them both safe, and he'd not fail. In the Razor's Edge lived many predators. Most Humans were woefully ignorant of the fact that they were at the bottom of a fairly long list. At least the People were not 'most Humans', and they treated the hunt with respect. Still, the blood would call to the others, and 'twas why they'd moved the hunt far away from their camp. He was grateful that Gheryh was so adept. Quickly, she tied the carcass o'er Ryygg's shoulders, and then mounted up just behind it, to allow them to leave the area with all haste. Even having led them a merry chase, the Kahyah had them back shortly after dusk.

They'd stopped in a cave she'd used afore, after clearing out a few unwanted guests, and soon returned there. The ellka were much larger than their ancestors of ancient times and their racks were all one piece, having a wide hard cap 'cross its head that held the huge curling branches of both sides together. 'Twas shaped similar to a ribcage, so that if turned upside down, could be used as the frame work of a crawl-in shelter. She'd refused to leave the rack behind, having some odd sense that 'twould be essential in the future, and although 'twas a tad difficult to balance during their return, she'd managed. The giant antlers were so hard, they were next to impossible to cut through and she'd never known them to break, even during the rut. They'd be safe left in the cave for them to retrieve on the return trip.

Ryygg preferred his meat raw, although he'd eat anything if he was hungry enough. Gheryh liked hers red in the middle with bloody juices running, but warm throughout. However, she'd decided the delectable aroma would not only make her mouth water in anticipation, 'twould not be worth the risk on this mission, therefore they were both eating raw, although she had dried and salted provisions to look forward to, and would be well stocked by their tribe kin when they were homeward bound. Still, she was concerned that as much as this one provided 'twould not be enough for her partner. She'd hoped not to spend much time hunting in order to avoid the others and still arrive first, but her current path was off the direct line they traveled and if she couldn't make up that time, the Hunters would most likely reach their destination afore them. In Wyndsyr Forest outside of King's Gate Village they'd find Artemis, Larken, and Matana, and the urgency of this trip gave them few chances to enjoy fresh meat along the way.

She was proud she'd been entrusted with this mission. At only thirteen winters, she'd been chosen as Liaison 'tween her tribesmen living at Evanntyr, and the People. Now fifteen, she'd made the trip several times. 'Twas a long journey, but an essential one. This time she was bringing back a most important guest. Everyone knew who Gabriel was, with the exception of Gabriel himself. To be trusted with his personal safety was more than an honor. She'd become an excellent survivalist and was confident that she'd not be followed, but she didn't know much about Gabriel's experience and was prepared to do some training on the trip.

As far as the Danoh was concerned, if the Hunters couldn't see her, neither could anyone else. 'Twas a challenge Gheryh had accepted with enthusiasm. She'd make her father proud, and Gabriel's return to the People would be safe. No outsider would know where he was, even if someone knew who he was. Secrets had a way of speaking loudly to those from whom they were supposed to be kept. She hoped the boy would have time to grow into his destiny afore they were discovered, but Gheryh knew eventually they'd have to openly enter the war. The Evil One had come as the ancient Battle Commander predicted, and the Hoard was making it their mission to destroy all the prophesies they could.

Of course, since most of them had to do with their demise, she supposed 'twould make sense, but she knew they'd like nothing better than to kill the True King. When the time came, Gabriel would be returned to Kadoor. 'Til then, he'd be kept hidden in the heart of the Razor's Edge.

Chapter Three
An Angry Child

LATER THAT EVENING

~~~~~THE PAINTED ONE'S CABIN~~~~~

Mikkal woke in a cold sweat, jerking upright, pushing away nightmarish hands touching his naked body... again. Clenching his teeth to keep from screaming out in sheer revulsion, he shivered with the rise of the gooseflesh o'er his youthful muscles and smooth skin, his heart hammering in his chest so loudly, he was afraid 'twould awaken Artemis. As his eyes adjusted to the darkness he discovered he was still in the cabin and not out in the woods wondering how he'd gotten there, but for the life of him he didn't know what put the fear of Hades into his soul, nor could he recall the details of the increasing nightmares. O'er the past winter they'd gone from the occasional sleepwalk to near nightly confusion and horror. He needed rest but was afraid to try again this night. He'd felt, more than heard, the whispering demands of his tormentor. She wanted him to bring her something. Something potent, something foul, something even Artemis didn't talk about. He knew everything she had in her cellar, every powder, every herb, every concoction, and he knew for what they could be used. Or misused.

There were still several marks afore dawn and dressing quickly, he reached under his desk for the vial, absent mindedly tucking it into his pocket. Then he crawled out the window onto the narrow ledge. Leaping effortlessly to the nearby tree branch, he shimmied down the broad trunk and crouched low at the base, listening to the sounds of the night. There was always a presence in the distance that couldn't be explained, watching him but never making itself known. 'Twas not the normal animal life teeming in the forest, but since it didn't hinder his travels, 'twas eas-
~~~~~

ily ignored. Quickly, he headed into the trees toward the castle, drawn there without reason. Artemis forbade his travel to the village, but he was close to thirteen winters now, and she wasn't his real mother. He could take care of himself. She'd taught him much about her profession as well as fighting, hunting, and survival. He was quite agile and stronger than most his age, and he wanted to take control of his life. 'Twas something happening to him; he needed to learn why he was being led to Evanntyr, and why he felt so violated each time he woke, invisible hands touching him, voices telling him to do terrible things. He'd not even told Artemis about the nightmares, stubbornly keeping the knowledge a secret, for he'd have to admit to having done something very wrong.

<center>~~~~~DOWNSTAIRS IN THE STUDY~~~~~</center>

As was his way, Larken stood behind her when she turned about at the whisper of his breath on her ear. "How do you do that," Artemis asked, annoyed. "Next time you might be met with my dagger!"

He disregarded the question and the outburst, 'twas simply a matter of skill after all. He was quite talented and also knew that Artemis's reflexes would not allow her to strike him, no matter how surprised. 'Twas past midnight and the woods were dark enough to make his travels less complicated. Even though he liked teasing her, he was here to discuss the boy and 'twas going to be a difficult discussion indeed. He stepped back and took a deep breath afore he spoke. "'Tis as you feared, he's been to the castle. Although you should be proud, he moves as a spirit wind through the trees and if not for our Beasts he would've lost me more than a few times. They've been following him. Even so, he's not seen me or the Kahyah, and still has no idea of their existence." 'Twas remarkable really, as large as they were it should be more difficult for them to remain unseen. He rested one foot upon the chair he'd pulled out from the small table. Leaning forward he crossed his arms o'er his knee and looked at her solemnly. He knew she understood the gravity of the situation, but he fully expected a retort of defensive protection. He didn't have much time afore dawn and he steeled himself for her response.

"He's an angry child," she began, but to his utter surprise she continued, "and I've been losing control o'er him for the last winter. If he continues along these lines he'll eventually come face to face with Shytin, or worse yet, Gabriel. But then, either meeting would have disastrous results." 'Twas obvious her admission was difficult. Having the boy here o'er the long winters had given her life a new purpose, fulfillment, and companionship. At least, 'til the past few moons.

Larken sighed. Revealing she'd miss the boy was akin to acknowledging she loved him, as well as admitting that she was lonely. Although both from another world, their homeland deep within the mountains of the Edge, he had Matana to keep him company and remind him of his origins. Artemis was alone out here, with only the company of their Night Beasts and the ones who came seeking her skills, 'til that fateful dawn Mikkal was birthed. She'd thrown her heart and soul into raising the boy, teaching him what he'd need to know in order to stay alive. She'd not intended to actually love the child, only to raise him and to use him to protect his brother to further the prophesy. Neither twin had knowledge of the other, but her strategy to stay aloof toward the younger, had failed her miserably. She had indeed become a mother Kahyah and despite her words, he was concerned she'd place Gabriel in danger by raising her hackles o'er Mikkal's future. 'Twas a future decided long afore his rather violent entrance to the world, and one that could not be altered.

Stepping closer, he gently cupped her face in his hands and lifted her hazel eyes to his. "I don't wish to make you feel inadequate. You've been an excellent Claim Mother, and you've taught him well. But he's headstrong and needs a man in his life, Artemis. 'Tis time to send him away, my friend."

"Larken, we send Gabriel to the People to continue his journey into manhood and for his own protection, as he begins to show likeness to Bryard, and if he stays our deception may be uncovered. With Gabriel gone we eliminate half the problem. But sending Mikkal away will be yet another rejection in his mind. 'Twas not his fault he was second born." Artemis recognized she was losing in this dispute and sullenly she accepted Larken was correct. She smirked at the notion that her present arguments were reminiscent of his at the time of the births, when she'd been the one to present the side of reason to him. She sighed in resignation. "Where do we send him? Gabriel will soon be living with the Daggogh, a strong young man already in the making. Who will be able to rein in Mikkal's anger? Who can heal his heart and guide him in his journey to manhood? I've done my best but I fear I've failed," she stated gloomily.

"You've not failed. He's always been a challenge, even to himself. He's the one rejecting you. You've given him your knowledge, your heart, your very soul. Despite your original resolve to use the boy, you've kept him safe and have never allowed him to go without. I know you've grown to love him as your own, but remember he's never been yours; his destiny lies in another direction. The prophesy shall not be thwarted. 'Tis time for him to go to Drekinn. 'Tis time for him to go into Training with the Clan."

The Healer dropped her gaze to her feet and sat down heavily in the chair opposite. Swallowing hard, she willed away the tears threatening to spill down her cheeks. Trying not to clench her jaw she was able to bite out just one word. "When?"

Larken's heart was filled with compassion for his lifelong friend, and his voice was firm yet kind when he replied. "Gheryh travels even now with a full hunting party from home. She should be here for Gabriel by the end of the next moon. Mikkal needs to be well on his way afore then. The twain cannot meet, even by accident. I believe we've been fortunate thus far, but I doubt we have much fortune left us."

Artemis looked down at her hands, now clutched in her lap. "Agreed. The sooner, the better. I'll speak with him in the morning and he'll be ready to embark soon after. But how do we get him there? Neither of us can leave, and we dare not arrange for Hunters to guide him, for he must not know of our tribe. 'Tis a long, dangerous journey in these times and he's never traveled so far alone afore. And there's no assurance the Clan will accept his petition for Warrior Training as well as the fact that being an Outlander he'll have to prove himself worthy." The Healer's thoughts spewed forth in a rush of ideas, one after the other with increasing speed, her voice growing more frantic with each word 'til Larken leaned forward and placed one finger 'cross her lush lips to gain her silence and attention. Upon feeling his touch, she stopped abruptly and met his gaze.

Slowly and eloquently, he answered each of her concerns. "His journey will prove his merit. You've taught him honor, and he'll not betray this. His skills will see him there, and the anger will subside out of necessity as 'twill not put food at his fire and he's smart enough to understand that. He may not have traveled so far, but he has been on his own far longer than 'twill take. Speak to him in the morning, I'll return the following dawn. I'll lead him through the worst of the mountains, and since he knows me not, tell him I'm your hire, a freelance huntsman from the village. Just in case, I'll come in disguise. The Kahyah can continue to protect him 'til he gets to the Plains and still return afore me." Larken sighed. "He's been to the castle, and we know not exactly what he's experienced. We can only pray we're not too late." Artemis nodded in agreement. She could no longer trust her trembling voice.

Her head turned swiftly to the slight knocking sound from upstairs and she leaped up, securing the study behind her. Climbing the stairs quickly and quietly she went straight to Mikkal's room at the end of the hall. She saw only darkness under the door, and after opening it a mere handbreadth she watched the boy for several moments as he lay still under his covers, his chest rising and falling rhythmically in sleep. Suddenly he sat bolt upright, pushing away invisible cobwebs enveloping him. His eyes opened, and he stared uncomprehendingly afore the light of recognition shone. Falling back to his pillow he pulled the covers o'er his head. "Did I wake you again? Go away, just another dream. I'm fine."

"Good night." Artemis spoke into the shadows and having received a groan in response, she closed the door and went back downstairs, wishing he'd confide in her. 'Just another dream', was all he ever said.

~~~~~~~~~~

Larken was still waiting. "Do you think he's been out again?"

"I don't know, I can't tell anymore. He has to go soon, I fear for his safety. Something is happening and I don't understand what 'tis."

Larken nodded his agreement then left through the window, melting into the night.

~~~~~~~~~~

Mikkal rolled o'er and propped his chin on his hand. Had he actually gone to the castle? 'Twas like a dream 'til he'd found himself climbing back in through the window, making a sound that would betray his indiscretion. Mayhap he'd just been outside as he'd often found himself afore. He'd barely managed to cover up and slow his breathing long enough to satisfy Artemis, but many questions ran through his mind. Had the beautiful woman come to him again, meeting him under that moss covered windowsill, mesmerizing him with her gaze, her sensuality? Drawn to her as if he had no will of his own, his yearning was stifled as her perverted desires soaked into his skin like stinging nettles, her touch cold as ice. He was appalled, nauseous, disgusted, yet he couldn't move, couldn't defend himself, couldn't turn and leave. She'd forced him to lie down with her, forced him to... but he'd not wanted anything to do with her, unable to stomach her increasingly sickening demands. He'd felt her fingernails shredding the skin on his back as he'd tried pushing her away. As his shirt tore, the vial dropped to the ground and reaching for her treasure, she'd let him go. He'd run all the way home, her manic laughter shrill in his ears. That is, if he had gone, which he wasn't certain of anymore. Mayhap 'twas another nightmare. But his back burned. Getting out of bed, he began to undress. Pulling his torn shirt o'er his head, 'twas damp, and he stared at it in his hands. Even in the darkness, he could tell 'twas blood.

EVANNTYR

~~~~~THE BEDCHAMBERS OF THE QUEEN~~~~~

</div>

Koryl gloated o'er her success. When she'd first uncovered evidence that Mikkal was the First Born, she'd considered simply killing him, but after catching him within the otherworld, controlling him was so much more fun. And after all she'd made him do, 'twas her steadfast belief that if he was ever found, he'd never be crowned. "'Tis mine! At last, the Veil Grit is mine again. That stupid Healer. She's been very careful not to release this since your conception, but she knows not the hold I have o'er the boy. I don't care if I never discover of what 'tis made, there's enough here to do one more, and one more is all I need do." Propped up upon several pillows in the enormous canopy bed, Koryl spoke with triumph in her voice, her long shapely legs sprawled apart as she caressed her naked womanhood. Staring at the tiny vial of dull yellow crystals, she ignored her young son standing at the footboard, fumbling with the ties of his pants, his lips quivering in a perverse mix of anticipation and loathing. The excitement she felt with her success soon had her body shuddering to her own touch, the sense of power she obtained from manipulating others, stirring a madness of need. Her fingers wet, she licked them sensuously, finally acknowledging Shytin's presence. "Do you want this? Get on your knees and beg."
~~~~~

He was so hard now, 'twas painful. Still fumbling to untie his pants, the building adrenaline gave him the strength to rip them open and he pushed them down to his ankles in annoyance, releasing his throbbing member. Shytin was not built as was his father, but then, Koryl wasn't certain who his father was. Tall, pasty pale, and skinny in puberty, he responded with disdain, "What I want, is the crown. We now have the means, when will you let me ascend?"

Her eye twitched with the need to punish him for his insolence, but the very thought of such was exciting, and her voice became low and husky with renewed hunger. "Soon. The timing must be perfect. 'Twill not be long, tonight mayhap. But 'tis my decision, not yours. Prove that you're ready and I will put you on the throne. Now, beg."

THE FOLLOWING DAWN

~~~~~THE CABIN~~~~~

</div>

Mikkal strapped on his weapons, carefully tucked the extra dagger that Artemis had gifted him into his pack, and tied the full length hooded and fur lined cloak around the straps. He'd watched her make two matching cloaks, thinking she was fulfilling a consignment. He was pleased that she'd given him one, wondering to whom had gone the other, for 'twas beautifully crafted and helped him blend into the forest with ease. She'd warned him the winters north of the Plains were even harder than they were here at home. "Drekinn can get completely snowed in, sometimes for moons, and they can't leave their fires." She'd told him many things, her voice trailing off at the end of every new revelation, her eyes glazing o'er. He'd not said anything. Shock, most likely. He'd always known he'd be leaving one day to go out into the world and make his own path. 'Twasn't as if she'd not prepared him for this, he just hadn't expected it to be this sudden, or to hurt this much. He'd fully expected to be ready, eager, excited, not this mind numbing, make-his-head-spin pain
~~~~~

that not only took away his voice, his reason, his every argument, but his very breath. He was afraid if he opened his mouth to say anything, he'd break down in tears, and that was simply unacceptable. She expected him to be Warrior material. Warriors didn't cry. When they'd finished talking the morning afore (or rather, when Artemis finished talking and Mikkal finished listening), he'd grit his teeth, firmed his square jaw, and pushed his half eaten breakfast away. He'd thought he was being punished for sneaking out again. Mayhap she knew he was visiting the castle against her orders, but then, mayhap leaving would make the nightmares stop. Standing up awkwardly, so tall already that he towered o'er his Claim Mother, he went upstairs in silence. He'd not spoken a word to her since.

He looked around the tiny room that had been his refuge for all his thirteen winters. For the story of his life 'twas a tad sparse in belongings, but he'd never felt deprived. Despite their reclusive existence, Artemis was not poor and she'd ensured that he'd had everything he'd needed. He'd never wanted much. There was always, in the back of his mind, a sensation of being split in two, as if he shared another's soul. As a child, he'd thought he could almost see the other, but just last winter when he'd attempted to use Artemis's special potion to open himself fully to the otherworld, the nightmares had begun. 'Twas an offence for which she'd never forgive him, if 'twas ever discovered.

He sat on the bed and bounced a few times, the memories of helping her make the mattress as clear as the day 'twas done. 'Twas a pleasant memory he now wanted to forget. She was pushing him out of her life. He looked out the window at the tree he climbed to sneak in and out. He'd learned to climb that tree at just five winters. Standing up, he walked to the desk and spread out some papers he'd been writing, his thoughts unfinished. Mayhap 'twas for the best. Artemis hadn't neglected his education and he was fully literate. When he got settled somewhere, he could begin anew. He opened the squirrel cage in the hutch and released the creature. "Don't get yourself eaten too quickly. Try to stay alive at least long enough to find a mate. Everyone deserves someone special in their hearts. And if you tell any of your friends that I was so soft I saved your stupid ass and healed that broken leg, I'll deny it. Now get out of here. 'Tis time you were on your own. Like me." He sighed as the little beast sat on the desk, seemingly listening to his words, and he lifted him up and placed him on the window sill, giving him a slight push afore he finally leaped to the tree. But there he sat, and the two stared at each other for awhile. When he heard the huntsman arriving downstairs, he turned away from the confused creature, grabbed his pack, and walked out without a glance o'er his shoulder, closing the door behind him softly as if 'twould make his leaving less final.

Chapter Four

Divide and Strengthen

~~~~~DREKINN~~~~~

Corbyn's ebony feathers gleamed in the candlelight of the wall sconce upon which he sat in the hallway of the Dragon's Den. He'd just flown in from the Razor's Edge, having completed a protection Spell o'er Mikkal and his traveling companion. There was trouble brewing in the mountains but he'd not had time to uncover its roots. He was fairly certain the simple Spell of distraction would suffice. 'Twould have to, he couldn't do anymore now, he was expected elsewhere and was late already. Whomever sought after the boy would be blinded to his trail and he'd be able to travel as safely as 'twas possible through the treacherous range. Preening his left wing, he carefully avoided dipping it in the wax. He'd chosen the perch for the dramatic impact and 'twould have been most inconvenient, as well as embarrassing, to have such an mishap. 'Twas sometimes difficult to maintain the proper respect from Humans when your preferred Shift was that of a raven. Although, if he'd known how Humans felt about him, and ravens in general, he'd have been quite impressed. He was feared by most, greatly respected by some, and a few actually trusted him. The Battle Commander fell somewhere 'tween the latter two options.

Grifynn was brusque, as he was in a hurry to get to the Pits to supervise the morning katas."What do you want from me now? 'Tis not time for our change, so what brings you here?"

Corbyn had long ago learned to ignore his gruff nature, once he'd proven beyond a shadow of a doubt that he could be trusted, and that he did have an appreciation for his assistance in their lives. He cocked his head and stared at the big man, his beady eyes glistening eerily in the flickering light. *"Mikkal."*
~~~~~

Genuine confusion flashed o'er the Commander's face. "Who?"

"There comes a boy to Drekinn, seeking petition to Warrior Training. He'll need assistance as he has reached his thirteenth winter. He's a strong young man with excellent potential, and he will be needed by the Brotherhood. Mayhap he could be tutored."

Grifynn contemplated the words of the Raven. On the surface 'twas a simple request however, he knew the Fay well enough to understand 'twas never simple, he'd not be given the whole story, and he was most likely being manipulated into doing something that could end up very badly for him personally. But he also accepted that if he didn't take heed 'twould be Flame to pay, mayhap for all of Kadoor. 'He will be needed by the Brotherhood.' Time and again 'twas proven, the Fay knew things about the future. Somehow, this Mikkal would be linked to him and/or the Clan, and he must advance through Training and take the Oath. He sighed. "I'll have Aalanna tutor the boy. She's had many such private students. She's an excellent, and very patient, teacher." With extreme skepticism, Grifynn added, "Of what exactly, is he lacking?"

"The boy is literate, however, he's never ventured outside his own world. He will need history, economics, and the social arts. He has many skills to share, many which will bring him favor with the Brotherhood. But his life has been very secluded."

"So, what you're saying without saying it, is that the boy has no patience and little control o'er his temper. He's probably good in a brawl, but mayhap he's also somewhat impulsive?"

The Raven smirked at the Commander's accurate interpretation. Grifynn had come to know him well o'er the many winters they'd worked together. Mayhap too well. He Responded after a slight hesitation. *"Something akin to that, yes."*

Grifynn's eyes narrowed and his jaw twitched. He leaned as close to the Raven as he could and in a threatening voice he declared, "If he harms my mate, I will kill you with my own hands."

Backing off, he resumed his frustration with yet another request by the Fay, and continued, "But, I've promised your death many times afore and my words seem always to fall on deaf ears. Oh you've never lied to me, you merely leave out major details. When and where? Is he coming to me, or do I have to seek him out? How hard am I going to have to work for this?"

"You will not need to look for him, he will come to you quite soon," the Raven Stated as he took flight and disappeared down the hallway, leaving the Commander to wonder exactly who was this Mikkal, and just what was he going to bring to the Clan and the Brotherhood. Corbyn flew quickly out of the Den and set his course to the east. He had no time to congratulate himself on having completed one more step to the fulfillment of the prophesies. He was meeting with the Highland Ancients at Flight of Fire Keep on a volcanic island set in the middle of the Dragon's Tears, an uncharted ocean with its waves lapping upon the shores at the edge of Darkling Forest beyond the Raptor's Talons. Even with his speed Magically enhanced 'twould take him near a sennight to get there. He'd hoped to be there by now, but when he'd learned of Mikkal's travels he'd taken a side trip so he wouldn't have too much trouble on his way to Drekinn and getting into Training. Would his encouragement ensure the boy's acceptance? 'Twas no guarantee, however, 'twould surely be sufficient. Now he had another task to which he must attend. He had to convince the Ancients to join the Fay and recreate the LifeBond with the Dragon Clan. The Black had returned and the war was forthcoming yet again. He set his sights for the distant Keep of the Highlands and let no other thoughts disturb his efforts.

THE FOLLOWING NIGHT

~~~~~EVANNTYR~~~~~

</div>

The Sorcerer stood in the open shower, buckets of heated water pouring o'er his head from above, as he lathered up to remove all scent of Koryl. He was meticulous in his cleansing ritual, he
~~~~~

wanted nothing to distract him. He'd left the witch on the floor, her cries twisted from passion to despair. It made his mouth water to watch her grovel. But he had a task to finish and a meeting to attend. 'Twas amazing how much information one could obtain from someone, when given the right incentive. His preferred incentive, of course, was torture. He was very good at that. In fact, torture was far more satisfying than sex lately. He shook his head. Sex used to be so much more. His brow furrowed. When had it lost its glamour? He'd given the bitch a good workout and she'd given every bit back, but he'd not been able to... He shook his head again. No matter. The mercenaries he'd hired on his way to Evanntyr should be arriving soon. Their mission? Bring him the First Born (although they knew not his identity). His destination? Apparently, Drekinn. The boy had been under their very noses all this time, and once he learned who'd been hiding him, there'd be Flame to pay. He'd suspected for some time that the boy was alive. 'Twas quite fortunate that he'd uncovered Bryard's attempts to locate the whereabouts of his 'True King' during his last visit, meaning he knew better, too. But this evening was eye opening, as he'd also discerned the Queen's belief that she'd found the First Born winters past. Mayhap 'twas time to eliminate Bryard. Permanently. Shytin was much easier to manipulate. And Koryl? He smiled wickedly.

<div style="text-align:center">~~~~~THE TRIP TO DREKINN~~~~~</div>

Mikkal and the huntsman faced each other 'cross the glowing coals of the campfire. Neither of them had said much in the several dawns they'd spent together. The huntsman was from King's Gate and was quite accomplished, even as he was quiet. However, Mikkal considered himself skilled as well and had attempted to take o'er the trip from the beginning. Strong feelings of betrayal had no vent other than this man and this situation, and so he'd chosen to take out his annoyance by leaving him behind. But traveling through the Edge was dangerous and most wouldn't even try, taking the Razor's Cut 'tween Lorelei and King's Gate instead.

Being alone in unfamiliar territory hadn't worked out very well, and finding himself totally lost, he'd been most grateful by the time the huntsman found him again, tangled hopelessly in a mass of briars at the bottom of a ledge. Several marks did the huntsman assist Mikkal out of the briar patch and now he sat eyeing the other, eating what he'd been handed, bandaging several lacerations upon his arms and legs and applying salve where he'd run into burning nettles. The sensation brought forth an unwanted memory. From the beginning he'd hidden the scratches on his back and now had reason to continue to treat them openly, although they were healing well. As long as the huntsman didn't look too closely, for they were of obviously different ages, his older injuries would go unnoticed.

Finally, Mikkal could tolerate the silence no longer and he blurted forth sarcastically, "I suppose I should thank you." No response. The huntsman didn't even lift an eyebrow, just continued staring at him, chewing thoughtfully. In a sudden fit of temper Mikkal stood up and yelled, "What do you want from me?"

In a quiet, calm voice, he replied, "What makes you think I want anything?"

Mikkal started to respond, but abruptly discovered he had no answer. He sat back down. What did he think the other wanted, and why would he think that? After much introspection he finally admitted, "I was wrong. I have difficulty containing my temper at times. And I'm impatient. Thank you for searching for me, you could have left me out there and simply returned. No one, not even Artemis, would have known." He didn't say what he wanted to say at the end of that sentence, 'or would have cared'.

"I would have known."

'Twas as if he'd been punched in the stomach. If he'd been blessed with a father, he would've wanted him to be like this man, honest, intelligent, kind, and yet strong, independent, confident.

The huntsman gingerly picked out another large chunk of the snake from the hot coals. 'Twas longer than he was tall and had taken both of them to carry the monstrous carcass back to camp after they'd killed it in a nearby stream. Licking his fingers to cool them, he shared the portion with the boy, who stood up to meet him coming around the fire. Compassion in his eyes, he completed his thoughts. "And she would've known. And she cares very much." Mikkal felt his knees buckle.

O'ER A FORTNIGHT AFTER MIKKAL'S DEPARTURE

~~~~~THE DRAGON'S DEN~~~~~

</div>

Grifynn was shocked. "Bryard dead? That can't be. He was in perfect health when I was there discussing our contract. 'Twas just three moons ago." As Battle Commander, he couldn't afford many friends, and the High King had been one of the closest, as well as a strong ally to the Clan. He sat down at his desk and stared suspiciously at the paper the Runner from King's Gate had given him just a quarter mark prior, but 'twas clear he wasn't comprehending what he saw.

Aalanna gently pulled the paper from his fingers and summarized the contents. "It says he died a fortnight past, and they held the coronation immediately. They've arranged an 'open house of mourning' o'er the next six moons to ensure all the Clan leaders can arrive to 'pay their respects and recognize the coronation', but that Bryard's body will not be available for viewing." Looking up, she was at a loss to fathom such nonsense. "No guests for the coronation? Bryard's body not available? What's going on out there?"

Grifynn slammed his meaty fist down on the heavy oak desk. "Recognize the coronation, my hard cock! They want to make sure we all swear fealty. I refuse to swear fealty and drag the Clan under that parasitic blood sucker." His lovely mate massaged his neck trying to soothe him, or at least calm him down a bit, as he was about to explode in anger.
~~~~~

Her voice soft, she asked, "Mayhap he was taken ill as the report suggested?"

"No!" Standing up so fast and with such fury in his heart, he knocked his mate o'er, immediately regretting his actions. With lightning like reflexes he grabbed her to prevent the fall, but not without bruising her arm. 'Twas shameful. An angry man did not make rational decisions. He sat back down and drew her arm to his lips, kissing the red marks that would soon turn purple, Aalanna having already forgiven him. He rolled her arm o'er to his cheek and she hugged his neck tightly. Taking a deep breath, he began again. "He was younger than I, and I've never known him to be sick a day in his span. And now, that two faced, back stabbing worm he claimed as his son, sits upon the throne. When last we spoke, he confided that he'd always known in his heart Shytin was not of his blood, and that the First Born was still this side of the Veil. He'd been searching covertly for proof, but was concerned he'd opened a doorway to disaster. I tried to get him to tell me what was happening and he made a vague reference to thinking his life might be threatened, which he later denied. He wanted me to follow the prophesy and find the True King if anything happened. I thought he was just being suspicious. I should have paid him more heed. 'Twas obviously murder."

"But you can't prove that from here, and 'twill be a delicate state of affairs into which we're about to step, my love. We must go without delay, and you must be prepared to use good sense. We know not for certain what happened, and we know not of what Shytin and Koryl are actually capable, although 'tis difficult to believe they'd do such themselves. If 'tis true and he was murdered, we need solid evidence. If we show reservation without, he could turn on us and the Clan. And remember, like it or not, Shytin is High King now. His word is law."

"You've always kept me focused, my dear. I'll make the journey to Evanntyr tomorrow; I can handle this alone."

"'Twould not be appropriate for you to go alone, Grifynn, I'm your mate and Koryl may use my absence as an excuse to claim insult. Besides, we have to show trust to put them off guard. For many winters you've suspected that she was manipulating her son, and if they would do this heinous deed to put him on the throne, we're all in danger. Furthermore, I can cover for you while you do a little snooping around. Only if you uncover proof, can we even consider protesting the coronation."

"We're the largest and most powerful War Clan in all of Kadoor. The prophesy says we shall help the True King ascend the throne. But if I'd known the little bastard and that witch mother of his, were going to do this..."

"No one knew Koryl was this desperate, or this wicked. And technically, the prophesy refers to the Clan helping the True King regain his rightful throne, which speaks to me as though these events may be unfolding as they should. Also, have not reports surfaced from the Warriors stationed there, that Dragons have been sighted from the castle? 'Tis relevant?"

"For the past two winters, several sightings in that region have been noted. I think 'tis highly relevant, and I'm uncomfortable they've not returned to Drekinn. I'm concerned the Dragons seen o'er King's Gate herald the return of the Evil One." He became quiet for just a moment and then his entire countenance changed as he made his decision. Standing up, he took her tiny hands in his and pulled her close, giving her a slow, deep, passionate kiss. Then he turned her around, smacked her backside playfully, and pushed her toward the door, saying, "Pack for us, dear one, I trust your judgment." She was just about to feel true relief with this change of mood, but then with a glint in his eye and a sinister tone that made her shiver, he continued, "I'll gather our escort. We leave at dawn."

EARLY SUMMER
A FORTNIGHT LATER
~~~~~EVANNTYR~~~~~

Matana's tears flowed unchecked down her reddened cheeks, and she sniffled softly into the handkerchief afore pushing it back into the pocket of her apron. Larken pulled her close and hugged her tightly, then Gabriel joined them. He'd just returned from a trip to Lorelei, and although 'twould have taken the length of time he'd been gone, Gabriel doubted the story. Larken had actually guided Mikkal almost to the northern border of the Edge, returning as quickly as he could, once confident he'd have little difficulty traveling alone the rest of the way to Drekinn. At least he wouldn't have the Spring Melts to deal with any longer. In truth, the boy should have arrived by now. They'd discussed his agenda once he got there, as Mikkal had never been to a village afore. He'd been given enough coin to live well, but 'twas to be kept a secret for his own safety, and therefore 'twas up to him to make his own way while petitioning for Training. Along the journey Mikkal became more open and seemed to be excited about his new life. Larken was relieved, as was Artemis when he'd told her. But Mikkal held a grudge and he'd not once said he loved his Claim Mother or that he'd miss her, and she'd been devastated.

"The boy does love you, 'twas clear by his reactions, he just can't bring himself to say the words."

Bursting into tears she exclaimed, "I may never see him again!" Then she ran back inside.

Gheryh was at the cabin when Larken arrived, but preferred to sleep in the woods with her Night Beast who was enjoying a reunion with the two belonging to Larken and Artemis. Most of the evening was gone after catching up on the news from home, and then he'd learned about Bryard. The High King was dead. Word was that he'd died suddenly in his sleep shortly after he'd left with Mikkal, and 'twas said the coronation was held the second dawn. With this unexpected loss of a most beloved ruler,
~~~~~

followed by such an abrupt and strange coronation of his son, rumors abounded. The Queen Mother was stifling them with threats of treason, and many had been taken to the dungeons already.

Larken caught Artemis's expression and saw that which he feared. "I know not," she said. "Matana could find no information about the death. 'Tis very quiet at the castle, at least since the first few marks of his Passing. But it did sound suspicious of the Veil Grit, so I checked my supply. 'Twas short one vial." She shook her head. "'Twould have only taken one."

In agreement, he affirmed the obvious. "It had to be Mikkal, could've been no other."

"I can't believe he'd do that willfully. Koryl must have some kind of hold o'er him."

"'Tis too late to worry about now, and if she has such a hold o'er the boy, we didn't put distance 'tween them too soon. May he be safe in Drekinn. We'll just have to deal with the consequences, knowing the prophesy remains intact and 'tis as it should be. Shytin had to take the throne for Gabriel to make his claim, but 'twas not in my wildest dreams 'twould be as this."

After accepting the situation as best they could, and discussing the near certain end to their presence in King's Gate within their watch, along with safety concerns surely forthcoming with the change of leadership, 'twas understandable that Gheryh needed to leave soon. She'd waited two dawns for Larken to return afore taking Gabriel, knowing they'd want to say their farewells, for which Larken was grateful. But he couldn't avoid the inevitable any longer and alone in the dark of the new moon, he'd gone home to get the boy. 'Twas his turn to shed tears and feel the sting of separation. "Come my son. 'Tis time to meet Gheryh, your guide." Gabriel's eyes glistened, but no tears welled o'er. He pulled on the new cloak his mother gave him. 'Twas full length, hooded and fur lined, and of excellent quality. He knew Matana had the skill to make it, but how had she hidden it in the making?

And 'twas evidence that she'd known of his leaving long afore they'd informed him. 'Twas not like the ones the other boys at court wore, 'twas unusual in the style, functional, simple, and similar to the shirts she made for him, allowing him to melt into his surroundings. 'Twas one of the best gifts he'd ever received. "I'm ready, father." Turning, he kissed his mother on the cheek, told her he loved her, then shouldered his pack and walked out the door.

~~~~~~~~~~~

Grifynn led the way to Evanntyr on a black War Horse stallion, with Aalanna riding side by side much of the trip. Their journey took them 'cross the Great Plains of Drekinn, past Lorelei, and through the Razor's Cut to King's Gate Village. The Commander set a fast pace, but 'twas a hard ride with the expectation of comfort and courtly extravagance at the end. However, they arrived at Evanntyr within a fortnight to a shameful lack of protocol. Barely imbedded within the castle, they were taken afore the new High King in the throne room, and without ceremony, were forced to prostrate themselves and swear fealty for all they represented.

The entourage from the Dragon Clan were the first to arrive but they were soon joined by many others, all treated in the same manner. There was much grumbling about the unusual and unreasonable fealty swearing, the lack of appropriate observance, and the general substandard conditions in the castle. Grifynn had to keep his wits about him at all times, for the mood was foul. Yet try as he might, his senses far superior, he found not a hint of proof as to the reality of the situation. The staff, the peasants, and the visiting landed, Clan leaders, elders and mayors alike, remained tight lipped, unwilling to speak their minds. 'Twas a palpable fear throughout the castle that he'd not encountered his entire span of days, a rather lengthy time, considering.

The young King showed himself to be impulsive and immature in his words and deeds, clearly influenced by his mother. No
~~~~~~~~~~~

one managed to speak with him alone 'til Aalanna, using her natural outgoing charm and sociability, struck up an innocent conversation while Koryl was briefly indisposed. Upon returning, 'twas plain the Queen Mother and her son were not in agreement with regards to her company. Aalanna tried to take her leave but Shytin forbade it, and there ensued an awkward power struggle she'd hoped to avoid. However, Koryl eventually accepted the situation simply because she couldn't discern any treachery in their acquaintance.

Aalanna's heart went out to the boy, for his loneliness and insecurities initially shone through the outer facade he attempted to portray. Could they have been wrong? Mayhap the boy was in such a state from losing his father, for thus far there was no evidence to suggest 'twas not a natural death, however, 'twas impossible to elicit anything revealing from Shytin, with Koryl at his shoulder from that moment onward. This actually helped their cause and Aalanna assured her mate that she'd do everything she could to keep them busy while he continued his clandestine efforts. Aalanna spent many marks entertaining the new King, but a sinister side began to emerge. As the days stretched into sennights, his hidden nature exerted itself and her discomfort grew. Nevertheless, she felt her mate was taking a greater risk day after day, so she persisted. If Grifynn had known of her anxiety, he would have left the castle without delay.

With Aalanna's successful efforts, Grifynn followed every lead, no matter how slight, even extending their stay under the ruse of discussing business with the new King. The Dragon Clan provided his Warriors, and although they'd enjoyed a healthy contract with all the Kings of the past, he sought to ensure the new one was of the same mind. But what he really wanted was to locate the Healer who might have seen Bryard, as well as the Cleric who'd presided o'er the coronation. Eventually, he had to admit that he'd failed to find that which he needed in order to prove foul play had a hand in the death, and in less than a moon they were forced to pack up and go home. Nevertheless, the apprehension that lay o'er Evanntyr raised more questions than answers. Despite his skill, all he'd uncovered was proof that Dragons were visiting the castle, as well as a mysterious man so menacing that no one would name, let alone discuss. Great fear followed that one.

<center>~~~~~DREKINN~~~~~</center>

Mikkal leaned the broom against the wall and practically tore off the apron, hanging it haphazardly upon the hook. Cleaning up had taken longer this morning than usual, but he was finally finished. On his way past the stoves he grabbed half a loaf of day old bread, tore it open and shoved some roast inside. Dipping the loaf into some gravy, he slipped quietly out the back door of the inn. Eating quickly, he raced through the alleys of the Port District toward the High Gate. 'Twas not yet dawn but he knew well the way, even in the dark.

Running was his favorite time, his personal time, his endurance increased tenfold in the fortnight since he'd arrived, as this had become his daily routine. The Port District was terraced with the lay of the land from the flat top of the ancient mountain, downward along the southern border of the village as it wrapped its way to the Sea of Dreams. The inlet was created by a natural coral reef, bordered by cliffs along both the northern and southern edges, where lay the docks. 'Twas all uphill to the High Gate, with many alleys, rooflines, fences, and rock walls of varying heights, that led the boy to perform flips, jumps, rolls, dives, cartwheels, and all manner of acrobatics. 'Twas not only a good workout, but provided a more direct route allowing him to avoid the normal back and forth walkway, getting him to the Den in less than half the time. Today he'd petition the Training committee, just as he did every day since he'd arrived. Today he'd be accepted, he could feel it, just as he felt it every day. But afore even that honor, he'd wait in the observation stands of the Pits and watch the katas, fascinated, imitating their moves, learning, practicing, preparing for his chance. Mayhap he'd see that boy who looked so much like him. Since he had no real family, he'd never met anyone with similar features, and 'twas intriguing.

Halfway through the district, he heard them. Several boys were bullying a younger and much smaller boy as he was going about his morning chores. They wouldn't get away with it this time. Just a few dawns prior, he'd found the lad cowering behind some crates in an alley, nose bloodied and eye swollen. Rychard had been afraid to go back to his employer in fear of punishment for not only an incomplete task, but loss of the coin with which he'd been entrusted. Mikkal had been late to the Den that morning as he'd unsuccessfully attempted to track down the assailants, afterwards assisting his new friend to get his chores done, paying for his purchases with his own coin. Bullies were something new to him. He'd decided he didn't like them at all, and being rather quick tempered and intolerant of wrong doings, he set out to put a stop to their deeds. Surely if they did this to Rychard, they were doing this to others. Even though they were older than he, Rychard told him they were of similar size.

He slowed down and very quietly approached the area. When he heard the little boy's squeaks of protest abruptly turn to pain, 'twas more than enough for Mikkal and he burst upon the scene without a glance. 'Twas a dead end alley into which five boys had cornered Rychard, each taking turns pushing him around. His lip was cut and bleeding, pants ripped, with his bag on the ground, coins spilled everywhere. Mikkal cared not that he was vastly outnumbered with no weapon to even the odds. He rained fury upon the boys, grabbing them by the pants and literally flinging them into the walls and o'er the garbage bins, ducking, swinging, connecting with feet, fists and elbows time and again, his anger fueling his strength. Suddenly, Rychard was at his side, hugging him and telling him they'd all run away, and that he was a hero. Hero? The boy was just lucky he'd regained his senses quickly enough so as not to hit him, too. "Rychard, are you alright? Did they hurt you badly?" Mikkal wiped the corner of his own mouth and glared at the blood on his thumb as if 'twas impudent of it, to have been there. After all, he had no memory of receiving such a blow, or any blow, from the others.

"I'll be alright, and I got my coin back, thanks to you."

He helped the boy recover his belongings from under the trash bin where he'd been trying to stay out of the way of Mikkal's offensive. "Who are these boys, Rychard? Are they Clan?"

"Oh no! Well, not most of them. They're travelers, outsiders. They come in with the tides, with the mariners. But lately it's always someone, and I seem to be everyone's target. Can you teach me to fight like that? I'm afraid they'll try again and you won't always be around. And you know, we're almost the same age. I'll probably never be as big as you."

"Didn't you learn how to fight in Early Training?"

Rychard stared pointedly at Mikkal afore responding. "I'm not Clan either, and I'm an orphan. I missed out."

Mikkal was late again.

CHAPTER FIVE

Lost and Found

~~~MEANWHILE, A FEW DAWNS AFTER
LEAVING KING'S GATE~~~

Gheryh sat on her heels beside her bedroll, munching on some roots she'd dug up earlier. She was acutely aware of her father's command not to help Gabriel make his self discovery, but he was very curious and she wasn't certain if 'twas more persistently frustrating or innocently amusing. She glanced at the boy of thirteen winters and imagined herself on her first journey at the same age. Handsome and well muscled, he still appeared quite young. Had she looked so young? Surely she'd not been so sheltered. Much was expected of this one and in her opinion 'twas wrong to keep the truth from him, but 'twas not her decision. Still, mayhap she could lead him without leading him, after all, they were just having an innocent conversation. "You ask many questions without asking. You seek answers in casual responses to leading comments. For what do you search? What troubles you?"

Gabriel was a good judge of character, and having already decided Gheryh was trustworthy, he chose to be straight forward. "I search for knowledge. I know that with which I've been presented all my life, is somehow lacking. I don't know exactly why I feel this way, I just know I'm different from the rest in my world. And if that wasn't bad enough, I seem to be missing a part of me. 'Tis as if I live another life somewhere, my soul split in half." He lowered his head, lost in thought. "Larken and his mate are good people, intelligent, loving, kind, yet we look not alike, and they live secret lives they think I know not about. My education has been solitary despite the other boys at court, and I've been presented many courses of study they have not. I know more than my parents think I do, but I know not all." He cast his gaze upon his guide, sensing
~~~

her emotions, and choosing his next words to elicit that which he sought, he continued. "And I won't more than mention being sent to live with the Daggogh, whom I've never even heard of afore. Trying to protect me from the chaos at court since Bryard's death, somehow doesn't adequately cover this situation. Protect me from what? Too many questions, Gheryh, and even your answers are vague. I seek the truth. Will I find it with the People?"

She hesitated, but was wise of her own accord, and her response was not a recitation of another's thoughts. "'Oft times, truth depends upon both the speaker and the listener, and the impact of truth depends on its timing. I believe you will find the truth you seek, when the time is right. Other than that, 'tis not for me to say."

Satisfaction shone in his eyes. "You've said much. You've revealed that I have a purpose yet unknown, my life is in danger, and that you, and mayhap all of the People, know more about me than I know myself."

"Wild guessing is usually dangerous as well, but your reasoning is astute. May I suggest that you keep these thoughts to yourself? Surely you've not confided in anyone at the castle?"

"No, I never felt safe there. You're the first person to whom I've said anything in my entire life. I pray I haven't misplaced my trust."

"You chose well, m'Lord." Her words stung her own ears as she'd spilled forth the appropriate title for one of his station, immediately regretting them. But how does one take back words?

Surprised, he questioned, "M'lord? You're my elder, I should call you, m'lady."

Thinking quickly, she replied, "I am a Hunter. You are from the court of Evanntyr. But, don't get used to that. Once with the People, you're nothing again and will have to earn their respect." Watching the emotions play o'er his face, she was confident she'd managed to cover acceptably, sensing her blunder had gone unnoted. Fortunately, the boy was still a bit shrouded in the sorrow of leaving his home and family.

"No concerns there. I've felt like nothing most of my life. But I shan't be that way for long. I have plans."

Gheryh was surprised by this admission. What would make the boy feel like nothing? Or was that one of his ploys to elicit more information? She chose to ignore the first comment, focusing on the last, as she stared at him meaningfully. One would hope the boy who'd be upon the throne one day, was of the highest integrity. And if he ran off on some self indulging mission afore... "Plans have a way of changing as we age."

"And with the truth..." he replied immediately, his gaze locked onto hers, daring her to answer and not ignore him.

She could tell he knew the truth when 'twas told. 'Twas obvious he was strong willed and yet, not reckless. The traits he'd displayed o'er their journey, along with this conversation, gave her much hope. She dared to say what she felt. "Yes, plans change with the truth."

Releasing her gaze, he glanced down and sighed, the power play ended for the moment. "I really need to know. How long will I be kept in the dark?"

"As long as it takes. In the meantime, you'll be prepared for whatever life throws at you. You've much work ahead, and you'll enjoy living with the Daggogh. You'll feel welcome, your arrival has been long awaited."

Uncharacteristic self pity took root. Fueled by recent events near o'erwhelming, and with his future in the dark, he snapped back, "And to think, I just learned about all this within a few mere marks of being thrown in head first."

"Sarcasm does not favor you," she said, then bit her tongue afore she repeated her previous slip.

He recovered quickly. "You're right. 'Tis what 'tis and I shall make the best of it."

Her reply was filled with compassion. "Things will change soon enough and 'twill be the end of childhood. Do not hasten such. Live each day as it presents itself to you, for once 'tis gone, 'twill never be lived again."

"Although I fear my 'childhood' has already ended, you are most wise, Gheryh. I wish to learn from you."

"And 'tis a wise man who knows from whom he can learn. Now. Running silent does not include long conversations. Sleep for awhile. We rise with the moon and travel through the night. Silently." Her tone did not allow refute, and although only two winters his elder, Gabriel did as she said and was soon asleep. Gheryh caught her partner's eye, giving him the responsibility of waking them both within a mark, and keeping watch as they rested. She was fatigued and not sure she'd waken on time, but she needn't have been concerned.

Ryygg cast his glance o'er his shoulder when he felt her rise. Quietly he stood up, stretched slowly and yawned, then disappeared into the forest to reconnoiter while she gathered their belongings. Gabriel woke without her nudge, which made her smile. The Kahyah returned as quietly as he'd left, conferring with Gheryh while the boy finished packing. Ryygg was impressed with her plan, and the trip wouldn't even take that much longer than their usual return. He'd found the Hunters the previous dawn and explained the plan to their Night Beasts, who couldn't divulge their secret as they had no translator. Even so, he'd not revealed their path, ensuring their safety first. But the Beasts could encourage their Handlers to follow them, and their trail would be well covered, in case they were needed. He chuffed, pricked his ears, then followed Gheryh and the boy into the night.

<center>~~~~~EVANNTYR~~~~~</center>

The Sorcerer stood at the window and glared, as the entourage from the Dragon Clan finally left the castle to return home to Drekinn. They'd arrived a mere dawn after the return of their messenger. The Runner would have taken a fortnight to get there, and 'twould have taken a fortnight hard ride back. They must have left immediately. He'd been prepared for their presence, along with all the others however, their extended visit had made it more difficult for him to complete his business. Angrily, he Called to the Dragon he'd sent with the mercenaries.

Long after midnight, when all in the castle had retired, he stood at the same window and stared into the night. He hated complications and he'd just been presented with another. The Dragon he'd sent to keep watch o'er the mercenaries had reported they'd lost the boy and his escort, but then he'd found strangers traveling deep into the Edge. 'Twould seem the mercenaries thought the boy had switched traveling companions. This was not what his source had revealed, and now he wished he hadn't already killed him in order to ensure his silence. He watched the Dragon fly off into the distance with instructions to gather the reinforcements from Tupry he'd previously hired to replace any of the men who might be lost in the chase. He'd also set a Spell upon the beast to allow him to scent the boy through his father. 'Twas not an easy Spell to cast and had taken much from his depleted resources. 'Twould not last for long, but 'twould be worth the risk if they located the True King afore anyone else. If the boy was with these strangers, 'twould soon be confirmed.

~~~~~SOMEWHERE IN THE DEEP OF WYNDSYR FOREST~~~~~

The leader of the group of men leaned o'er the fire and tore off a piece of one of the rabbits sizzling on the spit. He'd just received some interesting news and was most aggravated. They'd been a'field for o'er a moon and this mission wasn't going as planned. He carefully assessed each of the sixteen men eating and working around the camp. All he could hear o'er the crackling of the fire was the rough, rhythmic scraping of blades being sharpened upon whetstones. As he stood silently, his jaw set, he waited for their attention. Soon all eyes were upon him. His nose was flattened from past injuries, his voice nasal. "I think we must concede that we've lost the boy. As you know, Rinny and Birt never came back, and I sent two more pair who also went missing. By the time 'twas confirmed and I'd sent yet another pair of track-
~~~~~

ers, our quarry had vanished, although they found what re-mained of the last pairs. I've also discovered that our employer hired reinforcements, and I'm leery as to why he felt that we'd need such, as he apparently made these arrangements afore we'd even left Tupry. Thus far, we've lost a total of eighteen men, the six trackers and the rest having never returned from forays on their own. Some were hunting, some were pissing in the woods. They. Never. Came. Back." His eyes scanned the men and found the two who'd just returned with their gruesome report. Still un-settled, they sat with their backs to each other, weapons in hand as if expecting a Troll to attack. "And tonight I was told two of the horses are missing, as well as more than a few of our hounds. 'Tis not in my plan to continue the search, as 'twould be a convenient way for someone to knock off a few more of us." This last state-ment was to everyone's relief. The men didn't say a word, their eyes diverted from their leader's heated gaze, as they continued tending their weapons. No one wanted to be chosen to go back out on the search. In point of fact, no one wanted to leave the fire alone, no matter upon what task.

The man continued. "We all knew the risks, however 'twas ob-vious the boy and his escort were heading straight to the Great Plains of Drekinn and then they simply disappeared. It should've been relatively easy to find them again, even given a two day head start, yet there's been no trace 'til less than a mark ago, when quite by accident we've learned that we have an audience. 'Twas through no fault of theirs, and 'twas most certainly through no skill of ours." He glared at them afore continuing. "'Twas the Dragon. He smelled something in the forest from on high. Seems we're given new information by random chance, and after a bit of snooping around we now know we're being watched by at least two men, mayhap more. They're following us, and I believe they're responsible for thinning our numbers. And, they're not from King's Gate, nor of Lorelei or Tupry." Speculative whispers resounded and the speaker finally raised his hand for their attention once again. "I've heard about a mysterious tribe of humans who live deep in the Edge, and one thing is certain. They do not allow outsiders into their midst. We already know the boy must be suspect of the High King's seed and therefore worth far more than we're being paid, and 'twould make sense that if they're covering for him, he means much to this tribe as well. These hunters must have switched the boy we seek with a false trail. I don't think the one we're being paid to bring back is going to Drekinn at all. I think these others are taking him deep into the mountains."

Unconvinced, one of the men spoke up. "I think we lost the one we're being paid to bring back, and now you want to try to find another to take his place. After all, our employer is not going to pay us 'til we return with the prize. But 'tis one very large flaw in your thinking. You've not mentioned a boy with these hunters."

The first man nodded his head. "Under other circumstances I'd say you were right, no visual, no quarry. But there are too many questions here. What happened to the boy? We can't even find his escort. Now we've picked up followers and why exactly would they be following? And they've been most determined to keep us from following them. C'mon. They're hiding something. Or someone. Either way, if we've lost the boy we still need an income, and I think we may have fallen into a treasure trove. On the other hand, if we've found the boy we'll get the income we'd planned, plus more upon negotiations for our added trouble. And, we still have the Dragon, if he'll cooperate. He's not exactly on our payroll however, which brings up another point. 'Twould behoove us to fulfill our contract, as we have no idea how loyal this creature is to our employer, although he's just as guilty for losing him in the first place. He's attempting to scout around. Although he's reluctant to land, for some reason he thinks he can track him now by scent alone."

The others conferred amongst themselves, shaking their heads and emphasizing their opinions with raised voices and mugs, as they heatedly discussed the situation. None of them wanted to return to Tupry empty handed. The likelihood of their 'audience' having something worthwhile, seemed to rise as a quarter mark dripped past.

Finally, a chosen speaker stepped forward. "We're in. We find out what they're tryin' so hard to hide. Then we kill 'em. Hopefully, in that order." A chorus of voices all in agreement, rang out from around the camp.

CHAPTER SIX
Trouble on the Trip

Using the guttural language of the Kahyah, Gheryh spoke with Ryygg. "Why were you gone so long? Are they still following us?" The Night Beast had left two dawns prior and 'twas now past midnight of the approaching third. She was relieved to see him, yet his demeanor spoke volumes in foreboding. Her back to the boy, she searched her partner's eyes.

'Twas a significant delay in his response. "I had much to observe. And yes, they follow us still."

His tone made her stiffen. Mistaking the implication, she asked apprehensively, "How many?"

"As we already knew, they began with no less than thirty in their company. But they came not from King's Gate. They're from Tupry. By the time I traced them down, the Hunters had killed a total of thirty six and all their hounds and horses. However, they've gained Human reinforcements. I counted nineteen at their fire afore I returned. They're not far behind, nevertheless, I believe we're safe through dawn."

She shook her head. They'd originally assumed the trackers came from King's Gate, but Tupry was closer to Lorelei than 'twas to the castle. And they'd been traveling near a moon. How did they get here so fast? Tupry was a known black market town for those who wanted something they shouldn't have, and a hideout for those who could be paid to provide such. These men must have left Tupry afore they'd even departed King's Gate. So. They were mercenaries, not Hoardsmen. She was supposed to let the Hunters take care of any followers, but a very bad feeling crept up her spine as Ryygg continued silently willing her to ask the obvious question.

Evading, she asked, "Any Dragons?"

Ryygg shook his head. No, he hadn't seen any, but yes, he'd heard them talking about one that might be helping them. Still he waited for the question he didn't want to have to answer.

Finally, she asked. "Are they safe?"

His jaw tense, eyes burning with rage, Ryygg replied, "They're dead, but their bodies were not alone. From the carnage I observed, the Hunters and their Beasts did not go easily Past the Veil. 'Twas where they took mayhap sixteen with them, the others were killed prior. 'Twas difficult to sort through, but I could smell the Dragon."

No longer able to stand, she sat on her heels and hung her head, staring into space while trying to find her voice. Trembling with emotion, she replied, "I'm confident they put up a righteous fight, but they were only two. The Danoh didn't want a large hunting party, felt 'twould draw too much attention. Apparently, we drew too much anyway." She looked up, resolute in her strength. "Nevertheless, I'm actually surprised to discover they sent this many to take us down. They must know something. But how? And who would pay mercenaries? I like it not, yet I can think of no way to get a message to Larken. They could be in danger too, but we must go. They're on their own."

Ryygg was proud of his Handler. She had not the scent of fear about her, just determination, and mayhap indecision. Trying to read her unspoken thoughts, he asked bluntly, "Should I kill them?"

Her hesitancy evaporated as she regained her feet. "There are too many, and they've proven even a Night Beast can be o'erwhelmed. We have no idea if they're expecting more reinforcements and I won't lose you. No. Kill only in defense of our retreat as we make haste. Our mission is to get Gabriel safely home without leading the others to the People, and that is what I intend to do." Resolve filled her roving eyes. "We change course immediately. We take the short cut."

Ryygg sat down hard, shaking his shaggy head. "Through the abyss? Very risky. You and I are the only ones who've ever made it through, and the Danoh is still ignorant of our daring. If something happens to us within the chasms, we'll never be found. And may I remind you, it's not exactly short."

What the Kahyah had referred to as 'the abyss' was officially known as Abysmal Gorge, a terrifyingly steep, deep, and treacherous multi-cave and chasm region. 'Twas the home of many nightmarish flora and fauna, some found nowhere else in all of Kadoor, a region through which no one other than Gheryh and Ryygg had safely crossed and everyone avoided, for all those who tried, died. "Better to lose the three of us without anyone knowing what happened to Gabriel, than to lose him to those men. And 'tis short, 'tis a direct route home. If we go around the mountain we have fewer places to hide, and 'twill take o'er twice as long with those trackers on our butts. Besides, you doubt our ability to cross again? We've done it many times afore!"

Ryygg's voice was brooding. "We've not done it 'many times', we've survived it twice, and only because you insisted, and it seemed like a good idea at the time. As I recall, we near Passed on both crossings. And if a Dragon does come, we'll have even more difficulty defending ourselves, adding one more hurdle. Frankly, I prefer my odds with those men."

Gheryh stubbornly countered. "I don't. The plan was to travel by stealth, not fight our way home. If we leave now we can lose them with ease, and even on the slim possibility they're able to enter behind us, they'll not survive. And Dragons never travel this deep into the Edge. They're afraid of the forests and there's few places for them to land. On the other hand, you and I alone cannot take on nineteen men, with possibly more reinforcements coming. And how many hounds and horses did you say they had? Furthermore, we must protect Gabriel. We'd be o'erwhelmed as were the rest, and our mission would be for naught."

Sullenly, Ryygg responded. "None." She was right of course, her reasoning sound, but he still didn't like the idea.

True consternation covered Gheryh's face. "What?"

Narrowing his eyes, he repeated himself. "None. They have no hounds or horses, the Hunters killed them."

Exasperated, she threw her hands in the air. "Is that all you got out of this entire conversation?"

Gabriel had been watching and listening to the peculiar behavior 'tween his two traveling companions, and 'twas evident something had changed for the worse. He'd already decided that they were talking to each other, and he had a pretty good idea they were discussing him at the moment. From their inflections and posturing 'twas clear his life, as well as theirs, was in danger. Standing behind her, his voice cracking with puberty, he said, "I can swing a decent sword."

Spinning around in surprise, Gheryh repeated her earlier question in Common Tongue, "What?"

Gabriel cleared his throat and began again. "I said, I can swing a decent sword. Larken taught me how to fight. This is about me and people are going to die. I need to participate in my own defense. And are you really talking to the Beast?" Once more hearing her father's warning to keep their exchanges to herself, a flash of guilt swept her senses and she snapped, "Does it look like I'm talking to him?" Afore the boy could respond, she spun back to Ryygg and continued their private dialogue. "We shall do what we must and prepare for the future, when we join forces with the Clan. My father cannot deny this now. The People fool themselves if they think to stay on the sidelines of this war. 'Tis looming ever closer and 'twill soon land in our laps."

Turning back to the boy, she began to collect their gear, switching languages flawlessly. "Gather your things. Leave nothing, not even footprints. No torches. We travel dark and silent from here. Keep your weapons sheathed and your hands and face covered. We don't want the moonlight sneaking through the canopy and glinting off the steel, or your pale skin. You ride for the first few marks while I backtrack to set a false trail. Once I catch up, Ryygg will cover us the rest of the night. We must be long away afore dawn."

Gabriel began to protest that he wasn't that pale, but then he took another look at the 'Gogh. He'd been proud of himself when they'd first met. He'd not even stared at her, however, he hadn't really thought her appearance so odd. She looked a lot like the other female living in the cabin, the one they called the Healer of the Forest, and he'd actually met that one in the castle afore. She was simply different. Appearance didn't make or break a man, their character did, and he trusted his instincts more than his vision. Her skin, hair, and clothing were dyed, cut, and wrapped, seemingly to blend into the surrounding brush. Even the weapons he'd seen thus far, were perfectly camouflaged. Why, she could probably stand out in the open and remain unseen as long as she didn't move.

Her appearance reminded him of his cloak. His mother and father were good to him, but it seemed he'd always known they weren't his real parents. Still, Larken had taught him much and he'd felt loved and wanted for the whole of his short life. He'd miss the man. One of his most important lessons was to be patient, listen far more than you speak, choose your loyalties carefully, and pay close attention to body language, tone of voice, expression, and emotions. Be always prepared for the worst. His intuition was strong, for which he was grateful, but still, there was so much yet to learn. So many changes. He stooped o'er and quickly gathered his few belongings, helped brush away the evidence of their stay, then accepted her knee up onto Ryygg's broad back. Taking a double fistful of thick mane, he drew a deep breath, and although he was an excellent rider, 'twasn't going to be like riding a horse. He hung on tightly, and for the first time since this adventure began, instead of feeling sadness about what he'd lost, he felt keen anticipation.

CHAPTER SEVEN

Abysmal Gorge

They'd taken twice as long to reach their destination than she'd thought 'twould take. Gheryh was even more confident that she'd chosen correctly, for trying to shake their trackers had proven a more difficult task than either of them anticipated. The mercenaries were tenacious indeed. Gheryh whispered as they listened to the beating of wings approaching from the distance. "A Dragon? They actually sent a Dragon into the forest for us? 'Tis desperation they show, they must know our secret." Although they'd managed to lose the men, 'twould be more difficult to lose a Dragon. Not all of the mountains were forested, but she'd hoped the Hoard would take a lot longer to come to that realization. And the abyss was only heavily forested in some areas. However, they wouldn't be visible from the sky for much of the crossing. She still liked their chances this way.

Gabriel was confused as he expected to see a canyon somewhere. But what they now faced was a solid wall of thick undergrowth into which they were evidently about to venture. Gheryh had already warned Gabriel to stay close. "'Tis imperative we not become separated," she'd said. After she'd laid the false trail and caught up with them, she'd sent the Beast to retrieve the ellka rack. With Ryygg gone o'er a sennight, they'd had some close encounters with the mercenaries who'd split up and were casting about hoping to find them by chance. But they'd successfully managed to give them the slip and Ryygg met them soon afterwards. Gheryh had secured the huge rack squarely 'cross his shoulders so he was balanced, and they'd traveled almost nonstop 'til arriving at the wall.

After ensuring everyone understood the plan, Gabriel lined up behind Gheryh with the fearsome Night Beast bringing up the rear.

Using her machete she vigorously attacked the twisted vines, creating just enough space for all three of them to enter. Amazingly, the brush seemed to heal itself, growing rapidly to fill in where they'd passed through, leaving not a trace of their entrance. 'Twas so fast, Gabriel had to literally hang onto Gheryh's quiver or the vines would grow up 'tween them and he'd be lost in brush, totally blind to direction. He couldn't see anything above or to either side of them, and he had to keep his eyes riveted to the ground to avoid tripping and falling on his face, which could be fatal as the vines grew at such a rate they'd impale any living creature in their way. Initially he'd attempted to assist her with his sword, but there wasn't room enough to swing and he was afraid of injuring one or the other of his guides, if not himself. She'd assured him, without stopping her assault upon the living barricade, that his assistance wasn't necessary and encouraged him to simply keep up with the pace she'd set, manually rerouting the vines behind them as they grew. He felt the warm panting breath of the Kahyah upon his back and knew the great Beast was having as much trouble as was he, the encumbering vines aggressively attempting to close up their path. The Night Beast uttered some combination of growls and chuffs that Gabriel recognized as speech, to which he expected the 'Gogh to respond. She'd seemed surprised that he'd known they were having an intelligent conversation the other night, but he'd kept to himself the inability to decipher their exact words. Using his heightened intuition, he'd watched their body language and listened carefully, as was his habit. Very good at making accurate guesses, he could then draw more information through leading statements. Gheryh didn't disappoint him, and he wondered of what they said.

"How much further, Gheryh? 'Tis much more difficult with another 'tween us, and carrying this rack is about to break me. The vines grow quickly and I'm being inundated back here!"

"Stop whining, at least you don't have to cut the Flaming things! They spit at me, and my skin is burning already. 'Tis all I can do to keep it out of my eyes."

"Are you sure there's no Fearyn among these?"

Grunting with her efforts, she replied, "'Tis not known to grow among other species. It requires much more light and prefers open high grounds and solitude. Besides, these have no thorns, just this gods awful burning sap. We're safe from the poison of the Fearyn here, but soon…"

"'Tis exactly as the last times. How did we manage to find this place afore?"

Gheryh didn't answer. She was getting too tired. 'Twas so thick, the light of day barely shone through. Their feet were dragging, all of them having more trouble stepping o'er the tangles. Thinking back to their first crossing, she recalled the stories she'd heard of the abyss. And then there was the need for shelter from that group of outsiders they'd near run into. Being farther away from home than they were supposed to have been, they'd had no back up, no Hunters to protect them, and they'd been desperate. She'd hoped that at the very least the vines were in themselves a provider of refuge, and at the best 'twas the legendary wall. Once through they'd realized the dream of a lifetime, but had to use every bit of knowledge and skill to survive. The first time was sheer dumb luck. The second? An experiment. The third? Her gift to Kadoor.

Abruptly, Gabriel lost his grip on the quiver as Gheryh lurched ahead and disappeared. With his great nose, the big Kahyah shoved him onward afore the wall completely closed. Stumbling, he stepped onto solid rock as if he'd just crossed a threshold from night to day, Ryygg right behind. 'Twas so sudden, the sunlight blinded him and he blinked several times as his eyes struggled to adjust. The 'Gogh was squatting at a rock formation halfway to the edge of the cliff upon which he now stood, catching her breath and rubbing some kind of powdery substance onto her arms and legs where the sap had begun to raise welts. Still breathing hard, she passed a handful of the pale brown powder to the boy, who looked first at her hand, then at his own arms and legs, and realized he was covered in the ugly welts as well, and they were beginning to burn. "We were not prepared for this journey. 'Tis as the first time. We scored better the second, but I'm in no mood for another test." She smiled, then went to check the pads of the Kahyah. Carefully, she inspected each paw, four times the size of her own hand, afore gently setting it down. "I wish you and I had such fur," she stated, as she gave the Beast a clear bill of health while picking off clumps of hardened sap.

"How 'tis possible we're not burned to a crisp? You cut through a solid wall of vines, we should've been showered with sap. Yet we're relatively unscathed," Gabriel observed.

"The vines self-seal injury with their sap, creating a clear bandage. 'Tis only dangerous to bare skin when 'tis still wet, but since you were behind me and it dries so quickly, you didn't get much. I managed to save some from the second trip and found at least one very practical use." She stared at the powder Gabriel was using and then smiled in such a manner, he knew what she meant. This powder was made from the sap of the vines that caused the injury. Amazingly, the welts were gone as he rubbed it off. "The first time we did this, I suffered through days of natural healing 'til I discovered some of the dried sap stuck in Ryygg's fur and powdered it. And afore you wash, rub dirt everywhere you used the powder. Ryygg burned his tongue from accidentally licking a tiny amount off my arm. Apparently, it regains its original potency with hydration other than the fluid of the blisters of burns and bites, and I can only surmise that water and spit might have similar results. The second trip I cut a few sticks, and since they seal themselves, I now keep some in a pouch in my kit. There's much in the land of the People which causes harm, and much which takes it away. We merely need to listen, observe, learn. All we require is here, with us. Nothing is as it appears on the surface, and everything has a purpose."

Gabriel was still amazed at the healing properties of the dried sap after what it had done to his skin in its original form. After both of them rubbed down with dirt, he watched her take some new cuttings and very carefully place them on a rock. When the ends were sealed, she gathered them and put them in a small bag inside a pouch that hung at her hip. She also took the dried sap that had dripped onto the rock, and placed the pieces in the bag with the cuttings. She caught his eye and saw the concern. He had much about which to be concerned, what with being hunted by mercenaries in alliance with Dragons, out in the field alone for the first time in his short life, feeling ill equipped to handle the looming battle, and now facing the legendary abyss. She'd made an effort to prepare him for their crossing, making sure he understood the gravity of the situation, while at the same time trying not to cause panic. Attempting to portray some sense of future while shifting his thoughts away from their present, she stated, "I'm not a practicing Healer, although all Hunters have basic training. I carry only that which I may not be able to find in the field. 'Tis not wise to be without a medicine bag. But each of the People carry their own, stocked with what they feel are their greatest needs. It may be interesting to you to learn what other Hunters carry with them. Soon, we'll be able to do that." She stood up and brushed off his pack, then helped him hoist it to his shoulder afore doing the same with her own.

The boy recognized her encouragement and was grateful. "I'll do my best to be a help and not a hindrance to you, Gheryh. I very much want to meet the People."

"I will get you home safely, Gabriel. We're not lost yet. But we very well may be, if we don't move. I hear not the mercenaries but we're open to the skies above."

As if on cue, the shriek of a Dragon came from on high and they scrambled under the edge of the vines. The voice of the creature boomed in their ears as he made his pass, and they had to link their elbows around the larger stalks to keep from being swept off the ledge by the powerful backbeat of his wings. Ryygg was further away and hadn't been able to sink his claws into the threshold where the dirt and rock met, preventing the vines from growing all the way 'cross. Losing his footing, Gheryh screamed through the wind, but nothing could stop his slide toward the edge. The Dragon flew so high that he was a mere speck to their vision while Ryygg thrashed and clawed, his entire body splayed out, completely visible to the Dragon as he set up for a second pass. Having sighted his quarry he dove, plunging swiftly toward the struggling Kahyah. Gabriel threw himself toward Ryygg and grabbed hold of the rack with both hands, lying spread eagle upon the rocky surface, but only managed to slow the Beast. Like a human chain, Gheryh grabbed Gabriel's ankle and then linked hers together in the vines, scraping them open, the burning sap oozing onto her exposed skin. She didn't let go. His slide finally stopped, Ryygg regained his footing and scrambled back up the ledge. Gabriel rolled o'er, and panting, saw the Dragon still plummeting toward them, so close now he could see the glint in the creature's eyes, his wings laid back against his flanks. Gheryh hugged her partner while tears ran down her face to be absorbed by his heavy mane, her burning skin all but forgotten as once again they sought cover under the edge of the vines. 'Twould do no good.

Of one accord and with speed unimaginable, Gheryh nocked an arrow, and after plunging the head into one of the vines to coat it with the sticky sap, she let it fly toward the Dragon. Aiming for its eye to damage the brain, she hit true, while Gabriel tried to pierce the creature's side with his sword. 'Twould have been useless, since the sword would have bounced off the Dragon's scales, but Gheryh's arrow sunk deep and the creature rotated away from them, exposing his underbelly as he fell onto the ledge. Gabriel ran and shoved his sword through the underarm into the ribcage, hitting the heart. This slowed the Healing even more, and although the Dragon seemed to be mortally wounded, they both knew that they could not be killed unless their heart was removed or so damaged as to never beat again, or they were decapitated. Both strikes injured key areas for the Healing, and if they were lucky they'd have enough time to actually force him Past the Veil. But if he fell o'er the edge he'd Heal himself, and they'd be battling again. 'Twas understood they'd get no second chance to survive.

The Dragon slammed down, rolling toward the edge in a repeat of the Kahyah's previous scramble, only he wasn't actively trying to prevent the fall. Ryygg grabbed him by the neck with his teeth and pulled with all his might. Gheryh and Gabriel both grabbed legs, but Gabriel saw 'twas ineffective and ran back to the wall. Cutting a long piece of the vine, he wrapped it around the Dragon's back legs, then anchored him to a large rock. Meanwhile, Gheryh was doing her best to hack out the heart while Ryygg was ripping and tearing away at his neck in his effort to behead him. But even with sluggish Healing and the strength of the jaws of the Night Beast, progress was slow. Gabriel grabbed his sword off the ground where it had fallen and helped Gheryh, who yelled at him to get more sap. Running back to the vines, he slashed several thick pieces and brought them to her as fast as he could. His hands burning, he gripped his sword tighter and watched as Gheryh coated the edge of her own with the sap, then plunged it into the heart. The accursed brute shuddered. "We don't have much time! We have to do more damage, I can't cut it out quickly enough!"

Gabriel followed her lead and they took turns cutting, coating, slashing, she at the heart, he in the eyes to keep the Healing at bay, 'til the beast finally stopped moving. He drew one long, trembling breath, his head jerked up and back violently, and then he lay motionless. Since she could still see him and trusted not the evil thing, they continued their efforts, this time with Gabriel helping cut through the hide. Rewarded a few moments later with the heart in multiple, bloody, and severely burned and blistered pieces at their feet, the carcass of the deceased creature became part of the rock formation to their vision.

"'Tis a foul trick, he disappeared," Gabriel panted in disbelief.

"No, the remains of Magic bearers cannot be seen by humans."

She leaned o'er and looked about to drop to her knees as he replied, "'Tis a good way to confirm their deaths, then."

Sitting down afore they both fell down, she barely managed to respond, "Yes, 'tis indeed."

Still, Gabriel was infinitely curious. "Why did he not simply Flame us?"

Her breath still coming in gasps, she did her best to answer. "They seem to have both a deep respect and a great fear of the forests. I can't explain." She shook her head to indicate she could no longer talk, and covered in blood, heavy breathing was all that could be heard. The fight replayed itself in her mind and she was amazed they'd been successful, each of them having had a part in the killing of the fetid thing. Gabriel worked well beside her, Ryygg was at the head... she squinted as she remembered... the creature threw back his head... and as the shock of the battle wore off, she realized they were alone. "NO!" Leaping up, she frantically searched all about the remains, but no Night Beast was to be found. "Ryygg!" She cried several times for her partner and friend, but only the echoes of her own voice did she hear in reply. Gabriel crawled to the edge of the cliff, wary of the crumbling rock, and peered o'er.

Just as the edge began to collapse under his weight, Gabriel heard Gheryh shouting from behind, "They're coming through!" But 'twas nothing he could do about it, as he slipped head first and tumbled o'er. Free falling, he heard a voice as if from inside himself, yelling for him to reach out. In so doing, he suddenly grabbed Ryygg's rough, thick coat, stuck by the rack still tied to his shoulders in the tangled branches of an old scrub tree growing out of the side of the cliff. "Hang on, boy!" Gabriel didn't have to speak his language to understand the sentiment. The Beast had been knocked unconscious initially, and now struggled to regain the footing he'd had against the cliff wall just prior to being jerked by the addition of the boy. Once steady again, Gabriel climbed 'tween him and the rock, standing on Ryygg's muscular back legs, a death grip upon his mane. With widened eyes and no ability to speak, he stared at Ryygg in astonishment, shaking uncontrollably.

"Gheryh? We're alive, stuck on a tree."

"Ryygg? By the Ancients!"

"Don't come to the edge, I can't hold all of us like this."

"They're cutting through. They don't understand the danger, they've failed to keep together. Some have fallen, I can hear their death screams."

"Go to the tree, any of them who manage to survive, will follow."

"I won't leave you!"

"You must. 'Tis impossible for us to climb up, and you can't climb down. They won't find us here. Wait at the cave of the Eoche, if you can. If not, keep going, we'll find you, I swear it! Now go!"

Gheryh jumped up, rapidly checking her supplies as she bolted down the steep and ever narrowing trail 'tween the wall of vines and the cliff edge. She was grateful for having picked up her pack prior to resting. Hearing angry shouts coming from behind her, she didn't stop or even look back. Some died, but the ones who made it through were now out for revenge. Their experience had made this more than a job. This had become a grudge match.

'Twas no need to try to get their attention, there was no other path. The first 'bridge' stood around the third corner, allowing her time to 'cross afore the men saw how 'twould be accomplished. 'Twas a huge tree which would have taken at least a dozen men linking hands to surround, with one very long and very large branch laid o'er the chasm to the far edge, creating a natural bridge. The branch was inviting and 'twould be easy enough to walk 'cross. But 'twas heavily o'er grown with what the People called the Fearyn, a thick, waxy leafed vine. Its highly toxic, finger length thorns, hidden by its large, deep purple flowers, were fatal with the slightest scratch. She also knew two more things: 'twas no other way 'cross this section unless Ryygg and Gabriel were successful, and the branch was hollow.

<center>~~~~~THE TOWER OF EVANNTYR~~~~~</center>

The Sorcerer was livid. He'd Received a telepathic message, but 'twas so far away he couldn't Respond. The Dragon had found the boy, his scent true and pure of Bryard's seed. The First Born lived. Unfortunately, the dimwit failed to Share his location at that time and shortly thereafter, he'd Heard the beast scream in defiance. Through the Spell linking them, he'd Shared in his death as he'd been forced Past the Veil, and 'twas most painful. Yet, how could that happen? How could one young boy, kill a full grown Highland? And where was the True King now? His lip curled in disgust. It seemed he'd have to depend on the mercenaries after all.

<center>~~~~~THE FEARYN LOG~~~~~</center>

Gheryh scrambled around the tree, and using her hands and feet, she dug through the underbrush to open the hidden entrance to the hollow log. The flowers of the Fearyn were beautiful, the purple so dark 'twas almost black, but preferred to grow only in direct sunlight, and even avoided where 'twas shadow. Still, she had to be careful not to get scratched by the thorns afore she was safely inside. Fortunately, both the entrance and the exit were close to the bottom of the branch where the vine was thin. The opening within the branch was so spacious she could stand up and run, although she did have to watch her head. The Kahyah could have squeezed through, had he been there. He'd done it afore. She rubbed her eyes hard. Tears would alter her vision and mayhap get her killed in the exit.

By the time she was 'cross, they still hadn't come into view. Taking a moment to search the cliff face opposite, Ryygg and

Gabriel were gone and the scrub tree on which they'd probably been caught was partially uprooted. Had they fallen or were they somehow climbing down? Then she heard the mercenaries. With some difficulty, she counted at least sixteen. If all nineteen whom Ryygg saw at their fire had made it to the wall, they'd lost mayhap three cutting through. She grinned. Then she ducked as the blade whooshed past her right ear, lodging in the tree behind her. Turning, she yanked it from the trunk (the People never left good weapons) afore running into the brush heading for the next 'bridge', the cave of the Eoche.

THE DRAGON'S DEN

~~~~~THE OFFICE OF THE BATTLE COMMANDER~~~~~

</div>

Thoughts of their stay at Evanntyr haunted Grifynn. His lovely mate had been upset since their return, but she'd given no reason. Shaking his head, he decided 'twas most likely fatigue from the extended journey. He looked up at the boy standing 'cross from his desk. "So. You say your name is Mikkal? You're an Outlander, correct? I understand you've been petitioning for Warrior Training. I also heard you helped a young lad in the Port District recently."

"Yes, Sir. On all points." Mikkal was elated. After making daily petition since his arrival and fully expecting to continue for moons unending, he was called in this morning to interview with the Battle Commander himself. He now stood afore the most powerful Warrior he'd ever expected to lay eyes upon, and although he had many questions, he knew instinctively to keep them to himself.

An unruly auburn curl escaped its leather tie and Grifynn impatiently tucked it behind one ear. He'd been watching the boy since their return, keeping tabs on his petitions and activities, both in the village and in the Port District. Wary of the Fay's warning, he had to concede Mikkal had merit and should be allowed to train, but he couldn't start off by spoiling the lad.
~~~~~

Training was hard, the hardest thing any Trainee ever attempted in their lives, and the Dragon Clan had a perfect record to maintain. No one had ever quit, all taking the Oath unless they'd Passed during their time in Training due to sickness or accident. 'Twas why the process was so closely controlled, so regimented. His gaze unnerving to most, the boy had yet to flinch. 'Twas a good sign. "Outlanders have no blood allegiance to the Clan. 'Tis why we rarely consider them. However, there are Outlanders in the Brotherhood. And, if you're accepted to Training you'll be behind, as you've already seen your thirteenth winter, correct?"

Again, Mikkal affirmed the question, barely able to hide the grimace elicited. Surely he wasn't the oldest Outlander ever accepted?

"No. You're not the oldest ever accepted."

Well, that was disturbing. 'Twas as if the Battle Commander had read his thoughts.

"Mayhap I can, and mayhap I cannot read your thoughts, but I can certainly read your face. And again, you're not the only Outlander with whom I've dealt."

'Twas a lengthy pause following, to which Mikkal eventually felt he was required to respond. He licked his dry lips and stated, "I'll remember that, Sir."

"Have you ever gambled?"

The question was totally unexpected. "Gambled? Uh... no Sir. I've played games, but I've never been in a village afore Drekinn."

Brusquely Grifynn grabbed the quill pen from the ink well on the corner of his desk and tore a strip off a piece of parchment. While writing something in a flourishing script, his voice deep and booming, he replied, "Well then, 'twill be a learning experience. Teach you to keep your thoughts to yourself and not spread them all about by your expression. In the meantime, I have an arrangement for you. If you still want to be a Warrior, that is. I need your loyalty to me, the Clan, and the Brotherhood. You need to become known to one and all, as well as knowledgeable in our principles, our ways."

His eyes bright, Mikkal was filled with confidence. "You want me to prove that I mean what I say, and that I won't be a detriment to you later. You want me to give up my past and become a Clansman through and through."

"Precisely."

Mikkal grinned and stepped forward. "I've nothing to give up, Sir. What can I do to prove my allegiance and become one with my new home and people?"

Grifynn found himself liking the boy and couldn't help but be amused by his enthusiasm. He'd always wanted a son, yet the prophesy stated 'twould be otherwise. Proof reading the brief note he'd written upon the piece of parchment, he then handed it to Mikkal. His signature gave him access to the castle. "Well my boy, first you'll move into the Den this very morning. Be quick about it, I've made arrangements for you to begin classes with a tutor this afternoon. Following supper, you'll meet me and some of the other petitioners, in the third room off the main Mess Hall in the barracks, for a little game of chance. Then we'll see."

THE DRAGON'S DEN SEVERAL DAWNS LATER
~~~IN ONE OF MANY READING ROOMS
OFF THE MAIN LIBRARY~~~

</div>

Mikkal had interviewed so many people, his head was swimming. Surely most of the current petitioners on the rosters had come by to visit already, but mayhap he was becoming delusional. After posting the development of the program all o'er Drekinn, the Port District, and the Den, he was a tad disappointed that more of the Warriors and Clansmen hadn't come to make application, but mayhap he'd not given it enough time. After all, 'twas only the first day.

Grifynn had tasked him with creating a program to identify those children missed by the Early Training of the Clan, teaching them the ways of self defense and honor. He'd hoped, 1) to avoid
~~~

the bully mentality by catching them early and making them a part of something more important, 2) to identify those who were not going to change, and, 3) to give the others the tools with which to deal with that reality. Life wasn't easy, and trying to control the bullies would prove useless in the end. Every child should be prepared to deal with all kinds of people, for all kinds of people would they confront throughout their span of days. Grifynn gave Mikkal relatively free rein to set up the program, recruit his own trainers, gather and enroll the children, teach the Clan about it, and make it self-sustaining so that he'd have the time when 'twas earned, to enter Training himself. As Mikkal was learning, 'twas a mind boggling concept. But, he had only himself to blame, for his actions caught the attention of many in Drekinn, and they all expected him to do more.

Resting his head on his forearms, he closed his eyes for 'just a moment'. Drifting off he suddenly saw 'the other' as he slipped o'er a crumbling cliff, caught a glimpse of a huge furry creature attached to the rock wall behind him, and screamed, "Reach!" His eyes now fully open, his heart pounding, he could still see the beast with antlers growing off his shoulders, hanging from the side of a cliff while he watched 'the other' falling close by. Facing the wrong direction and tumbling headlong o'er the edge, he couldn't have known what to do, and grabbing the creature was his only chance. Had he done so? Was he quick enough with his warning?

"Hello?" A tall blonde girl walked through the doorway, and Mikkal rubbed his dry eyes. Another one. She was very young, pretty, but not muscular. She definitely wasn't the petitioner type, but wasn't exactly the product of Early Training, either. 'Twas likely she was an Outlander herself.

Still distraught from the harrowing fall experienced in his dream, he read from his jotted notes. "Hello. Would you like to teach? Do you like to work with children? Do you know how to fight?" He continued to list his primary questions, the ones he hoped would separate the potential teachers of his program and the ones who would not be an asset, but his mind was elsewhere and he didn't even wait for her to answer. Thus far, he'd not asked anyone his secondary questions.

"Whoa! I have no idea what you're talking about. I heard someone yelling in here. Thought I'd see what was going on. Are you alright?"

"Nightmare. Sorry." Finally casting his gaze back up to her, he explained his task. Even though Grifynn had required this, 'twas a concept he'd actually suggested, helped develop, and for which he'd become quite passionate. The girl sat through his dialog, listening intently to the end. Then her face took on a familiar look of pity and he waited for the negative response. Flame it all, he needed at least one other person to help him start this program, and thus far not a single suitable candidate had been identified. Mayhap he was being too picky. No, children were special, the program was worthy, and he knew the type of teachers he wanted. He just hadn't found them yet. He would. He braced himself.

Sitting still, she considered all he'd said afore she spoke. She sat up taller, pulled her shoulders back and with a voice full of confidence, crisp and clear, she stated, "First of all, never apologize for yourself. If you truly have to apologize, you should've pulled your head out of your arse afore you spoke, or did, whatever 'twas for which you felt the need to apologize."

Mikkal chuckled under his breath. The girl had nerve. She'd go far in life with such an attitude if 'twas not all a front.

Without missing a beat, she continued. "Next, yes. I've always wanted to be a teacher. I plan on being a Master Educator. I will be the youngest Master ever, and my specialty is children. I'm already in classes, but I'm intrigued by your concept. I wish I'd come up with the idea. I want to join you, if you still have room."

He certainly wasn't expecting that response. He shook his head. "Room? Yeah, well, how many winters have you seen anyway? And what's your name?"

"Twelve, but I don't believe that makes any difference, you aren't much older. And my name is Tyrza."

Knowing he'd found his program coordinator, with a widening smile he replied, "Well, Tyrza, welcome to one of my nightmares."

<center>~~~~~THE ABYSS~~~~~</center>

Where were they? 'Twas marks since she'd arrived at the cave's entrance. The abyss was a series of four deep chasms, as if a huge Dragon had pushed off from the side of the mountains, leaving the slash marks of his hind foot as scars. 'Twas impossible to traverse unless you could fly, so one had to travel to one end or the other of each chasm to go around them by going through the mountain itself, emerging on the other side to continue the journey from chasm to chasm. The first crossing was made close to the southeastern end, via the Fearyn log. To reach the next 'bridge' she had to travel back southwest, to the closest end of the second chasm, taking her about a sennight, although they'd taken less than three dawns to travel the same distance in the past. But then they'd not been followed by a group of men trying to kill them. There were three more chasms closer together after this one, with about a dawn 'tween each. The only good part was that they were traveling gravity assisted, attempting this the opposite direction was not a pleasant thought. In point of fact, knowing the path as she did, Gheryh wasn't even sure 'twas possible to traverse the other way.

After several dawns avoiding the mercenaries and the unique dangers of the abyss, she'd arrived at her destination anxiously waiting for her companions to appear, worried they wouldn't. She'd tried all her tricks to throw off her trackers, with little success other than to slow them down. Ryygg promised they'd catch up if she had to proceed without them, forgetting one very important reality. Gabriel may understand that Ryygg could talk, but she knew that he didn't understand what Ryygg said. That meant he couldn't tell the boy how to get through the next cave alive. She had to wait and hope by the Fates that the mercenaries wouldn't find them or the path they traveled.

She'd held her hands o'er her ears as they'd started 'cross the log. At least four of them died, either from the poison of the thorns or from the fall off the log immediately after the poison entered their system, leaving them burning from within, their nerves a'Flame, afore the rest discovered the way. That left mayhap thirteen on her trail. Still too many for her to take on alone, but with Ryygg? No, she thought, she'd let the next 'bridge' thin their numbers even more. Within the abyss were many trails but there was only one safe path, if any could be thought of as safe. 'Twas the least dangerous, the only way anyone had crossed with their lives, and she and Ryygg were the living proof of that claim. They'd either discover the correct path, or they'd be lost forever. But once they caught up, she'd have to forge ahead. And, she'd have to get through afore they entered or her fate was sealed as well. The Eoche did not suffer visitors well.

Peering o'er the edge, she watched the water falling down the cliff into the distant pool below. 'Twas enormous, and 'twould take her several marks to swim 'cross. The pool flowed o'er its outlying edges in multiple smaller falls eventually leading to the river beyond. If there was another way to get to that pool, they could avoid the Eoche altogether. Mayhap 'twas where Ryygg and Gabriel were now? If they yet lived, could they actually be ahead of her? Suddenly her thoughts were interrupted by the sound of distant rustling and 'twas now or never. Pushing aside the brush covering the low entrance to the cave, she shoved her pack and weapons in front of her as she crawled through.

SEVERAL DAWNS PRIOR

~~~~~'TWEEN A ROCK AND A RACK, OR, 'TWEEN

A RACK AND A HARD PLACE~~~~~

</div>

Ryygg tensed as the tree began pulling away from the cliff wall. With grim acceptance he huffed, "Hold on, I fear 'twill be
~~~~~

a rough ride." Gabriel's expression showed agreement with the plan he understood all too well, along with a healthy sprinkling of fear. Then, 'twas the crack of the roots followed by the jerking of the antlers as they dropped branch to branch 'til the last one gave way, throwing them into free fall. Tumbling downward, Ryygg managed to turn them so the boy was cradled against his belly, letting the heavy antlers take most of the beating against the rock. Gabriel began to think they'd never hit bottom, bashing against outcroppings time and again, scrub brush tearing at his limbs, his face protected by the fur of the Beast's heavy mane. He abruptly determined 'twould not be fair to survive such a fall, only to die upon landing.

He'd not had time to look down to see what awaited them below, his view had been obscured by mist anyway, and 'twas honestly too far to have seen much from the ledge. He thought he heard the rush of water getting louder. Soon near deafening, the pair dropped feet first into a deep pool fed by a towering waterfall. Down, down, down they plunged, the height from which they began, making their dive seem never-ending. Ryygg wouldn't let go, fearing they'd get tangled in the rack and both drown. Finally, their descent slowed and they began to rise again. Separating, Ryygg struggled to distance himself from Gabriel, allowing him to swim upwards unimpaired. By the time the boy broke the surface he thought he'd died, gasping for breath, his lungs screaming for air. 'Twas a candle drip afore he realized the Night Beast was not with him. Frantically he looked about and then his worst nightmare of late, became reality. Ducking under, he saw the Beast through the crystal clear waters, still struggling far below. The heavy antlers were solid and had no buoyancy. Ryygg was strong, but he was losing the battle to rise to the surface with the rack, and he couldn't remove it by himself.

Promptly shedding his pack in the shallows, Gabriel dove back down and tried to help him swim. Grabbing the Beast's flailing paws he pulled, but only succeeded in slowing them both down. Gabriel went back up for a breath and then dove again, this time, grabbing the rack. Ryygg was weakening, losing consciousness. Swimming strongly, Gabriel pulled with all his might, and finally managed to get the water logged Beast to the surface, but Ryygg wasn't breathing. Terrified, the boy dragged his new friend further up the shore. Tugging and pulling, he managed to get a large round rock under the Beast to apply pressure to his abdomen, rolling him side to side 'til he vomited a rush of water, bringing the gasp he so wanted to hear, but he was afraid to stop. Continuing to push the Beast side to side, he soon heard a weak growl. "Enough." Although 'twas very soft, Gabriel caught the gist and fell backwards to lie exhausted in the sand. His own breaths ragged, he could do no more, and closed his eyes in gratitude to the One. His friend would live.

<center>~~~~~THE CAVE OF THE EOCHE~~~~~</center>

The entrance was small, but 'twas much larger at the exit. A bioluminescent fungi covered the walls, maintaining a constant, low level, blue-green light, allowing her to pass through without the need of a torch even with her mere human vision. This was very good, for she didn't want the heat to attract attention. Not far into the cave gushed the headwaters for the waterfall, the river flowing from just inside the entrance as a small spring, growing rapidly afore it burst through the wall close to the opposite end.

As far as she could tell, the Eoche were blind even though they had eyes, and had no sense of smell. She was unsure about their ability to detect temperature changes. They seemed to hunt strictly to vibration and were deadly accurate. Looking like a hybrid of spider and scorpion, the giant insect, half the size of her Night Beast, had an exceptionally hard exoskeleton with multiple long scraggly hairs sprouting from their lower legs. They had no teeth and used their spiked tails to inject a venom which would paralyze their prey, afore using their razor sharp jaws to cut them into tiny chunks they could stuff into their mouths to swallow whole, all while their victim was still aware. The Eoche didn't rush their meals and once stung you could only hope they'd start at your head to kill you quickly, for 'twould take too long to bleed to death. Although not truly vicious unless defending themselves, they were always hungry and would not stop eating 'til 'twas nothing left to eat, leaving paralyzed prey waiting for their turn. 'Twas a survival technique, since they never left their cave. Living off stray creatures drawn to the water, it could be erratic timing 'tween meals. Fortunately they were extremely rare, found nowhere else on all Kadoor as far as she knew, for they were not easy to kill. They had only one small area the size of a coin on the top of their heads 'tween their eyes, that would do the job if directly penetrated, and this they fiercely protected with their stingers.

Standing just inside the entrance, she picked up her pack and weapons slowly so as not to make any noise that would vibrate through the rock, attracting attention. Silently she waited for several long breaths afore she began to move. Stepping lightly and being careful not to slip, she stayed close to the water as 'twas the safest place to be, mindful of the location of the insects moving through the cave. They avoided the water, obtaining their hydration needs from the blood of their prey. The Eoche crawled 'cross the ceiling, and the distant walls were covered in places, blocking out much of the light, making an already eerie situation even more so, with the flickering shadows thus produced. Warily she navigated the distance, her eyes roving everywhere, trying not to trip o'er the insects as they walked beside or in front of her. Time moved as slowly as did she, but her resolve was solid. 'Twas nerve racking, even though she'd done this twice afore, and then she'd had a huge furry companion with her, actually making it more difficult.

As the river became wider, the rushing waters louder, she continued moving silently for the Eoche were so in tune with their environment they took immediate notice of the slightest changes. Yet even though her presence created nominal changes in certain aspects, the vibration of the waters helped disguise them.

The journey was taking its toll and she was tempted to jump into the river and fall with it by the time she arrived where it burst through the wall. But 'twouldn't work, since the falls traveled down a series of ledges afore hitting the pool below and even if the descent didn't kill her, the landing would, for the base was rocky, becoming deeper only much further out.

'Twas then that she heard them. The mercenaries entered the cave and they were oblivious. 'Twas both good and bad for Gheryh. Her passing would now be more scrutinized, but their passing would be terminated. Mayhap the Eoche would rid her of them all.

'Twas just a heartbeat afore she heard the scurrying of the creatures as they began to hunt together, and not long after, the terrified cries of the men as they fought and died against this unknown enemy. Gheryh couldn't take the time to try to see what was happening behind her, she had to complete the last quarter of the distance to the exit afore she was also discovered by the insects. Listening to the men's shrieks made her grit her teeth. Blocking out the noise, she concentrated on keeping her pace steady and silent, for fear led to panic, and panic was her greatest enemy now. Unexpectedly, she heard the sound of splashing. Someone had gone into the river to evade the Eoche. Or mayhap they'd fallen in, paralyzed. That one was blessed, for instead of being carved into bits one small piece at a time, he'd have the luxury of merely drowning. The light at the end of the cave was just ahead, but curiosity about the splashing made her lose her focus.

Abruptly, she felt something touch her leg, then her hip. An Eoche rubbed up against her thigh. Accidentally stumbled upon by the insect on his way toward a potential meal, she rolled o'er with the pressure as smoothly as she could. Breathing slowly and evenly, she laid perfectly still as she soon found herself under three more, and if she tensed or resisted in any way she'd be attacked, with no chance of killing them afore being stung. She could hear the men coming ever closer as they fought through the nightmare. Using only her peripheral vision so as not to move her head, she saw some of them holding up their paralyzed companions as shields, the hapless men getting struck again and again, not even able to scream in pain or horror.

The Eoche nudged her limp body as they stepped o'er, the sharp tips of their legs digging into her skin, the long hairs tickling her chest, thighs, and belly. One after the other crossed, as she prayed they'd not realize o'er what they stepped. Finally, the last one was well past and she dared to look about. Several of the men were still coming, walking back to back, using their human shields. The rest of the Eoche were eating in the distance. The men dropped their shields to the nearest insects as a way to escape, and they began to eat. Gheryh stood up and ran to the exit. They'd seen her, she had to hurry. Pushing through the undergrowth, she was out and racing down the next path in a heartbeat. She didn't take the time to look back. She had no idea how many were still in pursuit, she'd not actually seen the whole party, just the closest ones. If sixteen or seventeen entered, and she saw at least four being used as shields, there could still be more than ten coming. Where was Ryygg and the True King? Had she made a horrible mistake taking this route? No. She refused to second guess her actions now. Besides, the abyss was helping her eliminate the enemy. Regardless of the outcome, considering their numbers she was certain she'd chosen well.

<center>~~~~~THE POOL AT THE BASE OF THE FALLS~~~~~</center>

Although neither of them had escaped the harrowing fall without some injury, most were minor due to the incredible resilience and strength of both his partner and the rack. However, Gabriel quickly discovered that Ryygg was much worse off than was he, bleeding profusely from a deep gash in his hind leg. Leaving him lying on his side in the icy water slowed the flow considerably. Gabriel was taught the Healing of the Painted One, even though he wasn't aware of this at the time, and although not as knowledgeable as Mikkal, he was familiar with the medicinal arts and with emergency field dressings in particular. "I must find something to pack the wound and stop the bleeding. Don't leave the water 'til my return, unless of course, I don't return. We must also avoid hypothermia."

Ryygg knew the boy couldn't understand him so he thought to himself, 'what else would I do?' Still, he gave the impression of waiting for acknowledgement and/or approval of the suggested plan of action. 'Twas sound, so he repeated his thoughts aloud which seemed to satisfy the boy who nodded affirmatively afore striding into the surrounding woods. Shortly after, he returned carrying an double armload of a yellow flowered plant, cattails, and moss. "I hoped to find something to help with the pain, but no luck. I'll keep trying. In the meantime, I found goldenrod. 'Twas unexpected this late in the season, and I'm very grateful. 'Twill help avoid infection as well as help to stop the bleeding." He encouraged Ryygg to drag himself out of the water after doing his best to clean the wound, and once on the shore Gabriel patted the area dry with large leaves and the soft spongy cattails. With a rock he crushed the goldenrod and layered it upon the moss, then packed it in the wound. He frowned, as 'twas far deeper and more serious than he'd originally thought. Applying additional layers of the absorbent cattails fluffed and spread flat, then more leaves, he tied the bandage in place using lengths of the youngest, thinnest and most pliable vines he could locate. The whole process took much time and although Ryygg never protested, 'twas apparent he was in great pain.

Gabriel was exhausted by the time he'd finished, and both of them required rest. The rack still tied upon his shoulders, Gabriel was about to remove it when Ryygg stopped him, as 'twould have been too difficult for the boy to carry alone. "'Twill be needed soon?" Ryygg nodded his head to show he'd guessed correctly. Since 'twas obvious neither of them could do anything for awhile, Gabriel prepared a fire to dry their belongings and warm them both, and decided to pass the time by explaining how he'd learned some medicine from his parents, whom he now knew were of the Daggogh, and that 'twould be necessary to allow the wound to heal for a few days in order to keep the bleeding at a minimum afore they continued their journey, for the Beast had already lost much of his Life Source. As Gabriel talked, Ryygg answered, and he told the boy what they faced and where they had to go from here. 'Twas a sort of kinship that relayed the essence of his words to the other, if not the exact content.

They stayed in the area for several days. Gabriel built a lean-to shelter, fished to supplement their supplies, and kept watch for predators during the long cold nights. Working with Ryygg to regain his strength, he helped him walk to the pool to drink and into the woods to relieve himself. Using the rack as a stabilizer and lift, 'twas not as difficult as he'd thought 'twould be. Initially the bandages soaked through several times a day and he changed them frequently, then daily as the drainage slowed. After much exploration in their surroundings he'd found a plant used as a pain reliever and to reduce swelling, which had the added benefit of helping induce sleep, although he couldn't recall the name. Gabriel vowed to himself that when they got out of this situation he'd learn everything he could about medicinal plants and trauma care.

Even though the boy couldn't understand, to alleviate his boredom and worry Ryygg told him many things, including the fact that he was the First Born, the history of the Night Beasts and of the People, all about the Word Sayer, and their previous crossings of the abyss. Toward the end of the third day he guessed that Gheryh should be about to travel through the cave of the Eoche, if she didn't wait much longer for them. But 'twas no way to get back up there. However, he thought he knew a way to meet her at, or near, the next 'bridge'. They'd need to leave soon. They had to reach their destination afore Gheryh, for he had no way to tell the boy how to get through the cave safely, let alone how to find the entrance. No, they had to catch up with the Hunter or they might very well die here.

~~~~~MEANWHILE, IN THE CAVE~~~~~

The Eoche struck and the Human dropped at just the right angle, pushing the insect off balance. Its tail to the growing river, it took several awkward steps backwards trying to avoid the inevitable, afore it fell in. The Eoche were not swimmers and hated the water. It had actually never ventured so near afore, 'twasn't blood and therefore 'twas no need for sustenance. But now, completely out of control, the Eoche was swept along, bobbing up and down, swirling under the rapidly moving waters, unable to reach out and grab hold of anything, unable to stop its plight. Flailing legs did no good, the others wouldn't help even if they knew how. It could not reach the bottom, and could not pull itself out. Within moments, the ill fated insect was pushed through the wall with the explosive force of the water, and plunged downward toward the pool far below.

Several times the waters fell onto outcroppings or ledges where its legs brushed against weeds or rocks and it tried to drag itself out, but to no avail. The rushing water pulled it under, back, and around, again and again. Blind and out of its element, its natural senses depended on its ability to comprehend the surrounding vibrations, and now outside for the first time in its life, adding the deafening waters of multiple falls, its world became a madness of vibration that could not be interpreted. Totally disoriented, the insect shut down its senses while the currents dragged its yielding body for leagues, taking numerous days, through the pool to the falls, o'er multiple ledges, waterways, into a river, and finally to the Ocean of Fears beyond.

Eventually, and miraculously, the insect was caught in the net of a family of fishermen. Several generations of experience did nothing for their ability to identify the creature they had to cut out of their net. Originally appearing dead, by its looks alone they determined 'twas very dangerous, and so they had it caged afore it regained its senses. Fishing was a hard occupation and Shytin had imposed heavier taxes when he'd taken the throne,
~~~~~

making it even more difficult to eke out a living. After discussing the find with the rest of the family as well as the villagers, they decided to take it to the new High King. Mayhap he'd reward them.

<p style="text-align:center">~~~~~BELOW THE FALLS~~~~~</p>

Gabriel woke up to Ryygg's paw upon his chest, his big nose a handbreadth from his face. As soon as he opened his eyes the Beast simply turned and started to walk away, leaving their campsite. Gabriel quickly packed their gear and all the wound care supplies he'd accumulated, then ran to catch up with him. 'Twas time to continue the journey. He sighed. These past few dawns were the closest to paradise he'd ever been, and he would miss this special time together with the Beast, but reality was a Flaming hard taskmistress and they had to return to her. Gheryh was out there somewhere, hopefully still alive, and she could probably use their help. He was certain the Beast had told him that, as well as something else. Something he'd known in his heart. Something of which everyone seemed adamant in their efforts to keep him ignorant. By all the fires of Hades, he'd know the truth when they arrived at the Daggogh village, or he'd move on and make his own way. He'd had enough.

<p style="text-align:center">~~~~~THE DRAGON'S DEN~~~~~</p>

Mikkal was elated. Not only was Tyrza a good teacher, she was a fantastic organizer, and after less than a fortnight she'd practically taken o'er the entire program, getting it up and running efficiently. The Clan rallied behind their efforts. There were volunteers to identify the children, sign them up, ensure their arrival, teach a variety of classes, and follow up with the Commander. After a brief discussion, Grifynn agreed to his request to name Tyrza the Director, which suited him fine. And once she was accepted into full time education classes she'd have this program self sustaining. 'Twould give her a huge head start on her requirements, literally pushing her ahead of her classmates by o'er a winter. All he had to do now was a little promotion and supervision. That, and teaching one class per sennight. The children loved Mikkal and although he tried to act as if 'twas a chore, he fooled no one, especially not Rychard. 'Twas an added benefit that while working with the children he could escape his daily lies to himself, and the need for them.

<center>~~~~~THE ABYSS~~~~~</center>

After o'er three days of hard traveling, they reached yet another cliff. This time, they could see beyond the abyss, above the forest canopy. 'Twas an awe inspiring view. But in this region Gabriel had learned that awe inspiring meant much danger, and he remained vigilant, worried about his slow moving friend. Ryygg knew they were late but he couldn't walk any faster. If Gheryh had traveled uninjured and without significant delay, she would've arrived within the first dawn. Would she be able to wait for them? With the added responsibility of protecting the boy, he was grateful, but feeling guilty, that the men stayed on Gheryh's trail and not theirs, leaving them with just the local inhabitants and dangers, creating enough of a challenge for the unlikely pair. Focused upon finding their way to the next crossing through totally unfamiliar territory, and unable to tell Gabriel of their need, he hoped she'd not forgotten to gather the sage. Padding up and down yet another cliff edge, he was finally confident they were in the correct general vicinity. Lying down to relieve some of the pain in his haunches, he used his superior vision in an effort to locate his Handler.

<center>~~~~~THROUGH THE NEST~~~~~</center>

Gheryh's skills were tested as she traveled to the next stop. 'Twould have taken her a day at most, but with human predators on her trail, the trip took o'er thrice as long. All the while she tried not to think about her friends. She could do nothing but hope they'd be there when she arrived, because if they'd found a way to get to the cave of the Eoche, they'd not have made it through the feeding frenzy, and there was no way to warn them. Of course, even that depended upon whether or not they yet lived.

Nearing her destination, certain the last of the mercenaries were close behind, she had to risk exposure to look for her friends at the edge. Somehow, she had to let them know that she was alive and well. They would've expected her two days prior, would they have attempted to go through the nest alone?

"Gheryh! O'er here!"

Gheryh cried aloud, but remembered to speak in Kahyah Tongue, the mercenaries ignorant of such, had they been able to hear. "You made it!"

She was concerned they'd be caught out in the open, but Ryygg and Gabriel were on another ledge and she was stuck opposite. They'd gone too far east and if they tried to backtrack they'd find themselves behind the mercenaries. A passable trail mayhap once used by mountain goats, barely showed from their angle, leading 'cross to her location. 'Twas difficult, but with Gheryh guiding them, the echoes of their chuffs and grunts reverberated as if an entire pride of man eaters was on the hunt. 'Twould mayhap, keep them safe from discovery for awhile. Slipping a few times and barely avoiding falling off the edge, she held her breath and tried not to scream as she watched, 'til they finally made it to where she stood.

Gheryh grabbed the rack still attached to Ryygg's shoulders, and yanked hard to assist him up onto the ledge where she hugged him 'til his eyes bulged. She didn't question Gabriel, simply giving him a nod of approval as she quickly checked the bandage for drainage. Reaching for her pack, she untied three tightly wrapped bundles of sage and handed one to each of them, Ryygg mouthing his around 'til he found a comfortable and secure position. Then she climbed up a tree, cutting the longest vines she could. Dragging them clear of the branches, she went to work setting up for their rappel. "'Tis an opening in the side of the cliff, down there." She pointed to a small outcropping against the sheer wall, but Gabriel was dumbfounded. There was hardly room for the three of them to stand on that ledge, let alone a Beast rappelling. How was that going to work?

As if she'd heard, Gheryh answered his unasked question. "The last two rappels I had to lower him with a figure eight harness of vines. He could help keep himself away from the wall, but 'twas not the safest or the most comfortable, and he near fell out as well as almost dislocating his shoulders afore we managed to get him to the ledge. I thought we could lower him using the rack here, and 'twill certainly work better at the next crossing." Gabriel had been rappelling afore and once he realized the plan, he promptly assisted. When he was ready, he helped Gheryh with Ryygg's set up. But the vines they'd originally used to secure the rack had finally had enough and broke afore they'd finished. Remembering how he'd stood and then fallen, cradled in the Beast's legs against his belly, Gabriel took the rack and instead of trying to tie it onto his back again, which he thought would have the same result as a figure eight of vines, he turned it to face the Beast, who squeezed his upper body inside as if putting on a coat backwards. 'Twas similar to being in a full harness but with a wider chest piece. Ryygg liked it as 'twas fairly comfortable and easier for him to hold onto with his forelegs, giving him some sense of control. Gheryh and Gabriel tied the vines to the rack then looped them around a tree, and Ryygg stepped off the edge backwards, his hind legs pushing against the wall just as the others would soon do.

Afore long he was at the ledge in front of a tall narrow cave opening. There was no other way to get there, unless one had wings. Gheryh and Gabriel soon joined him. They retied the rack to Ryygg's shoulders, then Gheryh sprinkled each smudge with a sedative powder from her bag afore lighting them. "I killed two of the men last night, they'd gotten close and I was tired of not knowing exactly what we were up against. There's still eight left."

She looked at Gabriel as she hurriedly gave her directions. "'Tis a nest we enter. Giant red and yellow wasps the size of a grown man, with stingers like daggers. They can punch clear through your body, and the venom would then be the least of your problems, although 'tis known to cause instant and extremely violent seizures. The sage will calm them, the sedative an added boost to keep them calm after we've passed, for the nest is quite large. See there? That shadowed section free of brush?" This time she pointed far below to the bottom of the cliff, and slightly off to the west. "'Tis where we'll exit. There's no way to get there other than through. They'll ignore us if we keep quiet. Although 'tis practically a vertical descent, and we'll be climbing down the nest by sliding on your belly, like the staircase of Flight of Fire Keep, you must not step on one or touch them, and watch your footing. If you slide into one of the egg tubes, the wasps will seal you in without delay and you'll be eaten by the larvae, despite the effects of the smudge." His eyes shone with determination to do everything he'd been told, but 'twas becoming o'erwhelming. Her voice was encouraging as she finished. "This is next to the end of our crossings, our last stop is the river."

A river? That seemed easy enough. With that thought in mind, he followed Gheryh inside the nest, Ryygg right behind.

<center>~~~~~~~~~~</center>

Gabriel was not very experienced in rock climbing but he was a quick study and 'twas very good, as Gheryh had to assist Ryygg to avoid him sliding into the larvae tubes while they cautiously and laboriously worked their way downward through the nest. The huge wasps crawled everywhere, but the smoke from the smudges kept them lethargic and seemingly unimpressed with the intrusion. The only disadvantages were those which could not be avoided. Their smudges, with the added sedative, allowed the mercenaries who followed to pass with less difficulty than they would have otherwise, and they'd not been able to free their rappelling lines, clearly showing them the entrance. Still, with no idea of what they were about to encounter and being o'er two marks behind, although eight men entered the nest approximately the same time the companions exited, only four would survive. Per numbers, they were close to equal ground. However, Ryygg was weaker than ever after the long and difficult descent, and in agonizing pain. The bandage had fallen off, 'twas soaked so with his Life Source, although the packing remained in place. Nevertheless, blood dripped steadily down his leg, which would leave a trail anyone could follow. Gheryh wasn't certain he could defend himself, let alone help with the last of the mercenaries. Not knowing how many would survive the nest, she chose to continue forward instead of making a stand. Wasting no time trying to conceal their path as they headed for the last crossing, Gheryh hoisted one side of the rack to her shoulder while Gabriel lifted the other, relieving some of the weight to keep Ryygg moving. Basically dragging the immense load, they traveled non-stop through the night. The headwater of the last 'bridge' was less than a dawn distant.

THE FOLLOWING DAWN

~~~~~THE MOIRAA RIVER~~~~~

</div>

"Are we there yet?" Gabriel was completely out of breath. Gheryh was, too, and giving one more push through the brush, they felt sand under their feet, both losing their grip upon the rack simultaneously. Ryygg was so weak he couldn't stand upright, and dropped heavily to his chest with a huff.

Gheryh didn't bother using their private language. "Sorry, my friend." Then, looking at the boy, "We're close, but we can't cross here."

Gabriel pondered what she'd not said. Why not here? As they all caught their breath, he sat in the sand staring at a fairly narrow river with gentle white water caused by a series of almost evenly spaced boulders, some of which one might be able to jump 'cross, although 'twould be slippery. 'Twas a beautiful, although narrow shoreline on both sides and even if one avoided the rocks, it couldn't be that deep. 'Twould seemingly be easy enough to walk
~~~~~

or swim 'cross. Without a doubt, it appeared that 'twould be the easiest 'bridge' of the entire journey. Calculating how difficult 'twould be to drag the Beast through the waters, he felt confident they could be on the opposite shore in less than half a mark, even if they had to do all the work themselves. Headstrong, but not stupid, he waited to hear what Gheryh had to say. He'd learned 'twas nothing as it appeared in the abyss.

He hadn't long to wait. "We have to go, those men will be very close. We traveled slower than could they after all, and with no time to hide our tracks our only chance is to fool them into the river, thinking we're within their grasp." She began to strip, tossing a few non-essential belongings and her meager upper coverings onto the beach, while Gabriel took the hint and did the same. When he began to remove his boots, she stopped him, saying, "No, they'll be in too much of a hurry. Leave only your shirt at the waterline, but don't disturb the surface." She carefully and swiftly cut the vines and released the rack from Ryygg, leaving them on the sand as well. Then she and Gabriel hoisted it 'tween them while Ryygg gathered himself. Following back into the brush up river a short distance, they began to climb once again. Gheryh ran back to hide their trail into the brush making it appear they'd gone directly into the river, afore returning to the pair and continuing the climb. After half a mark, they heard the mercenaries at the river's edge. Although their words were muffled, 'twas obvious the ruse had been successful and they listened to their excited chatter. At about the same time the men came through the brush, Gheryh, Gabriel and Ryygg climbed out onto the ledge far above. Looking down, they could see the mercenaries about to enter the water after having found the mess they'd left. "There's no need to hide once they enter the river. You might want to watch this, while I prepare for our crossing. 'Twill be most rewarding."

Gabriel peered o'er the ledge and watched as the four survivors prepared to enter the waters of the Moiraa, then he helped Gheryh secure the rack to Ryygg in the same manner as he'd used it to rappel to the nest, however, she had him twisted to one side leaving the other open like a giant hook. Gabriel's eyes were drawn back to the river when he heard the first spine-chilling scream. He saw three of the men still fighting for their lives. They were already too far from the shore to return and could not reach the boulder to get out of the water. Intently, his eyes searched for the cause of their demise and suddenly he was rewarded with a clear though brief view of the namesake of the river. 'Twas shocking. Gheryh continued her preparations, not even bothering to look o'er the edge, while she explained. "The Moiraa are enormous flesh eating eels that live in the deep channels around each of those boulders. They'll only travel so far from their homes, therefore, they're not often found outside of the headwaters, and the vast majority of their species is located here. They have hinged jaws like snakes and can swallow a full grown man whole. They use their needle-like, razor sharp teeth, to latch onto their prey and drag and hold them under the rocks in deep water, but they don't wait for death to occur afore eating unless 'tis an abundance. Four men is not an abundance given the numbers of the Moiraa, and they will fight o'er the bodies, ripping flesh and limbs." Gabriel listened to the lessening commotion as the men were taken under water, and soon the river flowed red with blood.

Turning away, he tried to figure out how they were going to 'cross. Gheryh stated, "This is why we brought the rack." The huge curls of the antlers seemed inviting, and then she walked to the edge, pulled her bow, nocked a bolo arrow with an attached line, and took careful aim. The arrow sung through the air, piercing a tall pine on the other side, the bolo netting wrapping around the thick trunk. He helped her pull the line tight and ensure 'twas solid, then secured it to the trees behind them. They were high enough that they would avoid the water entirely, and if they didn't get stuck in the middle, they'd all be safely 'cross soon. Hooking the open side of the rack to the line, she layered Gabriel 'tween her and Ryygg, and then without warning they were off the edge and sliding o'er the river, gaining speed and momentum. Using the rack turned out to be both good and bad, increasing the ease and safety of crossing, but their speed was uncontrollable. Ryygg held out his legs and hit the tree first. Even with most of the blow cushioned by the rack, 'twas the final straw for the wound. They cut themselves down and checked the river. No survivors could be seen. Nothing could be heard.

~~~~~~~~~~

On the cliff above the Moiraa, Gheryh finally considered them safe. She used the last of her sleep inducing powder to prepare for suturing the wound as 'twould be extremely painful given the supplies available in her pack. But if they didn't close it now, he'd bleed out and Pass the Veil in a very short time. Dangerously weak, Ryygg closed his heavy eyelids, but 'twas doubtful 'twould be enough to last through the process. Gabriel remembered the plant he'd discovered in the woods surrounding the falls and went to look for more. Gheryh was completely focused upon her lifelong friend. Fatigued, anxious, weakened herself, she didn't notice the man sneaking up behind her 'til 'twas too late.

~~~~~~~~~~

When Gabriel returned, the plants tucked into his pockets, the last mercenary held Gheryh at bay with a knife hovering o'er Ryygg's head. She couldn't understand how this one managed to avoid serious injury other than a severe rash from the vine sap. Sheer good fortune probably, but Gabriel's reaction floored her. Barely looking at the Beast, he stared arrogantly at the ugly blisters upon the man's chest and arms, chuckling all the while.

The man sneered, his flattened nose creating a nasal whine. "What are you laughing at? I don't think you're showing the proper respect here. In case you haven't figured it out, I'm going to kill your friends."

Disinterested, Gabriel shrugged his shoulders. "That rash will kill you first, if you don't treat it quickly. You've reached the final stage. 'Twill be a most repulsive death."

Worn out, confused and angry beyond belief, his eyes roved from one to the other with growing doubt. Mayhap he'd chosen the wrong victim. He flashed the knife menacingly from Ryygg's drugged form to Gheryh, all the while keeping his eyes upon Gabriel. "And I have your Healer at my mercy!"

He smiled. "She's not my Healer."

The man was truly shocked, he'd thought the boy was a willing travel companion. Mayhap he'd made another mistake? Gheryh wasn't certain if Gabriel recognized the man was in no danger of Passing from such, 'twas the same rash they'd endured entering the abyss even though he was unusually sensitive. She barely caught Gabriel's fleeting glance, but he turned away afore she could question. 'Twas something going on in that boy's brain and he was either turning on her, or playing his role to the hilt. She could only hope 'twas the latter.

Nervously the man demanded, "I invoke the truth of the Healer. 'Tis correct? 'Tis fatal?"

Gheryh trusted her instincts and since Gabriel's words were outright lies, 'twas certainly a con. Obviously the man didn't know she wasn't really a Healer and therefore not bound to their oath. She hoped she understood where Gabriel was going with his ruse as she chose to reply as if she were. "The rash is a simple thing. I have a powder in my bag that will stop the itch and dry the blisters within a quarter mark."

Gabriel's tone oozed sarcasm. "She didn't lie. She does have a powder that will do just what she says, but 'twill not treat the poison inside. She wants you to Pass. She won't even have to lift a finger. And if she doesn't treat you properly, you'll go Beyond afore the rash disappears. Consider how much more of your skin is now covered than when you came through the vines. 'Tis getting worse."

The man was shaken. With growing fear in his eyes, he began sweating profusely. The sweat increased the pain and itch, causing new blisters to literally bubble o'er his arms and chest and even began spreading to his neck. 'Twas obvious that he struggled with the decision but finally he growled, "Get the powder. No tricks, or I'll kill the animal."

Gheryh dug into her pouch, pulled out the powder and then poured some into the palm of his hand. He looked questioningly from the boy to her, while she gave her directions. "Rub it into the rash, make certain you leave no unbroken blisters."

Afore he could do as she said, Gabriel jumped past Gheryh, pushed her aside, and knocked the powder out of the man's hand, yelling, "No! Were you not listening? It has to be treated from the inside."

Gheryh fell backwards and sat in the dirt with angry disbelief upon her face. "You betray us," she hissed.

He glanced at her disdainfully. "She gave you the wrong powder, 'twould have done nothing for the rash but help spread it, and you don't have another quarter mark to wait. Furthermore, you swallow it, you don't put it on your skin."

Grabbing her pouch, he took a lump of the fresh sap she'd recently harvested and powdered it on a rock. Gheryh couldn't speak. She was dumbfounded at what she imagined was about to happen. Gabriel finished his task, carefully scraped the 'new' powder into his palm and handed it to the man, who was frantically scratching the worsening rash. Offering him his water bag, he said, "Put it on your tongue, then chase it with this. Tastes nasty, so drink fast."

The man wasn't a complete idiot however, and he stared at the powder in his hand suspiciously. "You do it first. You take it, or I'll kill her."

Gabriel didn't even bat an eye. Scraping more of the powder into his own hand, he did what he was told, then took a big drink. Gheryh was horrified, and held her breath for several heartbeats, but nothing happened. Her expression was misread by the mercenary, and 'twas all the proof he required. Needing relief, he grabbed the water from Gabriel and tossed his head back to down the powder. Suddenly he coughed, attempted to clear his throat, and then tried to swallow again. The two of them watched the dying man, his tongue and throat swollen with the rehydrated powder, liquid fire burning all the way down his esophagus and into his stomach. He coughed again and spewed blood everywhere, then he gasped with widening eyes, his hands on his throat as he eventually only gurgled, bloody froth upon his blue lips. 'Twas a most ugly demise. After they'd stripped him of all his valuables, they kicked his corpse o'er the edge to the river below, where he quickly became eel bait.

Gheryh kneeled beside Ryygg's still sleeping form and stroked his mane affectionately. "I'm really impressed that you remembered about the sap, 'tis good to know we can use it like fresh from the vines. 'Tis easier to carry in dried form. And I had no clue 'twould kill, I'd never have thought of using it in that way. I would have thought the moisture of the blisters would do the same thing, but mayhap 'tis neutralized by the salt, as neither does sweat rehydrate the powder. I wonder if another liquid would serve to affect the poison quality? Mayhap blood?" Gheryh was excited, for they'd probably found a poison that would help to kill the Dragons. Mixed with a few other noxious ingredients, namely the Veil Grit, she felt they were onto something very good. "You had me there for a moment. I'm sorry I doubted you. You showed much courage."

"Courage? I'm ashamed to admit that I was terrified." He shrugged his shoulders. "'Twas a gamble. I recalled you telling me about Ryygg's tongue. I wasn't certain how much to give him and that 'twouldn't be diluted with the water, but I thought he'd be able to avoid the consequences without. And I take that as a compliment of my acting skills. My father would be proud."

"A gamble? 'Twas a stroke of genius." She stopped and gazed at him. "And courage is not the lack of fear, my friend. 'Tis the ability to do what's needed, regardless. Are you alright?"

"Do you mean, am I alright with having caused that man's death? Yes. He threatened you and Ryygg, he would've tried to kill us regardless, and then he would've gone after the People."

"Good. But what about the dose you took? How did you pull that off?"

He opened his other hand and showed her the powder. "Simple deception. Sleight of hand. I was taught by one of the best, you know. Larken is a man of many talents."

Gheryh stared at the boy with respect, then gathered her supplies to suture Ryygg's leg. She admired his cool exterior and the control he'd displayed. He'd just killed in self defense for the first time, and showed little affectation. 'Twas both good and bad for the boy King-to-be. Such a burden was not wished upon the young, but his reign was destined to be fraught with chaos and death. He must be prepared to be a war time leader. She'd thought the People were going to have to help with that process, but after this experience, well, mayhap the One True Liege had already taken care of that for them.

~~~~~THE DRAGON'S DEN~~~~~

Mikkal was very proud of the way the Outlander Early Training program was accepted, and how quickly it came together. Tyrza reassured him of their ability to continue successfully, leaving him free for his own Training to begin. Grifynn was well pleased with how much the pair managed to accomplish in just a few dawns, and arranged for Mikkal to continue tutoring with Aalanna after his classes designed to allow him to enter Warrior Training when he was up to par. His schedule full, his time precious, he taught as he was able and kept tabs on the program. He fell into the rack well past midnight most days, and was up and working again afore dawn, never happier, never more at peace with himself.

~~~~~THE VILLAGE OF THE DAGGOGH~~~~~

Once clear of the abyss, the three traveling companions made good time back home, where they were greeted with cheers. They'd dragged Ryygg on a travois most of the way, but he'd insisted upon walking into the village on his own. Word spread quickly about their journey, and the remains of the two Hunters and Beasts were found and retrieved within a moon. Gheryh and Gabriel were truthful about their route, leaving out their prior experiences, and the Danoh never questioned. The most exciting information was not the ability to cross, 'twas the new poison. Dragons had been seen o'er the Edge, landing in the meadows and other open areas, and the People would soon have to engage. The information Gheryh and Gabriel brought back was most valuable, and a party was sent to the vines to retrieve as much of the dried sap as they could carry. Every Hunter was equipped with the new powder, as well as briefed upon the most effective methods for bringing the huge creatures down. But the Danoh still advised hiding as opposed to open fighting, wanting to remain outside of the war as long as 'twas possible. Their new guest would need time to grow into his destiny. After all, a boy of just thirteen winters had yet to reach his full physical strength, and he'd need that to defend himself once he returned. Although Gheryh was in favor of overt attack, she didn't oppose her father's decision.

<center>~~~~~GHERYH'S CABIN~~~~~</center>

They'd just lit the home fire, relaxing for the first time since they'd left on their mission o'er five moons past. Gabriel stood looking out the window. He'd be staying with his new friends 'til he'd successfully constructed his own living quarters. Gheryh and Ryygg had lived alone since she'd become a Handler, but she was frequently absent. Therefore her shelter was small but suitable, the mantle made of mud bricks impressed with shells and leaves, the fireplace and hearth made from limestone with fossils aplenty. Her furnishings were sparse but functional, handmade and well decorated. She'd stuffed their mattresses with goose down and had an extra one rolled up behind the divider which she laid out in the opposite corner for their guest. Ryygg dragged his own closer to the hearth. Gheryh was exhausted. She wasn't hungry, she was cold, and she closed her eyes to let the warmth of the blaze soak into her arms and legs. Deciding the boys could get their own evening meal if they so desired, she allowed herself to drift off to the repetition of their journey playing through her mind.

Ryygg limped stiffly 'cross the room and laid down on her feet, his head in her lap, soulful eyes gazing at her. Uncharacteristically apologetic, he stated, "I told the boy. He needed to know."

She near went cross eyed when she opened them and found Ryygg nose to nose. More than a little irritated at the interruption she stated brusquely, "What? What did you tell him?"

"What do you think I told him? His destiny is set and he is of age, he certainly needs to know his future is not his own afore he does something he cannot live down." Gheryh struggled to achieve an adequate level of alertness in order to follow the conversation. Still somewhat drowsy, her brow furrowed, Ryygg took advantage of her slowed senses. "I told him he is the First Born, of course."

Sitting bolt upright, her eyes flew open. "You didn't!"

Ryygg sat back on his haunches. "I did. Ask him."

In disbelief, she spun toward the boy. "Did Ryygg really tell you that you're the First Born?"

"Yes, he did," Gabriel declared while behaving as innocently as possible, as if he'd known that already. He'd thought 'twas what the Kahyah had said during their time alone, therefore he wasn't really lying. But without Gheryh to translate, confirmation was a surprise. Ryygg had actually been quite vocal while pushing him toward the self discovery of which Gheryh was forbidden to assist. The Night Beast had no such fetters. Still. He truly was the First Born? The Fates had thrown him to the Water Dragons this time.

"Wait. How could he have told you anything?" She turned abruptly to her partner, who sat with a triumphant smile upon his furry face. "Ryygg?"

Ryygg made no attempt at denial. Moving stiffly off to the side 'tween the pair, he watched their faces, enjoying the conversation. Even Gheryh had told him that the boy should know his destiny. He'd just manipulated it for him to learn earlier than he might have otherwise. "I told him many things. Most of which went in one ear and out the other, as is typical of a boy of thirteen. We were in a most desperate situation and had to pass the time somehow."

"But. I. He couldn't. I mean, you can't. I'm the only one who… oh Flame it all. I just told him! You did that a'purpose!"

"Well, don't feel too badly. To be precise, I did tell him, 'twas no lie. You just translated."

Gabriel put his hand upon Gheryh's shoulder, gently turning her to face him. "I won't say anything if you won't."

"Agreed," she replied without hesitation.

CHAPTER EIGHT

The Ties That Bind

SEVERAL MOONS LATER
~~~~~THE TRAINING PITS OF THE DRAGON'S DEN~~~~~

Rakkah dropped the tip of his dulled practice sword to the sand and momentarily steadied himself upon the hilt while he caught his breath. His heart pounded to the beat of the drums and pipes, the constant background rhythm setting the pace for their work-outs. Sweat dripped into his eyes and he ripped off the soaked band impatiently, wringing it out and wrapping it back around his head. This one was giving him a hard time, not like all the rest. Not only had the boy recently been admitted as a level ten Trainee, a full two levels beneath his own, he was showing rapid improvement. Given his natural strength and coordination, his potential was near limitless. 'Twas what the Trainers had said about him, when he'd begun.

Most Trainees accomplished a level promotion per winter or winter and a half, but Rakkah had managed to climb two levels in just o'er one and was pushing hard for the third. However, most Trainees entered at ten to twelve winters, but his entry had been delayed. He glanced at his selected partner for the day. Not un-like this one, he thought. Finally he had some decent competi-tion, and mayhap 'twould help him push through even faster. 'Twas going around that Mikkal had seen just o'er fourteen win-ters, an Outlander who'd traveled alone to Drekinn, living and working on the docks and petitioning since the day he'd arrived. Outlanders weren't often accepted and were under more scrutiny than most 'til they made it, if they made it, all the way to Warrior Training, the promotion from level one. However, Mikkal was being treated as a born and bred Clansman, even being tutored by the Commander's mate. 'Twas downright odd. Stranger still
~~~~~

was their resemblance to each other, as well as having similar temperaments. Each with comparable strength and build, tall and brawny with the same rich brown hair and sea green eyes, under Mikkal's 'twas dark and puffy, and he'd just stifled another yawn. Rakkah couldn't pass up the opportunity to tease him. "Can you not put forth a bit more effort? Your weariness cannot be from training, therefore, you'd not be so tired if you didn't wander about all night, instead of sleeping like the rest of us."

Mikkal was mortified. He'd been putting forth all his effort in order to impress the others, and he'd thought he was doing rather well against the more experienced young man looking down on him as he kneeled in the sand, his heart still pounding. Not to mention the fact that he'd not known he'd been sleepwalking again, and it made him nervous that this one had such familiarity with his 'affliction'. Instead of admitting to his own lack of experience, he chose to address the other problem. Barely audible, speaking under his breath, he replied, "I can't sleep, I know not what's going to happen to me once I close my eyes, and I know not where I'll wake." 'Twas easy to see that Mikkal was troubled, and 'twas clear to Rakkah that he wasn't faking the sleepwalking. Thus far, he'd been the only witness to the nocturnal activity and at first he'd followed out of curiosity. Just the prior night he'd led him back to his barracks, sacking him out in the bunk next to his own for the boy's protection. Rakkah had never been close to anyone, considering none to be a true friend. Although he got along with the others during Training, on his own time he was distant and reclusive, and the rack beside his had been empty for many moons. The change in his demeanor had not gone unnoticed, and the Trainers attempted to encourage this budding friendship by pairing them in the Pits. Though 'twould seem they'd have done better to try to pair two wild boar, as the rivalry 'tween them began straight away and only increased as the day lengthened.

Dismissively, Rakkah replied, "You're not working hard enough. If you're tired, you'll sleep."

Mikkal was not only embarrassed now, he was getting angry, but more so with himself. For some reason, gaining the other boy's respect was suddenly very important. Standing his full height, he didn't bother to control his volume. "I'm still stronger than you are! And, I'm a winter younger!"

"'Tis an audacious claim from a piss ant," Rakkah spit forth, his fuse just as short. Yet he wasn't genuinely angry, for which he was somewhat puzzled.

Mikkal pursed his lips and grit his teeth to counter his fatigue. Stepping closer, the two never taking their eyes off each other, he growled, "Who are you calling 'piss ant', Troll face?"

That crossed the line for Rakkah, who was actually self-conscious despite his uncommon good looks, and he issued his challenge. "Draw then, and strike me down to your size, if you can!"

In less than a candle drip, Mikkal drew his sword and struck viciously. 'Twould have caused heavy injury had it landed, but Rakkah expertly sidestepped, bringing his own sword up and around to smack flat sided against Mikkal's shoulder, knocking him off balance in an age old fighter's insult. Although he didn't end up face down in the sand, and was even quick enough to avoid Rakkah's next strike, Mikkal's temper boiled o'er, and all his training thus far was tossed to the four winds as he let loose his pent up frustrations. Raining a hail of strikes upon his partner, who managed to block most of them while making numerous strikes of his own, each eventually disarmed the other. But neither would surrender, and unrelenting they rolled upon the sands in a furious fist fight. The Trainers said not a word, watching closely without interfering, as 'twas felt the workout would do them both a world of good. 'Twas late and there'd be time tomorrow to correct the outburst. Shayla the Healer heard the commotion from her clinic and stepped out in anticipation of injuries. From 'cross the Pits her eyes met those of the Battle Commander observing the situation from afar, and although she didn't always approve of their methods, she respected their outcomes, and stepped back inside in response to his nod of dismissal. But none of the other fighters said or did anything, most of them ignoring the ruckus as they continued with their own endeavors, unwilling to waste any of the waning daylight.

Surprisingly, the end result was not the need of a Healer, for once exhausted they rolled groaning and gasping to their backs, and stared at the open sky above for several heartbeats. Dusk was upon them, yet, 'twas as if time itself had stopped. "Piss ant," wheezed the elder of the duo. "Troll," was the other's gasping reply. Suddenly bursting into laughter, they picked each other up and brushed off the sand. 'Twas the first time either of them had even smiled during Training, let alone laughed out loud, and it caused a ripple of startled silence through the Pits as many dropped their practice swords to stare at them strangely. Even the voices of the drums and pipes ceased. Their Trainers sent the others a warning glance and harrumphed to get the pair's attention. The eldest and tallest of the trio, Elder Warrior Tannyr, who specialized in swordsmanship, kept silent along with Warrior Gwynn, home from active duty 'tween deployments, who spent most of her Training time guiding the lower level katas.

Both of them deferred to the dark blonde, heavily built Elder Warrior Regynn, specialist in hand to hand and martial arts training, who asked, "Who started this and why? Warriors don't fight amongst themselves. And although you're not Warriors yet, this may go in your records."

Mikkal didn't even blink, although one eye was swelling shut anyway. "'Twas me. I did it. I pushed him into the fight. He was only defending himself."

Rakkah was shocked to hear the ease with which the other attempted to protect him, and while he nonchalantly inspected the bruising on his shoulder, he responded just as quickly, "No, he had no part in starting this, I teased him into fighting. You know my charming nature."

The three Trainers gaped at them. They well knew both their 'charming natures' and their quick and selfless responses were somewhat unexpected and highly prized. All Warriors could be difficult men and women, for they lived and trained hard, knowing they'd most likely Pass the Veil hard, and 'twas not that they wanted submission. The two would be excellent additions to the Brotherhood but the art of fighting required emotional control and they thanked the One True Liege for bringing Mikkal to pair with Rakkah. They sparked off each other but 'twas not destructive. Their minds of one accord, they rendered their verdict. Tannyr stated, "'Twould appear as if both of you were at fault, and neither." Regynn continued, "Since no real harm was done, mayhap we misunderstood the gravity of the situation, although we warn you this once, against lying." Gwynn finished, "Get thee to the showers and then to supper, for dawn arrives all too soon."

Much relieved, they joined the others. Warriors in residence, on leave, or 'tween duty, Trainers, Trainees, and a few house staff keeping up their skills, all stripping out of their sweaty work out gear and stepping under one of the many naturally flowing spouts pouring forth from the far end of the Pits. Some wide enough for several at a time, no one had to wait. For a spring fed system, the water was oddly moderate in temperature, cool but not freezing in the winters, and wouldn't give you a headache when you drank from it in the summers. 'Twas a gift never questioned, merely appreciated. House staff hurried about, handing out slices of hand milled soap, and once everyone was finished there were fresh towels and clean clothing as they shook the water from their hair in a sparkling spray of moisture from a multitude of heads, both male and female. Drying themselves rapidly, they dropped the towels where they'd stood and dressed as they left the Pits to go to supper in the Mess Hall. After which, the Trainees and Warriors would retire to their barracks to spend several marks cleaning and caring for their real weapons afore they hit the racks.

Long past midnight, when most were sleeping soundly, the two sat on the edge of their bunks, their voices low, getting to know each other, gaining mutual respect and trust. They talked about anything and everything, and even went into detail on all the gossip concerning the pregnancy of the mate of the Battle Commander. Finally, the moment of truth was upon them, and Mikkal was the first to reveal his inner most secret. "You know we were both born about the time foretold in the True King Prophesy." He looked o'er his shoulder to ensure none were listening, then scoffed, "The story told me was that of a babe born to a peasant girl who Passed the Veil giving me life. I'm quite certain there's more to that tale. But I was raised by a Healer in Wyndsyr Forest, outside of King's Gate. 'Twas a solitary existence 'til last winter when I was sent to the Clan to become a Warrior. The sleepwalking and nightmares had already begun. Seems I'm always drawn to Evanntyr. I thought they'd stopped when I came to Drekinn."

Prompted by his new friend's admission, Rakkah countered, "I've never told anyone this, but yours is a similar story to my own, although I can't say I've had the same experience with sleepwalking. I was told that I was born to a bar wench somewhere in the middle of the Ocean of Fears off Port O'Kings. Had she stayed, we'd both been killed in Koryl's upcoming, and now infamous, royal hissy fit to clear the castle and all of King's Gate of Bryard's concubines and bastards. She gave me to a family in Port O'Drekinn, and was never seen or heard from again. She didn't leave any information, not even her name. I can only speculate on my blood parents, but the ones who matter, Claimed me, and I was raised as a Clansman to become a Warrior."

In a hushed voice, Mikkal blurted forth, "I believe I was sired by Bryard."

"As do I," Rakkah replied without hesitation.

Relieved, Mikkal nodded his head. He'd noticed their resemblance instantly, 'twas as if he'd been looking in a mirror. "You don't think..."

Rakkah cut him off firmly. "What? That you or I could be the True King? Hades, no."

Mikkal sat upright and stammered with feigned lack of care, "Oh, well of course not. No. That couldn't be. I just wondered."

Rakkah realized the boy really had believed he could've been the True King. Thus far, Mikkal had shown himself to be ruled by his emotions and doubly impulsive, and he had to make sure he didn't bring disaster upon himself or the Clan. "'Tis obvious you were sheltered and therefore, may not have been aware of the happenings in the outside world around the time of our births, so let me enlighten you. Infants and toddler boys who were even suspected of having been sired by the High King, died with strange illnesses or in accidents by the drove within the first winter after the birth of Shytin, regardless of their age. In the following few winters, anyone who was rumored to be of his seed, mysteriously Passed as soon as the knowledge was revealed. I haven't heard of any such deaths recently, and I'm fairly certain most of them weren't actually blood to Bryard anyway, but I've kept my past to myself. I think you should, too. There's no need to tempt the Fates unless something happens. Besides, we aren't positive of our sires, and there are many here who have no past. Our lives begin and end with the Oath, but in order to take it, we have to survive Training.

"Agreed. But what happens if I start doing it again? What if I sleepwalk?"

Confidently, Rakkah replied, "I'll stop you, just as I have since you moved into the Den. End of problem."

"You didn't even know me then. I was just on the prospects list, another petitioner. I didn't even sleep in this end of the barracks yet. Why would you do that?"

"When I first laid eyes upon you, my brother, as you stepped through the Main Gate and gazed in wonder upon the tapestries, I knew our destinies were interlaced. We are blood, of that I am certain. The One True Liege sent me to protect you for a greater cause, and I always complete my mission. Now, rack out, we need to get some sleep."

Clasping arms in a Warrior's embrace, they embarked on one of the most enduring friendships in the history of the Brotherhood. Each trusting the other with their most personal secret. Each trusting the other with their very lives. Not just as brothers in arms, but as brothers in blood.

<center>~~~~~THE DAGGOGH VILLAGE~~~~~</center>

The sensation was strong, but without its usual frantic quality. Still, it woke Gabriel and he rolled o'er, blinking as his eyes adjusted to the darkness. Shivering in the pre-dawn chill, he got up, wrapped his cloak around his shoulders and added another log to the fire pit, stirring the coals. He squatted beside it to warm himself as the blaze took, and squeezed his eyes shut to focus his thoughts. 'Twas not déjà vu, for he re-lived not something or somewhere he'd been in the past. 'Twas as if he was actually somewhere else at this very moment. Seeing the world through another's eyes, in another's body, speaking with another's voice, he tried to keep his eyes shut in order to extend the waking dream. There was a boy sitting 'cross from him, similar to his own appearance, and they were whispering to each other in the darkness of some kind of sleeping quarters. He strained his ears toward the conversation and caught something being said about the High King. Shytin, or Bryard? He couldn't be certain, 'twas gone as quickly as it had come.

Every time this happened he felt strong emotions pulling him in different directions. 'Twas great turmoil that one felt. Shaking his head, he shut his eyes once more, willing the image to return, but after several moments of nothing, he took a deep breath and gave up. These waking dreams were not Visions either, but something else. He'd not told anyone about them, but he'd had them for as long as he could remember, always fleeting at best. The 'other' seemed close to him, in need of him, was so alone his soul cried out for him, but he didn't seem to know about Gabriel, and Gabriel didn't have enough information to begin to find the other. There'd been several episodes throughout his span of days, and always with some grievous decision or event in the other's life that he believed caused the sharing of their spirits. Mayhap he was wrong, for this time 'twasn't grief he felt. 'Twas a peace, almost hopefulness. Who was he? Why did they share what they did?

Dawn was approaching and he focused his thoughts away from the other as he prepared for a demanding day. In less than a mark he tested for Handler in his first solo hunt with his own partner. Traddya, a Kahyah bitch, would be at his side and he'd made every effort to ensure they were familiar with each other, so they'd have no difficulty through the trials. He was pleased to work with this particular bitch as she'd recently become the mate of Ryygg, the big male who worked with Gheryh. Traddya was being 'given' to him if he passed today's testing. Most Handlers took their tests at ten or eleven, but he'd only arrived with the People last winter and he'd had to accomplish much in just a few moons in order to achieve this honor. Already past his fourteenth, Gheryh had praised his work in hunting and handling skills, even going so far as to tutor him with Ryygg. 'Twas largely due to her efforts and faith, that he was being given this chance. He didn't want to fail her or himself.

<center>~~~~~EVANNTYR~~~~~</center>

The fishermen had presented Shytin with a most interesting and rare insect they'd reported snagging in their net along the Southern Slippes, many leagues southeast of King's Gate. Their claims altered not, even through much torture. Apparently, they'd spoken the truth. So, this Eoche had somehow gotten lost. But from where 'twas caught, 'twas no way to determine from whence it came, or how it ended up in the Fears. Although he'd never laid eyes upon one, the Sorcerer immediately realized what 'twas, but what he really wanted was the location of the nest. Still, even though he was disappointed, possession of one Eoche was better than having none. After killing the two men who'd brought him the insect, he sent Dragons and Agents to complete the wash at their home. Men, women, children, all perished without knowing why. Then they razed the village, leaving nothing but a'Flamed rubble. No one with any knowledge of the Eoche was to remain alive.

The blacksmith forged an iron cage with bars tight enough 'twould not allow the tail to get through, and the insect was pushed into the farthest corner of the dungeon. During the transfer only three of his men were stung. Watching the feeding process with excitement, he'd allowed the insect his fill afore shutting the cage. Elated, the Sorcerer was quite certain he'd have an inspired use for the Eoche eventually.

CHAPTER NINE

The Dragon Lives

A WINTER AFTER BRYARD'S DEATH
~~~~~THE DRAGON'S DEN~~~~~

The Summer Solstice was upon the 'morrow. The Faire opened the previous dawn but Aalanna was too pregnant and uncomfortable to walk about as she pleased, and stayed inside most of the day. Even though 'twas quite late for teaching, she was grateful for the boy's company for she didn't expect Grifynn home for some time and she really didn't want to be alone this night. During the Faires he'd keep watch o'er all the visitors, maintaining the peace. She loved being his mate, but there were times she wished he wasn't so dedicated to his position. She ran her hand o'er her taut belly. Had it already been nine moons since they'd returned from Evanntyr? 'Twas a full winter since the death of Bryard.

Sitting forward in the chair, she leaned sideways as far as she could, in order to determine if his eyes were open or shut. He seemed much older than fourteen, but he'd just begun to nod his head again as if he were a small child. "Mikkal?" Aalanna flicked his ear with her finger to wake him. She'd been tutoring him at night for the past several moons, but 'twas as if he never slept. Extremely dedicated and very skilled with weapons already, he was a handsome boy with good coordination, grace, strength, and reflexes. A natural Warrior. But he also harbored a darkness inside, and he struggled to keep the anger caged. However, he seemed to be handling himself well lately, and she'd never mentioned her concerns to Grifynn. She didn't want to see the boy's dreams dashed. She had faith in him, he just needed more time to mature than some. And Rakkah needed him as well. 'Twas remarkable how different they both were, since they'd become best friends. The two were good for each other. She flicked his ear again, a little harder. "Mikkal!"

Mikkal practically jumped out of his skin, blurting, "Yes'm?"

Aalanna reached o'er the boy's hands and folded the book closed, placing his pencil at the top of the table. Driven to excel, he far surpassed most of the others now, but he'd not wanted to quit their sessions. "Go to bed. 'Tis past midnight and you have morning katas, then hand to hand in less than four marks. Get some rest."

"No! I'm sorry I fell asleep. I can do this, I can, please... don't push me away..."

'Don't push me away.' Aalanna felt the anguish in that plea, and it near broke her heart. The pain in this one's past must be unbearable. She wished she knew what demons plagued him, she wished she could help more. "No, my boy, I'm not pushing you away, I'd never do that. You've done well, and we're finished for the night. In fact, you're far ahead of the others, and I don't think we need spend any more of your nights in study. But that doesn't mean you can't come see me when you want. We're friends now. Come to me whenever you're troubled or just need an answer to a question, any question, and I'll do whatever I can to help."

Mikkal sat back and pushed the chair away from the desk. He hung his head, staring at his boots. "You've done more than is required for any Trainee. I know 'twas for Rakkah, but I do appreciate everything. I won't bother you any longer."

"Oh poo, Mikkal, I've tutored many others, not just you. And I believe you're implying you aren't the one benefitting. If so, you're wrong. I did this for you, not for Rakkah, not because Grifynn told me to do so. I did it because you are worthy of being a Warrior, and I want you to fulfill that quest. 'Tis honorable, and you have a Warrior's spirit. I believe in you. And you are now, and have never been, a bother."

Mikkal wanted to let the welling tears flow down his cheeks, but he couldn't show that kind of emotion. He wanted to take the hug she plainly wanted to give, but he couldn't. 'Twas reminiscent of when he'd left home. When he'd left Artemis. He'd wanted to hug her, feel her hold him again, tell her how much he loved her, hear her tell him the same. Instead, he bottled it up inside and grit his teeth. He was going to be a Warrior no matter what he had to do, but 'twas good to hear that she felt him worthy of such. It lessened some of the pressure he'd placed upon his own shoulders. He had to make Artemis proud, he had to make amends for betraying her.

"OH!" Aalanna abruptly grabbed her swollen belly and gasped.

Mikkal sounded as if he'd known all along that she was in labor. "Another pain? How long 'tween them now?" His knowledge of medicine was reassuring, his calm demeanor inspired confidence.

Although he had his personal demons with which to deal, he was a good young man at heart, and she answered his questions as if she was speaking to the Healer herself. "I've been in labor most of the day, but I believe the little one is getting impatient. I think I need Shayla, and the Battle Commander is not yet back from his duties."

"I'll get her for you."

"No! Please don't leave me, I don't want to be alone." Aalanna was young, without a hand maiden or family assistance, but she was unwilling to admit fear.

With the confidence of experience, Mikkal's voice was comforting, despite her concerns. "This is your first baby, correct? You should have plenty of time, I shan't be gone long."

But all comfort dissolved as her breath was taken away from her, and she bit back a scream of pain.

Mikkal stood up rapidly and reached for the woman. "Put your arms around my neck, I'll carry you to her. You'll be safe with me."

Even pregnant, the mistress of the Den was a tiny woman, the boy-to-be-Warrior strong and determined not to fail his

Commander. But as soon as he lifted her, she went limp in his arms. Carrying her into the hall, he barely got past the doorway when he ran headlong into what might as well have been a rock wall. His eyes traveled with trepidation upwards past the leather breast plate, into the heated gaze of Grifynn himself. Stammering, the boy transferred his burden to the huge Warrior, who took her easily into his muscled arms, and then they both stared at each other, watching the water run down their leathers, pooling on the floor. Aalanna was still unconscious. "Mikkal, run! Get Shayla and bring her to me now. We will meet you on the way to the hospital," he yelled at the boy's retreating backside, following as fast as he could. The picture of strength, he was terrified. This child meant everything to his people and would be his first, but Aalanna had to live for she was his life.

By dawn of the Summer Solstice, the healthy lungs of the long awaited infant protesting the cold afore being wrapped and handed o'er to the new parents, could be heard far and wide. A mighty roar of approval and good will resounded throughout the Den, and then all of Drekinn and the Port District soon joined. The Battle Commander and his beautiful mate, both much loved and respected, had a daughter, the answer to the prophesy. With flaming red hair and piercing blue eyes, Darque Aalanna Grifynn, AKA the Dragon, had entered Kadoor.

~~~~~~~~~~

'Twas a mere moon afore the People learned of the birth. Throughout the Razor's Edge and the Raptor's Talons, from village to village then rippling outward to all Kadoor, the word was spread, "'Tis done, the prophesy begins. She has returned, the Dragon lives!"

<div align="center">

SIX MOONS LATER

~~~~~EVANNTYR~~~~~

Shytin defiantly addressed his mother, hoping he'd not pushed too far, but craving his desire. "You promised me a Queen of my own choosing. I have chosen." 'Twas his first real demand, and thinking he'd obtained her consent simply for the audacity of the deed and the control she'd gain, he continued staring at her, nervously awaiting her response.

Standing afore his throne, she was silent for several long breaths. Shytin began to sweat afore she finally deigned to answer. With a knowing smile and a sickly sweet voice, she spoke. "You have chosen well, my son. I will make the arrangements as soon as she has rid her body of yet another of Grifynn's spawn." Wickedly, she was the one who waited now.

Shytin realized the price of such a victory and didn't keep her waiting long. Submitting, he stated, "Thank you, mother. I will be most grateful." Bowing his head so she could not see the look on his face, he swallowed his bile and tried not to shudder. He'd get no sleep this night. But he had his memories to help him through to the dawn. When the Battle Commander of the Dragon Clan appeared at Evanntyr o'er two winters past to swear fealty to the new crown, he'd brought his beautiful mate, Aalanna, whom Koryl had always hated without explanation. Shytin had spent as much time with her as possible and she'd seemed quite cordial, her noble and friendly nature drawing him like a moth to the torch. She was a true lady. Oh, he'd been completely aware of the fact that Grifynn was trying to find evidence of wrong doing in Bryard's death, for Koryl had Seen such, but he'd found nothing. They'd made assurances by 'holding' anyone who might talk, threatening others with the lives of their families. 'Twould have been particularly gruesome for those who helped the Commander in any way. When they'd finally left he was determined he'd have Aalanna as his own. He'd even argued that taking her afore she had her first child would prevent the prophesy, however, Koryl had steadfastly refused. Soon after their return to the Clan, 'twas announced Aalanna was expecting. Shytin fantasized the child was his, and such made the long nights with his mother more tolerable. Three moons after the birth of Darque,

Aalanna was once again pregnant, and his fantasies drove him mad. The more he fantasized, the more he wanted her, and finally he'd made his request a demand.

O'ER SIX MOONS LATER

~~~~~THE DRAGON'S DEN~~~~~

Mikkal stirred in his sleep. Restless again, Rakkah opened his eyes to see his brother was already up, dressed in britches and boots and walking out of the barracks. Rakkah got up, and hastily donning his own pants, he followed him to the Mess Hall where Mikkal poured a mug of milk and downed it in one chug. Then he went to the Commander's quarters. Aalanna had just given birth near a fortnight prior to another beautiful girl they'd named Storrm. Rakkah knew Grifynn wasn't home at the moment and Aalanna should be alone with the babies. But Mikkal never hurt anyone in his sleep and he wasn't worried. Standing against the wall out of sight, he watched as Mikkal stepped up to the guard outside the door, who moved aside for him to knock. He then entered her quarters, coming out again within a few heartbeats. Mayhap she wasn't home, either? Mayhap she'd left the babies with a nanny. No matter, he continued to trail after Mikkal for o'er a mark as he wandered to the library, then to one of the alcoves in the Great Hall, then finally back to the barracks. Rakkah was appreciative 'twas non-eventful, and after seeing Mikkal back to his rack and ensuring he'd stay there for the rest of the night, he fell out as well.

~~~~~~~~~~

</div>

Immediately after Mikkal left her quarters, Aalanna grabbed her cloak and checked on her daughters in their adjoining bedroom, giving them both a kiss. Darque stood up holding onto her mother's hand, a question on her face. "Ama?"

"Ama is going out for a bit, someone needs to discuss some personal issues. I said I'd meet him. I won't be long, my darling. I love you!" And then she turned and walked out the door,
~~~~~~~~~~

blowing her eldest daughter a kiss, which Darque attempted to catch. Stepping outside, she informed the guard that she'd return shortly.

~~~~~~~~~~

Aalanna arrived at the chosen thicket away from the prying eyes of both the Den and the village. Mikkal had been quite distraught about something, feeling he couldn't talk where anyone might hear. Aalanna had agreed to meet him, but where was he? Suddenly, she saw him striding through the trees. "There you are," she began, her guard down, trusting completely. He didn't even give her time to finish her thought afore he grabbed her, and she melted in his arms with the surge of Magic, her memory erased of Mikkal's participation. It all happened so fast, the Sorcerer hadn't needed to speak, which was good, for 'twas difficult enough to pull a Human Shift without adding the extra burden of voice. Besides, even though Mikkal had no clue about what he'd done, he'd done it well. Koryl would be proud. This kidnapping had been too easy. He carried his burden to the waiting Dragon and mounted. They'd be at Evanntyr by morning. No one would see them. No one would ever know what had happened to Aalanna, including Aalanna. She'd be mated to the King in two dawns giving him time to reject her, which was the hope of Koryl, or time to prevent her from rejecting him. Threatening the prophesy, the Clan, and those she loved, would accomplish that task with ease. He almost pitied her. Almost. But he pitied more the Cleric already in the dungeons, as his death would quickly follow the ceremonies. He'd been so helpful with the coronation, but when the Brotherhood began to search for Aalanna in earnest, there must be no one with any information to provide.
~~~~~~~~~~

General Gunnarr

PART TWO

The First Winter Of The Black War

Chapter Ten

The Black War Begins

16 WINTERS LATER
~~~~~FLIGHT OF FIRE KEEP~~~~~

Corbyn stood afore the Highland Counsel once again. Exceedingly handsome, his dark eyes flashed as with lightning as he spoke, his voice deep and resonating in the massive chambers. "The Mighty Maahayyel must agree with the Fay now, 'tis time to join the Clan. 'Tis time to recreate the LifeBond."

Maahayyel, as the rest of them, was well aware that Corbyn was the heir apparent of the Fay, even though he was in exile, however, they trusted him far more than his father and therefore, they'd agreed to hear him out. 'Twas not the first time Corbyn had come afore the Counsel with this same request. Mayhap this should be the last, she thought. She leaned toward her elder sister, Kaahayyel, and after a brief Exchange, she spoke with a slow and clearly majestic tone none could miss. "And you are certain the Dragon Clan will stand with the Highlands?"

"I have followed them since the Last Holocaust, as have you, Matriarch. The Humans of the Dragon Clan are trustworthy and highly skilled. They are the best of the best. Joining with them through the 'Bond, we have a very good chance to do that which we failed to do afore. 'Tis the only way to defeat the Black, once and for all."

After the Counsel conferred for close to a quarter mark, during which time some heightened emotions were evident, Maahayyel once again turned her attention to their honored guest. "Although the Highlands had hoped never to be forced to this Magic again, we must agree with the Fay. The situation has become more unstable, the Hoard gains in strength daily, their atrocities ever more depraved and brutal, and there appears to be
~~~~~

no one to stand against them. 'Tis time to recreate the LifeBond. We shall make contact through Kallyr, the Seer of the Dragon Clan. He should have little difficulty deciphering our Message. We shall ask for a meeting with the Clan's Counsel. We shall offer them the Magic. But we must also say 'twill soon be need of the return of the High Races Counsel, and Mankind must be represented once more."

Corbyn nodded and sighed. He'd won a huge victory getting them to agree to finally bring back the ancient Magic. For the most part, Mankind was still ignorant of the return of the Black, although Grifynn might know more than he let on, for he was brilliant. However, as he'd pointed out afore, 'twas a fine line 'tween brilliance and insanity. Nevertheless, bringing back the 'Bond was nothing compared to what he thought 'twould take to bring back the Counsel. Oh, he was in full agreement with the Matriarch that it must return. And soon. He sighed again. First things first. "A fortnight to get the message through to the Seer and meet with the Clan Elders, leaving a fortnight at most to gather the Warriors for the effort. We have just one moon afore the winter solstice. We'll need every advantage to guarantee our success."

Maahayyel nodded her agreement, and the Counsel was dismissed to begin their tasks. Corbyn dove headfirst out the window of the Keep, his Shift so fluid 'twas a marvel to be observed by any who happened to catch the view. The Raven flew off 'cross the Dragon's Tears toward the Far Northlands upon the horizon. He had some business to which to attend afore his presence would be required in Drekinn.

A SENNIGHT PRIOR TO THE FIRST LIFEBOND
~~~~~THE BLOSSOMING OF THE PROPHESY~~~~~

The Ancients requested thirteen candidates to stand for the ceremony, and Grifynn fielded fifty fighting men and women in response. The battle drums and pipes resonated from around the Pits below as Corbyn observed the Warrior sisters, at just sixteen and seventeen winters, continue their reign of victory to prevail o'er their opponents, fighting through the eliminations to earn the right to take the 'Bond with the Highlands. Storrm was an excellent swordsman, graceful, fluid, defensively without equal, waiting patiently for her opportunity to appear, winning each of her trials with fair ease. She had an odd idiosyncrasy of maintaining a running and irreverent dialog while fighting, making her observers laugh and her opponents lose their tempers, and their advantage, oft times giving rise to her opportunities. But Darque simply terrorized them with her swift and brutally offensive approach. Her blade sliced through the air so fast she gained her victories near afore the fight began, and Corbyn wondered if the 'Bond could actually enhance such incredible raw power and skill. Nevertheless, she remained true to her namesake, of whom she'd yet to learn, having no stain of arrogance or conceit. She was a fighting machine, dedicated to the Clan and her Oath, determined that she and Storrm would be first to take the Cut. For Darque, in line to assume the position of Second in Command, 'twas her duty to her fellow Warriors, not some kind of ego challenge. As things appeared, he had no doubt she'd accomplish her goal.

Corbyn spread his long wings, soaring high above in his preferred Shift as the Raven. Repetitively circling the Training Pits of the Dragon's Den, his feathers gleamed in the sun's rays. So much had happened here, so much was yet to happen. Here be the Dragon, but where was the True King? And could he prevent the death of life? The Fay were the strongest of the Magic bearing Races and considered themselves the keepers of the prophesies. Self appointed of course. Well, somebody had to do it, for they'd learned during the time of chaos afore the High Races Council was created, that prophesy did require a certain amount of assistance or evil reigned supreme. 'Twas a test of faith. Those faithful facilitated the side of their faith, while those who had none gave up their freedom of choice, accepting whatever happened, which wasn't often that for which they'd hoped. Therefore, he'd done what he could toward that end, knowing all the prophesies fit together, requiring each to blossom to fulfill the others. No prophesy was guaranteed, but 'twas indisputably certain that if they didn't occur, disaster upon a grand scale would follow. 'Twas how the Black initially rose to power, and although the Highlands shouldered the blame for his deeds, Corbyn knew the Fay were just as guilty. But all of that was ancient history and quite another story.

His thoughts returned to the current triad. How long had he waited and watched and hoped and pushed the Fates toward their realization? Soon Darque would be set upon her path of destiny, if nothing else went wrong. He'd known from the moment she was but a few marks birthed, that she was the answer to the prophesy heard by all the Races at the time of the Last Holocaust. 'And there will be a girl child born to the Race of Man, of Dragon Blood and Dragon Seed, with flaming red hair and piercing blue eyes, who will take up the Sword and lead the Races from near extinction into a New Beginning.' She'd certainly fit the physical description. With an unruly mop of the richest copper red hair he'd ever seen and blue eyes that pierced his very soul, 'twas merely curiosity she'd shown as Gunnarr the Mighty Blue, High Prince of the Highland Dragons, used his Magic to enlarge the space of her tiny bedroom within the Den, thus allowing him to stand his quite impressive height without banging his head against the low ceiling. With her sparkling eyes she'd tracked his every movement, and when he'd laid talon upon her, bestowing the vow of protection of his Race, not even a whimper was offered. The scar upon her right thigh bore the resemblance of a Dragon, (giving rise to her Battle Name of the Dragon), but 'twas the Dragon blood running through her veins that Called to the Raven, longer and louder than did that of her kin.

Watching o'er Storrm, his current obligation, he fervently wished his cyclical curse to serve a Warrior 'til he could no longer prevent her Passing, had not included those he considered of royal blood. The sisters of Aalanna Grifynn were more than special, with direct lineage back to the beginning of the Council, and 'twas particularly distasteful to him to involve them in his fate. And, they were the only representatives of their Kind known to be in existence. However, the Morrigan (from whom Storrm derived her Battle Name) owned his curse, and he had no choice but to participate as she directed.

Nevertheless, despite the energy charging the atmosphere with all these happenings, 'twas something else that bothered him, something despicable occurring in another place. 'Twas something that had to do with him, which he'd undoubtedly discover long after the fact, as usual. Flame the curse, it stifled his senses. He'd need to slip away, this distraction was too persistent to be ignored. He'd endured the curse long enough to have exposed all the loopholes, and was confident he'd be able to make at least a token investigation into this most troubling matter, without missing any action with Storrm. After all, he'd not even found the need to make his presence known to her yet, although Shayla had already detected him. He'd not be able to avoid that confrontation much longer. Why did Humans have to complicate everything so? Banking into a change of direction, he left the Pits behind as he took wing toward the far horizon.

<center>~~~~~THE ISLAND OF DREAMS~~~~~</center>

The following dawn, Corbyn landed upon the highest branch of the oldest and tallest pine tree on the island, outside the Royal Library of the Sprites in Dream Hold. Adjusting for the sway from the steady sea breeze, he scanned for leagues around. From here could be viewed the entire island, and what he saw and Felt was most disturbing. The Sprites were a serene, nature loving people, maintaining the peace through the strength of their forces, ever ready to repel the outside world, and always standing firmly together. Now heightened emotions, chaos, fear, rage, disbelief, indignation, and anguish, emanated from all around. Troops secured the Hold and were moving their search further outward. He listened carefully, almost reluctantly, chilled by what he heard. The heir apparent and the 7th Egg had disappeared less than two dawns prior, along with the Captain of the Sprite Elite Guard, Caleichante, a highly respected, trusted, and extremely accomplished fighter. Piecing the story together he discovered that an initial investigation found Kevon's blood, giving rise to the belief that the boy was seriously injured, with the implication that 'twas of Calei's doing. If she was innocent and the Prince was indeed injured, how had it occurred, and why not take him immediately to the Skald instead of this disappearing act? But even worse, it looked as if she took Bryynn with them. Corbyn was dumbstruck as his long time friend was being accused of such wrongdoing. He heard nothing to indicate they had any evidence of her guilt, but they were in lynch mode. Lord Rohar had just ordered she be 'brought in with prejudice', translated to dead. Something was seriously wrong here and he would uncover the truth. He began his own investigation, opening his senses to follow the sequence of events, and hopefully, discover how they'd managed to completely vanish on an island. Wherever they were, he had to locate them afore the team being organized at this very moment. And somehow, he had to do that while attending to the Dragon Clan. He fluffed out his feathers, lifted his beak, and smiled to himself. He loved a challenge.

~~~~~THREE DAYS DEEP IN THE FAR NORTHLANDS~~~~~

Calei hugged Kevon against her chest, the saddlebag with the Egg held tightly by the Prince, as they rode her Water Dragon, Shlyyn, sliding 'cross country away from the shore into the deep forest. As soon as they reached the first small village, she stole a horse and sent the Slyder back to the sea for more information. They rode for marks as she took them as far from their landing point as possible without traveling too far from the shore, so she could stay in touch with Shlyyn. There'd been a well in the last village, but 'twas much distance 'tween populated regions this
~~~~~

far north and not all Water Dragons knew the location of every well, unless they'd built it themselves or had utilized it in the past. With winter set in, and having no idea where the next well might be, they were on their own and needed shelter and rest soon. They'd be hunted, and she suspected a squad was sent out for them without delay. Her only hope was that they were still focused upon the island. 'Twas her best guess that when they began to search the mainland, which was inevitable, they'd assume she'd traveled deeper.

Still unwilling to risk a fire or Magic, she'd managed to steal some blankets and wrapped most of them around Kevon to ward off the increasing chill. She'd just gotten the Prince to sleep and was rubbing down the horse with some evergreen branches when she felt the whisper of air waft against the side of her neck. Turning swiftly, her sword was in her hand and she near skewered Corbyn as he glided in, Shifting back to his real form mid-air to step lightly 'tween her and the boy. Although he appeared unruffled, her heart pounded. "Why are you here, and how did you find me," she demanded, unsure of his loyalties. Keeping her sword in her hand, she edged her way around the Shifter, their gazes locked.

Corbyn merely cocked his head and sighed. Her thoughts greatly saddened him. He'd not doubted her. But she was coming off a battle, and he did have a certain reputation. Still... "Myrrdin sails the Krakken northward even now, from Port O'Drekinn to Port O'Teliv, where he will set anchor offshore and try to await your arrival should you not show within three dawns from whence they dock. He's not been home, yet he seeks answers, for Islyth discovered one of her treasures missing from her stash in the grotto and informed him. Myrrdin realized 'twas a message, given this particular item, and he began his search upon the sea." Winking, she smiled and nodded her acknowledgement as she re-sheathed her weapon. Corbyn had discovered the missing sunstone with Islyth and recognized her cry for help, obscure as 'twas. He'd used his senses to Feel her need, and told the Water Dragon she must report to the Ship's Master. "I would have wasted much time had I not made that discovery, but still, I wasn't certain that I'd find you first. You are a most difficult woman to locate when you don't wish to be found, so I recruited your cousin's assistance. If you hurry, you can catch him afore he anchors offshore." He glanced one more time at the Prince, now sleeping fitfully. The pain was somewhat lessened by his Spell. His heart beat stronger, his breathing less labored. "'Twill not last for more than a few moons, and 'twill deteriorate rapidly when it does lose its strength. Still, if Bryynn hadn't interfered, we'd have lost him."

She picked up the saddlebag and held it in her own lap as she sat down beside the boy, and proceeded to tell the Fay everything that had happened in Dream Hold.

"You did the right thing, Calei, you could nothing else. 'Twas not in your power, and you managed to save both the Prince and the Egg by your actions."

Relieved by his approval, she was still concerned. "I didn't want to believe 'twas you, Corbyn, but you know Bryynn could only be removed by one of royal blood. We've been friends a long time, although you're the only Fay I've seen since the Last Holocaust. But his eyes... I did not mistake them." She cast her own eyes down, so uncomfortable was she by her next question. "Are you confident your brother is dead?"

Shaking his head doubtfully, he did not take offense. "I've thought I was the last of the Fay for so many winters, I no longer know. But I cannot and will not believe 'twas Brannyn, either. On the other hand, I have no explanation, since there could be no other."

The awkward silence that followed told Calei the subject was closed, but she trusted 'twas not the Fay in front of her, whom she and the Prince had encountered. "How did they not find the blood of the invasion force? And how could they have seen ours?"

"I fear there is a spy amongst the Sprite Nation, I could sense the animosity, but was unable to pinpoint the source afore I left the island. 'Twould have been child's play to create a Suggestion Spell so none would notice other than what the Brewer allowed, after destroying the bodies."

She nodded. Of course, 'twas so simple. She'd thought the Assembly infiltrated, but hadn't uncovered any solid evidence afore their flight. And if they were focused on the high emotion of the loss of the Prince and the Egg, they wouldn't even notice the Spells. Stroking the boy's hair, she whispered, "What can I do for him, Corbyn? 'Tis sealed his fate?"

"Not sealed, but his days are surely numbered. 'Tis a question of when, not if. He will die if we cannot rid his system of the poison."

"Who can do such?"

After a slight hesitation he said, "There is one. I believe you'll find the answer you seek with Myrrdin. And I believe you need to drop your cargo."

"What? Drop the Egg? Why? Where would he be safer than with us? Unless you mean to take him, which I'd welcome."

"You must drop the Egg and I can't take him, for the same reason I cannot help you more at this time. The Evil One pursues me and the Egg. With the two of us together, neither stands a chance of remaining safe. My hand cannot be on your doings, I've done enough by lessening the boy's pain. I can only hope 'twas not a mistake. But time is of the essence, and Bryynn is a burden you do not need. His only chance is to be hidden where no one can see him, Hear him, or Feel his presence."

"But such interference would also mean great danger to him."

"You have no choice."

Calei's voice raised in sarcastic retort. "And do you have a suggestion as to where I might find such a hiding place?"

The Fay remained ever calm. "Yes. I suggest you bury him in the Bog."

Incredulously, she responded, "The Bog of St Swiftyn's? He'll drown!"

"His shell is moisture proof as long as 'tis unbroken, and he can Feel his danger and keep from hatching 'til your return." Corbyn hoped he was right. If Bryynn did hatch under the Bog he would drown, for he'd have no sense of direction. And even if he could determine which way was up, newly hatched he'd be too weak to dig his way through the top layer of debris in order to take his first breath in time to survive such a traumatic entrance to Kadoor. But, why complicate things any further? Prioritizing, 'twas no doubt the Prince would die soon without treatment, but the Egg was not in any present danger other than from being found. And the Bog would cover his Allure, effectively hiding his presence from the Evil One. At any rate, this visit must end, as he Felt the draw of the curse pulling him back to Drekinn. Turning, he made his Shift and flew off through the gathering darkness, giving his final words of advice. *"Watch your back, Caleichante. The recovery team sent for you does not seek answers, only your blood and the return of what you have taken, both boy and Egg. If they succeed, the Prince will surely Pass. Now go. Get thee to the Krakken."*

<center>~~~~~THE LAIR OF THE HOARD~~~~~</center>

The Black was once again angered by his report. 'Twas becoming a habit for that one to balk at direct orders. His lip quivered o'er a loose fang as he watched the Sorcerer take his leave, backing away and bowing humbly as if 'twould make a difference. If he failed him again, he'd roast him alive and make him share in the feast afore being allowed to Pass. Grumbling, he sauntered off down the cavernous hallway in search of entertainment and nourishment. As he'd just noted, they could very well be one and the same.

The Sorcerer backed away from the Evil One, rushing out of the Lair and making his escape as quickly as possible. He was pleased he'd been able to hold the groveling to a minimal level in order to gain the Black's approval of his original mission. Sent to retrieve the 7th Egg, he'd had another scheme, one that would gain him the revenge he'd sought for so long. He'd implicated Corbyn the Fay in the abduction, and although the boy should have Passed immediately, the death of the heir apparent was ensured. Further, he'd succeeded in framing the Captain of the Guard as a thief and murderer. His Sprite nemesis held no more o'er him, his infiltration in the Assembly complete, without those two standing in his way. He laughed out loud. He was very good at making things appear to be that which they were not. There was another advantage to the way things worked out, and that being the Egg was now safe from the Hoard, as he wanted to use Bryynn himself. 'Twas one who could retrieve it for him, even now in place. Nowhere could the Captain hide the Egg, that his spy would not discover. Now he just needed that child, Fryya. Koryl had promised him the girl, winters past. He not only wanted her for his own perverse gratification, he believed that with her, he could gain control o'er Grifynn, as well as use her to get the Eye, which was proving to be more difficult to obtain than he'd thought. He needed Grifynn to tell him how to break the prophesy and where the True King could be found, among other things. He'd come so close to capturing the boy several winters past, but he'd slipped the noose just as 'twas tightened. He ground his teeth with the memory of that loss, and vowed once again that soon he'd be freed of both Corbyn and the Black, leaving him the unopposed supreme ruler of all Kadoor.

<center>~~~~~THE CAVES OF DREKINN~~~~~</center>

'Twas a moon since the first 13 Warriors took the LifeBond with the Highlands to enter the Black War. Forging new pathways, each learned to deal with their enhanced senses, strength and speed. The Highlands gave up their infinite lifespans, and by Sharing with their Human partners, if not killed in battle or accident, both would now live a mere several hundred winters together afore reaching their final sleep. Being part Dragon, Darque and her sister had latent Magic of their own, and after taking the 'Bond 'twas beginning to show itself. However, 'twas as confusing as enlightening to the girls, as they had yet to learn of their hybrid genes.

But this night was special. Just falling asleep upon the ledge outside their cave after another exhausting day of searching for the Hoard Lair, only to find refugees of horrible slaughters, they awoke to a desperate Cry for help resounding through the cosmos. 'Twas the Voice of Walkyr, the boy Seer. Experiencing his Vision as reality, he Screamed into the night for someone to 'help the girl'. Although he shared not the enhancements, including the Link, his Cry was so loud, so emotional, that Darque and Gunnarr picked it up through their own senses.

Flying swiftly, they plucked his slender frame from the edge of the well in Drekinn Square, just afore he would have plunged headlong into the darkened pit, surely causing major injury if not instant death. Then, with their passenger secured they flew swiftly to Kaddart. Led by the boy's Vision, they were too late to save the village, but managed to rescue the girl. 'Twas Fryya, sent there to die, the entire village destroyed to silence her witness. Darque lost one of her blades in the battle against the Hoard Dragon they forced Past the Veil that day. He was their first kill, and 'twas there that the first Dragon's Eye since the Last Holocaust was created. Found by Gunnarr amongst the remains as he salvaged fangs and talons, he was well pleased to have acquired such a jewel as a binding gift for his lovely mate, saving it for a more appropriate moment.

When news of the girl's harrowing escape from his clutches reached the castle, the Sorcerer wasn't certain if he were more angry or pleased. He'd lost her to Shytin just after Koryl had finally given her to him, the jealous boy using an opportunity he'd been trying to orchestrate. Backed up against the wall, he had to order her killed, but instead of doing so outright, he'd devised the scheme in Kaddart, secretly hoping she'd be rescued. After all, if she was still alive, he might yet get her back. And, he had no doubt that he'd exact his revenge on Shytin sometime in the future. He never forgot, or forgave.

He'd sent spies to the Clan, who'd not been able to penetrate their defenses. The Black decided 'twas a job for a more talented spy. The Sorcerer reluctantly volunteered, but after infiltrating he saw a greater opportunity. Continuing his personal vendetta, he thought to lower the moral of the Clan, break their trust in each other, and foster fighting amongst themselves. 'Twasn't easy to move around as he was hounded by a tiny Green named Haniyyah, and her huge Human 'Bond, Axyl. Time and again he was almost caught, barely escaping the tenacious pair. He'd expected to have to avoid the Battle Commander, who was legendary in his skill to ferret out spies, however, 'twasn't long afore his suspicions were confirmed. Grifynn was dying.

In and out of the Den he ran his forays of deceit, but truly no information did he manage to gather that was useful to the Black. His temper was a'Flame as he attempted to please his master while trying to make his own gains, particularly the kidnap of Fryya and Walkyr, who at only six winters was an extraordinary Seer. But Darque moved the children into the castle and hired a personal bodyguard for each after his initial failed attempt, and he'd not even gotten close again. His disguises were good but apparently not good enough, and if discovered he'd not live to see another dawn. His own torture techniques came from his perverted enjoyment of the effects, but those of the Clan came from loyalty, honor, and the Oath of the Brotherhood, making getting on their bad side something to be very much avoided. 'Twas also most grievous to him that their One True Liege seemed always to thwart his efforts, hindering his every move. His own Kind had no need of a strong deity, but if they did, he'd seriously consider the One, after what he'd observed.

~~~~~~~~~~
~~~~~~~~~~

Near a winter passed as the LifeBond Teams gained experience and skill, practically stumbling o'er the Lair of the Black multiple times, while the Sorcerer deterred them with his most potent distraction Spells. He continued to work very hard to destroy the Clan from within, but angry with his lack of success, he'd exploded and killed Darque's favorite War Dog out of spite. Implicating Storrm, he'd been rather proud of himself 'til 'twas obvious the Warriors saw through his tirade and he feared he'd given away his most effective advantage. Now 'twas understood they were dealing with a Shifter. So, again, he tried to blame Corbyn. If he couldn't break trust 'tween the Warriors or the Clansmen, he'd break trust 'tween them and their strongest ally.

<center>~~~~~THE THRONE ROOM OF EVANNTYR~~~~~</center>

The great hall was empty of all but the three conspirators. The Sorcerer had just returned from Drekinn and had devised a bold plan. Scornfully he stood in front of the King, the Queen Mother in the chair beside the throne, as he gloated o'er the pain 'twould cause. Having planned his revenge for some time, he savored the moment. "'Tis simple really. In order for our offensive to bear fruit against the Clan and the Brotherhood, we need to cut off their heads; separate them from their Commanders. Not only can we bring Grifynn running into our trap, 'twill have his Second and Third following close behind."

Shytin glanced suspiciously at his mother afore answering. She nodded her approval. With his petulant whine, he questioned, "How do you propose to do that? Grifynn isn't stupid. And neither are his daughters."

"Grifynn is a man ruled by honor and chivalry. His daughters are like him." The Sorcerer couldn't hide his knowing smirk as he delivered the blow. "You have his lifemate in the Tower."

Shytin's face became a mask of fury, his eyes burning hatred at being reminded that he'd kidnapped the mate of another, wedding her illegally, keeping her imprisoned for seventeen winters. He bit his lip to keep from saying anything, as he waited for more on the plan. The Sorcerer elongated the wait, letting him simmer in his emotions. Then he continued, "Beat her, bring the Commander here, and his daughters will follow to protect him. 'Twill then be easy to kill them all. Three against your vast army? He knows she's here. Let it leak that she's going to be executed, but don't give him enough time to arrive for a rescue effort. In the meantime, we launch our attack upon the Clan while they're away from the Den."

Shytin's already pale skin turned pasty yellow, his eyes widened, and he had to bite his tongue to keep from disagreeing. He glanced at Koryl, who was now grinning in delight. He had never hit Aalanna, she was his treasure. If Koryl made him do this, he'd leave her in the dirt. He was through with the Queen Mother. They were taking his most prized possession. He was backed into the corner facing both her and the Sorcerer, and he couldn't say anything that would show his opposition. He attempted to counter. "They have Dragons, they could be here very quickly."

"Grifynn has no Dragon. 'Twill take him at least a fortnight, and that, after he discovers her plight, which of course will already be too late. He won't be able to get here for at least a moon. We can kill her within the next fortnight at our leisure, and still have time to prepare for their arrival. A public execution after the beating would be suitable, no one will recognize her anyway. He'll be so devastated that he'll lose his mind and will be easily taken down." The Sorcerer was confident in his assessment of Grifynn's mental status, he'd seen the decline o'er the moons he'd been spying in the Den. This would do it for sure. 'Twould be his final doom.

~~~~~~~~~~

Brannyn eavesdropped upon this conversation from the hallway. He had to get word to Grifynn that his mate was about to be executed. Although he too, understood the mental status of the Commander, he also knew the personal fortitude of the man. 'Twould take more than this to destroy his mind. But, he had to try
~~~~~~~~~~

to save Aalanna, and it couldn't be by his hand. There was more to her than anyone understood. She had but one chance. He'd offer the Commander an arrangement. One through which he'd not return. 'Twas no other option. He was dying anyway, giving him the Magical boost to save his mate would merely make it happen sooner. He palmed the blade he'd found at Kaddart. 'Twas one of a matched set of four belonging to Darque, but 'twas not that fact which made it valuable for his current need. 'Twas the fact that it already had upon its edge the Life Source of a Dragon and his own, and by adding that of the Commander's mate he could Link with him to deliver the blade and explain the pact. When Grifynn added his blood, 'twould seal the Spell. All he could provide was the opportunity, 'twas up to the Human to make it work. If he failed, his very spirit would be imprisoned, and the Resistance would be hard pressed to survive such a devastating blow. 'Twould do no good to attempt to visit Aalanna afore they beat her, although 'twas not easy to ignore and allow to happen. He'd leave and take care of the arrangements, assuming she'd be ready to participate by the time he returned. A certain Ship's Master of the Krakken and his Tie would be most helpful, for he had but a sennight to get Grifynn to the castle to accomplish his goal.

<p style="text-align:center">~~~~~THE SEA OF DREAMS~~~~~</p>

Myrrdin found no fault with asking Islyth for the favor. When Brannyn came to him seeking safe and swift passage for Grifynn to the castle, he'd been intrigued with the happenings at Drekinn, seeing clearly as had the Fay, the blossoming prophesy. He would've given much to know just what Brannyn was up to, but not asking too many questions was how he and the crew of the Krakken made a living. Besides, he had a fair notion of what the Fay was about, regardless of how tight lipped he'd been.

Myrrdin had faith in the Water Dragon with whom he'd Tied at her hatching shortly after he'd moved to the Island of Dreams. An excellent hunter, she was also smart, brave, and loyal. She actually made good decisions on her own, not like most of the others, but then, he'd never treated her as a child in need of constant supervision. He'd treated her with respect, as a thinking individual, a working partner, and she'd responded in kind. Yes, he was concerned whenever she was in the Fears, because the Water Dragons were not easily pushed to aggression, including self defense. 'Twas a characteristic he'd tried often to circumvent. That was not to say they wouldn't defend their Ties, friends, or family members, something they'd do with a vengeance, their terrible jaws and claws making short work of anything that happened to be in the way, even their spit could cut a man in half. But not to defend themselves. And if caught alone, they were unusually easy to force Past the Veil. Nevertheless, he had no doubt that whatever creatures lived in the depths of the Fears, they'd not catch Islyth. There were many wrecks in the waters along the rocky Southern Slippes coastline where she could hide quite easily, but following the coastline took far longer and had its own problematic currents, tides, cliffs, and other dangers. She'd often enjoyed playing there, finding things she wanted to keep, and he allowed her to stash them in the grotto under their island home. She knew each and every one of her treasures and could tell if anything had even been slightly jostled from when she'd last visited. She'd wondered if she'd ever see her sunstone again, but it had gone to a good cause. Calei was as much her friend, as Myrrdin's. Standing on the foredeck, he tied his long black hair in a single tail with crossed leather strips, his matching eyes and pale skin in stark contrast where it could be seen under his black leathers. The Elven Prince took a deep breath of the salty sea air, then turned and barked his orders. His Sprite crew leaped into action as they set sail to Port O'Drekinn.

~~~~~THE OFFICE OF THE BATTLE COMMANDER~~~~~

Grifynn sat shaking with emotion. His tears soaked into the oak flooring beneath his desk, his heart about to break. He'd
~~~~~

known for some time that he had no more winters. The Link was clear, the messenger concise. Take Darque's blade offered as confirmation of this unfolding tragedy, for the Vision was surely Aalanna, beaten, bruised, adding a touch of her Life Source to the edge of the proffered blade to prove 'twas truth. His Dragon senses assured him 'twas her blood, could be no other. Brannyn presented him the chance to save her, but 'twould be his last mission. Resolutely, he'd accepted. Adding his own blood would seal the Spell and there'd be no turning back. He had 'til dawn to board the Krakken, soon to be docked in the port, and hand o'er the blade as his passage to Myrrdin the Ship's Master. Then he'd be taken to meet the next leg of the journey to Evanntyr, somewhere in the middle of the Sea of Dreams. He could only hope they knew what they were doing, for he had mayhap a sennight to prevent Aalanna's execution, and the opposition didn't know yet, that he was coming. He'd make certain they'd regret what they'd done. 'Twould be a night to remember, his final act, a one man extraction mission amidst a blood bath.

<p style="text-align:center">~~~~~LATER~~~~~</p>

Managing to send both his daughters off on separate missions which would not have them back afore he was long gone, he fingered the tag he'd worn since afore the Last Holocaust when all this began, the etchings so faded he could no longer read the words, the name forgotten many lifetimes past. 'Twas his most treasured possession. He'd leave it for his sister, Shayla. 'Twas the only memento they had left them from that time. Several strands of hair stuck and tangled in the chain as he ripped it off o'er his head. Folding the necklace neatly, he laid it upon the desk. She'd understand.

No note. The spy or someone else might find it afore he was ready, so what could he leave his daughters? Their favorite story, the scroll he'd written by his own hand, detailed pictures decorating every page, lifetimes of sketches added. The story of the

300. A favorite from his own childhood, he'd read it to his daughters from the time they were born, and they'd know 'twas his encouragement to keep fighting, stand strong, and never ever give up. His daughters were the only hope of Kadoor. There was no more he could teach them or give to them. Adjusting the scroll oddly upon the shelf to draw Darque's attention, he looked about the room one last time, then turned and ducked through the secret panel behind his bookcase, the passages eventually leading to the docks.

~~~~~A FEW MARKS LATER~~~~~

The Sorcerer had entered the room immediately after the panel sighed shut. He had much difficulty with this Shift, Storrm was not an easy Human to impersonate. He'd managed to get into the Commander's office only to find he was gone, but he'd acquired an even higher prize indeed. Grifynn's hair would prove most valuable. Tucking it into his pocket, he put pen to parchment and used Grifynn's seal on the fake orders, handing them o'er to the first Warrior he'd met in the hall to deliver to Axyl. They'd be sent to Byndynn Forest up north and ambushed, leaving the Den completely unprotected. They'd not survive the three waiting for them. Darque was still mapping the forest further north and not expected back for at least another two dawns, and Storrm and the rest of the Teams had been sent to the Darden region about the possibility of locating the Lair of the Hoard. Oddly enough, 'twas there, proving Grifynn's senses were still sharp, but they'd be called back afore they'd even arrived. Then he'd haughtily walked out of the castle and into the surrounding woods for the last time. Meeting the Black himself, they made haste to Evanntyr, thinking they had a full moon to prepare.

~~~~~THE NEXT DAY~~~~~

Darque arrived home early, but something was amiss. She and Gunnarr found the Den empty, every Team out on a mission her father had manufactured, leaving only Haniyyah and Axyl, however, they were missing as well. She'd Heard the shrieks of anger and pain from the little Green and they'd taken flight north to assist in what was certainly a vicious battle. Calling for backup, she'd discovered Storrm and the Teams were close to the Darden region, too far away to offer much help, but she'd managed to divert them back northward. Still, she and Gunnarr could and would arrive afore them, and while Haniyyah was fighting for their lives, Axyl's voice could not be Heard. But if Han was still alive, so was Axyl. She prayed for them to hold on as they flew with all speed.

After a hard journey taking several marks, Darque and Gunnarr burst upon the grisly scene. The Sorcerer had b'Spelled three of his Dragons to allow them to Flame within the forest, even though the Aversion Spell continued to cause them much anxiety. Mayhap 'twas why they'd not finished the pair as of yet. Axyl and Haniyyah had thought they'd received orders from the Battle Commander himself, to fly directly to this location to meet a new contact with information about the spy. But when they'd arrived, they'd been ambushed. Han was inundated, severely injured already. Battling alone, straddling her unconscious 'Bond, she protected him courageously from the three cowards attacking from all angles. Darque urged Gunnarr for more speed, but 'twould still be too late afore they could engage. Suddenly Haniyyah inhaled deeply just afore she was engulfed in Flame from a united frontal attack, and Darque thought the little Green was no more. A mere heartbeat later, she belched forth the largest, longest stream of Flame that any Dragon had ever spit, squelching their incoming. With Gunnarr streaming from behind, they took out all three of the enemy, sandwiching them 'tween their infernos.

'Twasn't long afore Storrm and the other Teams arrived and they loaded Haniyyah and Axyl in the slings to carry back to the Den and the Healer. Most of the next day was gone by the time they arrived and while Shayla went straight to work, Darque left the Healer to her task and hurried to her father's study. He'd sent all the Teams out of the Den at the same time, and on a wild goose chase no less. Not even to mention that they'd come close to losing these two, and might still. By the Ancients, what the Flame was he doing? Angered by the events of the past few days, let alone the past few moons, she discovered her father was absent. Answers were sparse, but after opening her senses within his office, she learned where he was going, if not why. Dawn would break within a mark. Calling to Storrm and Mystynn to meet her on the Great Plains of Drekinn, they took wing to Evanntyr.

CHAPTER ELEVEN

Memories of Regret

~~~~~THAT NIGHT~~~~~

The dull russet colored scales of the Dragon were covered in a thick layer of bat guano and dust. The shimmer of Allure which bespoke the health of all Magic bearers was gone, assisting her camouflage in the darkness. Many, many, many winters past, she'd curled her emaciated body into the farthest corner, away from the iron gate of the dungeon cell in which she'd been imprisoned for what seemed like forever, and simply stopped.

Prior to the Last Holocaust, when she was young and impulsive, she'd slipped away from her mother to follow her heart. How many times since that fateful night had she wished she'd listened? But she'd been in love and hadn't believed the Ancients when they'd warned her about the flagrant lies of the Hoard. Her life was turned upside down, her father had disappeared and they'd feared 'twas the Black's doing. Not long after, when Kaahayyel Felt his violent Passing, she'd abdicated her position as Matriarch to Maahayyel, and gone into seclusion to mourn. She took another deep breath as her mind wandered back to that time once again. 'Twas ever thus when she awoke from a long period of stasis, and try as she might she could not prevent the past from assaulting her present. Painfully, she relived how she'd been deceived, misplacing her trust and finding herself drugged and b'Spelled, captured by the Evil One. At first they'd kept her heavily sedated to prevent her from using her formidable Magic against them, and barely conscious, she'd been transported from place to place, finally ending up in this cold dark dungeon.

Her thoughts returned briefly to the present. Why had she awakened? Using only her common senses, she blinked her dry eyes several times and squinted to see past the bars. The well in
~~~~~

the middle of her view hadn't changed, but she couldn't see beyond the stairs to whatever lay above. There 'twas again, a sound; the rhythm of the ocean waves, the water lapping against the rock. And there, the smell of brine. Her brow ridges furrowed slightly as she tried to comprehend. It could be coming from the well, however 'twas fresh water. But the energizing affect of these sensations was short lived in her weakened condition, and her mind drifted yet again into the distant past.

Barely able to open her eyes at times, their brilliant luminescence slowly faded to a hideous yellow tint through the ages. Her Human captors kept her starved, not only to weaken her Magic, but to force her into submitting to their heinous plan. She was the daughter of an Ancient and a Matriarch, and they'd rightly expected her to be more powerful than most, for through her they'd hoped to gain a foothold into the upper echelon of the Highlands. But she'd refused to submit, steadfastly risking decapitation or having her heart carved from her chest, preferring death to betrayal. Winter after winter she'd survived torture and chaos, dehydration and starvation, solitary confinement and misinformation. Still, she wouldn't participate in the capture of her own family. Finally, she was weakened to the point she couldn't maintain her Life Force if she stayed constantly aware, and she didn't even have the strength to reach her final sleep. If she'd tried to Pass, she'd be forever wedged in the Hades of the Fade. Stuck 'tween this world and Beyond, she'd have no chance of ever getting her revenge, and no one would know what had become of her. She'd shunned her familial position and responsibilities, leaving their burden upon her little sister, to what end? Now she'd give anything to join the war effort and fight against the Black to redeem herself, if only in her own eyes. Utilizing a boost from the strongest Life Forces available (unbeknownst to the donors), she'd set a self-renewing Spell to constantly gather and channel energy to help her sustain. Allowing the Humans to think they'd finally forced her Past the Veil, she'd closed her darkening eyes.

Calling forth every bit of Magic she had left, she plunged inside her own being, thrusting herself into an unfathomable state of stasis. Never afore had a Dragon gone so deep. She wasn't even certain it could be done. But through the centuries she'd awakened a handful of times and gathered her wits about her. The discovery that she remained in the same place had been a small victory. Apparently the Humans, with their relatively short span of days, had forgotten about her. There was a taste of fear in the air that was obvious enough using only her common senses, and she knew they thought the dungeon haunted and did not frequent here. But she had not the strength left her, to escape. Unable to do more than maintain her stasis, she'd draw comfort from sensing that her mother and siblings were still alive, and then she'd go back down.

Once again the Dragon's thoughts returned to the present. She wearily lifted her muzzle off the damp stone floor, snorting with as much vigor as she could muster, clearing her nostrils and sending a cloud of dust billowing 'cross the cramped space. Inhaling slowly, deeply, she took her time, for time was all she had left. Her wits awakening as lethargically as her body, she wondered how long it had been since she was last aware. What had brought her out of the depths? Oh yes, there'd been something. A sound of water lapping, the smell of brine. Now she heard soft footsteps. A Human? Here? Her Spell had been drawing power from the Life Forces of every living creature who'd ventured into this section of the dungeons for centuries. Animals had long avoided the area, and the Humans hadn't understood why they'd become so weakened. Some even dropped dead upon descending, and therefore few now dared. Mayhap even her Spell had weakened to the point of being ineffective? If 'twas so, she had to fully awaken, try to gain back her lost mobility and move her great bulk closer to organics, for she could draw nothing from lifeless stone, iron, and dried timber.

Struggling to clear her vision, she could just distinguish the Man climbing out of the well and jumping quickly to the floor.

As she watched, the shimmer of the Magic that enveloped him, allowing him to breathe beneath the surface while in contact with its creator, was shed like dripping water, leaving him completely dry. She knew he wouldn't be able to hear her, let alone see her, for 'twas obvious he embarked upon a mission of his own, his full attention to his task. Still, 'twas interesting. Her cousins, the Water Dragons, had created the wells in order to travel safely inland. But to utilize the Well of Evanntyr they would've had to traverse the Ocean of Fears, and that bespoke urgent need. Yes, she'd known she was in the King's Castle since shortly after being transported here, despite their efforts to keep her ignorant. However, 'twas not a Sprite who'd just climbed out of the Well, and 'twas odd that a Water Dragon had allowed a Man to ride. Where was her Tie? Were the Sprites and Man now allies in the war? Apparently much had happened during her incarceration. She needed to learn more, and with growing curiosity, and a bizarre familiarity with his scent, she watched the Warrior gulp down the contents of three small vials he pulled from his boot. Then drawing his sword, he rapidly disappeared up the steps. Losing sight of him as he ascended into the diffuse shadows, her endurance failed and she slipped back down.

<div align="center">~~~~~~~~~~</div>

Grifynn dismounted the Water Dragon at the edge of the well and jumped to the floor. Shaking his arms and legs to regain normal sensation, he reflected on the journey. 'Twas exhilarating, and he wished he could learn more about the strange creatures of the water, but 'twas not to be. Tugging forth the three vials from his boot, he threw back his head and chugged them. The surge of strength he acquired from the Blood Elixir would have to be enough for 'twas all he had left, and his span of days would end this night. His plan didn't include leaving the castle alive, just ensuring that Aalanna did. Beyond feelings of regret or remorse, he accepted that he'd never see Drekinn or his family again, or know what would become of his legacy or the prophesy. He'd done all he could, 'twas up to his daughters now. All that mattered was finding and saving his lifemate afore he Passed the Veil. Once the word rang forth that he was here, 'twould be a race to the Tower afore they killed her, but he feared not, for nothing would stand in the way of his objective. Grabbing his sword, he climbed the stone steps two at a time and entered the castle. He could've gotten there without anyone the wiser, he was quite familiar with the layout of Evanntyr, but the blatant bloodshed would divert attention away from his real plan. He'd not only rescue Aalanna, but ensure her safety and escape after his death. Therefore, he welcomed the fight. They would pay dearly for what his mate had endured.

<center>~~~~~THE WELL OF EVANNTYR~~~~~</center>

Islyth shook off the Allure she'd carried o'er the Man, allowing the water to enfold her, making her near invisible. As long as a Water Dragon was wet they'd blend into the background as if one saw straight through them. But if moving they'd appear as a rippling outline to anyone or anything paying attention, making the need for added Allure necessary at times. As she watched the Man drink something he'd carried in his boot, she pondered the circumstances. Her Tie was the Elven Prince Myrrdin, Ship's Master of the Krakken, the pride of the mariner fleet of the Sprite nation. He'd asked her to bring this Man to Evanntyr and then wait for a Female to return in a mere few marks. The trip took a very long time and 'twas a lot of directions to recall for the average Water Dragon, but Islyth was not average. She was one of the first batch of hatchlings to be brought forth in life with the assistance of the Sprites after the Last Holocaust. The 'wild' birthings were not so fortunate. The aftermath of that time was terrible, such destruction, contamination, so much life lost, both in the seas and on the land. Her memory was far superior to the 'naturals', for which she was grateful. Still, 'twas another normal characteristic of her Kind to be somewhat distractible and when she lost sight of the Man as he ascended the stairs, her attention immediately began to drift.

She'd long avoided this area, as the Ocean of Fears was not safely traversed and the Well of Evanntyr was distant and rarely used. Hanging in relative boredom o'er the edge by her forelegs, her ears flared out to the whisper of a sigh coming from one of the cells in the far corner. This area should be completely unoccupied, but there could be no mistaking the sound. 'Twas something very much alive and very large, o'er there. Hauling her long body out of the well, scraping and pushing herself 'cross the rock, she was careful not to use her teeth. The mortar of the wells was made from Water Dragon spit, and the only thing that would cause it damage was Water Dragon jaws along with the special enzymes produced in their salivary glands. Their saliva could create and destroy, depending on how 'twas used. Mixed with water held in one of their stomachs, they could make their spit into a fluid sword, slicing through and felling the largest trees or piercing rock. Used with caution, they'd created the wells. Sprayed forth, 'twould stick to a man or beast like a net, allowing them to capture without injury. They were unbelievably accurate, spitting great distances, and there was no rival for the strength of their bite in all of Kadoor.

Water Dragons were not as large as Highlands. If Darque were to compare them to anything, 'twould be to an average War Horse, mayhap a tad longer, not including the tail of course. Her neck was graceful, about a quarter of the length of her body, tapering to a shortened, somewhat triangular head, with a blunted muzzle. Her nostrils were long and at the front and toward the top of her snout, so that she could stay mostly underwater and still breathe, and she could close them tightly. Her jaws were muscular and she had a frill of translucent skin around her neck and behind her flat pointed ears which she could roll and lay back alongside her head to keep out the water, appearing as if she had horns with a flouncy collar. Her eyes were extremely large, almond shaped with slit pupils and a double lid for added protection. All Water Dragon eyes were shades of greens or browns with gold or silver flecks which matched their scaly hides. Islyth was a Green/Gold, meaning she had green eyes and scales, with gold flecks. Her body was long and sleek, very powerfully built, with short thick legs and large rounded paws with sharp claws. She had several rows of wickedly pointed teeth with short fangs, and a serrated dorsal ridge as sharp as a saw blade beginning just in front of her hind legs and running all the way to the tip of her long tail, which was slightly longer than the rest of her put together, and was used to help navigate and increase her speed through the water. The ridge was about two handbreadths tall at the peak (about at their hips and base of tail), strong but flexible, and could be laid down when they were relaxed or being ridden, so 'twas safe to ride at the shoulders or just behind the front legs. They were not big enough for extra passengers for long distances, but with the ridge kept flat against their spines they could take an additional rider for awhile, as long as the Dragon didn't lose his focus during the trip, as when the ridge was thrust out into full extension 'twas sharp enough to slice through near anything. They'd made a pact with the Sprites, but it still took a strong Tie to keep them focused to avoid such 'mistakes'. Their toes were webbed, and they had a tough but narrow webbing that was actually scale-less skin stretching from their ankles and wrists to their torsos. These, along with short, wide wings, allowed them to sail through the air quite a distance after surging up out of the water with incredible speed, but they couldn't actually fly like the other Dragon Races, for their wings were not as flexible, being more like fins, having to survive the harshness of their usual environment. They were considered the fastest animals alive in the water, but on land they were cumbersome. Affectionately known as Slyders, they produced an oily substance from special glands along their sides that allowed them to avoid chaffing their underbelly as well as quicken their movement as they'd glide along, pushing themselves with their feet.

Unlike the curving, back and forth pattern of a snake, Slyders preferred to propel themselves by pushing with both front legs, followed by both back legs together, which created a fairly straight, smooth path, not unlike that of a giant snail. The oil dried and disappeared quickly, leaving no tell-tale sign of their passing. Not the most efficient method of transportation, but then, they were water creatures and 'twas why they built the wells. They had no special fighting prowess, only their extreme speed in the water, their spit, and their formidable bite, claws, and dorsal ridge for self protection. Their main defense was a strong run-away-and-hide-ideation, which usually worked, unless they forgot what they were doing and got sidetracked. 'Oh look, a jellyfish'. They were greedily curious, excessively friendly 'til they established one as an enemy (usually too late), and loved anything shiny. Despite all these characteristics, Water Dragons were not slow, nor were they stupid. They were loving, loyal, highly intelligent, exceedingly inquisitive, but naive creatures, and their naiveté led many of them Past the Veil much too early. Myrrdin taught Islyth to be wary of everyone and everything first, to ask him when in doubt (most of the time), and to conceal herself 'til she was certain. This habit elongated her life, saving her hide many times through her rather lengthy span of days.

Islyth's attention returned to the corner. No more sounds emanated from that direction, but, true to her nature, her curiosity had her sliding toward the cell. The door was completely rusted shut so she laid on her side, pushing and clawing at it 'til eventually she was able to break it about half way open. 'Twas just far enough to enter. As big as she was, she could flatten herself and squeeze through some very narrow spaces. She listened. She crawled on all fours, closer to the corner. She saw the strange shape in the guano and dust and furrowed her brow ridge for a moment. Suddenly she realized what the pile of garbage represented and was shocked. A Highland! Her head tucked low, her chin stuck forward, she squinted. A Highland? "Be you dead?" She asked simply in her childlike voice. She was perplexed. Getting no response, she crawled closer, then sat up on her hind legs holding her tail with both paws, and chewed thoughtfully on the tip as she pondered this find. "What you doing here?" Still no response, although she could see the snout clearly where the dust was scattered. Mayhap the Dragon had moved when she'd dropped off the Man. She rocked back and forth nervously, her head moving side to side as she considered what to do. Dropping to her front feet, she moved a little closer, then sat upright once more. Maintaining a comfortable distance, she stretched forth one paw, gently poked at the mound of filth three times and said, "'Lo? Be you 'live? Who you be?" No reaction. She held her paws against her chest, wrists folded back to back as she thought. She wiped her snout with her elbow, then returned to her previous position. She squinted some more. Then she remembered if she could smell the Dragon, she might be able to recognize who 'twas. She waddled closer, leaned forward, and slowly lowered her snout 'til 'twas just above the cleanest spot she could find. Inhaling deeply, she choked on the remaining dust and fell o'er backwards, sneezing and coughing. Her eyes wide, she scrambled quickly and turned back to face the possible threat, but there was still no response from the other. Calming herself, she let the breath invade her nostrils, her mouth, her throat. There was something quite familiar about this scent. Highland undoubtedly, but anyone with any intelligence could see that from the shape. No, her scent was unmistakable as well. Yes, 'twas female, but 'twas more. 'Twas similar to one she knew. After thinking very hard, Islyth gasped and her eyes crossed with the revelation of whom she stood afore. She was in the presence of royal blood. This had to be the long missing and much loved Synahmarr, the 'Crown Princess' of the Highland Matriarchy. "How... how you get here? Never mind, how I get you out?" She was no longer thinking about her prior mission, her prior orders, even if she could remember them. This find superseded any other command even her Tie could have given. She'd never found a greater treasure. 'Twas nothing more important than returning to the Krakken and locating the Mighty Maahayyel to tell all of Dragondom that Synahmarr was alive. But from what Islyth could sense, not for long.

Sliding smoothly 'cross the stone, she went back to the well. Reaching up, she hoisted her bulk o'er the wall, diving head first into the cool water. Swimming swiftly straight down to the curve, she 'flew' around the loops and changes, through the underground river system which eventually led her back to the Fears. At full speed, she may be the swiftest creature here, the only Magical creature here, but her Magic was not at its peak and she was certainly not the biggest. Alone, she was as likely to become fodder for another as she was to make another her fodder in her own waters. Many Water Dragons were lost to the terrible creatures of the deepest ocean on Kadoor in the early days of the aftermath. 'Twas as if the bottom of the Fears opened up during that time, spitting forth the most vile of all things ugly. At least they stayed in their own territories, seemingly unable to withstand the changes in pressures of the other great bodies of water. Even the Mariners respected this region. Her route was relatively safe as long as she stayed close to the surface and watched her back. Islyth was very good at that. 'Twas why she yet lived, when all of her hatch mates were long gone. She could not Call to Myrrdin yet, she had to get out of the Fears afore she could risk using any more Magic than her own Allure, hiding her presence from all but the hardest scrutiny. "Must tell, must tell Myrrdin, must tell, must tell Myrrdin," she kept chanting to herself, so she wouldn't forget.

Islyth flew through the waters 'til she was marks away from Evanntyr, the Man, and the Highland. Her single minded mission consumed her; she had to find Myrrdin to tell of her discovery. But would she be too late?

~~~~~THE HALLS OF EVANNTYR~~~~~

Darque and Storrm followed their father's path through the castle. 'Twasn't difficult. 'Twas painted in blood and paved o'er with dead men and body parts, to which they added a hundred fold. Traveling a'Dragonback from Drekinn as soon as they'd discovered he was gone, 'twas a race against time afore they'd lose him to Shytin and the Black. His disappearance had them trailing days behind, but Gunnarr and Mystynn were two of the fastest Highlands ever to take wing and they'd caught up to just after his arrival. 'Twas a well laid trap to divert all of the leadership of the Clan, but expecting the Commander and his daughters to arrive the following moon, the Black had to scramble to take advantage. Not happy about yet another blunder, the surprise to his own forces could work to his advantage as well. There was a spy amongst the Hoard, but his detection efforts had thus far been unsuccessful. This timing would guarantee that no one was aware of the attack, and no one would be prepared. Although Darque remained unaware of the extent of the battle to come, she was aware 'twas a diversion and knew what she was doing. She just wasn't certain if her father did. So many secrets, so many questions about his life, her life, even the history of the Clan. Why was he here? Why now? It didn't matter, he was her father and she'd do anything to try to save him. Her battle cry echoed through the halls of the castle as she and her sister fought the bloodiest battle of their lives. But, 'twas merely the beginning.
~~~~~

CHAPTER TWELVE

The Power of a Name

~~~~~SEVERAL MARKS LATER~~~~~

"She's gone." Aalanna's words fell softly upon Grifynn's ears as she finger combed his blood drenched hair, his head resting on her lap. Surprised to see her mother, Darque recognized her and 'twas gratifying. She'd followed Grifynn as he'd battled his way through the castle, fighting incredible odds to reach her in the Tower. She loved her mate more than her own life and using her daughter's boot blade, 'twas her choice to join him when he crossed Beyond this night. Darque had given her the blade just afore escaping through the window, leaping into free fall where Gunnarr caught her and was taking her home to Drekinn. Soon she'd face her first trial as Battle Commander. The most epic battle of the ages, sure to be the most horrific since the Last Holocaust, and Grifynn wouldn't be there to lead the Clan. Instead, he'd chosen to lay down his life to rescue his mate.

She didn't blame Darque for arriving a fraction of a moment too late to prevent the soon-to-be fatal strike upon Grifynn. The King's Agent was too far away, even with her enhanced speed. Thinking her father already Past the Veil, Darque had instantly taken her rightful field promotion and acted as Death Avenger, beheading his killer. Aalanna smiled grimly. 'Twas not just the girl's duty. No, she'd seemed to relish the strike. Dare she say 'twas fulfillment within the deep recesses of Darque's blood red eyes? Mayhap 'twas just the Battle Lust raging, but there was something strange about the girl, her movements, her appearance, and 'twas not all rationalized as benefits of the LifeBond. What was it, as she'd made her dramatic entry just in time to witness her father's demise? What caused the illusion of heat waves lifting off her body as if she'd become living coals, her Sword
~~~~~

glowing as if just pulled from the forge. No, she shook her head again. 'Twas just a Warrior in full Lust. 'Twas the dust settling from the door through which she'd broken. But if truthful with herself, 'twas the shimmering image of a huge Dragon o'er her daughter, enveloped by a spirit thing that vanished almost as soon as 'twas noted. Her unique birthright enhancing her senses in a manner similar to the 'Bond itself, she knew there was something. Even the face of the Agent reflected astonishment in that single candle drip. 'Twas a Vision? She'd not had a Vision in many winters but 'twould not explain whatever the Agent saw.

Spitting blood with his efforts to speak, Grifynn broke through her chaotic thoughts. "I still breathe upon this side of the Veil. My heart still beats, but not for long. Aalanna, you must swear!" Dragged back to the moment, her face became a mask of concentration as he wheezed forth, "Promise you'll not, by your own hand, follow me Past the Veil." His glazed eyes riveted to his beloved, but he could no longer see; pain and determination reflected there as his body temperature continued to rise. Aalanna's eyes widened as she pulled back her hand in alarm from the increasing heat of his skin. "I surrendered my own life to come here and ensure yours. Promise me, woman. Go inside the walls, get thee to the well. Safe passage awaits you there. I Pass soon, but you must live."

"My love, I..." Aalanna stuttered, watching in stunned apprehension as tiny wisps of smoke began to curl off Grifynn's leathers. The acrid stench of singed hair permeated through her senses and she could see the shimmer of Allure lying o'er him like a blanket. "What's happening?" she whispered with confusion and disbelief.

Grifynn resisted the inevitable. Grabbing her hand, he squeezed hard, hurting her fingers, yanking her face closer to his. Panting, he gasped, "Your real name is Aalanna Myriam Treygyn. You are the key, memorize these words. 'I will journey to St Swiftyn's for the shortest day of the sun. The path will shine through the eye made wet with your tears, and you will come.

Thus shall be restored my heart, for even the Veil cannot keep us apart.'"

She could barely think past the name he'd just uttered. "But, Myriam is your name, 'twas your mother's name. Grifynn Myriam Baadyyn… that would make us…"

He had to get her past the disclosure. 'Twould be time enough for her to understand, now 'twould suffice to simply remember. "We did nothing wrong, my love. Believe me, trust me." Then he implored her, "Repeat the poem, commit it to memory." Aalanna's eyes burned, her heart hammered in her chest as she sputtered back the words. His poetry was rough, but 'twas necessary, as it made his commands easier to recall, and she'd need all the help she could get after what she'd just learned and would soon learn this night. Her destiny was just beginning. He should've told her winters ago but he'd never found the time to discuss the past, and now time was gone. Making her repeat his words thrice, he gave her hand a final squeeze, then shoved her toward the fireplace. "Hurry. Do what I said and remember, our love shall open the path." Then he closed those striking blue eyes forever.

She didn't want to let go, but the decision was taken away from her as his body darkened and the heat became unbearable. She'd be scorched if she stayed, and she'd promised. His hand went limp and his head fell off her lap as she scrambled out of the way. 'Twas so quick, everything happening at once, she couldn't even think, only react. The boots of the King's Agents echoed into the Tower room as they ascended the spiral stairs on their way to fulfill their orders. Jumping to her feet, she felt for the lever hidden in the stonework at the edge of the hearth just under the mantle, pushing it with all her might. A cool puff of musty air sighed against her face as the secret panel opened to reveal the passageways which honeycombed the entire castle, known only to a select few. Turning to sweep her gaze o'er the room to make certain she'd not been seen, she was practically blinded when Grifynn's body burst into flames. The opening was small, within the hearth itself, and she stepped o'er the hot embers of last night's fire, slipping through quickly and closing it from the other side. She heard the quiet 'snick' of the latch falling into its secure position telling her that she was safe for now. There were spots afore her eyes from the blaze, but even so, she was certain his body was completely burned to ash. 'Twas similar to the fireworks of the Greening Festival held in the spring, only much hotter. Yet almost as soon as his body ignited, the fire died in a puff of smoke, leaving only a blackened silhouette upon the stone. 'Twas Magic, she was certain, for could be nothing else.

Backed up against the hard rock, she allowed herself to slide down to the floor and wept silently, 'til she had no more tears. Her youngest daughter, Fryya, had frequented these passageways, using them to visit Larken and to listen and learn all she could about the castle afore she'd escaped. But Aalanna had never attempted them, for her fate was sealed, and if she'd ever been discovered missing, Shytin would have declared war against the Clan to destroy the prophesy. At the time, she'd felt 'twas her duty to protect them. Now, she realized she should have at least studied a map. 'Twas so dark she couldn't see her hand in front of her face, and even if there were torches available, she knew not where they were bracketed. Fryya never carried one, she seemed to be well oriented in the dark. She'd never realized just how well.

She stood up, felt along the wall, tried to remember from whence she'd come and which way she needed to turn to get out of the Tower, but directional sense failed. 'Twas so puzzling, all the stones felt the same. Was she facing the hidden doorway, or had she slid down beside it? The dark, damp silence slithered into her soul, the space seemed to compress smaller and smaller as she began to feel buried alive. Her breath stuttered, rising doubt fueling panic. Reaching deep within for calm, she forced her breathing to normalize, slowing her racing heart. She was the mate of a mighty Warrior and would not shame his memory. Standing up, she took the blade out of the sash at her waist. 'Twas warm and comforting in her grasp. Even though there was no difference to her vision, she closed her eyes to increase her other senses and soon chose her path. Feeling along the wall, she stepped confidently o'er fairly even ground when suddenly her foot met empty space and she fell backward, the blade clattering into the darkness. Sitting down hard at the head of a roughly hewn stairwell, she checked to ensure she wasn't injured and was grateful she'd not continued headlong, as 'twas spiraling downward at an astonishing pitch. Regaining her wits, she felt around for the blade; she had to find it afore she continued. 'Twas a painfully slow process as she crawled this way and that, careful not to miss any part of the area. How long had it been since Grifynn...?

Abruptly she heard something down there somewhere and she froze in place. 'Twas the sound of muffled footsteps. After quite some time there was only silence, but how could she be sure they'd gone? Now the blade was even more important, and she almost cried aloud when her fingers touched the steel. 'Twas peculiar. The blade had rested upon the cold stone for a very long time, yet, 'twas still warm in her hand. She shook off the odd impression and returning to the stairs, she slowly, warily, began her descent. 'Twas tight in places, her shoulders almost touching both sides simultaneously, and 'twas obvious few could fit in this part of the passages. Carefully feeling for each step afore committing, 'twas silent below. Foreboding filled her, thinking 'twas an Agent awaiting her at the bottom, and although she wasn't a Warrior, he'd soon regret his choice of allegiance. Nevertheless, she had two promises to keep; she'd not be taken alive, and she'd not die. She lifted her chin at the irony. For the first time in o'er sixteen winters, she was in control. Her self confidence grew as she continued downward to whatever the Fates had in the making.

<div align="center">~~~~~THE OCEAN OF FEARS~~~~~</div>

Islyth had chosen the faster route, cutting 'cross the vast expanse of open water instead of navigating the irregular shoreline, so when the huge shadow rose from the depths behind her, 'twas upsetting but not entirely unexpected. Abandoning her Magic to gain more speed, she'd thought to outdistance it afore she was spotted, but sadly, as soon as she dropped the Allure, two more shadows rose just under the first, bearing down upon her route. There could be no doubt. They'd not only seen her, she'd become their target. She couldn't make it 'cross the Fears to the shallower Sea of Dreams in time, and if she hid along the coast she'd be stuck in an even worse situation. Without another thought she changed course and fled as fast as she could, back the way she'd come. Literally swimming o'er the rising leviathans, she flew through the cold waters in a direct line to Evanntyr, just clearing the Slippes and entering the underground river system ahead of their flailing, poison spiked tendrils.

MUCH LATER

~~~~~DAY OF THE BATTLE~~~~~

Synahmarr had been awake for less than two dawns, of this lone fact she was certain. At least a dozen breaths had passed through her great lungs since the Man emerged from the well. Her senses focused, her long tongue licking out just the tiniest distance from her lips, she could still detect the faint taste of brine in the air. The sea water had clung to the Allure that protected him and allowed him to breathe on his journey as they swam through the long underground rivers from the Ocean of Fears, finally climbing up out of the fresh water well in the center of the dungeon, the Allure dispersing. However, she was mystified that the familiar scent of this Man was such an ancient memory. No Human lived so long. Mayhap she was not yet fully alert and mistaking him for one of his ancestors.

She cast her attention back to the well. The Water Dragons built them, clawing and digging from the underground rivers, pushing the rock and mud upwards. Using their saliva as the mortar, they created a surface structure that was next to indestructible. The wells were their gates into the mainland from the seas and oceans of Kadoor, allowing them to travel inland in relative safety without an open river. Water Dragons were awkward on land and hard to miss if dry (unless they were very still), becoming invisible only when wet, and they were not gilled like fish. They required air to survive as do all mammals, however, one of their specialties was their ability to stay underwater for up to a moon at a time, 'breathing' with Magic 'til they'd finally exhaust their strength and require that breath of reality (and of course, they'd be ravenous, as using one's Magic always increased one's appetite). They could keep another being alive underwater as well, as long as they were touching skin to skin, but 'twould deplete their Magic proportionately faster. The wells dotted the land, and most of them had become of central importance to Mankind, helping them to survive the Last Holocaust as they established their villages around the unfailing sources of fresh water. There were many yet to be discovered.

As her brain began to function more clearly, she concluded that the being she'd seen last night was indeed a mere Human. Details of his appearance flashed in her mind. 'Twas a big muscular male with long unruly auburn curls, dressed all in leather. Curiosity sparking, her senses awakening further, she braced herself to lift her head slightly. 'Twas almost more than she could manage in her weakened condition, the layers of filth weighing her down like an anchor.

There 'twas again. Leather boots on stone, quietly descending the stairs. Was he coming back? She listened intently as the soft footsteps set a stealthy and erratic pattern, stopping, then starting again, step by hesitant step. As they came closer, she focused her attention toward the place her cell gate was the last time she'd been aware and was rewarded with the sound of creaking and the grating of metal on metal as 'twas opened, the ancient hinges protesting their use. She moved not a muscle, barely lifting her outer eyelids to avoid being seen by whomever was about to invade her space, although she wasn't certain if their luminescence was even enough to be noticed by Human eyes. Her great nostrils flared delicately as the gate allowed itself to be pushed open about half its normal distance afore it stubbornly refused to move any further. A tall, lean, shadowy figure slid through, then shoved it closed again. After a heartbeat, the figure slid down the wall to the dusty stone floor and slumped in fatigue.

As potent energy surged into Synahmarr, she heard, "Dragon dung, what more?" 'Twas a rhetorical question whispered with growing frustration from a youthful, and most definitely feminine throat. Reeking of blood, sweat, and Battle Lust, the scent of fear was noticeably lacking. Admirable for a Human, she thought, even as she realized that at this close range the girl was being rapidly sucked dry of her Life Force, and there'd soon be no stopping the flow afore the Veil. Making her decision, she raised her head and fully opened her eyes. As the girl's energy transferred, Synahmarr couldn't explain the enhanced affect of this Life Force o'er most that she'd fed from, but she hadn't felt this strong in many winters. 'Twas something special, as if she'd tasted this afore. And then her memory failed, as did her effort to stand. Only able to lift her head high enough to get her chest off the floor, she began to Sing. 'Twas a quiet Song, one that no Human ear could understand , soothing the girl sprawled out on the floor 'til she lifted her own head and looked around in bewilderment. The Dragon fell silent as the girl scrambled to her knees, her back pressed hard against the wall. Face to face, the girl's head thrown back and the Dragon's chin tucked low, they stared at each other in the shadows of the late afternoon light, cast through the narrow windows in the thick stone high o'er head. Still, there was no fear from the Human. Interesting. Synahmarr risked much to allow this one to live and if she screamed in panic, they'd both be found. 'Twas obvious now that the girl was hiding as was she and that they were on the same side of this war. She was glad she'd had the strength to save her, even though that strength had come from the girl herself. But the stare down couldn't continue as 'twas exhausting, the eons of inactivity slamming into her, the short lived burst of energy spent. Her source for that energy was removed from her Spell and without it, she dropped back to the floor in a heap.

~~~~~ELSEWHERE IN THE CASTLE~~~~~

Aalanna stepped carefully through the pitch black of the passage. She didn't want to twist an ankle, or worse yet, break one. She'd never be found. The muffled footsteps were gone by the time she'd made her way to the bottom of the stairs; apparently though, she wasn't the only one here. But the path she'd just descended had not been traveled within her lifetime by anyone other than Fryya, and her newly awakening senses told her that few actually traveled anywhere within the walls of the castle. 'Twas a deep aloneness here. Oddly, since learning her real name, 'twas as if a memory was just out of her reach, tickling her psyche, taunting her, empowering her as never afore. Feeling as if someone were beckoning her to follow, she forgot Grifynn's order to go straight to the well. With mounting anticipation that she was being led to a discovery of great significance, she slipped the blade back into her sash. Her senses provided a map enabling her to step this way and that, totally blind, avoiding hitting her head on low ceilings and her ankles on outcroppings in the rocky walls. Three more flights of stairs did she descend, none as steep or long as the first, and taking the turns as she felt directed, she finally stopped, then reached forward expecting to find the lever at her fingertips. For all she really knew, 'twas Shytin's bedchambers. She paused, then placed her other hand upon the wall aside the lever. The room beyond spoke to her of antiquity and abandonment of long standing. She grasped the lever firmly and pushed hard. Slow with age, the mechanism wasn't completely stuck by a total lack of use and she stopped again briefly as the thought occurred to her that she might not be the only person seeking ref-
~~~~~

uge here. Sensing not another being nearby, she pushed the lever the final distance flush with the stone, and a small, narrow opening appeared. She stooped low and stepped through.

Once inside, after carefully closing the doorway, she felt for the torch. Using the flint within the bracket, along with Darque's blade edge, she soon had light by which to see. Setting it back on the wall by the hearth, she looked around. Dust covered every surface, thicker in some places than in others, but 'cross the room at an unusual, hand carved desk, she noted a minimal amount of dust as if 'twas used occasionally, wiped clean by leaning sleeves. As she walked closer, gazing around in wonder, she saw shelves stacked with tubes and containers and funnels and burners and bowls of all sorts and sizes. There were books and scrolls and parchments, dried up ink wells and pens and lots and lots of small bottles and boxes with labels neatly written in a beautiful, but seemingly foreign language. Peering at some of them, she thought she could make out a familiar letter or word, but on the whole nothing made sense. Setting the blade down, she stepped o'er to the bookcase behind the desk when she noticed one was surely out of place, and reached up with both hands. As she pulled the heavy book toward her, a thick folded parchment fell to the floor. Pushing the book back in place, she picked it up, and knew this was why she'd been brought here. Blood wax sealed the aging parchment, keeping it safe from scrying. She broke the seal, pushing the crumbling bits of wax o'er the blade on the desk, then unfolded the parchment and stared at the words. 'Twas a royal birthing certificate, recording the date and exact time of the birth of... Gabriel? But 'twas a full three dawns afore the birth of Shytin. Her eyes flew open and gooseflesh covered her arms. 'Twas reality. The prophesy of the return of the True King. This information would get her killed as surely as the prophesy of her own daughter.

Suddenly, she heard the faint whisper of stone moving behind her, and she thrust the parchment into her bodice. Turning to the hearth, she was confronted by a tall man with long brown hair, unfolding himself gracefully from the narrow opening, holding a dagger. Startled, her reflexes delayed, she turned to grab her own but he crossed the short distance too fast and stayed her hand. "I waited for you for some time, in the passageway beneath the Tower. When you didn't come, I thought I'd missed you and was concerned for your safety." He stared at her with uncertainty. Not wanting to suspect any wrong doing, he prayed she was the woman he knew and respected. But how had she come to this place? "Many winters I mapped these passages, and many more afore I found this room. 'Tis the study of Sarai, the ancestor of Shayla the Healer." He shook his head. "I'm the only one who's entered here in centuries. And you simply stumbled upon it?"

Relief flooding her heart, she burst forth, "Larken! I'm so grateful to see you! I haven't laid eyes upon you in so long. You've changed little, and much. I did come through the Tower passage, I thought I heard footsteps but they'd moved on by the time I got to the bottom, and I knew not to expect assistance." She shrugged her shoulders. "I felt drawn here, as if being directed."

Her face was unreadable, but Larken found no fault in her story. He bowed his head in deference and stated, "My Queen."

Suddenly angered, her patience broken, the need to talk to someone, anyone, was too great. "No, Larken, I was never the Queen of Evanntyr. 'Twas always Koryl. She used her insatiable appetite for sex to fuel her black arts and control the King. She began with Bryard, but he eventually wanted nothing to do with her increasingly twisted desires, so she continued with her son and then helped Shytin kill him to place the boy on the throne. The more perverted the acts, the stronger the energy she so reaped, and she's been abusing Shytin since he was but nine. She has total control o'er him, although with me, he did try to break the leash. His touch was nauseating, yet he attempted to treat me well." She paused, and sweeping her hands down her body, she continued, "This wasn't what he craved, and he came to me infrequently because of impotence. With one exception. I knew I'd become pregnant with Fryya the night Grifynn found me, and I had to convince Shytin the child was his or we'd both be forced Past the Veil. I had a Vision of what he required in order to be functional. 'Twas depraved. I hated it, but 'twas successful and he was never even suspicious. In point of fact, he paraded his 'success' in his mother's face, which all but got me killed anyway, and made me fear for Fryya's life. She did not get away too soon."

Aalanna stopped to take a breath. Nervous energy had her spewing forth her thoughts, but she'd best bite a loose tongue, lest she say too much. Larken had been supportive o'er the winters and little she'd said thus far was beyond his knowledge, but did she really know her allies? She avoided touching the parchment in her bodice and hoped he couldn't see any evidence of its location. She turned away sighing, barely lifting her eyes to the shelf to ensure the evidence there was also minimal, and then finished. "I am the mate of a mighty Warrior. I will not shame his memory by accepting the title of Queen of Evanntyr."

Larken was understanding. She'd been through much and yet still held her head high. "He is Passed, then?"

"Yes," she stated softly.

"And Darque?" The question was fueled by more than curiosity. 'Twas an attack in the making and the Commander's absence might tip the scales away from the Clan.

"She travels even now, to lead the battle."

Nodding, he recognized 'twas good. "Her skills are excellent. I was entranced as she fought her way through the castle to get to you. She will prevail, there's nothing for which to worry."

With regal poise, she responded. "First, remember that she was following Grifynn. She had no idea I was there. Second, I shall remind you that I am of the Dragon Clan and we do not worry about battle. And then I shall simply say, as for her fighting skills, she is her father's daughter." Aalanna's confidence and pride couldn't be more obvious.

Larken was pleased. Despite the gravity of the situation, Aalanna could still take o'er with her imposing presence, and still found humor in life. She was not only a true Clansman, she was an amazing woman. Not unlike his own Matana. Thinking of his mate brought his attention back to their current circumstances. "Come, I'll take you out of the castle to a place of safety in Wyndsyr Forest. But we must hurry. After you, m'lady"

"I think not this time. You know the way better than I. After you," she said politely, with a grin on her face and upright hand.

As soon as he turned his back to lead her to the doorway, she realigned the parchment, but couldn't fit the blade into her sash quickly enough without displacing what she'd just concealed, which would make it show clearly through her fittings. She couldn't draw attention to it on the desk as 'twas covered in blood wax, and Larken may have noticed that as well, so she reluctantly left it behind. Somehow, she knew the parchment was the more valuable, but just barely. 'Twould be safe there, given the bits of blood wax were still potent enough. Mayhap one day, 'twould be recovered. Glancing o'er his shoulder, Larken warned her to stay close, afore he extinguished the torch. She could hear the sigh of the movement of the stone, the breath of air puffing against her body as she followed him into the inky blackness, needing no warning to remain silent.

<div align="center">~~~~~A FEW MARKS LATER~~~~~</div>

Aalanna was utterly disoriented. They might as well have been walking in circles for all she could tell. Laying her hand on Larken's shoulder, she asked, "Where are we?"

"Near the northwestern section of the lower chambers of the castle. We have to climb a few flights of stairs, then another hallway and a tunnel afore we exit outside the ward along the outer wall. 'Twill require darkness to 'cross. 'Tis not long now, and I'll scout afore we make a run. We must watch for peasant eyes as well as Agents. You can run a short distance, can you not? I should have mentioned it earlier."

"Do not fret so. I can run as fast as need be, to keep pace with you."

Larken beamed at her tenaciousness. "I believe you're armed, m'lady? You may wish to keep your blade at hand for the rest of this journey. We can leave no witness to our departure."

His question was unexpected, her alarm genuine as she stumbled o'er her words. "My blade? I'm not in the habit... I haven't carried one since afore I was abducted..." At the reminder of that event, gooseflesh began to rise, but calming her senses she avoided the powerful backlash of a potential Vision. Hesitantly, she finished her thought, "I must have left it in Sarai's study." Her brow furrowed, she knew she'd have to explore that time in her past once again, but not now.

"'Twould be suicidal to return this night. Take one of mine, I'll obtain another for your personal use." With feigned seriousness, he performed an extensive courtly bow, and stated poetically, "'Tis better to lose one's knife, m'lady, than to lose one's life."

"Ever the Court Jongleur. Even though 'tis practically an unforgivable offence to leave behind one's source of protection, you graciously and humorously manage. I thank you."

His sincerity matched hers this time. "M'lady, you are revered by many, a source of wisdom, hope, and strength for more than you realize. Gracious, and yes, humorous, in the face of great loss, tragedy, pain, and even certain death. I can be no less."

CHAPTER THIRTEEN

Goldenrod

MUCH LATER
~~~~~THE WITCH'S DUNGEONS~~~~~

Synahmarr felt something wet upon her lips. Scarcely able to open her eyes, she licked forth her great tongue and tasted something sweet. The girl sat cross legged upon the floor beside her. "'Tis mead. I had the flask in my boot last night, seems to have made the journey well enough. Try to drink." The girl had dripped a small amount of the tantalizing liquid upon her muzzle in an effort to waken her. Apparently, considering how damp she was, she'd been trying to wake her for many marks. Relief clear in her voice, the girl lifted the Dragon's muzzle in order to help her swallow. Struggling to open her mouth, she tried to get more of the rich fluid upon her long tongue. She savored the delicious flavor, craving the wetness, the honey richness, but she was severely malnourished and couldn't tolerate much.

"Steady there, don't gulp that. 'Tis plain you've not eaten in many moons, if not longer, and I can see we'll need to build you up a bit afore we start on solid food." The girl shifted her weight and pulled her hand out from under the Dragon's chin afore she continued. "Although, I haven't exactly a lot of experience in Healing. And you're damp because I found a bucket at the well and cleaned you up a bit, hope that didn't make things worse. I was quite worried there for awhile." She sighed, placed her calloused hand upon Synahmarr's snout, and then continued, "I am a Warrior. My first employment was as a personal bodyguard for the daughter of one of my Commanders. Nothing happened. Then the biggest battle since the Last Holocaust was breaking, I ran out of the Den to join the fray, and head long into a seemingly never ending stream of refugees trying their best to push me back inside. I couldn't swing my sword, couldn't get out of their way, so I tried to find out what they knew. Anyway, long story, I got my butt captured afore I was able to do much. Then a Hoard Dragon picked me up in her filthy talons and bore me here. I missed the most horrendous battle of the ages! And I thought I'd be broken in half by the time she finally dropped me in the ward. But at least I knew where I was, and the Agents are so poorly trained I didn't have much difficulty escaping. I waited just long enough to find out what I could and at first it seemed that they were taking me to the Black himself. He was here! Or at least, I thought he was. Anyway, turned out he wasn't and they didn't know where he was or when he'd be back, or even if he was coming back. Apparently, he's not been here often. So I decided 'twas time to part company. As I was carried down the hall, I took advantage of a darkened alcove, slammed the prick down and relieved him of his blade. He won't be telling anyone what happened. But I didn't want to leave the castle, I wasn't certain I was the only captive, and I thought there might be more here than meets the eye. I chose to hide in the dungeons. 'Twould be the last place they'd look. Most would avoid where they were being taken, try to get as far away as they could, and besides, I learned from their conversations that they think this part of the dungeons is haunted and they won't come down here. You know the rest. Here I am." She moved closer to the Dragon and waved her hand dismissively. "I figured out the whole Life-Force-sucking-Spell-thing while you were asleep, I'm certain that's why they all think 'tis haunted. I've seen the 'Bond, you know."

Wearily, the girl reached up and pulled out her hair picks, setting loose her long, golden mane o'er her face and about her shoulders, flowing down the full length of her back. She slid her fingers through the thick tresses and pushed them up and o'er her forehead to get them out of her eyes. Her hair was so flaxen, it almost glowed in the shadows. Looking directly at the Dragon, she took a breath and stated with a crooked smile, "I guess we're in this together now my friend, for neither one of us seemed to be in the right place at the right time, and 'tis obvious we're both unknown guests with invisible chains." She gazed off into the shadows. Quietly, she continued, "I used to dream about what I didn't have, fighting against what I did have and what I was given, thinking 'twas not good enough. O'er the last few marks trying to wake you, hoping you were alive, I realized I was given all I ever needed and more, and I was blessed. I have to admit I have a lot of regrets, much of which to be ashamed, and now I'm just grateful that I'm still this side of the Veil. And I began thinking we're each exactly where we're supposed to be, for mayhap together we shall find a way to turn the tide and rejoin this war effort." Smiling at her new friend she stated simply, "My Battle Name is Goldenrod. But you can call me Mynx."

<center>~~~~~A FEW MARKS PRIOR~~~~~</center>

The Dragon had no intention of returning to the battle after dropping off the Warrior. Known as the Sentinel, the act of audacity took a heavy toll on her Magic, ensuring the Agents hadn't realized she'd had no authority to take the prisoner, let alone 'encouraging' them to give her away instead of simply killing her. And she'd had to keep the Warrior from freezing without warming her so much that she was aware of the Magical assist. Filthy and exhausted, she was well pleased that the Fates handed o'er such an opportunity to further a prophesy near and dear to her heart, while remaining undercover. Now she required food and sleep. Flying toward her private den, deep in Wyndsyr Forest, her scales glistened their amber hues in the mid-afternoon sun. 'Twould not be too difficult to fake participation, since the Hoard lost the battle already, and those who had fought were either dead or in hiding. She smirked, relishing her latest triumph, counting the days to the death of life.

A FEW DAWNS LATER

~~~~~WYNDSYR FOREST~~~~~</center>

The Battle for the Dragon Clan had been devastating, but they'd been the victor. Expecting to catch the Clan unaware and
~~~~~

without leadership, the Hoard abandoned the fight prematurely due to the ferocity of the unanticipated defense encountered. Unwilling to die for their own cause in order to finish the annihilation of the Clan and their Warriors, they'd tucked tail and fled, hoping that time would complete their mission for them. After all, they'd lost a proportionate number of their own, and in fact, the Predator knew the Hoard lost far more than the Black would acknowledge. He knew. He'd been there, while the Black vacated early.

Thinking back made him angry; looking forward, angrier still. Dyrrk arrived at dawn as planned and their meeting began typically. He reported the Clan survived, although barely, and that Darque the Dragon flew in late. As Commander she'd rallied the Resistance to win the battle. But he knew not how Darque came by her field promotion, only that Grifynn had been forced Past the Veil the night afore and that she was already making changes and provisions to ensure their survival. The Predator knew how she came to rank. He'd been the one who'd ensured Grifynn could make his attempt to rescue Aalanna. Things hadn't worked out quite the way the Black wanted. Oddly enough, since he'd joined their cause, things rarely worked out the way the Black wanted. He was going to have to be more subtle. Catching his breath, he laughed maniacally. Subtle? After what he'd just done? The Predator stooped o'er, staring at the blood on his boots, unable to raise his eyes to the carnage spread all about, even though 'twas of his own making. Their meeting was interrupted by two Hoard Dragons suddenly appearing where they weren't supposed to be, and although they each forced one Past, Dyrrk missed his strike and was Flamed full stream. Still alive, they'd known the fight had drawn the attention of the Destroyer, who was on his way at this very moment.

Brannyn was forced to kill Dyrrk with his own sword, his only friend, his liaison to the Clan, a Warrior faithful to their cause since childhood, who gave up his life in order to maintain their secret and allow his partner to continue their mission. Alone. His selfless act brought forth the emotion locked inside, never afore revealed or exposed, not to be trusted. The Fay had turned away from strong emotion since the time of Chaos and the High Races Council. Magic was strengthened by such and even more so by blood, and if one wasn't strong enough to handle the power surge, erosion and perversion of one's Magic resulted. The Black took advantage of this, luring his followers with the addictive attributes of power and control, but they didn't realize that ultimately, they were the ones being controlled.

The Fay heir apparent risked all to share his life and experience true love with Hellyn, the most beautiful female of their Kind, but things got out of hand and he was cursed and exiled. Brannyn followed in his footsteps, orchestrating his own exile in order to infiltrate the Hoard, seeking to break through and learn to control emotion. Only Dyrrk knew his true identity. And now he was dead. But his friend's death was not in vain, as he would soon take his promotion to the highest position yet, Third Fighter, AKA Second to the Destroyer, the right hand of the Black himself. And he'd broken through and conquered strong emotion, at least temporarily. 'Twould be difficult to sustain, but 'twas a beginning. The heady influence was surely addictive and he now understood the pull, but his mission would not be compromised. The strength of the experience and his ability to use it gave him much confidence, and although he'd be tortured by guilt for some time to come, he praised Dyrrk's sacrifice and courage, and would always remember. His mission, their mission, would succeed.

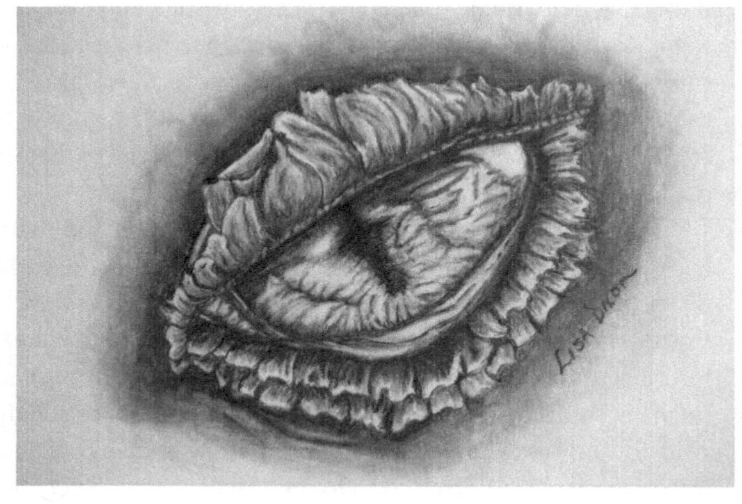

The Dragon's Eye

Beyond The Battle For The Dragon Clan

CHAPTER FOURTEEN

Telling the Tale

A FORTNIGHT SINCE THE BATTLE
~~~~~THE WITCH'S DUNGEONS~~~~~

Mynx offered the rat to Synahmarr, hand feeding it slowly, bit by bit, to avoid regurgitation. Initially, she'd given her what she'd pinched from the kitchens, but although 'twas easier for Syn to swallow, 'twas not as beneficial as was freshly killed, raw and bloody. Sneaking out of the castle to hunt was not her first choice for safety reasons, but bugs, small mammals, as well as birds and bats, were beginning to return now that the Spell was dispersed. They'd discussed having the Dragon delve back into stasis mode so the Warrior could safely leave her there, escape the castle and find out what had happened to the Clan. Mynx could then return with a rescue party. But try as she might, Synahmarr just couldn't sustain the Spell again. Mynx was concerned, but the people of Evanntyr and King's Gate Village were highly suspicious, being sandwiched south and north 'tween the Southern Slippes coastline of the Ocean of Fears and Wyndsyr Forest of the Razor's Edge, two of the harshest environments on the mainland. Mayhap folklore and actual history would be sufficient to maintain their privacy. Although Syn had tried to talk her into leaving anyway, Mynx refused.

After getting every morsel of the rat down her throat and being fairly certain 'twould stay in one of her stomachs for the time being, Mynx leaned back against Synahmarr's neck, settling herself into the cradle of her great paws to keep her butt off the cold stone floor, and was rewarded with a comforting sigh. Telling stories was not one of her talents, but the Dragon was infinitely curious and her lack of energy didn't allow her to do much more than listen when awake. Mynx worked hard to help her gain strength, knowing she had to get more solid food into the great beast, but 'twould take time and time was a commodity in short supply. So every day she set snares made from her own hair, and snuck up the stone steps to the lower levels of the castle into the storerooms and kitchens, where she'd audaciously dip broth as well as taking whatever else upon which she could lay her hands. Synahmarr hadn't questioned her absences since she slept through most of them, but she asked from whence the multitude of supplies came and was understandably apprehensive of being detected. She didn't just fear the loss of her new food source, she actually liked the girl. Mynx assured her she'd not been seen, however, she couldn't continue the raids or they would be discovered, and what small offerings her snares provided wasn't going to be sufficient for both of them once the Dragon was able to consume more. If they had to stay much longer, she'd have to risk leaving the castle to hunt. That wasn't the hardest part, though. Getting back in without being seen was the trick. She was seriously concerned about compromising Syn's hiding place.

In her forays thus far, she'd o'er heard much. There were no other prisoners at this time, the last were rumored to be a Team from the Dragon Clan, who'd arrived a fortnight after the 'Bond and were tortured throughout the night afore finally submitting to the Veil. 'Twas supposed to be a secret, but 'twould have been impossible to keep such from the staff.

She learned little about the Hoard and the Black, but there seemed to be a visitor who did frequent often, seemingly as a liaison 'tween the Black and the King. Known only as the Sorcerer, he was greatly feared. He spent days secluded in some other part of the northern dungeons, conjuring and brewing potions and what not. 'Twas said he was looking for a child who used to live in the castle, and some kind of rare jewel. She had to think 'twas Fryya, but the jewel had her stumped. He was known to spend a great deal of his time with the Queen Mother and Shytin often joined them. No one was comfortable with their visitors, and everyone tried to keep clear of the questionable activities. She'd also heard that the Agents were still searching for 'the escaped Warrior' in Wyndsyr Forest, and most recently she'd learned that the Healer known as the Painted One would be brought in soon for 'questioning'. Mynx knew not this Healer, but from what she gathered, she was remarkably talented, revered by all, and held no allegiance to Shytin. If she could be rescued, 'twould be very good for Synahmarr. Although the Dragon heaped praises upon her, reminding her that even her Battle Name bespoke healing prowess, she wasn't likely to live without much more help than Mynx could provide, and she didn't want to lose her new best friend.

Taking a deep breath, she gathered her thoughts to tell the tale. What had happened o'er the past fortnight? She so hoped to hear more information, anything about the Clan and the aftermath. If not for her new friend she would've returned by now, but she couldn't leave the Dragon. As for the battle, Mynx pieced together that the Black disappeared early, not to be seen since. After leaving his Hoard without direction, they'd soon folded. But the destruction was believed to be complete. And what about the King's Men who'd been there? None had returned. 'Twas rumored the Clan and the Warrior Brotherhood were no more. What if she were the only survivor? She shook her head to clear her thoughts away from such, and proceeded to regale the Dragon once again, with what she did know about that fateful night.

As she relaxed into the narrative, she felt drawn into the past, speaking as if reliving the events as they'd occurred, while Synahmarr listened enraptured.

<p style="text-align:center">~~~~~MYNX'S TALE~~~~~</p>

Mynx struggled to avoid being crushed in the claws of the Hoard Dragon. She could barely breathe, the wind chill during this seemingly never ending flight had her teeth chattering and her lips turning blue, and she was losing the feeling in her hands and feet. But by the 7th Egg, she was alive and still armed, having retained her boot blades in the scuffle with the King's Agents.

The cold of flight was piercing, she hadn't thought of that aspect of the Teams' new lives since the 13 of First Flight had taken the 'Bond. Given the twin's link she shared with her brother Mace, she knew the second ceremony had already been held, but Mace hadn't gotten the chance to release his Blood Call. There'd been some kind of problem and the ceremony barely ended without loss of life. However, she also knew there were 13 new 'Bonds headed into the battle at this very moment. 'Twas why she'd been so eager to get out there, she had to find Mace. She'd been employed by Darque herself, to protect Fryya and Walkyr the boy Seer, but Cayell shared that duty. Once he took o'er, having been released by Shayla, she'd charged out of the Den to join the rest of the Brotherhood in the battle.

Her body shaking uncontrollably, nausea rising with the uneven beating of the great beast's wings, hypothermia began to set in, and she wasn't certain where she was or what she was doing. She tried to concentrate on remaining calm, conserving her strength for when she'd get the chance to use it, reorienting herself to stay alert and ready to fight. Breathing deeply, she held off the nausea while she recalled leaving the children in the care of Cayell. She was one of the last of the Warriors to spill forth from the great gates, most of the others already out in the fields facing the Dragons who'd come Flaming into the Port District. Focusing on her actions, she attempted to analyze them, to learn from her mistakes. She was determined she'd not die in her very first battle.

'Twas a mere half dozen Warriors at the Gate defending the Clansmen as they entered the Den, but despite being a War Clan no one believed such a battle would come to Drekinn. Chaos reigned and the Warriors had their hands full. Mynx was caught up in the push trying to go against the flow of refugees and since there was nothing she could do, she started helping them get inside. During this struggle she heard some interesting information that led her to suspect there might be foot soldiers, mayhap approaching from the northeast, which would place them upon their flank. With all the Warriors engaged o'er the Port District, a human contingent might compromise the Den.

Her training screamed 'twas a feint in action. Afore she felt confident to relay this gut feeling to her Commander, and only the One knew where he was, she needed more evidence. Slipping away from the Main Gate and leaving the rest of the villagers to the other Warriors to secure, she ran as fast as she could in the opposite direction of the heat of battle, praying she'd not be forced Past the Veil with everyone thinking she'd turned coward. She had an idea of where a large group of men could be hiding, but who were they and how had they gotten there without being seen in the first place? A lurching drop and subsequent painful jerking rise in altitude, gave her the answer. They were King's Men and they'd been flown to the battle under cover of a Mask. She took several more deep breaths and focused on mind o'er matter to relieve the pain and keep sharp her wits.

As soon as she cleared the main throngs of refugees, she ran to the first barn, confiscated a horse and rode off toward her destination. In the distance were a group of large dwellings built relatively close together, where several families had lived many generations. There were barns, stables, shelters of all kinds, and groves of fruit and nut trees. All this in combination would provide the cover needed for an invading force. 'Twould be where she'd find the proof she sought.

The land was full of tall corn, hay, and other crops, some in rotation soon to be harvested. Ditching the horse at the edge of the groves, she snuck in a'foot. Good hearing and a quick eye caught a foreign accent from male throats, although she didn't understand the actual words. She moved closer. Leaving the crop cover, she ran from stacks of hay to animal pens, then crawled to the nearest big barn. There was no sense in looking for the residents, they'd be dead already. Using her dagger to enlarge a hole at the base of one plank, her eyes widened as she counted o'er two hundred men in there. Without regard for secrecy, she leaped up and fled toward the crops again. She had to get back, she had to confer with the Battle Commander. Distracted in these thoughts she ran straight into the back of a large company of King's Agents already marching toward the Den. Quickly stopping her forward momentum with a shuffle in the dirt, she smoothly pulled her sword from its scabbard at her hip, and without another sound she engaged the surprised men. Her skill was exceptional, but she was young and had never been in actual battle afore. Frustrated with the affect of Battle Lust upon her control, she only managed to best eight of them afore two more factions came up behind her and she was taken. The siege was on, and she'd failed. The entire force of King's Agents were on their way to join the Hoard, and no one knew they were coming.

Still, it took six of the big men to hold her down and disarm her, and not so delicately, either. She spit in their faces and thought to herself, 'Oh great. My first Battle and I get captured afore I barely blood my sword. Some Song my Legend will be.' Her feet were crossed and bound, her hands trussed behind her with cord, and her body was held above their heads like an offering to the gods. Within moments, a female Hoard Dragon with amber hues to her scales, swooped down and grasped her in her claws, lifting her to the heavens with ease, taking her who knew where, and for what purpose.

For awhile, she tried to see where they were going but 'twas impossibly cold and her eyes streamed tears. What little she did manage to see didn't help much, as she'd never seen the land from this height afore, and they were traveling too fast. She soon gave up and let her instincts guide her. They were traveling ever southward and that meant toward the Razor's Edge and Evanntyr.

She spent the travel time critically assessing her situation. She was lucky they'd not just killed her. Why take her captive?

Regardless of their reasons, she couldn't count on luck to keep her alive next time. She didn't think she could take the Dragon alone but she was confident she'd handle any and all humans, given she didn't freeze to death first.

Mynx cursed her luck. She'd fought long and hard to get where she was, and where she was, was humiliating. Her teeth were now chattering so hard, she wondered if they'd break. She couldn't feel her skin, her arms and legs were going numb. Breathing was becoming ever more difficult, and she feared she'd gone blind, but couldn't open her eyes in order to confirm that suspicion. 'Twas no way for a Warrior to Pass the Veil. She'd rather they'd forced her Past during the fight, sword in hand. She'd lost that sword, but still had her boot blades. At least, she thought she yet had them. She was having trouble remembering details.

Mynx knew she was an enigma to people. Most weren't certain if they liked her or not. She'd never felt at ease with others, was rather shy, and usually kept to herself, talking little unless asked a direct question. 'Twas an attitude easily misinterpreted. And she wasn't exactly pleased with her first assignment, a child's bodyguard. She'd viewed this employment as a relatively boring babysitting position that needed not the skills of a highly trained Warrior. She was ambitious, eager to excel, to show the others they'd not been wrong about allowing her to join the Brotherhood. She wanted to feel like she truly fit in, almost obsessed to prove herself worthy. Mace never seemed to have any insecurities or difficulties making friends. He'd always been there with her, never leaving her behind, ensuring she kept up with her studies and that her skills were honed to perfection. 'Twas his doing that they'd advanced together, taking the Oath upon the same day, entering the Brotherhood as equals. But she still felt a chasm of doubt 'tween her and everyone else, a feeling of inadequacy that drove her to the edge of recklessness more often than she could recall. Surely the Fates hadn't meant for her to earn her way this far, and then simply Pass without making her mark? Vaguely, she realized if she did Pass, no one would even know what had happened to her.

Another sudden jerking drop and then steadily lowering altitude, brought her thoughts out of the ditch of despair and self centering ideation. Vaguely she thought she heard a voice in her mind telling her that she must live, for she had a greater purpose soon to be revealed, making her realize she had much for which to be grateful. Still alive, she'd venture to guess she was one of the fortunate this day. 'Twas little to do with her skill. Or mayhap 'twas. She'd fought hard and well, killing several, setting up disorder within their ranks afore being taken down. The smell of their fear was palpable. The King's Men weren't Warriors, didn't have the training of the elite of Kadoor. They were bound to make a mistake and all she had to do was be prepared to take advantage. She'd played a part. She could only pray 'twas enough to help her brothers in arms, in some small manner. With these thoughts came a rising sense of hope. She'd always wondered how her future would play forth. Mayhap her destiny would be fulfilled with this capture. There'd been rumors of a Hoard alliance with King Shytin, the Team sent to Evanntyr having never returned. And what other reason could there have been for the Agents at the Battle? Someone needed to get into the castle and find out the truth. She could and would be that someone. With growing awareness that the Fates had placed her exactly where she was needed, she devised a plan.

A heartbeat later, Mynx hit hard on her right side upon the cobblestone in the open ward, knocking her breathless. The jolt was painful, but now fully alert, the gasp that followed helped to increase her circulation and she rapidly regained mental focus. Battle Lust loomed once more, but this time she was prepared for the effects and welcomed them. Barely opening her eyes, she quickly assessed the situation. Her ankles were crossed, but they'd been quickly trussed without taking off her boots, and she'd managed to maintain some slight degree of laxity during that process. Like as not, she still couldn't pull the blades hidden on the inside of each boot due to them being made of Clan steel and the high probability of cutting off her own foot in the process. Once she could untie herself, then 'twould be no problem. She'd been roughly searched and they'd disarmed her of her heavy weapons, but hadn't checked further. Negligent of them. A boon for her. 'Twould be little difficulty slipping her bound hands forward, as she was quite flexible. She just required the right moment.

Being in the open wasn't the best scenario for her coup, so 'twould be wise to allow them (or encourage them, if need be) to take her elsewhere. But she was prepared to fight here if they didn't, for she'd not be simply executed. She bit her tongue to keep from groaning, willing her sensation to normalcy as she felt the tingling that bespoke the swiftly returning blood into her extremities. Fighting with numb hands would be more difficult, and she already faced problematic odds. The Dragon apparently had dropped her and then flown away, leaving her in the presence of several human captors, all seemingly disorganized and appearing confused with her abrupt, and apparently unexpected, arrival. Was she the only captive? Had these men been at the battle or were they left behind? She wondered how long she'd been in flight, and whether the Agents knew anything about what had happened.

She couldn't risk moving to try to see the sun in order to get an idea of the time. She laid very still, concentrated on controlling the Lust and pretended to be unconscious, knowing if she couldn't pass on that acting, she could at least pretend to be stunned by the drop. At any rate, she had to make them perceive her as less of a threat. 'Twould be evident she was a Warrior, there was no hiding her distinctive attire, coloring, and build, all classic Dragon Clan, which put the fear of Hades into most. 'Twas very useful when the odds were against them, which in their experience was most of the time, however, in this case 'twould be more helpful if they thought her completely incapable of self defense. Her shoulder ached and her fingers and toes practically screamed their protest, but 'twould not be for much longer. The stone of the ward held the heat of the late summer sun, warming her skin and clearing her mind now that she was no longer airborne. With the air cooling about her, 'twas likely late afternoon. A whole day. She grit her teeth, listened intently, and did her best to appear non-threatening.

Oddly, she was somewhat ignored for awhile, the initial moments stretching to half a mark. She was beginning to wonder if they simply forgot about her. But while she waited to spark someone's, anyone's, attention, she was privy to much gossip. 'Twas yet another overt indicator that the King's Men were not well disciplined. She was able to gather some information and 'twould have been much, had any of these idiots actually known anything of importance. They were certainly free enough with their tongues. Frustrated, she discovered none of them had left the castle for the 'big battle', and therefore none of them knew much about what happened. What they did reveal made her blood boil, and when one finally checked on her, she was a'Flame with anger but held her tongue, maintaining her pretense of being unconscious through shoulder shaking, followed by a few hard kicks to her legs. Fortunately, she was still pretty much fetal, providing some protection for her gut from his irritation, but her legs took a beating and 'twould show clearly for awhile upon her fair skin. Some of the sting was softened by her leathers, some by her sheer determination not to cry out, and some by the fact the kicks were a tad halfhearted in her opinion. Now she could show a man how to kick like he meant it. She tried not to smile as she thought about what was to come, and very soon indeed. Hopefully, to this particular Agent.

A gravelly male voice met her ears. "She's no threat in this condition, likely near death from the cold. The Dragons haven't returned, although 'twould be to my liking if they stayed away forever, but the others haven't returned either, and I've seen none of the rank or file since they left. So why did that one bring her here anyway? We weren't planning on taking any prisoners and 'tis not like we can ransom her. What the Flame were they thinking out there? I'd like to take her to the Witch's Dungeons, dump her tall ass down the stairs. Might be lucky and break her neck. Otherwise, wouldn't be long afore the spirits did our job for us. But I suppose I'd be whipped when they found out. I'll chain her up in the interrogation cell. Old Cratz will give her a workout when she wakes. That'll take the wind out of her sails!" The man laughed wickedly along with the others within earshot, all evidently in agreement with his plan.

'Twas clear that the men of Evanntyr didn't use the southern dungeons, fearing ghosts, and they'd actually set up their prisoner holding and interrogation in the other sections, although Mynx knew Evanntyr had several dungeon sections as well as levels. What she found most interesting was that the area known to the commoners as the Witch's Dungeons, were actually the southernmost portion of the entire lowest sections, meaning in some places they hung o'er the Slippes and also contained the Well of Evanntyr. She'd heard the rumors from all o'er Kadoor, that many thought the wells were haunted. She wondered if this was an extreme case of that belief, or if there was truly something going on down there. She knew not why they'd been named for a witch, as she didn't know that any still existed. Mynx mused for a moment, thinking about the ancient Legends of the Witch Women of Rienne, or the Rashei D'Rienne. 'Twas said they had an extraordinary way with animals and could share their powers. They were also well known and often sought out for their mystical knowledge. Although they were highly skilled in the arts of healing and self defense, these were mostly disregarded due to the fascination in their other talents. Said to be psychic, they specialized in predicting the future.

Mynx listened, counting the voices. At least a dozen. If they all came along, it could be a bit more difficult to escape. She chose to keep up the pretense a little longer, hoping for a more favorable opportunity to present itself soon.

Suddenly, the man who'd been speaking, hoisted her up and o'er his shoulder with a grunt. By the Fade, she wasn't that heavy, but it seemed he wasn't much taller than she, his lack of conditioning plain. The hard edged leather and metal shoulder pad dug into her belly and she had difficulty relaxing and keeping her eyes shut. Her plan would work best if he was caught totally off guard, and not having much back up would be a blessing upon which she knew better than to count.

Mynx continued faking unconsciousness, despite the flood of Battle Lust inundating her senses. Decreased wind, sound, and light, along with the acrid smell of torches, indicated they'd entered the castle. Trying to establish their current location from the maps of Evanntyr all Warriors studied during Training, there'd be three possible gates from the ward to the side halls. She'd not been certain where she'd been dropped, but cautious glimpses gave her an optimistic view of being closest to the southernmost doorway, and since he hadn't walked all that far afore entering, she hoped they'd be close to the kitchens. 'Twould be to her advantage. Having already figured the time of day as roughly mid to late afternoon, the kitchens would be at their least occupied for a bit. There'd be an alcove coming up soon, and without any other voices or shuffling steps indicating they had company, 'twas now or never. She carefully opened her eyes and waited for the alcove. They were exactly where she'd thought. No one passed them in the shadowy hallway and although there was the sound of some activity in one of the scullery kitchens opposite, she was certain they were otherwise alone. Her senses told her they were indeed traveling northerly, and if they continued past the alcove 'twould be to the stairwell descending into the Pits of Hades, some of the most renown prison cells in all Kadoor, filled with ancient and grisly torture devices. The reality that the Warrior Team sent to the King to report on the first LifeBond had most likely ended their span of days in these very chambers less than a full winter past, made her shudder involuntarily.

The shudder caused her to slide slightly off balance o'er the Agent's shoulder and his automatic reaction to try to keep her there, would be the last thing the man ever did. Falling off was definitely not what she wanted to do and as she slipped, she jerked her knees up into his chest. Combined with her upper body weight o'er his back, he was forced to lean forward with a huff. Curled tightly around his now folding torso, she jerked her arm sideways and managed to sling her elbow around his head. Using gravity against him, his reactions throwing him off balance in his ill fated attempt to heave her back up on his shoulder, she tightened her loop, pulling down hard. Stretching out her long legs, she stepped smoothly onto the floor where she had just enough leverage, coupled with speed, and the Agent's utter surprise, to finish him. With one vicious pull, his chin was driven to his chest with such ferocity that he was rendered unconscious. Without stopping, Mynx let him go while she sat down and half rolled, bringing her arms around her legs in front of her again. She drew his blade, cut the tie around her ankles, and dragged him deeper into the shadows of the alcove, where she slit his throat with his own sword. That accomplished, she cut the cords tying her hands. Now she had three blades in her possession, although her lost Warrior sword was far superior to that which she now held.

All this she accomplished in the span of a few heartbeats. She peeked around the corner. No one in the hallway. She broke and ran back the way they'd just come, praying she'd find the stairwell to her destination afore she encountered more trouble. Passing the door through which she'd just been carried without running headlong into anyone, she soon felt a slight hitch to her breathing, along with a faint tingling sensation which she rationalized as the result of Battle Lust as she continued into the deeper shadows. Slowing down as she set distance 'tween herself and the kitchens, she passed several doorways which might have been storerooms, but 'twas obvious they were not used daily or even every sennight. The dust was thick in the corners where no boots stepped, the ceilings had webs hanging where no one had swept, and the bracketed torches upon the walls had not been lit in some time. Apparently, the staff came and went using their own torches, and only when they had to access whatever was in these rooms. Interesting. This gave more credence to the rumors of their fears of this part of the castle. Testing one of the doors, she cringed at the protesting noise and moved on.

The stairwell she sought should be coming up very soon. When she rounded the corner and ran into the huge timber door at the very end of the hall, her heart began to beat faster and she was somewhat dismayed at a sense of foreboding that seemed to come from nowhere. Instead of being fearful, she was puzzled, but Mynx had seen the return of the Dragons, along with the LifeBond, and being no virgin to Magic she speculated, if 'twas Magic here 'twould explain many things. If this was what the people of Evanntyr felt when they came this way, no wonder they didn't come this way often. However, instead of being put off by this revelation, she was energized, as 'twould provide the perfect cover. She'd stay in the castle, in these very dungeons, using their fears against them to her advantage. She'd learn all she could afore she returned to the Clan. She pushed the heavy door open, grimacing at the creaking and scraping noise the hinges made, and slipped inside. Shoving the door shut behind her, her first task would be to find a way to silence those hinges afore she was found. At the very least, the kitchens should have enough lard lying around to be of benefit, or mayhap lamp or cooking oil would present itself. She peered into the darkness waiting for her eyes to adjust, listening to see if her escape had been detected. As the shadows opened up to her clearing vision, she was on a broad landing with a wide stone stairwell spiraling downward. There was no light coming from any source at this angle, but from the maps she knew there were windows, albeit very narrow and high.

The area should be lit from outside in the outer most cells and especially around the well. Mayhap not this late in the day, however.

'Twas getting more difficult to breathe and her skin warmed and tingled faintly. 'Twas the Magic; she knew the difference 'tween good air and bad, but for some mysterious reason, she was drawn into the depths. Although it seemed to be affecting her, it had not the taste of evil, and evil she knew well since the war started. Determined to continue her quest, Mynx slid her foot forward cautiously 'til she felt the edge of the first step, and began to descend.

~~~~~~~~~~

"And you know the rest." She turned her head around to look at the Dragon, but her eyes were closed, her breathing even and unlabored at last. Not wanting to wake her, the Warrior settled back, closed her own eyes, and was soon fast asleep.

~~~~~~~~~~

Islyth lay quietly draped o'er the edge of the well, staying wet while she watched the sleeping duo. Her front paws were curled under her resting chin as she'd listened captivated by the story of bravery and fortitude. She loved hearing Mynx's tale every time 'twas told. She'd been witness to the Warrior's struggle to bring strength and wellness to Synahmarr, but 'twould not be enough. Surely there was something the big Dragon could keep down to give her more nutrition than broth and the occasional mouse or bird the Warrior fed her so tediously. Islyth slowly considered her options as she munched on a snack of fish wrapped in seaweed. How could she help the Warrior without letting her know of her own existence? Synahmarr was already aware of her, 'twould have been impossible to hide from such a one, but she'd not revealed her to the Human, out of respect. Islyth had come and gone, barely able to get to the ocean to hunt, the shadowy leviathans always hounding her, making it difficult to leave Port O'Kings. They shouldn't be there much longer. Mayhap soon she could try again. She took another bite of her snack. She especially loved the heads, and as she ate happily she didn't notice how boisterous she became, snorting and chewing 'til she suddenly noticed an open eye staring at her, and froze mid-crunch.

Synahmarr was awake, but not a muscle had she moved. Islyth smiled at the beautiful one, and drooled fish bits and mashed seaweed from the corner of her muzzle. Synahmarr smiled back, her eyes now sparkling with amusement at her cousin's reactions. She couldn't help but lick her dry lips with the thought of the delectable and highly nutritious treats so close, yet so far away. Islyth wiped her own mouth with the back of one paw, and licked it clean. Synahmarr could have Spoken to the other a very long time past, but 'twould have taken even more of her strength and she had none to spare. Besides, when dealing with Water Dragons, one needed to let them think 'twas their idea. She'd waited for just this opportunity to let the notion come to her naturally. Finally, she saw the light of awareness shine in Islyth's slitted eyes. Her head bobbed upright, she stuffed what was left of her snack into her mouth, downing it with one chomp afore plunging back into the well. Synahmarr's mouth watered with the thought of what was to come.

CHAPTER FIFTEEN

The End of an Era

~~~~~O'ER A MOON AFTER THE BATTLE~~~~~

Artemis ran back to her cabin faster than she'd ever run afore. She must be there when the Agents arrived or they might suspect she'd hidden something in the woods, which was precisely what she'd just done. All she could do was pray that Aalanna's hiding place hadn't been compromised as well, for neither she nor Larken could help now. Larken had tried to get Artemis to leave with him after they'd carefully concealed her most rare and dangerous stash of herbs, powders, concoctions, and dredges, leaving the most common and non-harmful in the cabin to be seen. She'd argued her absence would prove her guilt; they were only taking her for questioning. And she had to protect Aalanna. He'd argued back that although Aalanna was not the escaped Warrior like the Agents thought, she was a Clansman and could handle herself, and for all intents and purposes she'd been in hiding since escaping the castle and could easily continue to do so. Aalanna would be safe, but, he'd stressed, all those 'taken for questioning' thus far had perished in the Pits of Hades. "I will not abandon my post," was her last word. Then she'd turned and was gone. Larken returned to the castle and began immediately to find out all he could about what they were planning for the Painted One.

'Twas less than two marks later when they brought her in, shackled and hobbled like a common port thief. Her eyes were swollen and he could see the shadows of the darkening bruises upon her face. Infuriated, he struggled to remain calm, for his own life and Matana's were also at stake. He could do nothing if he was taken as well. They'd expected two, mayhap three Agents at the most, as well as much later this evening, and there
~~~~~

was no suggestion that 'twould be difficult. But apparently she was greatly feared, for the High King had sent a squad of heavily armed men, evidently with the notion that they were about to face a Troll. 'Twas clear the arrest was brutal and that she'd not been able to put up a fight. Shytin would pay for this. The People did not forgive such treatment. Larken spit and fumed. His information was lacking and Artemis paid the price. They'd been waiting for her when she'd returned. Already having ransacked the cabin, after beating her they torched everything. She had only the clothing on her back, torn and covered with dried blood. They'd even taken her medicine and charm bags.

Larken was a master of filtering the truth from rumor. He quickly learned that instead of taking Artemis directly to the dungeons, she was being held for court in a small, empty, windowless room off the side hallway. They were still afraid of her, of what she might be capable of doing to them, for if they didn't care she would've been handed directly to the Examiner. Within a few days, if nothing happened and they didn't forget about her, she'd be taken in front of the judge and charged with treason for having assisted a prisoner to escape, and would then be taken to the dungeons where she'd be 'questioned' as to the whereabouts of said prisoner. Ironically, although they were guilty of many things, helping the Warrior escape wasn't one of them. By now everyone was aware of the bungling of the Agents, knowing that the day of the big battle, a single, slim, female Warrior had bested her captors and simply vanished. Even if Artemis had known her location 'twould do no good, as her fate was sealed, and the Warrior was probably (hopefully) long gone. Still, if Larken could find her, helping her would pay tribute to his friend as well as support their allies. But first he had to free Artemis and try as he might, he couldn't think of a way to make that happen. Matana was a good fighter, but the guards would quickly o'erwhelm the two of them if they tried a frontal offensive. Disguise? Unquestionably. But he needed a plan to go along with the disguise and he was running out of ideas. Every scenario he imagined, ended badly for all three of them. Leaving Evanntyr was foremost in his thoughts. He decided he'd at least see if there was any evidence of where the Warrior might have gone after her escape, then find a way to get Artemis out of the castle. And where was Aalanna?

After some quick digging he had to admit, although there were some rumors of odd things missing from the kitchens, 'twas just as likely they were stealing for their own and he had nothing to even suggest the Warrior was still in the castle. He sighed and hoped she was free and safe, and then forgot about her. Now he focused on getting Artemis out of the holding cell. If they actually succeeded they couldn't just saunter out of the castle, and they couldn't disguise her sufficiently. They didn't even know if she could walk on her own or if she'd have to be carried. There was one chance. If they could manage to get her to a certain alcove close to the lower kitchens without being seen, the very one where the Warrior was said to have left the remains of her captor, they could duck inside the walls. Once there, they could hide for moons if need be, but getting her out of the castle and safely to Wyndsyr Forest was yet another story. And once they committed to this plan 'twould not be safe to return to their prior lives. They'd become instant renegades, despite their disguises. 'Twould be the end of an era.

Finally out of options, he and Matana decided to risk everything. 'Twas past time to leave King's Gate and return to the People. Disguised as Agents, their plan to convince the guards they were there to transfer the prisoner early, they had narrow margin for error in this ruse. Taking one last look around their quarters, they silently said goodbye to all their possessions and the only life they'd lived o'er four decades. They left nothing that would compromise their true identities or their plan, and all of Gabriel's mementos had been lost with Artemis's cabin. Turning their backs, they walked out. 'Twas shortly after midnight when the least traffic wandered the halls as they approached the holding cell with their fake papers. Matana had slipped a sedative powder into the kaafy served to the guards, which would make them less likely to question without becoming aware of having been drugged.

~~~~~~~~~~

Matana all but broke down when they entered the cell and saw Artemis. Her face was swollen, her eyes could barely open. Initially she didn't recognize them, even with their silent hand language. After a long moment, she nodded her head slightly and tried to make the sign for agreement, but her fingers wouldn't cooperate. 'Twas heartbreaking. She couldn't stand up on her own and needing to stay in character, they bullied her, making her whimper in pain 'til finally Larken snatched her frail body o'er his shoulder afore they stormed out angrily. The guards had barely noted their paperwork at first, but they examined it with an odd expression now, that told the pair they had to move quickly. As the sun dawned upon the guards, Larken and Matana rounded the corner and broke into a run. Artemis must have lost consciousness from the pain as she went limp o'er his shoulder for awhile. They stumbled down the stairs taking them three at a time and soon realized they were being chased, although silently, and only by the two they'd deceived. The guards were now in deep trouble. If they sounded the alarm they'd have to admit they'd let yet another prisoner escape, but if they lost them, well, either way meant a trip to the Examiner.

After much navigation, backtracking, and almost running headlong into a group of guards who'd just changed shifts, they found themselves at the alcove. Breathing heavily, they searched for the lever, to no avail. Larken whispered harshly, "It has to be here! I've mapped every entrance to the passages!" Frantically, he ran his hands o'er the uneven surface but could not locate the mechanism.

Matana replied with fear in her voice."They must have found it when the Warrior killed her guard here. Mayhap 'twas dismantled?" Larken knew that could be the truth of the matter. Even
~~~~~~~~~~

though Shytin was afraid of the dark and seldom entered the passages, he had personally destroyed every entrance he'd located (which were relatively few, and Larken had fixed them again) since Aalanna became pregnant with Fryya, eight winters past. Shytin had some notion that she might try to leave him, although he couldn't imagine why. All sarcasm aside, he was at a loss as to what to do now. They had nowhere to go and they could hear the Agents as they scurried closer in their search.

~~~~~~~~~~

"Quickly! This way!" Appearing out of the shadows just a few paces down the hall, the tall blonde hissed and gestured for the trio to follow. Surprised, but desperate, they looked to Artemis who shook her head in agreement, afore leaving the alcove to follow the girl. They passed the lower kitchens and then some storage rooms. As they continued, the hallway darkened as it seemed to collapse upon them in abandonment. The legends echoed in their minds, but they'd no other choice. They had to trust this woman. No, they'd put not their trust in just any woman. They'd put their trust in a Warrior, for clearly she was the fugitive and no bumpkin hiding in the corners, begging for coin. Hastening down the ever narrowing, twisting and branching hallway, they passed room after room, some with boarded up doors, the very walls falling into disrepair, the torches unusable or missing entirely from the brackets. No one came this way; no one had been this way in many winters. Why had he not noticed this afore? Larken realized he'd been close, but always his intuition, presenting itself as a prickly sensation and feeling of imminent death, had kept him from... now he understood. 'Twas a Spell no longer active. Were Warriors also Magic bearers? The legends of the People told that the Battle Commander was immortal, living lifespan after lifespan, but that didn't necessarily mean Magic. Besides, he'd recently been forced Past the Veil in this very castle.

The heavy oaken door materialized in front of them so abruptly that he ran into the girl's back, and dropped Artemis
~~~~~~~~~~

to her feet trying to keep his own balance. The Warrior shushed him with a look upon her face that gave no quarter. Matana crept forward and they all listened behind them briefly, afore following her through the doorway. They'd squirmed as she'd shoved it open but mysteriously the ancient hinges made little noise. More Magic? No. Larken noted the highly oiled mechanisms and recognized 'twas her work. She'd been here afore, and 'twas likely where she'd been hiding since her escape. 'Twas all making sense.

<center>~~~~~LESS THAN A MARK LATER~~~~~</center>

Mynx was well equipped, having practiced her stealth lessons frequently o'er the past moon, but she was no Healer. All the same, she did her best to apply emergency field dressings on the Painted One, and during their conversation she was shocked to learn that Aalanna had been held captive in the castle all this time, but not as shocked as they'd been to discover a Dragon in the dungeon. And they were even more shocked to learn 'twas the Princess herself, as well as the fact that she'd been there longer than they had.

Mynx sat back from her ministrations. Thoughtfully, she considered her state of affairs. She'd wanted the Healer to help her with the Dragon, but now the Dragon might have to help her with the Healer. Addressing the new arrivals, she stated, "She can't travel and 'twill likely be awhile. She needs to stay here with me. I can protect her and when she's healed, I'll assist her to escape." 'Twas a heartbeat afore they realized she was talking about Artemis, although 'twas apparent the Dragon was in the same condition. But they could see no way for the Princess to escape the dungeons, she'd been there since afore they'd completed building this section and she'd never fit through the gated doorways. "But you can and should go soon. They'll be searching for three, not two, making it easier for you to slip past the guards. Besides, with the obvious constraints here, I can't feed all of us for long. Stay tonight and I'll reconnoiter. When you leave 'twould be safest to take the passageways, there's an entrance under the stairs." Out of habit, Larken tried to fake confusion, but he could tell 'twas not successful, even though he'd truly not known of this entrance. "I use them to get around the castle, as do you. We've come close to running into each other on several occasions." Now he was even more confused. How had she managed to get around him without his knowledge? He had to admit that she was good. The urgency in her voice caught his attention again as she continued, "Get thee to the Clan and tell of our struggles. We need help."

Larken made a token effort to convince the Warrior to come with them, but he knew she was right and 'twas apparent she wouldn't budge. He marveled at her selflessness, her devotion to the Princess, and their commitment to each other. Still, Mynx was worried about the Clan, and about her Oath. She felt she'd betrayed the Brotherhood by not returning, and yet, she could not leave Syn. 'Twas evident she could've escaped long ago, but she'd given up her life for the Dragon's, with no guarantee either would survive. "I had no choice, really. I couldn't leave her here alone, to possibly die alone. 'Twas my fault she had to abandon her Spell. If she Passes, 'twill not be for lack of my support. Flame the Oath and Flame the Brotherhood if they don't agree with my decision. If I can return, I shall face the Battle Commander with a clear conscience."

Reflecting on the candor of her words, all eyes turned to the well when they heard splashing against the stone walls. Mynx approached, blade in hand. They watched with growing curiosity as a spray of water shot up to the ceiling and a huge fish came flying o'er the edge. Mynx had been prepared to catch something, but when she saw they were practically the same size, she allowed it to land upon the floor, where it thrashed about. Using her full body weight to subdue the giant fish, she made the kill quickly. Through some innate sense coupled with her ability to Communicate with Syn, Mynx knew who was providing the bounty, but in evident practiced acceptance of the phenomenon she shrugged and stated simply, "A gift from the One. I no longer question." She cut off the head and took it to the Dragon. Then she returned and finished cleaning the fish, carefully saving the tail, fins, guts, and even the skin, filling a large silver platter which she set afore the Dragon. While Syn slowly ate her meal, Mynx sliced the remainder of the fish into long layers, leaving the bones with a thin layer of meat on each side as yet another delicacy for her friend. Her head turned toward Syn as if listening, but no one heard a sound.

Her eyes pleading, Syn Spoke. *"Let me try again."*

"Are you sure? There's no hurry. I can start a fire, too, you know."

The unlikely duo stared at each other, Mynx with a smile o'er lying concern, Syn with yearning. *"Yes, I want to try."* Mynx nodded, then laid all the slices on the floor in front of the Dragon, who took as deep a breath as she could and... coughed. Mynx stifled a snort and didn't even attempt to cover her mouth with her hand as she broke into a giggle. Larken was appalled. Did that Warrior just laugh at the Princess of the Highlands? He heard a huff and a growl and a sound like someone choking all mixed up together and he stared wide eyed at the Dragon who was also laughing out loud. Despite the events of the past few days, 'twas funny and caught everyone off guard. Joining in the levity, their burdens were lightened for awhile. However, Synahmarr was so weakened by this, she lowered her head to her paws to catch her breath. Mynx had a worried frown upon her face when she next looked to the newcomers.

<div style="text-align:center">~~~~~~~~~~</div>

Synahmarr glanced up and winked at Islyth when she stuck her head o'er the edge to see if the girl had caught this one. She noted the size of each and frowned. Mayhap 'twas a tad too large, and being Human, she was not up to the task. But she apparently captured it, and immediately took the best parts to Syn. She was well pleased with herself. Her offerings had helped the Warrior to survive and the Princess to heal, and although she was still in danger of Passing, she was gaining slow but steady ground toward wellness, and the Warrior had not been forced to leave Synahmarr to go hunt. She smiled at the pretty one, and resting her chin on her paws, she Said, *"Islyth found rogue Human. Belong to these?"*

Synahmarr had to think about this revelation. A rogue Human? Even though she was fatigued from trying to fire the fish, she used the Link. The effort was great, but such practice was building her endurance. *"What makes you think she's a 'rogue' and why would you think she belongs to these, my dear?"*

"She hiding. Smell like that one. Been close they have." She pointed to Artemis. When the pretty one didn't respond, she saw that she'd fallen asleep. After thinking about it, she decided the fish wasn't big enough to feed Synahmarr along with all these new Humans, and slipped back into the well, heading for open water. What would Myrrdin do? She pondered his likely response as she warily navigated through the underground river. Which was more important? The newcomers or the rogue? They all fought against the Evil One but the rogue was alone, and Myrrdin taught her that Humans alone were more likely to be forced Past the Veil. Changing course, she wove her way through the channels away from the Fears, toward the last place she'd seen the Human.

~~~~~~~~~~~

When Mynx learned that the Healer of the Forest was being brought in, she'd jumped at the chance to get expert help for Synahmarr. But she'd been severely injured when taken into custody and then Larken and Matana beat her to the rescue. No matter, their plan had been a bit more discrete than the one she'd chosen. Ever the Warrior, frontal assault was her forte. She should have paid more attention during Stealth Training, although, she was rather proud of her performance thus far. Nevertheless,
~~~~~~~~~~~

'twould appear that she now had two patients for whom to care, for neither could leave on their own.

Artemis could hardly speak from the pain of the injuries and loss of blood she'd suffered. "They took my bag and all my supplies. Can you bring more from the cabin?" As the moments dripped past, she stared at Larken in growing disbelief, 'til the sun dawned upon her with what he'd carefully not shared. Whispering, she questioned, "Is nothing left?"

Larken hung his head. "After they took you, they torched the cabin and tossed in everything that could be moved from the yard. 'Twas fast and hot and I..."

"The stash?"

"Safe, but currently inaccessible. Agents scour the woods even now for Aalanna, although she'd not been found as of the time we left for your rescue."

Artemis took an agonizing breath and clamped her hand 'cross her mouth to keep from moaning aloud, but she could not stop the tears. Near everything was gone; her life's work, her books, herbs and medicines, with the exception of what they'd stashed which could still be found and stolen. All of her containers, bowls, shells, mortars and pestles, handmade clothing, bedding, pillows with intricately detailed needlework and pearling, furnishings, family heirlooms, possessions handed down from generations of previous Healers and those she'd been preparing for the following, mementos of Mikkal, even her weapons, all precious, unique, irreplaceable... gone. Several ribs were fractured and crying made her shudder in pain, the pain made her cry harder, and the harder she cried the more erratic was her breathing, causing a vicious cycle. Matana tried to console her, but even her touch was shunned. All the loneliness, stress and frustrations of a lifetime, the realization that she'd failed the People by losing such valuable history and knowledge, came crashing in upon her and 'twas no use. Raw emotions stampeded through her soul as her companions kept watch nervously toward the stairs, afraid someone would hear the rising commotion, feel the intensity of her despair, afore she'd cried herself into sleep or stupor.

Surprisingly, sudden calm prevailed through the dungeon as a soft, melodic voice rose in the background. Stunned, the trio turned and stared. The Warrior was hugging Artemis tightly, rocking her while the Dragon Sang. The power of the Song was legend itself and they could do naught but sit still and listen. Entranced along with Artemis, they soon all fell asleep. Except for Mynx. Sharing a special Link with the Princess that neither could explain, she saw to Syn's needs afore bedding down. Long into the night, Mynx pondered the revelation that her Commander's mate was in the castle all these past winters.

CHAPTER SIXTEEN

Islyth in Charge

THE FOLLOWING DAY
~~~~~WYNDSYR FOREST~~~~~

"Are you a Water Dragon?" Aalanna queried the adorable beast half visible, lying in the water on the river bank. Islyth was pleased, since she'd tried very hard to create just that look so as not to frighten the Human. Taking most of the previous night to find the rogue again, she'd traveled much further than she'd planned and wanted to get back to Syn as soon as possible. She had no idea how to communicate with Humans, they seemed rather ignorant of language, although it could be that she had to bare her teeth in order to speak out loud. And they had no ability to use the Link. But, appearing adorable had her unafraid, and she could then try to make her intentions known. Islyth wagged her head up and down in an exaggerated affirmative, which had the desired effect. "I am Aalanna. I know of your Kind only through myth, but I've always believed that myth speaks truth to some degree."

Islyth tried again, although she'd been trying for quite awhile to no avail. What was one more attempt? She was hopeful, since the Human wasn't afraid. Yet. Wrinkling her nose, she growled as clearly as she could, her lips pulled back, her long tongue slipping out 'tween her fangs and splattering saliva in all directions. She hated speaking out loud. She hoped the Human wouldn't run in panic. "Islyth. Am Islyth!"

She had to give the Human credit for bravery. Not only did she not run away, she showed no sign of fear. In fact, she came even closer while she responded. "Was that your name? Forgive me, I didn't quite catch it, please repeat. I promise to listen very carefully. I'm in dire straits here, I have no idea where I am, I've been on the run all night and could definitely use some help."

The Dragon was full of joy! She'd understood her! Well, at least partially. And then the most remarkable thing happened. Aalanna stepped right up to the her, reaching out her hand in trust. Islyth sniffed the tiny woman, and could sense she was more than she appeared. This was no rogue, and was no ordinary Human, either. The Dragon had met her Kind afore. 'Twas long ago and far from here. She furrowed her brows in concentration. 'Twas at St Swiftyn's! The Dragon gazed deeply into the woman's eyes, and was baffled. Aalanna didn't know her own heritage. Her tongue tasted the woman's skin and she inhaled her scent. Yes. Her distant memories were Altered, but 'twas another layer. A more recent memory was Blocked. Islyth knew this Magic. 'Twas Fay, but 'twas the taste of evil in the recent Block. Her brows furrowed once again. The Fay and evil didn't seem to fit together. The Fay and arrogance, on the other hand...

Their meeting was rudely interrupted by Agents charging through the forest, and Islyth did the only thing she could. Grabbing Aalanna's hand in her mouth, she yanked her under the water, taking her deep to avoid being seen by the bad men. All the Agents saw was what appeared to be a giant lizard, a non-sentient, distant cousin of the Dragons, snatching their prize. 'Twas a dangerous and deep river, but 'twas still odd for they'd never known the creatures to live in this region of Wyndsyr Forest. Still, no one was willing to enter the water, and all of them would later swear they had. They waited along the riverbank for marks. They searched for half a league in both directions. No Warrior. No remains of a Warrior. And there'd been only a strip of torn and bloody fabric floating to the surface, which they eventually took back to the High King as evidence of her demise. The Sorcerer was elated. He'd known all along 'twas not the Warrior, but Aalanna was his nemesis and therefore, her death was welcomed. She'd either drowned or was eaten by the giant lizard...

mayhap both. What a pleasant thought. The only other thing to bring such joy to his heart was the upcoming torture of the idiots who came back without completing their mission as stated.

~~~~~~~~~~

Aalanna didn't even have time to take a breath and she was under water, being dragged deeper and deeper by the Dragon. Her wrist ached in Islyth's mouth, sharp teeth pierced her skin, but she knew that Islyth wasn't trying to hurt her. In point of fact, she'd seen the Agents breaking through the brush and knew the Water Dragon was trying to hide her. The river had a fissure through which they traveled and they stopped momentarily afore entering to allow Aalanna to slide around to Islyth's back and hold on to her shoulders, her apron ripping while she maneuvered into the new position. Aalanna quickly wrapped a piece of the fabric around her wrist to stop the bleeding, but the majority floated away.

She had to maintain skin to skin, that much did Aalanna recall of the myths of the Water Dragons. And although she knew she should be able to breathe within the surrounding Allure, 'twas difficult to trust that knowledge. Finally, the decision was made for her as her lungs burned and she near exploded. Racing through underground caverns, she sputtered and involuntarily choked on her own saliva, while her eyes widened with the discovery that the myths were true. Soon she was breathing almost normally and clinging to the swiftly moving Dragon, hoping their destination was not back to the castle.

Very soon the darkness lessened and she could see daylight above. Exhausted from holding onto the Dragon's shoulders so tightly in fear of losing her grasp, she rolled off onto the ground as soon as they broke the surface. Amazingly, she was dry.

"Islyth sad."

Aalanna gasped, "Whatever for, my dear?"

The Dragon actually appeared to be pouting. "Scare you."
~~~~~~~~~~

Catching her breath she replied, "Oh no, my friend, I was just flustered with the circumstances."

Now the Dragon's expression turned to chastising as she responded. "You hold tight. Islyth not lose you. Work too hard."

Aalanna rolled o'er to gaze into the Water Dragon's striking eyes, the golden flecks shimmering in the waning sunlight. "Seriously? Oh. That would've been good to know afore we began this journey."

Islyth squinted at this statement. 'Twasn't as if they'd had any time afore they began this journey, in which to exchange such information. Humans were so strange. "Skin touch. All need."

"Oh my. I'll remember that if we ever do this again." Aalanna was still trying to recover from the perilous escape, while being as gracious and thankful to her new friend as she could manage.

But the Water Dragon didn't notice, other than that the Human was fatigued, although she never did understand exactly what made them fatigue so easily. "Do again. Not stay here. Islyth need rest."

Aalanna wasn't one to blame others and always took responsibility for her own actions. "Did I make it hard on you, as well? I so apologize. I didn't know."

Islyth was beginning to like this one. She seemed to appreciate her efforts, her needs, and her importance. She sat up on her hind legs and puffed out her chest in pride. 'Twas an odd situation for her to be in charge. With forgiveness in her tone she stated, "Islyth go, come back. You stay."

Aalanna repeated her instructions for clarity. "I understand. I'll stay here and wait for your return. Islyth? Is Artemis safe? I wasn't home, I was out checking traps, and then went to the river for fresh water. When I returned, the cabin was already afire and the Agents had taken Artemis. There was only one left, rummaging around for more to toss into the flames. I killed him and dragged his body into the forest. I searched the area, but there was nothing left. And then the forest teemed with Agents and I had to hide. I couldn't help her and I felt awful. She must have been arrested because of me. Do they still have her? What about Larken and Matana? Do you know them?"

"Islyth know. All safe." And then she was gone. Aalanna shivered in the chill air and was grateful for being dry. She had no idea where she was or how far they'd come, but if there were any Agents in the area, she couldn't have defended herself. She was exhausted from running and hiding, not to mention the underwater journey. She'd attempted to get her old fighting form back while living with Artemis o'er the past moon, but she wasn't a Warrior and she'd given all she had to give this day. But she had to get to Drekinn. She had to find something of Grifynn to use in the conjure, she had to get to St Swiftyn's. She had to... Aalanna fell asleep as soon as she closed her eyes. Sometime later, with dusk falling, she managed to drag herself up the bank and under a thicket of evergreens, burrowing under a layer of leafy branches to keep warm and hidden, afore falling asleep again.

<center>~~~~~THE WELL~~~~~</center>

So excited was Islyth about finding the rogue for Synahmarr, in an aerial maneuver similar to a recent fish offering, she burst out of the well almost smacking her head on the ceiling afore inelegantly gliding down to the stone floor and landing with a loud thump that shook the cell gates. Sitting up on her hind legs, she spit forth, "Forgot. Here be tight." She chewed on her tail with an innocent look in her widened eyes, as if she hadn't just scared the piss out of every Human in the dungeon, and awakened the Princess as well. Synahmarr stared at her cousin in delight, while the others just stared. Mynx recognized the awkward situation and knew instinctively what was required, although 'twould divulge her 'secret'. This could turn ugly fast, and the Water Dragon was very important to them. "Welcome, Islyth. I'm so happy you've finally deigned to let me see you. You are a most beautiful creature. Surely you bring much needed information to help us, that we could not have obtained without your skills."

Islyth opened her mouth and then closed it again. She was speechless. Her chest puffed out in happiness that the Human showed proper admiration, and now she couldn't remember why she'd not shown herself previously. The Human considered her necessary.

~~~~~~~~~~

After they'd all settled and discussed the situation 'twas decided that Islyth would assist Larken and Matana to escape the castle, thereby not risking them being seen or captured. 'Twould keep the ones staying safer as well. They'd meet where she'd left Aalanna, leaving Artemis behind to heal and help the Warrior with Syn.

Once Islyth delivered the pair separately, she returned to the dungeon with a load of fresh healing herbs and roots, a gift from Larken and Matana. The Night Beasts had found Aalanna and were waiting with her for their Handlers. Unable to get to the Healer's stash, they were able to locate one of many of their own, providing the three of them with sufficient clothing, weaponry, and food stuffs to make travel easier. Careful to avoid the King's Men scouring the forest, they started home to convince the Danoh 'twas time to join with the Clan.
~~~~~~~~~~

Chapter Seventeen
The People in Retreat

The Night Wings were bred by the People of the Raptor's Talons in much the same way, and for the same purposes, as had their cousins of the Edge bred their Night Beasts. Originally hawkers, through careful selection the Gordatch saved the bat-like creatures from extinction, during the process dramatically increasing their intelligence, loyalty, physical size, and hunting skills. With long leathery wings and tails, short legs, and near human eyes in a face similar to that of a fox, the Wings were half the size of their Handlers when fully grown, but only a fraction of their weight. Using their extraordinary senses, fangs, and vicious claws, a Night Wing could take down a mountain cat with ease, protective of their Handlers as well as excellent hunting partners. Their tough smooth skin matched their eyes, from medium browns to blackest blacks, making them difficult to see 'til 'twas too late, for they preferred to hunt in silence.

Bayl sensed the unfurling drama long afore his Handler, and gave him as much advance warning as possible. Kyrag took heed immediately and provided an elbow shove to assist his launch. They'd been working together since Bayl was born and had well honed their interactions. For a Human, the man was quicker than most, interpreting Bayl's needs and giving him his head during the hunt. But 'twas the first time Bayl had ever felt this much hatred raging in the air about them. His instincts screamed 'twas coming from what he'd decided winters past, was a rather large, slow, and dreadfully ugly version of himself. Incoming! He'd tried to tell the People. But only Kyrag seemed to understand, as he took Bayl's warning and began to rally the others.

Bayl soared into the skies in order to determine the cause of his distress. As soon as he rose above the canopy he felt a tightness in his throat and a searing heat that came with a blinding flash of light. Ducking back under, he'd just missed a stream of Flame shot 'cross the sky, inhaling the acrid stench. Gathering his wits he crawled up one of the tallest trees to investigate. A dozen Dragons were flying o'er, guiding many men on the ground as they traveled directly to the People. Rage burned in his heart as he watched the other Night Wings gather in the skies, and he took the lead. Attack! Their meager forces understood his body language and screech. They were not from this range, only accompanying their Handlers, escort to the Prima Danah and Prima Danoh of the People, Gheryh and Kyrag. 'Twas Gheryh's home village being attacked. Flying into the group of Dragons, he and the other Wings did as much damage as they could, targeting the eyes of the creatures, for 'twas the target upon which they could induce the most damage, causing much havoc. Although they couldn't injure the brains through the eyes, for their claws and fangs were not long enough, they could limit their vision and harass all efforts to use their Magic. Although these Dragons did not Flame directly into the forest, they seemed to have no qualms about trying to fry Bayl and his fellow Wings in flight and this must be avoided to protect the village.

Bayl heard the People fighting below, his Handler among them. Through the trees he saw some leaving for a prearranged place of escape and had to keep the Dragons out of touch or they'd Tell the men where they were going. Many of the People were already dead or dying, he could hear the Night Beasts screaming in anger and pain. Drink from them! Bayl shrieked his battle cry to the other Wings, but they needed no such encouragement and eventually their vicious attacks caused the Dragons to abandon their efforts. Flying back down he began to hunt the Human enemy. So many. Bite them, claw them, slash them, blood them, bite them again. This one, that one. More and more. Pain, weakness, numbness. Hit them again. Where was Kyrag? Time stood still as Bayl continued his strikes, terrifyingly lethal against those who came to kill them. Severe pain, falling, his wing yanked, held down, stabbed. Fight back! Fangs and claws out, Bayl forced the last of the enemy Past the Veil, but he was so full he couldn't fly. He couldn't even get off the ground. Crawling laboriously under some brush to hide, he fell unconscious.

~~~~~~~~~~

Much later, Bayl woke to discover the village smoldered in shambles, countless corpses littering the ground. Crawling o'er them he recognized many of the People, but many more were of the enemy. He and the rest of the Wings had blooded them in the kill. His large black eyes saw much butchery, much senseless slaughter, men, women, children, the enemy, some Wings, many Night Beasts. He lived yet, but the pain was so great 'twas certain his injuries were severe. No living thing was about as he searched for his Handler. Was Kyrag amongst the dead? Was his mate? Collapsing under some rubble, he fell unconscious once again. When next he woke, his mind was numb with the enveloping pain. He dragged himself o'er the carnage through the remains of the village, sniffing and seeking 'til he finally found that which he sought. His only chance of survival. The scent of his Handler.

A FEW DAWNS LATER
~~~~~ELSEWHERE IN THE RAZOR'S EDGE~~~~~

Gheryh spoke hastily with Ryygg. By now all the People knew she was actually speaking with the Kahyah in their special language, and 'twas an intelligent exchange taking place 'tween them. The Night Beasts apparently understood the Danah speaking in their own language, the results of which even the most skeptical had to admit were uncanny. The others sprawled on the ground and waited breathlessly, for 'twas the first rest they'd had in several days, pushing hard and fast in their retreat to safety.
~~~~~~~~~~

They'd acquiesced to the young woman's right of leadership for they knew not if the elder Danoh yet lived.

In the thirteen winters since Gheryh and Ryygg successfully returned with Gabriel, the People had stepped up their watch for others. 'Twas no doubt they'd come eventually, and they knew why. 'Twas the boy. But no one would have changed the past, nor did anyone regret accepting such responsibility even now. He was the True King of the prophesy and 'twas their solemn duty to Kadoor and the Dragon Clan, to keep him safe to accept their role in the fight against evil. The boy-to-be-King had lived and learned among them, growing into manhood, becoming a much loved and respected friend, a highly effective Hunter, even establishing himself as a Handler with his own Kahyah partner, Traddya. 'Til recently life had been fairly normal. But just a few dawns prior, and with very short advance warning provided by Kyrag's Night Wing and a besieged hunting party who died while covering the retreat, the village was brutally attacked, catapulting them into the war. If not for vigilance, none would have lived to tell the tale, and Gabriel would have been lost. As 'twas, the survivors scattered to previously selected places of hiding deep in the mountains to await word of their next move, and to make contact with the other villages, if possible.

Gheryh and her party had taken Gabriel. Traveling to King's Gate to pick up Larken, Artemis, and Matana, they'd practically run into the threesome as they were making their way home. To Gheryh's dismay however, 'twas not Artemis, but Aalanna who accompanied her tribe kin, and after hearing their experiences she wanted retribution and was hard pressed to divert toward her next destination. Kyrag convinced her 'twas wise to leave Artemis in the Warrior's care and head straight to Drekinn. Gabriel was surprised by their appearance, but Larken and Matana caught him alone and explained that Aalanna knew not yet his true identity and should remain ignorant for the time being. Their reunion was quietly joyous but brief.

Gheryh sent most of the survivors to another village with an escort, taking only Aalanna, Larken, Matana, a handful of Daggogh Hunters (including Gabriel) and the full hunting party from the Gordatch. Her mission was to make contact with the Clan. If all went well, they'd return with a new ally. She never dreamed 'twould happen in her span of days. The end of their presence at Evanntyr. Their entry into the Black War. And for her to be Danah? 'Twas truth she'd already accepted the Prima in a ceremony in her adopted village when she took her mate, Kyrag of the Gordatch, the People of the Raptor's Talons, in line for Danoh himself. 'Twas actually an incredible coincidence that they, along with a hefty Gordatch party of Hunters and their Wings, were here now, as they usually split their time 'tween the two mountain ranges, traveling from village to village, insuring all was well. Her position as Liaison had long past been handed down to another, when her personal duties mounted. She'd missed the journeys and the news from her friends, but she'd grown and become familiar with a much larger purpose. Nevertheless, a recent dream followed by an intense sensation she was needed at home, had them rushing back to the Edge. After arriving barely a fortnight prior, they'd begun to find evidence to suggest there was a spy amongst them. But she wasn't in a mood, nor did she have the time to think about such betrayal now. Although confirmation would be heartbreaking, she'd begun to feel the need to take Gabriel to the Clan anyway. O'er the past few winters, each trip was laced with increasing news of the return of the Black, the evil happenings, and then the most recent occurrence, the Battle for the Dragon Clan and the uncertainty of their survival.

Gheryh felt the sequence of these events was not a accident. Her village was targeted right after the Clan. The taking of the True King had been their objective. The People were in full, yet thus far successful retreat, with everyone fatigued as well as most of them injured. Food was as much a priority as shelter, and they had to keep in mind the possibility of a traitor still amid the survivors, as well as the potential of another attack. Ryygg disappeared into the trees to reconnoiter and hunt. He never failed to bring back something they could share for sustenance. Traddya threw him a look that said to be careful and that the young man would be safe in her care. No one would touch him, unless they were both dead. Bayl hopped his huge bat-like body 'cross the span of leaf litter and using his clawed wings along with his front and hind legs, climbed painfully up onto the back of the Kahyah, where he stretched out to sleep. Traddya sighed and rolled her eyes but didn't protest further, despite her own injuries. After being severely wounded wreaking much havoc on the Dragons and killing many of the ground enemy in a most ghastly manner, Bayl drank so much blood that night that he'd still been in a stupor just the previous dawn, when he'd finally crawled up to the Hunters from out of some underbrush, bringing a cry of relief to Kyrag who'd thought he'd lost him along with the others. His hide and wings were severely damaged, and 'twould take a few moons to heal enough for him to be able to fly again, even for short distances.

In the meantime, Night Wings were not very graceful on land. They were also not sentient and communication was difficult, although Traddya and Ryygg were managing fairly well. Bayl's needs were little. Sleep, warmth, and more sleep. Since they'd found him, or he'd found them, his preferred sleeping position was on Traddya's back, her thick fur providing a warm and comfortable perch, and was easier for him to maintain his grasp as they'd made haste. His nutritional needs were more than met for some time to come. Night Wings lived mostly on blood, which allowed them to share the kills without competition with their Handlers, and to fly with the lighter weight carcass. They'd also eat raw red meat, although they preferred the entrails, vital organs, even the cartilaginous parts such as the esophagus (hence derived their killing strategies), and fruits and berries of all kinds. They sometimes snacked on insects and loved the giant

Rochas, which presented a dilemma since the People considered them a delicacy. However, if any were around, Kyrag would more than gladly give his share to his partner in utter gratitude for helping them escape.

A dozen other Wings survived, but half of them were sent out to hunt the day prior and one hadn't been seen since. However, they were hoping he'd simply been distracted and would find them again. Gheryh was more concerned about the rest of the Night Beasts. Their numbers were uncertain, but Ryygg was confident he'd make contact soon. Their plan would have been implemented, if such as this occurred, and within a few dawns of such an emergency retreat, he should find them in the caverns behind the falls of Big Bear Canyon, waiting for orders. He feared they'd lost countless of their Kind. During the fighting he'd watched many being taken down with poison spiked bolo nets. These would've caused no damage if they'd been quite still, for the Night Beasts were covered with a dense coat of fur and a long mane. But as they laid waiting for help, the enemy simply skewered them on the ground. As they struggled to release themselves from the nets, the spikes found a vulnerable area upon their lower legs, pads, or faces, resulting in an agonizing death. Unable to defend themselves, they were also unable to take their killers with them. 'Twas a tragic end, and he was more than angry. They'd remained hidden from the outside world for multiple lifespans, and 'til now even the Dragons hadn't penetrated their screen of secrecy. By all reasoning they'd been betrayed from within, for how did the enemy know their exact location, let alone their weaknesses? He wanted revenge.

Chapter Eighteen

Trouble in Triple

<div align="center">~~~~~THE RUINS OF DREKINN~~~~~</div>

The feisty new Battle Commander had proven harder to kill than they'd imagined. The shortest Warrior of the Brotherhood, she was now on the Hoard's most desired list. Darque Aalanna Grifynn led her Warriors to victory in the Battle for the Dragon Clan, but even though they'd launched and carried out an incredibly strong and unexpected defense, they'd suffered heavy losses. Darque was a strategist like her father, and she held no delusions. 'Twas just as much to do with the Black abandoning his forces early in the battle, leading to his forces abandoning their efforts prior to completion, than 'twas to any of their battle tactics. Nevertheless, the Hoard suffered far more casualties than they'd anticipated and after several marks of some of the most brutal fighting in history, their survivors simply retreated with the Brotherhood hot on their heels. 'Twas reported to the Evil One that they'd decimated their enemy. Surely the Clan would die out through attrition, their numbers so few they'd not last through the upcoming winter, with only the old and infirmed left, the bloodlines broken. Now 'twas up to Darque to prove them wrong.

Fresh off the battle, her leathers still wet with blood, the survival of their Races upon her young shoulders, she and her sisters learned the truth of their past and their present. They were not human. Shayla revealed that the daughters of Aalanna Grifynn were Human/Dragon hybrids. This answered so many questions she'd had through her span of days, however a flood of new ones quickly followed. She wanted answers but 'twould have to wait. Darque's task was to fulfill her prophesy. She was supposed to 'take up the Sword and lead the Races to a New Beginning.' She wasn't certain how to interpret such. 'Twould be suicide to simply go out there alone, Sword in hand.

Afore the sun set the day of the battle, Darque ordered everyone to the extensive cave system that riddled the land under the Den and the village. The only way out for the humans was by flight, or through the Spell door in the dungeon, walking skin to skin with their Dragon 'Bonds, Darque, or one of her sisters. Given these limitations, many were left underground most of the time. She was satisfied with that, for 'twas quicker to get everyone undercover should the Hoard return. The only Warriors or Clansmen out now, were on search and rescue. A few were found alive on the battleground immediately after, and these were saved by the combined efforts of the Ancients, Darque's emerging powers, and Shayla's 'secret' red Blood Crystal salve. She hoped 'twould be a different story once they uncovered the lower levels of the port. Most of the excavation was going through the caves instead of from the surface, as 'twas safer. Thus far, they'd made slow but steady progress in all directions.

'Twas plenty of room in the caves, but how to farm and raise the herd beasts necessary to produce what they required, without being seen from the Plains or the skies above? The people could live underground but the animals couldn't, and not all crops would lend themselves to the hydroponics system Regynn started, already in place and beginning to sprout. She recalled how, within a few dawns after the battle, Regynn dragged her eagerly down into the belly of the Den to demonstrate his plans. Without using the Magic of his 'Bond, Sydrayyah, which would have been as a beacon to the Hoard, he managed to bring the sunlight into the darkness using an ancient technique he discovered in the library that involved a series of strategically placed mirrors, or highly polished shields, which bounced the light of the sun deep into the shadows. After receiving the Commander's approval, he'd set up the system, and although the light wasn't as above ground, 'twas sufficient to begin growing a variety of greens in long rows of tiered, waterproofed containers, floor to ceiling. Darque gave him free rein to build whatever he required, although 'twas limited by the distance from the initial source of the light. Since they'd not been able to get a crop growing above ground, he'd immediately begun building the systems in every opening, using every available space along every wall, every smaller cave, with dozens of salvaged shields. Still, 'twould be a small offering, but the greens were an important source of nutrition and even this small offering would be welcome.

~~~~~~~~~~

Darque's immediate problems were triple fold and she considered her priorities. Protect the Clan after the battle, change their strategies to fight the Hoard while vastly outnumbered, and keep the Crown occupied so Shytin didn't declare open war against them afore she was prepared to take on his forces, now aligned with the Black. Traditionally the Clan fought straight forward, stand your ground and/or rush the enemy, tactics which would be ineffective given their current circumstances. The Evil One had survived and evil fed on evil. They had no goal other than destruction and perversion, and their lack of trust for each other, along with their inability to collaborate, had previously made any battle strategies futile. Yet in the last few winters they'd changed their tactics and grown at a staggering pace. She believed the Hoard was now motivated and becoming ever more effective by Koryl through Shytin, and the prophesy of the return of the True King required that he be located in order to regain his throne, or at the very least show he yet lived, giving all Kadoor hope that they could defeat the Hoard. 'Twas daunting to say the least, but instead of feeling buried, she dug in and tightened her grip. Stubborn and high spirited, she was a solitary force with which to be reckoned and would not give up 'til she'd 'crossed the Veil, Sword in hand, dragging many with her. But although she was prepared, and could and did make the toughest decisions, it didn't mean she liked them. She was still a young woman who'd
~~~~~~~~~~

just seen eighteen winters, and despite the fact that the 'Bond slowed their aging process a hundred-fold, holding others' lives in her hands was not a responsibility she took lightly.

~~~~~~~~~~

Surveying their progress from atop the battlements, their first need had been defense of the survivors. Since they were sorely outnumbered, that protection depended on the Spell Shield o'er all of Drekinn, including the Den, the village, and the Port District, as well as some of the surrounding farmland. As had become her habit, slowly, respectfully, she acknowledged each of the six Free Dragons who'd volunteered for the duty, sitting alone, heads bowed, eyes closed. At equidistance apart, essentially in stasis to preserve their strength, in Communication only with each other, they Held the Shield o'er all the land. 'Twas an extreme duty, and no one knew how long they'd have to Hold. The Highlands hadn't even hesitated. Day after day, for moons on end, even into many winters, they'd live off the Spell they'd created and off each other in a continuous loop of power that none of them would survive once broken. They'd fight to the bitter end, but when the time came for the Spell to be dissolved 'twould be to the relief of the Six, as they'd become known, for 'twould allow them to reach their final sleep at last. Each had been grateful for the chance to make one final contribution afore they joined their already fallen lifemates Beyond. With so many dead, 'twould be a small risk that they had a potential 'Bond partner still this side of the Veil now, so none felt any regret or loss of that opportunity. For all intents and purposes, they'd Passed the Veil upon the day they'd set forth the Spell. They'd given up their names, their lives, their futures, even conscious thought, for her, the Clan, the Highlands, and all Kadoor. 'Twas their only chance to further the prophesy and defeat the Evil One, once and for all.

'And there will be a girl child born'. The words kept echoing through her mind, she couldn't sleep under the weight of such responsibility. There'd been nowhere to go, no safe refuge for
~~~~~~~~~~

so many, and so few. There were too many variables, too many unknowns, and no one to trust. They'd had to entrench, there'd been no alternative.

Darque clenched her jaw and hardened her gaze as unbidden, a single tear rolled down her cheek. 'Twas the cusp 'tween summer and fall, and the blazing sun burned o'er head, but she hardly noticed. The Six couldn't feel it; they'd never again feel the sun or the rain or the wind, or touch. In a dream-like state they had each other, intermittent at best, hazy, obscure and indistinct, preventing total isolation. 'Twas small comfort. They might as well be carved from stone.

The power emitted 'tween them crossed o'er the land visible only to those living beneath, the golden threads of shimmering energy pulsating as if alive. Gazing upwards, she likened it to a six pointed star of fortification stretched o'er all of Drekinn. A normal Shield was just an illusion that hid one's Magic and physical being, but wouldn't hold up to touch, dissolving like a soap bubble if stumbled upon. For her plan to succeed, they needed something stronger than that, something that would last far longer. Marauders must be kept out, as well as those who might try to come to their assist, let alone the possibility of the return of the Hoard to complete their mission. She wanted them to appear as they did right after the battle to discourage such efforts.

The first test of the Shield came within moments of its inception. Snaking forth from each of the Six, the glittering ribbons of energy surged upwards, reaching for each other and connecting o'er head with a sharp crack like a bolt of thunderous lightning. 'Twas a heated flash of blinding radiance, and then a shimmering umbrella fanned out, enveloping all of Drekinn and burying itself into the very soil, creating a dome of protection which was immediately followed by nothing. All that could be seen now, was the thin flickering lines of energy dancing o'er head. Was it even working?

'Twas then that the rogue Dragon came out of the east, obviously intent upon his destination, as Darque watched him approach. She didn't really know what to expect. What would he feel? See? The Shield should cause any creature great difficulty, forcing upon them an increasing sense of impending doom the closer they came, along with the visual perception of total destruction. The people of Kadoor were superstitious for the most part, and 'twas hoped 'twould become widespread that Drekinn was haunted with the spirits of so many who'd perished in the battle. That, and the difficulty actually penetrating the Shield, which would feel something akin to pushing against a thick walled bubble, draining any Magic one had (theoretically strengthening the Shield, while the conversion of too many, theoretically, would have the Shield breaking down on the surplus), while also causing much pain. However, if any 'tested' the Magic, the Shield's existence would be spread far and wide, leading to a large invasion force that would be its destruction. In other words, in regards to her position of Command, if anything ignored the 'warnings' and actually touched the Shield, it had to die, and that meant a fight. Magic, she frowned. Such a force to be reckoned with and yet so many issues. She was still getting used to how it all worked. 'Twas obvious the more she learned the less she knew, and she'd never understand it all. Nor did she want to, 'twas not worth the effort. Not for the first time, she had no regrets she'd not been blessed with more of the potent energy than that with which she already dealt.

What to do with the rogue? She didn't want to lose any more fighters, yet she had to trust in their skill. Of course, all of them were battle survivors and that meant they were all recovering from injuries of one kind or another, even if in 'Bond. They were hurting, and physically and emotionally exhausted. But they were hers to Command. Hers to order to their deaths to protect the Clan. She had limited resources, but more deaths were inevitable. "Abba, how did you do it? Winter after winter, battle after battle, knowing those you sent out might not return? Upon what do I base such a choice? And while I'm asking, the entire world is hoping I have what it takes to replace you. Whatever made you think I did?" Darque calculated her options, as she continued her musings. "I have no doubt that you faced much worse in the beginning, and you taught me everything you knew. Surely I can do as well." She could watch the rogue come in, see what happened. No other Dragons around. Then kill him if necessary. If not, his report by word of mouth might actually help them by scaring off others. Or, 'twould create a challenge to others to try to complete the salvage effort this one abandoned. Kill him? Let him go? Flame it all. Being able to see multiple choices was not always a good way to make up one's mind! She turned abruptly and hardened her heart once again. "By the Flame and the One True Liege, I do have what it takes and I will fulfill the prophesy!" Gunnarr lowered his chin and gazed into her eyes, his approval evident as she questioned him. "Do we have a true rogue, or a spy sent to reconnoiter?"

"I doubt this one is with the Hoard, Flame Spitter. He seems intent upon salvaging from the wreckage. He has no injuries to suggest he was in the battle, and his strongest emotion appears to be... curiosity."

As it turned out, the rogue didn't get close enough to touch the Shield and was easily repelled by the Push, as were a small group of looters the following dawn, afore they'd journeyed half way 'cross the Plains of Drekinn. 'Twas most encouraging. In the days following, her recognizance Teams reported that Drekinn was becoming much feared as if haunted.

Again, she returned her thoughts to the Shield. The Highlands had gone deep into their Memories, and although there were limits to even the greatest of the Greater Brews, they'd devised a much larger, stronger, more malleable Shield that would stand up to touch, would allow in the weather, birds, and insect life needed for crop pollination, would disguise those working outside if not too many at a time, and encourage the image of destruction as a painting never changing. New plant growth would be normal so they could try to grow crops. The Mariners were reporting ghostly images within the ruins which seemed related to having too many people working outside at once, and safety measures were implemented to avoid that reoccurrence. None attempted to clear the path of ruin which blocked the inlet of Port O'Drekinn, believing there was nothing left to even scavenge. Their own scents were Masked, but the Spell could not completely Mask the scent of other things that should not be in the given scenario, such as tanning leathers, nor could it disguise major changes to the landscape, such as reconstruction, as 'twould tax their powers too much, forcing the collapse of the Spell.

Darque would rather their focus be upon keeping the outside world out, therefore everyone spent most of their time underground. 'Bonded Teams could come and go carefully, as it took Magic to get through the Shield, similar to walking through the Spell door of the dungeon. In order to avoid anyone seeing the Allure of this process, she'd posted a division of Free Dragons as Sentries upon the other side at all times. No one came or went without their knowledge and authorization. When they did leave, 'twas to and from the Lair, to reconnoiter and to hunt, bringing back as much as possible with each foray. Most of the LifeBond Teams were doing recognizance and hunting outside, while most of the Frees were working on salvage and rescue inside. There'd been a few skirmishes with rogues who'd ignored the Push, and these were quickly and efficiently forced Past the Veil. Nothing flashy, avoiding Magic, simply get in and be done. 'Twas much easier and quicker when you had the advantage of numbers upon your own side for once. She'd like to avoid killing rogues when times changed, as she'd try to recruit them to the Resistance, but there was no opportunity for that now. One never knew which side they'd stand, and she didn't have the time or resources to ensure their loyalties.

Darque had allowed the building of adequate structures for penning herd beasts and chickens and other food animals, as they required the outdoors. The War Dogs had been returned to the Kennels in the Den, as had the War Horses to their stables. Their activity in the open was well supervised, although most of them were being moved to the Lair where they could be outside under cover of the heavy forest nearby, their riders with them. Warriors were out in shifts, never all at the same time, and the en masse katas of old were now held underground. The Battle Drums and Pipes could only just be heard from above, although they reverberated throughout the caves. This activity was actually helpful, as the Cave of Voices was familiar to the mariners and 'twas being said the Voices were louder and more ominous now, creating another reason to avoid them. The Den itself was relatively safe, but the only secure entrance or exit was through the Spell door. Fryya's duty was walking necessary personnel through that door. Storrm's primary duty was endlessly watching the skies. If she saw anything incoming she'd raise the Alert and all would race to shelter. Thus far none of the Hoard had returned, but Darque remained cautious.

So many were lost in the battle but immediately following, the surviving Warriors lined up to volunteer for the next 'Bond. Since they'd seen the advantage of First Flight and the new Stable in the battle, they were eager to join the Teams. Sadly, the Free Dragons had also been decimated and she wasn't all that certain there'd ever be another 'Bond. Somehow, she had to turn this around. Come what may, she was the key to their survival. This was her prophesy, such was her destiny. If only she knew the answers, if only she could See the future. 'Twas no room for error. She shook her head and gazed off into space.

Examining the Hoard's strategies, if any, she and Gunnarr were certain that Kaahayyel was tenaciously inundated as the only orchestrated attack against a single target in the entire battle. Darque was now certain that the Hoard's next target was Maahayyel. She and Gunnarr had determined the 7th Egg, containing his youngest sibling, the 7th Prince of a 7th Prince, was yet unhatched, but he wasn't where he'd once been. Apparently the Water Dragons, who'd supposedly been protecting their guest since just prior to the Last Holocaust, had actually handed the Egg o'er to the Sprite Nation, whom they considered their guardians and saviors as they were near destroyed during that time themselves and 'twas the Sprites who'd saved them. In truth, they'd saved each other, but 'twas history she'd just learned and didn't have time to think about now. The important part was that Bryynn's Egg was missing, although the Sprites had yet to acknowledge such. Gunnarr felt 'twas about the time of the first LifeBond, when their connection was suddenly and mysteriously severed. He'd asked many times for confirmation of Bryynn's safety, but the Sprites remained tight lipped, and silent was the Island of Dreams. For the Highlands, the search was on. Bryynn's Magic would be formidable once he grew out of adolescence and therefore, 'twas one of the Hoard's prime objectives to prevent his hatching. They'd managed to kill the Ancient, leaving only her younger sister with the strength to continue orchestrating the Brew for the 'Bond. 'Twas thought that without Maahayyel there'd be no more 'Bonds as well as no more Matriarchs. Bryynn would be able to Brew the Magic once he reached age, but 'twas doubtful the rest of the Ancients had enough strength for such powerful Greater Magic alone. Losing Kaahayyel in the battle was demoralizing to the Highlands, as 'twas to the Clan. Losing the Matriarch afore she could pass her power might very well bespeak the death of life, their ultimate extinction.

Darque couldn't believe 'twould be the end of them, though. There had to be another to take her place. The Highlands were a matriarchal society, meaning the lineage passed through the females, and they mated for life. Kaahayyel had been Matriarch, but when the Black killed her mate shortly afore the Last Holocaust she'd abdicated the rule to her younger sister. The youngest sibling was Maakayyel, who was male and therefore ineligible for the Rule. But Maahayyel had no female offspring, only the 7

Princes, Gunnarr being the eldest. During the battle they'd lost not only Kaahayyel but three of her five children along with their Warrior 'Bonds, including her sons Zayddarr and Krynnarr and her daughter, Shraadarr. There was another daughter, the elder of the two, Synahmarr, who actually was first in line for the succession but was long missing, and one last son, Fyndarr, in 'Bond with Tyndall from First Flight. They had to find Bryynn, they had to find a solution, and they had to try for the Third LifeBond. Add those tasks to finding the True King, and her 'need to do now' list was ever lengthening. She added another, the recruitment of as many Warriors as possible for the next 'Bond. She smiled grimly. There was no current lack of volunteers.

In the hallway outside her office were the lists of those still MIA. Running her finger from name to name and mouthing each somberly, she recalled two more, although they'd not seen the battle itself. The Brotherhood's most legendary and successful Stealth Team, Graasyn and Bastyen. The father and son Warriors had not been seen since they'd left on their assignment to Kaddart to investigate the death of Tannyr and Daayn's little brother, Tonn. 'Twas a fortnight afore the first LifeBond, o'er a winter past, and there'd been no communication from them since. Their War Horses never returned and there'd been no trace of them when she and Gunnarr arrived on their rescue mission of Fryya, amidst the Flames of Kaddart's destruction. None surpassed their skills; they were the best Whisperer's of the Veil of all time. She'd seen them force a man Past in a crowded room with no one the wiser. She needed their skills now. Where were they? What happened to them?

All the Warriors now had either a Striker or a Biter, weapons made from salvaged talons and fangs, although they just had enough. Fangs, talons, and teeth would survive the Passing only if not damaged, otherwise they'd turn to ash along with the rest of the carcass. They also had Thumpers, scale covered shields resistant to Flame. However, scales were even less likely to survive after death and were also in high demand. Since the remains of Magic bearers were camouflaged to humans, Gunnarr Brewed a Spell allowing all the non-'Bonded to perceive the reality on the battlegrounds. Even though they were a War Clan, 'twas still a shock to most, but 'twas necessary not only for salvage efforts, but also for identification. The only uplifting thing about the ability to see was the fact that there were far more of the Hoard laid out, than of the Resistance. But even that had taken several dawns to confirm, as no one could tell initially who'd fought for whom. There were so many bodies, so much blood spread o'er so much ground, 'twas beyond belief.

The salvage crews gathered everything that could be used, stacking the remains and firing them all together. The mass funeral pyres were no problem under the Shield, as they simply suggested the village was still burning in ruins. They'd been greatly saddened in that they could not better honor those who'd died fighting for the Resistance, however 'twas a monumental task and being the end of summer, clean up had to happen as quickly as possible. Those Free Dragons they could positively identify were taken back to Fire Heart, but 'home' was Drekinn for Kaahayyel and the others in 'Bond.

She shook her head and returned to her study. As Commander, she was painfully aware of the lack of telepathy 'tween the Free Warriors and Dragons, which she saw as a major obstacle to their fighting strategy. Without this communication, those with no access to the Link were at a distinct disadvantage. Since they couldn't place more in 'Bond for some time to come, they had to increase their ability to communicate. This she hoped they'd accomplish by a method suggested from the Archives. Hand signals had always been used by the Brotherhood, mostly by those in the Stealth profession, however 'twas not a complete language and didn't provide entirely satisfactory results. Just prior to the battle, Regynn had stumbled upon a silent hand language used by some throughout Kadoor prior to the Last Holocaust, which

Darque had been studying. Seeing the potential, she brought in Daayn and Kashiyann from Second Stable, along with Tyndall and Fyndarr from First Flight, to work on the signs, taking the task off the hands of Regynn, who's main concerns were in research.

Daayn grit his teeth thinking about the loss of his elder brother, Tannyr. "I agree, Commander. The lack of communication 'tween the Frees, along with the sluggish Link 'tween us and the Frees, hindered our fighting, and we lost more than we should have." He was adept at silent attack techniques. Not a frontal offensive fan, he'd been set to enter the Stealth program prior to volunteering for the 'Bond. Long an orphan, he'd lost his youngest brother Tonn afore they'd joined with the Highlands, and then Tannyr. He could never repay his brother for saving him in the ceremony when Kaahayyel had weakened. If Tannyr and the Ancient had not 'Bonded, he and Kashiyann would have perished together in the Magical fire. Tannyr saved them, but lost his life in the battle soon after. Daayn was all that was left of his bloodline.

Tyndall agreed with his summation. "'Twas frustrating not to be able to help direct and warn the others. With this type of language, our attacks could have been better coordinated." Her enthusiasm came from having been a teaching candidate aspiring in archeology and history afore entering the Brotherhood. Such a find represented treasure in her thinking. Her 'Bond, Fyndarr, was still in mourning from losing his mother and three of his five siblings. Darque handed her the ancient documents and skimming through them, her excitement grew. "Yes, I think this is the answer, but not just for the Frees. The Hoard would be oblivious. We can use this to avoid the Link so they can't eavesdrop. 'Twould save their strength and be of great value when in hiding. Their hearing is so acute 'tis impossible to even whisper without them knowing." They were all aware of the mechanics of Magic, requiring strength and health or 'twould weaken. They all wanted their Dragons to be in top shape if attacked and would rather not use up their strength on anything not absolutely necessary, the Link included.

Darque was thrilled with their reactions. "The task is yours. As you know, the Dragons have extreme dexterity, however there may be some signs they can't mimic. Arrange the language appropriately, incorporate the Stealth signals, then teach every Clansman and Dragon. I don't think I need mention this will not be shared outside our own. Use whatever resources you require."

Nodding their heads and stating simultaneously, "'Twill be done," they took their leave.

~~~~~~~~~~

Leaning forward at her desk, Darque watched as Regynn stepped through the door, jostling shoulders with the two exiting Warriors in his inattention. Slapping him on the back good naturedly, they were familiar enough with the Elder Warrior to know 'twas his standard, and was quickly forgiven. His long hair unkempt, a quill pen stuck behind one ear, he obviously hadn't shaved in days. Carrying several old scrolls under each arm, he also had three paperweights in one hand, and a mug of pale yellow liquid in the other. Darque wrinkled her nose as the faint odor permeated the office. "How can you stomach that yak piss you make? And when did you build a new still?"

Immediately realizing she hadn't meant that description literally, he continued with a wink. "I don't particularly care for liquor made from yak piss, although I've tasted it. 'Tis Vydna. And I never lost the old one. 'Tis in the library, and thank the One, sustained no damage during the battle. I hope to begin restocking soon as 'tis rather depleted at the moment. As you know, 'twas considered quite useful to the Healer afterwards. My recipe, along with my still, creates a rather high alcohol content."

"'Tis a wonder it doesn't create a hole in your gut."

Darque had tasked him with, among other things, the discovery of who'd once lived at the Keep so close to their new Lair. She didn't want to uncover a security issue now. She'd not had time
~~~~~~~~~~

to do the research herself and Gunnarr had only a vague recollection, but what little he'd known, peaked her curiosity. She recalled their conversation with amusement. "Why didn't you tell me you knew who'd lived there?" To which he'd responded with a look of complete innocence, "You never asked." She still wondered how she was supposed to ask anything if she didn't know what to ask. However, she was convinced the inhabitants could be a boon for the Resistance, if any yet lived.

Regynn enthusiastically dropped everything on the desk at once, cleared a space in the middle and unrolled one of the scrolls in front of her, laying a weight on each corner and his mug on the last, afore pointing to the center of the faded map. "I've found drawings of a peninsula, or large island close to a greater land mass, somewhere in the Ocean of Fears that literally seemed to disappear beneath the waves o'er night. But 'twas long afore the Last Holocaust." Picking up one of the other scrolls and unrolling it a bit, he gave the impression he was trying to read something.

After an elongated silence, Darque asked impatiently, "And?"

Shaking his head as if he'd just awakened from a dream, he replied, "'Twas referenced by a name I've been unable to translate, as of yet. I'm still working to decipher these documents." He waved his hand o'er the rest of the scrolls on her desk. "However, by every indication I believe 'twas the legendary Rienne."

"Rienne? Fascinating. So why are you telling me this, what has it to do with the Keep?"

Darque grimaced as he took several strong pulls of the Vydna, after which he wiped his mouth with his hand and grinned impishly at her reaction afore he responded. "One of the ancient scrolls suggests the survivors of Rienne took up residence in the Keep. I can find no solid evidence, just legends and myths thus far, but I'll keep looking. If truth, you think they yet live?"

"If they do, we must find them. Gunnarr believes the Rashei lived at the Keep. If the people of Rienne and the Rashei are one and the same, we need them on our side. 'Twould give the Resistance a distinct advantage."

Regynn nodded, gathered his things and took his leave, lifting the now empty mug to her in acknowledgement, afore returning to the vast archives once again.

<div align="center">~~~~~THE NEXT MORNING~~~~~</div>

Darque had spoken to her Warriors afore morning katas two marks prior, the sun yet to dawn. She had to get them all on board with the coming changes or they'd be defeated afore they began to fight back. She leaned against the desk and recalled her words. "Warriors never surrender. As long as our hearts beat, as long as we draw breath, we fight. But these are times of war and we are greatly outnumbered; more so than we've ever been in the entire history of the Brotherhood. To stand and fight openly as we've always done, is to stand and die, leaving all Kadoor at the mercy of the Evil One. The mission of the Dragon Clan is to preserve and defend, but we must live in order to fulfill that mission." She'd cast her gaze to every face present, all waiting for her to provide a solution to such a predicament. She'd taken a deep breath. "Today we learn 'strategic retreat'. Today you will learn the subtleties of deception. Today, we all become Stealth operatives." Standing her fully unimpressive height, their response made it clear her words had the effect for which she'd hoped. The Brotherhood would have to become more flexible or they'd not survive, and apparently, they wanted to survive. She'd addressed her first two issues, keeping them alive and altering their fighting strategies. Of her top three, that left only preventing Shytin from declaring war afore they were prepared. She'd have to give that one some serious thought.

<div align="center">~~~~~~~~~~</div>

Gunnarr and Mystynn had been away less than two dawns and Darque had yet to sleep. A fortnight after the battle, the six Highland Princes escorted the Ancients, including their Matriarch, back to their homeland to participate in a ceremony to accept their rightful ranks. He'd warned her about the possibility of problems with Sharing through their Link. The load upon her shoulders was heavy and she'd been working non-stop for too long. Needing to be alone for a bit, she'd hidden in her office. When the pain hit her so unexpectedly, she practically fell off her chair. Grabbing her chest, she grit her teeth to avoid crying out. She'd only just gotten back her breath when another slashing pain hit her hard. Eyes watering, sliding to the floor on her hands and knees, she fought to avoid going into the Lust. *"Gunnarr? By the Ancients! Are you injured? Can you not defend yourself?"*

She Felt his frustration. Apparently he'd unsuccessfully tried to Block this from her. In obvious misery he Stated, *"'Twill be fine, my love. I warned you afore I left. 'Tis the Ranking. I'm not being attacked, all is as it should be. I welcome this."*

"You're being stabbed and all is as it should be? Why aren't you Healing yourself? Wait. The Ranking? 'Twould seem you didn't bother to share a few of the details, most particularly the process."

His usual humor and teasing were absent, his Response curt. *"You must withdraw, I've failed my Block. I was thinking about you to focus away from the pain. I wish not to be an embarrassment."*

"Don't be ridiculous, I wouldn't withdraw even if I could. How can I help?"

After a moment of indecision, Gunnarr Spoke again. *"Distract me. 'Twill be o'er soon. A few marks, then I will return, enfold you in my wings, caress your sweet body, make love to you."*

"Vit'Tayach, I love you more with each passing day. My sweet, Share the pounding of my heart, it beats faster just thinking about you. Your scent, so warm and masculine, the smoky look in your eyes when you gaze at me with desire, the way you touch me... your tongue..."

"My tongue wishes to lick your entire body, and will do so as soon as I return." Success! He was himself again, tough, brazen, sexy. His confidence resounded in his voice as he Responded.

Darque Felt the pain again and was desperate to redirect his thoughts. 'Twas as if his chest was being used as a carving board. Teasing about making love had helped, but he needed more to endure such. 'Twas excruciating. She pushed her chair away from the desk and leaned back, lifting her legs to the desktop and spreading her knees apart. Opening her mind to her lover so far away, she relaxed and Shared her emotions, her sensations, her body's reaction to the fantasy she spun for him. His own emotions intensifying, she knew her diversion was doing exactly what she intended. His pain perception was now shrouded by his blatant sexual response. She could Feel his groan, his heart rate and breathing increasing proportionately as she caressed her muscled thighs, then upward 'cross her hips, afore slipping her middle finger under her waistband, teasing, sliding edge to edge, her palm against the warm skin of her flat belly. With both hands she loosened the ties and pushed her pants roughly down her hips a little at a time, first one side then the other, as her lover's attention became riveted to her movements. Slowly, sensually, one hand strayed further down into her pants as she spread her thighs wider, lifting her hips, the moisture already glistening, her body prepared and anxiously awaiting the coming invasion. She thought about Gunnarr touching her, his tongue warm and wet. With her free hand she reached up under the apron of her leather top, stroking her hot skin, working her way up her ribs toward her now aching breasts. Cupping them firmly, she gave careful attention to first one then the other, rubbing and squeezing as her own heart raced, a soft moan escaping her lush lips. As they parted, her eyes closed and she imagined Gunnarr's body o'er hers, felt his tongue tipping hers afore sliding downward to lave the junction 'tween her legs. She licked her dry lips as her fingers massaged the center of her desire. Spasms began to ripple through her body, gently at first, then in sync with the rhythm of her fingers, back and forth, in and out, faster, deeper, harder. She couldn't believe how wet she'd become, and she couldn't remain silent when Gunnarr Shared his passion. Feeling his rising fantasy orgasm, she exploded o'er the edge of ecstasy with a stifled scream. Finally catching her breath, she was shocked, and knowing he was in the presence of others, she Stammered, *"I meant only to distract you, I hope you didn't actually..."*

"Vit'Tayoch, I love you, my woman. You are always with me, in me, mine. You are more precious to me than anything else in all Kadoor, and I am astonished at the depth of what we Share. You most certainly succeeded in your efforts and I'll hold onto this memory for the duration. And don't worry yourself, 'twas all a fantasy here. You know my control. But 'twas a promise of more that I'll not hesitate to collect upon my return." His growl accentuated his pledge, and she Felt his desire rise again. This time he actively sought to distract her from his plight and she responded in kind, orgasm after orgasm, 'til exhaustion took her into sleep for the first time since the battle. Gunnarr was well pleased with himself. Through the LifeBond they Shared many enhancements, including a decreased need for sleep, food, and water, when not physically or emotionally strained. But eventually, all of them required these basic needs be fulfilled or 'twould come crashing down upon them with a vengeance. He'd been concerned about his lifemate, with so much pressure upon her shoulders feeling as though she wasn't meeting her own expectations, let alone everyone else's. After all, 'twas not every young woman who had to live up to prophesy that bespoke the salvation of their Races. Focusing on their love instead of his current reality, he smiled as the pain hit him again, this time as a wave crashing upon a distant shore.

CHAPTER NINETEEN

The Ranking of the Princes

'Twas good to have Gunnarr home again. His absence o'er the last sennight had taken its toll on Darque, her emotions running high anyway, trying to lead, manage, adjust, survive, without anyone being abandoned. She wasn't the only Warrior who'd suffered through the absence of their 'Bond, although hers was the only mated pair, but it couldn't be helped. Escorting the Ancients back to Flight of Fire and ensuring their safety, was as important as ensuring the safety of the survivors of the Clan, and therefore 'twas a necessary risk. The others had also managed to survive their separations and were elated to be back together again. She'd chosen to wait 'til morning to debrief them, as she needed to debrief Gunnarr now.

'Twas getting late and they'd just stepped into the office. Gunnarr turned to her and tried again. He growled something deep, low, and strongly accented in Dragon/Ancient Tongue that even Darque couldn't decipher. "I don't understand," she impatiently growled back, since the admission was difficult for the headstrong leader and she didn't want to waste time being annoyed about something he was trying to convey. He was different somehow, distant, troubled, almost shy in her presence, emotions he'd never displayed. His lagging composure centered on her approval or disapproval of what transpired during his absence, as if he was afraid she'd now find him lacking in some way. Still agitated from the separation, her temper only added to his confusion and she could Hear it in his thoughts: Would she still love him now?

His feelings scrambled and then he lifted his head and spread his great chest with the inhalation of an enormous breath. She hadn't expected to see anything, after all, she'd never seen...

catching sight of it, she began to shake. With trembling fingers she reached forward and gingerly touched the gash 'cross his left breast. 'Twas angry, red, newly created. She swallowed and then stood on her tiptoes to inspect the wound. 'Twas not just a random slash... 'twas several... a design... no, 'twas an insignia. Her memory flashed back to the first time she'd laid eyes on the Ancients standing in front of the Lodge, how she'd thought some of them had scars that appeared to be a'purpose, likening them to a military rank. "How..." she began as the sun dawned upon her, of what he must have endured in order to accept these cuts, holding off the Healing, allowing the disfigurement.

Her acceptance relieved him, his fears of losing her affection melted away. "My only regret was that you were not there to Rank me yourself. 'Twould have been your right as my mate, but even with the enhancements, your Human body would not have survived the heat, and there was no time to build a resistance. Maahayyel is ill."

Shaken further by this statement, with all the obvious implications of such, she replied quickly, "Ill? How ill? What do you mean?"

"Her Magic fails her. She is nearing her end of days. She thinks I know not. She thinks wrong. The Highlands may be led by the Matriarchs, but our military force is led by the Princes. With the Ranking, my Memories were opened and I am privy to much, even more than the Matriarch knows. I now hold the title of Gphlzxsyfzhtcht." And of course, Darque still couldn't understand, which made her squint in frustration afore Gunnarr spit forth, "'Tis similar to 'Battle Commander'."

Sensing his peevish attitude, she teased, "Battle Commander? Well, that's not going to be too confusing! We really can't both be known as Commander. If we have to use Common Tongue, and it appears that we do, then how about another title?"

He frowned while Darque tried not to smirk. "What do you suggest?"

"Ummm, well... give me a bit to think. In the meantime, what do we do to help your mother? And not to be callous, but will we be able to hold the 3rd LifeBond soon, or even, at all? How about General?"

"You really must slow down and stop jumping from idea to idea. You're making my head spin."

Now she was concerned. "I've never seen you in such distress afore, my love. 'Tis from the Ranking? Tell me about it, I wish to know all. I wish to have seen the ceremony with my own eyes."

Sighing, Gunnarr sat down and lovingly gathered his mate to his lap. "Then let me hold you while you close those beautiful eyes, little one, and Share with me, the Ranking of the Princes of Kadoor. Such has not occurred since long afore the Last Holocaust, during the time of the Great War when the Evil One gathered his minions and attacked the Counsel of the High Races. 'Twas a time of chaos in the world. Avyndarr, my father, was 'General' afore me, his brothers all older. But he was a 7th Prince, his Magic strong. In our society, birth order has little to do with Rank. 'Tis earned in battle. He took the Rank from his father, Solvyngarr, another 7th Prince, and held that Rank through the millennia, keeping the peace by strength. All was well 'til the Black made a pact with Humans and he led them like lambs to the slaughter with his lies. Avyndarr was the highest ranking officer to Pass the Veil, and he did so in the last great battle of the Last Holocaust. He Passed, but he injured the Black severely, sending him into hiding. In fact, he disappeared for so long, he was all but forgotten. I had not yet been Ranked, therefore, we entered a time without a 'Commander' to lead the Highlands. Given that there's been no true war since, my brothers and I were not able to earn our rightful Ranks. For many long winters throughout my youth I was displeased. For the first time in our history the Highlands had no high Command officers, because there was no war. 'Twas both good and bad. Most of the Races retreated just afore the Last Holocaust, leaving the Highlands alone to help Mankind survive. We split up with the ensuing peace and became reclusive. However, the Ancients knew the Evil One would return one day. But I digress, sweetness, let me take you back to the ceremony. Deep in the bowels of Fire Heart within the center of the Keep we stood, the Ancients surrounding us, Maahayyel wielding the ritual fang..." And Gunnarr proceeded to tell the tale, the agony as the Matriarch sliced through their flesh, the reciting of their Code, their Oath to defend, acceptance of their military duties, sleepless days and nights, each laceration opened again and again. Even without conscious effort the Healing tried to erase the wounds and in order to create the scars they'd packed each new cut with a paste created from the salt water of the Dragon's Tears mixed with the lava from the heart of the volcano. Forcing themselves to be still giving no outward display of pain, all six of the Princes received their Ranks during a period o'er six days, each a distinct and elaborate rune-like pattern, each pattern designed to be altered as they rose in Rank, Gunnarr's being the largest and most intricate. In Common, Gunnarr became Battle Commander, Mystynn, Second, Ragnyrr, Third, and then the little brothers each took something akin to a Captain's rank. The pride in his voice spoke volumes, the pain of a naturally healing mutilation of his chest still evident, although he acknowledged it not. A new era for the Highlands had begun.

He literally pouted. "I am dismayed the title could not be translated to Common with more accuracy. I feel that 'General' has less impact."

Slapping her hand o'er her mouth to stifle her laughter, she snorted afore replying. "Do you truly think anyone can look at you and not feel the impact? You need no title, my love, to strike fear in the heart of the enemy."

He locked his gaze to hers and with apprehension in his deep voice, he asked, "And you, Flame Spitter? When you look at me now, what emotion do I strike in your heart?"

She hesitated not. Reaching out, she placed her hand 'cross the wound and stated clearly, "Respect."

~~~~~FLIGHT OF FIRE KEEP~~~~~

Maahayyel dragged herself from the base of the stone steps toward the lowest ledge within the primal volcano. She was so weary she hadn't even noticed if others were present as she'd descended. Hundreds of ledges cut into the wall eons past, spiraled upwards at various heights from the center in an ever widening funnel to the very rim, but this one was hers. She was struggling to conserve the strength she gained from her visits here, and 'twas obvious she had little time left this side of the Veil. Two LifeBonds, the Draw for weapons, the Battle for the Dragon Clan, the creation of the Shield, the Ranking of the Princes... all requiring Greater Magic, Brewed within the last winter since they'd brought the Clan with them into the war, had taken much from her.

The Princes had just left, returning to their 'Bonds. She was so weary, so drained, so afraid of losing her personal battle and leaving this world without a new Matriarch. But with the loss of Shraadarr, to whom would their ancestors allow her to bestow her rule? For the last many winters she'd begged for knowledge, near demanding succor, but received only silence in response. At first she'd felt something promising when her childhood friend Sydrayyah had shown up, but she took the Warrior Regynn in the Second 'Bond and the sensation disappeared. There was something special about the big green, but 'twould not be the accession. Then there was potential felt with Daynahmyn, but 'twas more ominous than hopeful. Even her taking of Mikkal had been fraught with controversy. Speculation would follow for certain, but whatever that was, 'twas not the accession either. Time would tell where their destinies lay. Which left Synahmarr. If only she could trace her eldest niece. Syn was the most likely candidate as 'twas her right. She'd had the potential to be more powerful than
~~~~~

any Matriarch who ever sat the throne, and Maahayyel had always felt she would ascend the rule with ease. But where was she?

Dropping heavily into the depression, deepened and polished smooth from so many others lying here afore her, she peered o'er the edge. The bubbling inferno was compelling. All Highlands sought out the warmth of the volcanic heart of their homeland, the blaze rejuvenating their powers, strengthening their Magic. 'Twas their link to the energy of Kadoor. Every Race had a link, somewhere they could call 'home', each one unique to their Kind. All required returning to their link in order to sustain their Magic. Most would only require visiting every few hundred winters, but as one aged or became weakened with illness, injury, or heightened demands, one would require much more frequent visits 'til at last they helped not, for even the Highlands, with a lifespan some measured in eternity, had an end.

Maahayyel held no delusions. She'd been forced to soak up the heat every winter for the last few decades, and now 'twas all she could do to avoid visits more often than every full moon. Too much stress, too many battles, too heavy a load, shortened her span of days. But she'd never regretted her decision to accept the rule from Kaahayyel. The way things were going, she'd have ended up with it sooner rather than later anyway, and abdicating kept her sister alive much longer than she'd have managed otherwise. They'd planned the time for joining with the Warriors, hoping against hope that time would never come, but alas, the Evil One did return, plunging them back into the war. Gunnarr knew she'd not left the Keep in some time, but he was unaware of her current level of need, her rapid and certain deterioration beginning to show in the loss of Allure.

Synahmarr was still alive, she could feel her essence, but she'd never attempted to contact her people since the fateful day of her disappearance. She'd have to bolster her Magic, for finding her niece and stepping down afore the end was all she had left to offer. If Synahmarr wasn't strong enough to take her power, then she wouldn't be strong enough to perform the Greater Magic the Resistance so desperately needed. Time would tell, and her own time was ever shortening. She sighed deeply, closed her great eyes, and laid her head down on her paws. Stretching out her long neck, her nose just o'er the edge, she sniffed the sharp odor of the molten rock below, tried to will the heat into her body. Instead, she shivered. How long would it take this time, afore she'd feel warm again? Her Magic was failing her and when it did, 'twould fail all of Kadoor.

CHAPTER TWENTY

No One Left to Hear

Storrm entered the Commander's office as of old, no knocking, no introduction. Darque had intended to introduce some martial order for added protection against the spy, however, there wasn't enough manpower to allow for a steady guard, and no doppelganger events had occurred since the battle. With the exception of the few stray rogues and the occasional wanderer, there'd been no outside activity, either. Additionally, her Sword would tremble, grow warmer, and practically demand she take hold when danger approached. 'Twas almost as good as having her own War Dog. Almost. It still hurt to think about her favorite, Bensyn, who'd been viciously slaughtered. She'd always wanted her own War Dog. But being in 'Bond with all the demands on her time, she didn't feel she had the right to take on another responsibility. One day. When she could give the beast the attention it deserved. 'Til then, she'd depend on her Sword and Gunnarr. Not a bad combination, really. Besides, both Walkyr and Fryya had their own and since the pups never left their sides she got to enjoy them whenever the children were around. Growing rapidly, both far outweighed their handlers now, and would match them in height soon.

Yet such pleasant memories she could not sustain, and with the recollections of the battle still clamoring in her mind, she spoke thoughtfully to her sister. "'Cross the carnage and the rivers of blood, 'twas not just hatred that burned in the Black's eyes. Surely I watched him shift from arrogance to fear of the Fade itself. 'Twas not our arrival alone, which caused him to abandon his forces." She lowered her voice. "'Twas his own demise he Saw there." Shaking her head, she finished, "His fears give me some hope that we're safe from further attack for the time being."

Darque leaned forward, her feet no longer dangling above the floor, as she'd just built a platform to serve as a footrest. Her father's huge desk and chair had barely fit the former Battle Commander, but she was not her father. The diminutive but mighty Warrior who claimed the desk now, was unable to prevent the fatal sword strike of the King's Agent as Grifynn valiantly protected her mother. Darque had instantly performed her final duty as Second. Acting as Death Avenger, her Dragon Sword beheaded the assassin a mere fraction of a moment following. Aalanna refused to leave Grifynn's body and Darque was forced to escape without her after giving her one of her own blades and obtaining her promise not to be taken alive. Then afore the dawn broke 'cross the Great Plains of Drekinn, she plunged into the Battle for the Dragon Clan as her first Command.

Pondering the past and sorting out the future, her isolation was sobering. 'Twas truth she'd never had many friends growing up as the Commander's daughter, and with her training schedule there was little time to foster such. She and Storrm grew up inseparable but others were held distant, and she'd developed a not entirely accurate reputation as a hard ass. Although her Battle Name of the Dragon was thought by the other Warriors to suit her physical strength, steel resolve, and quick temper, Storrm, Gunnarr, and Mystynn knew her inner doubts and the heavy toll that growing up so fast since taking the 'Bond had placed upon her youthful shoulders. Despite what the others thought, she was not so hard assed as to be insensate of the multitude of events that had occurred o'er the past winter. And losing her father had been the single worst moment of her relatively short life, immediately followed by the loss of the mother she'd just found. Nevertheless, Darque was born and bred a Warrior, trained from birth to assume the position she now held. Had she ever seriously considered she'd fulfill her destiny in that regard? Most certainly. But not this soon. She'd passed her eighteenth winter and that meant of course, that Storrm was now seventeen, not that age mattered in the 'Bond. However, their births just one winter apart upon the same day, always fell close, if not during, the Summer Faire. But since the War began, no one had even thought about such. She sighed. Festivals and Faires were the best part of the seasons. She missed them. 'Twould be a very long time afore they'd have another, she'd wager.

Storrm sat gracefully in the leather chair 'cross the desk from her sister, tucking one long bare leg under her hip. "Agreed. When you made your challenge to the Black, Mystynn and I were engaged o'er the docks. Your description makes sense of what we felt at that moment." During the initial Flaming, the upper level of the Port District was collapsed per clever pulley systems, allowing the secret lower levels to survive mostly intact. Much was stored there and most slept in the lower levels, but they'd still lost much. Amongst the hardest felt was the Leather Master's shop, once situated in close proximity to the docks. Leathers were now in short supply and 'twould take some time to replenish, even though they'd begun stockpiling moons earlier. But they had more than just normal wear and tear to replace because the Warriors' garments suffered greatly from the corrosive attributes of the Flame during their salvage and rescue efforts, afore the rains had come to neutralize the acidic affects. Most of them had taken to wearing only the bare essentials to preserve their clothing for the upcoming cold weather, as much as to stay cool in the late summer heat. Clad only in a very short wrap skirt with raw, uneven edges, and a halter bra with leather laces and links of steel to hold everything in place, (little more than naked, actually) Storrm was indeed glorious. Her long red hair was, as usual, in multiple thick braids falling about her shoulders to her knees, and around her sculpted biceps she wore intricate silver, copper and bronze circlets woven in knotted patterns. Her deep blue eyes glistened with Allure.

For the umpteenth time since they'd joined the war, Darque could hear the prophesy repeat in her head. 'And there will be a girl child born of the Race of Man, of Dragon Blood and Dragon Seed, with flaming red hair and piercing blue eyes who will take up the Sword and lead the Races from near extinction to a New Beginning'. No real pressure here. She only had the remaining Clansmen, the LifeBond Teams, and hundreds of Frees, all depending on her to keep them from failing or succumbing to the Veil, and that meant she merely had to find a way to get them through the next few moons, then the approaching winter, followed by the winters to come, and prevent another attack by the Hoard, or find some means to defend against said attack with inconceivable odds against them. And that didn't even take into account the rest of the population of their world. But, without the Clan, Kadoor stood no chance against the Hoard, and to protect the Clan she'd do near anything. She thought she was doing everything possible, but would it be enough?

The chair opposite the Commander's desk was a massive leather wingback, ornately carved with ball and claw feet and Dragons climbing the sides sneaking up on the sleeping one stretched out 'cross the top, for an overall feeling of power, not delicacy. When one sat in it 'twould make some feel quite intimidated. Storrm leaned comfortably in the polished leather, relishing this respite, anything but intimidated. She was sweaty, dirty and fatigued. Her lightly tanned skin was the color of walnuts, her arms, legs and face bore a sprinkling of new freckles. Darque wished she could tan that well, be that long and lean, look that good even when that dirty. But the Commander didn't truly regret her muscled buxom curves, pale skin, or lack of height any longer. She was what she was, and Gunnarr loved her with all his huge heart. What more could she ask? Darque glanced back at her sister. She'd been working in the gardens, trying to seed several different varieties of vegetables from the meager supplies they'd salvaged. Those stashed during siege preparations were precious and not to be used experimentally. But the grounds were not cooperating and she'd come to report her findings as Second, to her Commander. She didn't want to destroy what was left of their seed with more failed efforts. There had to be a way to get a crop growing afore 'twas too late. Nevertheless, in order to achieve the amount of harvest they'd soon require, they'd need several rotated crops without fail, and the weather wasn't going to cooperate with that need no matter how much they could get started now. But anything would help at this point.

There were so many factors working against them and time was just one. Rain fell heavily within a sennight after the battle, effectively neutralizing the a'Flamed grounds, and the corrosiveness was no longer felt while working the previously rich soil. They could even walk barefoot and work barehanded. The rivers of blood should have helped to enhance, rather than deplete the soil, however, they'd yet to get anything to take root and they knew not the reason. Storrm suspected 'twas some combination 'tween the Shield, the shortening days, and the Flaming of the once fertile land. Even though they could no longer feel the effects of the inferno Brewed by the Highlands and spit forth in their fiery breath, 'twas obvious the ground was sterile, for the seeds they planted would simply rot. Darque knew she couldn't rely only on their stores. She had to find a more permanent solution. She'd even asked their young Seer, but Walkyr had not had a significant Vision since the battle, which she'd decided wasn't so bad. After all, 'twas often truth that no news was good news.

Darque and Storrm had initially discussed planting the area around St Swiftyn's Bog, but decided 'twould not only draw unwanted attention, 'twas too far north to help with the immediate problem. Still, Darque hadn't tossed out the notion entirely, as when she and Gunnarr performed their cursory exploration of the nearby deserted Keep of St Swiftyn's afore they'd built the Lair, they'd noted blackberry vines covering one of the walls. She was determined to go there again, to explore further. Those who'd once resided there had to have had some manner of gardening or foraging available to sustain such a large population, and there was no evidence their disappearance was due to any inability to care for their own. The Keep intrigued her, she wanted to find out what had happened to the people, and if 'twas still a viable option for colonizing. In his prior 'incarnation' as Battle Commander Baadyyn, her father had been a frequent visitor, but she knew nothing else after Grifynn took the leadership and forbade further travel there o'er sixty winters earlier. 'Twas as solid as the Dragon's Den, more so, given its location in the gorge, struck from stone, surrounded by impassable rivers and cliffs, with only one huge rock bridge and ancient stone slab gateway as entrance. The Keep was a veritable oasis of security in the mountains. She couldn't imagine the people of St Swiftyn's having been conquered by an opposing force. One thing the battle taught her though, just as Drekinn may have been impervious to any enemy a'foot or a'horseback, with the exception of the castle they'd been as sitting ducks to the aerial onslaught of the Hoard. Her beloved Drekinn was in ruins, and might never be rebuilt. Had the residents of St Swiftyn's met the same fate? She shook her head. There were no ready answers.

Tossing her braid o'er her shoulder, she stared at the ancient parchment that proclaimed her inherited title. Smoothing it flat with her hands on the desk, she read again how the first High King had bestowed the title of Drekinn Ri, or King of Drekinn, upon the first Battle Commander. Grifynn was Commander afore her, and she'd recently learned that he'd held that rank all the way back to the Last Holocaust. Corbyn had used his native Memory Magic to allow the Commander and his sister to live lifespan after lifespan, and no one ever suspected. But with Grifynn's Passing, not only had Darque taken that rank, she'd also inherited the undisputed leadership of the Clan, becoming the Drekinn Ri as well. She knew now that at the time of the Last Holocaust, Grifynn had been in his early thirties, having seen mayhap a total of thirty four

.

winters. The exact number was unknown for Grifynn himself couldn't remember the name by which he'd been called then, let alone his age. 'Twas too long ago. Shayla (the current and Senior Healer for the Clan) was his younger sister by a mere two winters, but she couldn't remember her name or exact age, either. However, Grifynn was given the Blood Elixir to extend his life and abilities, being the volunteer used in the experiments and the first to take the substance, whereas Shayla used a different drug (known as the Blood Crystal) that she created by altering the original formula just prior to 'all Hell breaking loose', and she appeared to be much younger by the time her brother was forced Past. By actually changing their DNA, she obtained similar benefits including greater strength, longevity and some enhanced Healing, along with limited use of the MindLink, but she hadn't suffered the same negative side effects as he, such as erratic aging along with growing paranoia. Episodes of physical morphing of his body as it attempted to become a full fledged Dragon caused him great pain and led to increasing withdrawal. His body couldn't withstand the punishment, and the more he used the Elixir to which he became addicted, the more he struggled for control. Ultimately 'twas his downfall. Yet he'd had no regrets. He believed to the end that had he not taken the Elixir, there would have been no Dragon Clan, nor the fulfillment of the prophesy, and the Black and his Hoard would have succeeded in taking o'er all Kadoor with the assault that catapulted them into the Last Holocaust. Mayhap he was correct, she thought once again. Darque missed her father. Grifynn was a brilliant man and she felt totally inadequate trying to fill his illustrious boots. The Bards were already sharing his Legend Songs, the music drifting through the caverns during late night gatherings after her Warriors had done as much work as they could and everyone was too exhausted to even sleep. Would her Song be one of such praise, or would it tell a tale of ultimate tragedy? Rejecting such speculation she renewed her fierce resolve, for if 'twas the latter, there'd be no one left to hear.

CHAPTER TWENTY-ONE

The Falcon is a Brat

"By all the fires of Hades! Could you not have written down something this important?" Completely frustrated, her temper flaring, Darque threw her hands up in surrender while barking at the memory of her father. With parchments, books, scrolls, and papers piled o'er the huge desk, as well as scattered 'cross the floor, she finally gave up all hope of locating any records of those who'd been deployed, or to where, prior to the battle. 'Twould appear that Grifynn had kept such knowledge, and much more, in his head. If only she could talk to him again. Chewing on her lip, she sat back on her heels and looked around the office. By her best conservative estimates there could be as many as one hundred Teams still out there, with possibly up to two hundred Warriors, as most were deployed in pairs and not all of them were home when the Hoard struck. With only three hundred Frees having survived the battle, gathering the rest would be most helpful, almost doubling their depleted ranks. However, they'd not yet reported and none had been found in their forays thus far. Thinking optimistically, she hoped they were in hiding and trying to return home at this very moment. But what would they do when they encountered the Shield? And would they believe the rumors of their total demise? She needed a break. Gathering everything she'd dragged out, she filed it all away again. Just as she finished, there came a knock on the door. 'Twas a welcome diversion.

The Warrior standing afore her now was her last prospect 'til chance took o'er, to supply some bit of information to help locate the Warrior Dyrrk, in whom she had a keen interest. "Do you have any information regarding his fate?" Darque had questioned many of the Brotherhood, even the Clansmen who might have associated with him during the aftermath, to no avail.

Dyrrk wasn't the only one still on the MIA list, but she was convinced he'd been involved in her father's disappearance the night afore the battle, elevating his level of importance due to the possibility of being linked to the spy.

"I've seen him not since shortly after the cleanup began." Puzzled, he thought back to the last time he'd seen the heavily built Warrior. "'Twas within the first sennight, just afore midday. We were salvaging in the farthest southern section, but when Myrta and her crew from the kitchens arrived with soup and bread, he was gone. I don't recall seeing him leave, and I hadn't really thought about him since. Sir, your orders were to keep track of everyone and everything. I was negligent. I will accept any reprimand you deem appropriate." Stepping back into battle ease, he awaited his Commander's decision.

Darque could sense his annoyance at being unable to supply more helpful information and that he was sincere in his self chastisement. But 'twas useless to chastise for such, everyone was doing their best, and not only would she not kick his ass for doing nothing wrong, she wouldn't and couldn't have him kicking his own. "My orders were to try to keep such tabs, but 'twould be impossible to do more. Maintaining constant vigilance for the return of the Hoard as well as focusing upon the enormous workload, is daunting to say the least. No, Warrior, you've done well indeed. You've given me more information than any other to this point, and now I have confirmation of his survival as well as a possible timeline to place upon his disappearance. If you think of, or hear of, anything else, make report immediately. Check the lists of the missing on your way out, and do the same with them all. Now go, get some rest and something to eat afore you return to your station."

Dismissing him, her thoughts returned to Dyrrk. Playing with a pile of newly salvaged Dragon teeth, she was baffled. All of her senses told her there was more to the missing fighter than anyone imagined. She'd had a fleeting thought in the beginning that 'twas possible he'd been the spy they'd failed thus far, to uncover. However, although she'd felt Magic about him the one time they'd passed close enough to touch skin to skin, she was now certain 'twas not his own, and therefore 'twould have come from some outside source with whom he'd been in contact. Their evidence suggested the spy was a Shifter, but he or she could have used a human counterpart. She sighed. Was anything certain? Her head hurt.

Absently sweeping the teeth off the desk into yet another basket in her growing collection, Darque mused o'er the missing. Although she wanted to account for them all, Dyrrk was not the only one at the top of her 'private' list. She was also very interested in finding out what happened to Mynx. Had she been so blind, had her senses been warped when she'd hired the tall blonde Warrior as bodyguard for Fryya, her own sister? Questions burned in her mind, but the biggest ones made her grit her teeth. Was Mynx the spy? Had she been affiliated with the spy? She shook her head. Could anyone be trusted?

~~~~~~~~~~

Brannyn had been waiting for just this opportunity. He'd been on the inside since the beginning, was actually under the Shield when 'twas Brewed, working alongside the Clan, eating with them, 'sleeping' in the same caves. Shift after Shift, using Memory Magic so as not to alert anyone, he'd listened and gathered much information about the new Commander, hoping against hope that he'd found another Human as trustworthy as had been his friend, Dyrrk. Thinking about his loss still brought great anguish, a sensation he now relished and utilized to keep his energy levels high. Watching the Mighty Blue exit the Shield to hunt, he knew she'd be alone for at least a couple of marks. He followed the Warrior into the office, quiet as a mouse. Of course, at the time, he was a mouse.

~~~~~~~~~~

Her hearing was so acute even distracted and fatigued, that she looked up instantly with the breath of air sighing within the room. Standing 'cross the desk was the same Warrior who'd just taken his leave. He cleared his throat to speak, but the look on Darque's face silenced him afore he began. Pushing back her chair, she fixed her eyes upon his, while reaching carefully for her Sword. She'd not heard him re-enter even if there'd been time, but if that weren't enough, there was something odd about his eyes afore he dropped his gaze. 'Twas as if a tempest brewed under those long dark lashes. 'Twas the tell of the Fay. Was the spy standing afore her now? She had no backup, for Gunnarr had just left and she didn't expect him to return for some time. On the positive side, she saw no ready weapon, and her Sword remained cool to her touch even though every hair on the back of her neck was bristling. Calmly, she stated, "It takes much Magic to pull such a Shift. By what name are you called?"

He had the good grace to be chagrined. He'd attempted to make his entrance a bit more normal, but he'd been so far removed from normal for so long, he'd forgotten the simple things in his haste to take advantage of the situation. Admitting to nothing, he tried to steer the conversation toward the recent topic. "Dyrrk was not your spy, and he's been forced Past the Veil."

Keeping her Sword grasped firmly in her hand, she licked her full lips and quietly reiterated, "You didn't answer my question."

"I came here at great personal risk to offer my help to the growing Resistance. I can tell you much."

Calmly she asked again, "And would that include who you are?"

His eyes gleamed with defiance. "I'm surprised you didn't first ask how I got here."

The stranger was proving to be stubborn, but the Commander was more so, and in such, she'd not be bested. "That would be my next question, although I believe I've already indicated some knowledge there. First, I'd say introductions are in order."

"Mayhap you'd be so kind as to re-sheathe your Sword while we discuss business?"

She smiled and lifted the Sword to lay 'cross her arm ready for action, although she moved not otherwise. Darque would not lose a battle of tenacity, however, she was beginning to enjoy the interaction. 'Twas stimulating. "Not as long as you bandy words about, avoiding answering my question. If you continue, I'll be forced to treat you as the spy and gut you where you stand, although I'd rather not shed blood in this office. 'Twould be unfortunate."

Chuckling softly to himself, he made his decision. His every sense told him that she meant what she said and would try to the Veil to carry out her intent. She could be trusted, and if she failed him down the road through some flaw in her Human bloodline, there was nothing to be done. He might as well cooperate fully and tell her everything up front. Such honesty would be refreshing. "I believe you are sincere, but you wouldn't get far. I do know you have much skill, m'lady Darque, but not enough to kill me. Yet. Mayhap I deserve such a fate. But again, not yet. And since I already know you, I shall introduce myself. My given name is Brannyn, but within the ranks of the Hoard, I am known as the Predator. I have recently taken my promotion to Third, or Right to Second of the Destroyer, whom you may or may not be aware, is Second to the Black. 'Twas my 'promotion' which facilitated my absence from them, which is the normal procedure within our ranks. And I do use that term loosely. You see, I have no intention of being caught off guard and losing my current status as did my predecessor. 'Twill require that I thin the Hoard of a few loose ends still loyal to the last Third. I have much to do afore my return."

Darque couldn't breathe, as well as having trouble finding her tongue. She simply stared at the man. His claims were remarkable, and if he was being honest, his information would be priceless, giving her the spy she so desired in Evanntyr. Realizing they were in some kind of Silence that she'd not created, she noted 'twas similar to theirs but 'twas as if time itself had stopped. "How long do we have? There's much you can tell me, if you speak the truth. But afore we begin, I think 'twould be a gesture of trust to show your true face."

Brannyn decided he might as well comply. Maintaining the form of another living being was draining him anyway. He dropped the Shift and stood afore the girl. Tall, with flawless bronzed skin seemingly aglow with Allure, his dark hair hung past his shoulders, straight and thick. Dark eyes flashed as he absently tucked a stray strand of charcoal hair behind one thick pointed ear, fanning back like a miniature wing. He wore a long black leather riding coat and thigh high boots o'er his tunic and britches. Slowly, he pulled off his gloves and tucked them into his coat pocket afore he looked her in the eyes. His handsome face, predator's stare, and deep voice, were somehow familiar. "Possibly several marks, forgive me for not knowing more precisely. My Magic has been heavily taxed lately, still, 'tis going to depend mostly on that partner of yours, as the 'Bond you share makes him resistant to the time loop I've created. I know you can't keep anything from him, but I wanted a chance to speak with you alone, prior to obtaining his hot headed input." Darque had difficulty keeping a straight face, as she knew well about Gunnarr's 'hot headed input', afore he continued. "I propose a truce. We need each other. I've been watching you closely. If I wanted to kill you, I've had ample opportunity already. This fact alone should be enough to gain your confidence. From what I've seen I believe I can trust you, but without Grifynn, I honestly have no other option. He was my only contact outside of the Hoard, with the exception of Dyrrk. With their deaths, I find myself in a most awkward position. There remains no one who can verify my identity, or my cause."

His voice made her heart beat a little faster, 'twas so... masculine. If she were still unattached... she shook her head. She was very happy as the mate of the High Prince, but 'twould be near impossible to ignore the attraction of the Fay. 'Twas exactly as the moment she'd met Corbyn, despite having been but a child. However, the seriousness of the subject being discussed drew her back to the moment, and to herself. She suddenly realized that he'd been the Allure she'd felt on Dyrrk. "You're Fay," she asserted, just to receive the confirmation.

"Yes."

"Then you know the Raven."

His eyes widened, his face flushed, and he felt like he was falling. Taking a side step, he blurted, "The Raven yet lives?"

Immediately, he clamped shut his mouth, but not afore she noted the surprise in his voice, and the flash of disbelief in the depths of his eyes. 'Twas high emotion. Mayhap even shock? She replied in a low voice, "I thought the Fay knew everything."

He sounded almost disgusted with himself. "We know much, we deduce more, but no one can know everything."

"Obviously. Another reason for needing my assistance, for 'tis my assistance you're here to secure, yes?" She smiled at him.

"You deduce much as well, although I wasn't exactly trying to hide my objective. I worked with your father toward the end of his lifespan. He was an admirable and intelligent man. I'd hoped we could carry on the pact we'd established."

'Twas touching to hear such high praise about her father. He claimed to have worked with him. Her thoughts jumped from one to another. The Raven had 'worked with her father' for much of his lifespan, and 'twas more than obvious the two Fay knew each other, or at the least, they knew of one another. Corbyn had been absent since the Shield was Brewed, telling Storrm he had business elsewhere, and the two would have missed each other. She kept herself composed despite this knowledge, as 'twas likely 'twould prove valuable in the future. "And were you involved in his death?"

"Straight to the point. I gave him the chance to save Aalanna from her execution. He took that chance, knowing he'd not survive."

Solemnly she replied, "Then you should know he failed to complete that mission afore he Passed."

He stared at her, his face unreadable. "He failed not."

Now 'twas her turn to be surprised. With brows furrowed and giving away her ignorance, she stated a bit too quickly, "I left him dead in the Tower, my mother with my own blade to join him afore the King's Men arrived. They're both Past."

"You left him, but he was not yet Passed, although 'twas not long after. And afore he died, he made her promise not to take her own life. There's more to your mother than even she knows. Much more yet to be learned, and quite soon, I assure you. She's safe for the moment. But I believe you wished to know more about Dyrrk," he baited.

What Darque wanted was more information about her mother, but 'twas clear that topic was no longer open. At least he said she was safe 'for the moment', whatever that meant. Information was beginning to pour in as if she were standing in the middle of Clear Water Creek at the start of the Spring Melts. In order to avoid drowning, she returned to the original subject. "You mentioned Dyrrk was dead. I'd hoped to question him about my father's disappearance. I want to know how he got to Evanntyr in less than a sennight."

Her analytical mind made the Predator optimistic about his placement of trust. Despite her youth, she was proving to be exactly what they all hoped, as well as the fact that she hadn't taken the bait and become demanding about her mother. 'Twas a very good sign that she placed the safety and needs of her Command above her personal desires. Humans, especially the females, seemed always to talk more than listen, at least 'twas so in his limited experience thus far. 'Twas a trait he despised. But this one was concise, logical, pragmatic, as well as stunningly beautiful without conceit. If she wasn't already mated to the High Prince, he'd have actually been interested. Distracted, he gazed into her shocking blue eyes, feeling drawn there as if he were about to plummet into a well. With some difficulty he regained his focus. Even though he'd be famished as well as exhausted when 'twas released, his Spell was tight and he began to relax. "Your father got to Evanntyr because I made a deal with a friend. And he traveled by Water Dragon. You look surprised. Would that be because you doubt the Water Dragons exist, or that you doubt I could have a friend?"

She snorted trying not to laugh outright. But she wasn't certain how much time they had, and 'twas much to be learned. "Would that also explain why his sensory trail ended at the docks where no ship was registered?"

"Yes, although I'm not at liberty to say more on that subject at this time." His grin lit up his ruggedly handsome face, and then he frowned. Continuing, he spoke fast and with distaste. "And yes. Dyrrk died by my hand. His sacrifice not only kept our mission a secret, it secured my promotion as well. I was greatly angered at being forced to this, but he was close to death anyway, and there was no option. The Destroyer was upon us."

Listening to both the words and the passion behind them, she hesitated afore responding. "I thought the Fay were opposed to strong emotion."

"Some think 'tis time we embrace it again, learn to control it as we once did in the distant past, to give us the power to defeat the Hoard." The Raven was one who felt 'twas time to use emotion to fuel their Magic once more. 'Twas one of the reasons he'd been exiled. His heart began to race, thinking of that time in the past. The Raven. Dare he hope Corbyn was still alive? He decided to redirect the conversation again. "I've taken many winters, given up my family, my people, my life, done much that is unforgiveable, in order to achieve my current position. If anyone else learns of this, my mission will fail, many will perish, and all I have sacrificed will be for naught."

Now was her moment. Walking around to the front of the desk, she stood afore the Fay and presented the first challenge to their potential arrangement. "The Dragons have the Link. Gunnarr has the best control, but 'twill already be two with the knowledge. You had to have known this afore, and were prepared to assume the risk. Now I propose 'twould be wise to draw in one more pair, in order to avoid another destructive occurrence such as you've just experienced."

Brannyn paused and Darque could sense the turmoil. Had she gone too far, too fast? If he felt cornered, he could simply use his Magic to try to force her Past the Veil. Would he consider her proposal youthful impertinence (he was truly ancient compared to her) or would he see the logic?

Initially annoyed with something akin to a sense of betrayal, as he absorbed the increased energy from the flash of emotion, he quickly saw the girl was absolutely correct. She was a wise one. The prophesy would prevail. "What do you suggest?"

Heartened by this acceptance, she added yet another proposal. "First, I want to secure our alliance. Whatever decisions we make will be mutually agreed upon and will not be broken by either party. Are we in accord with that?"

"Agreed," he stated with relief.

"Then I want to remind you that you had not only my father in your confidence, but Dyrrk. That said, I want to inform my Second in Command, Storrm. She will assume Command if anything happens to me, and in turn she would inform her Second. This is the only way we can have some kind of safety net for you. And 'twould be impossible to utilize any information you provide without her knowing from whence it came. After all, I can only work off 'instincts' for so long."

The Fay considered her proposal warily. "She is a winter younger than you, is she not?"

"Yes. But although nothing is totally foolproof, I trust my Second with my life and with the lives of the Clan. She would not fail either of us. Of course, this knowledge would be Shared through both our 'Bonds.'"

He barely hesitated this time. "Agreed."

Trusting her intuition, the fact that she felt his presence in this very office from afore her father disappeared, which confirmed the truth of his tale, and the fact that her Sword was still cool to the touch, she continued. "Then I want to know how to make contact with you, not just you making contact with me, simply appearing at will. I want to be able to track you somehow, to know you're safe, and 'twould be more useful if we had the ability to share information both ways. I want to establish an emergency signal, some way to protect us both. And, from what you've said 'tis clear you've been exiled from your Kind, mayhap even orchestrated that yourself in order to infiltrate the Hoard, and therefore, if things get too hot in there, you need to let us help you escape and come here. Come home."

Brannyn was taken aback. He couldn't believe his own ears. She was concerned for his safety, attempting to protect him as if he was one of her own. Not in a presumptuous manner, but in a truly professional and compassionate one. He'd entered her domain as a stranger and now he felt like one of her Warriors. She'd literally given him a home. He had someone who knew what he was doing and would mourn for his loss, not just for the loss of information, but for him. He could sense the truth of this in her words, her emotions, her body language.

She knew intuitively what he was thinking. "And don't believe for a candle drip that I won't have the nerve to send you back in there. We need the information. We will win this war. Many have already Passed and many more will Pass. We do what we must. No one's life is more important than winning against the Hoard, not yours, not mine, no one's." Taking one of her blades, she made a small cut on the inside of her right wrist and held her fist out toward him as he did the same. Entwining their wrists together blood to blood, the pact was sealed. "Now, tell me how you got inside the Shield."

"Well, that's not so much of a story. 'Twas sheer luck. I was here when the Shield drew down. I haven't attempted to leave, but I was hoping to be 'allowed' rather than experiment and possibly end up forcing my way through, as it might cause irreparable damage, or at the very least, might be noticed outside and 'twould spill your secret, leaving you unprotected. However, I do see mice and birds and insects freely traveling both ways, I'm just not certain any of those as a Shift, would work. 'Tis amazing, really, you and the Highlands have done here what has never been done afore."

<center>~~~~~~~~~~</center>

During the following marks, Darque learned many things, some of extreme importance and some just interesting. The Clan would not have to seek the True King, he would come to them, and soon. "Be watchful, for he will not appear as you'd expect," Brannyn warned. The Sorcerer actively sought the Eye and was already in possession of Grifynn's hair giving him the ability to conjure his spirit, for the Black feared Darque and the prophesy and needed Grifynn to learn her weaknesses.

The Water Dragons did exist and were Tied to the Sprites. Brannyn believed they'd be forced to enter the war shortly, with the Elves following soon thereafter. The 7th Egg was safe for now, but the bearers were not. Bastyen and Graasyn, her missing, father-son Stealth Team, were still alive but their destiny lay in another direction. In a ghastly revelation, Brannyn revealed that the Hoard became intoxicated on the blood of children and would actively seek them o'er other sources, even ones readily available. And, Mynx was not her spy. 'Twas the Sorcerer himself. She sighed. How could she accurately determine who was who, if she didn't know all the swordsmen in the Pits?

The time was gone so rapidly, she was amazed. Walking with him to the Shield, she let him through afore he released the Silence. He could have made it through alone, but his Magic was weakened o'er the past moon, and his efforts might have been a tad awkward. On his way once again, he Shifted. The Falcon flew high o'er head, 'crossing the Plains and disappearing o'er the horizon toward the Raptor's Talons. He had a few chores to accomplish, but 'twould have to wait for him to eat first, as he was starving.

Walking back to the Den, she suddenly realized they'd not established a method for her to contact him. Stamping her boot on the ground, she huffed, "Dragon dung, you are such a brat!"

The Falcon's wings beat smoothly, his beady eyes glittering in amusement.

Chapter Twenty-Two
Priority Shift

Relishing a brief moment of stillness, Darque closed her eyes and reached for her new necklace, the Dragon's Eye that Gunnarr gave her this very dawn in remembrance of their joining, as well as for her otherwise forgotten eighteenth winter celebration. Condensed to the size of a walnut, 'twas the most breathtaking and hardest known substance in Kadoor, and 'twas literally the eye of a Dragon who'd Passed the Veil. Holding many qualities, some practical, some aesthetic, and some mystical, it lay nestled 'tween her breasts in a forest green suede pouch. She thought it best not to advertize her new acquisition, as 'twas coveted by the Hoard.

Not just any eye would convert to such upon Passing. Many factors were involved, resulting in the rarest and most precious of gems. In point of fact, they'd not been seen since afore the Last Holocaust, although she believed more were hidden somewhere. 'Twas legend that the original Ancients kept great treasure stashes of inconceivable worth hidden throughout Kadoor, only to be lost during the aftermath. This one had been salvaged from the remains of their first kill together. The Hoard Dragon from whom this Eye came was about to toast Fryya during the Battle of Kaddart, where she lost one of her blades. She loved the Eye, 'twas stunningly gorgeous, her most prized possession, and touching it helped focus her thoughts.

Nevertheless, 'twas more than difficult at this moment to do just that, with these constant, nagging interruptions. Her Dragon Sword had been floating about the office just out of reach most of the morning, and she'd made little headway trying to conclude her reports. But 'twas faster than her enhanced vision and in order to stop the commotion and get some peace, 'twas time to fall back on patience and trust her instincts.

Truth be told, she was well known for her lack of patience while growing up in the Clan. Although, since taking the Oath, and believing she had that part of her character well under control, she grew dismayed at how impatient she became with her Sword's antics this morning. O'er the last few moons since the Draw imbued their hand crafted weapons with Magic, she'd been receiving an education in its 'personality'. 'Twas still an inanimate object, a weapon of cold steel, for nothing could bring life to the non-living. Be that as it may, along with powerful Ancient Dragon Magic, the Draw forged part of her essence into the very metal, giving it an eerie presence she oft times likened to having a petulant child strapped 'cross her back.

The Sword, now tapping rudely on the desk, was one of thirteen known to be in existence. With only twelve Warriors left to wield them, since Ariel was lost while bravely attempting to protect Kaahayyel, Darque had spent some sleepless nights pondering what to do with the orphaned blade. Vastly superior to ordinary weapons, a Dragon Sword could pierce hide, slice through scale and bone, and even damage fang and talon. Without them they stood far less chance of destroying a Dragon's heart or beheading one. All Magic bearing Races had some form of enhanced Healing, and such was quite advanced in the Highlands, however, Magic took strength and was most definitely a finite resource, varying greatly in potency with each user, and required replenishment. If a Magic bearer was weakened by hunger, fatigue, or multiple tasks, his gifts became sluggish and Healing was usually the first of the Magics to suffer.

Cutting through quickly by using a Sword was not the only way to win the fight. There were a few other strategies one could use, such as distraction. A Dragon's brain and heart Healed slower, since both were required to help Brew the Magic of the Healing in the first place, and if injured one might have time to finish off the beast using ordinary weapons. But a Dragon Sword could beat the Healing, and if wielded with skill, could force the beast Past the Veil with all haste. This gave a much needed advantage to the swordsman, and Warriors were the best swordsmen in all of Kadoor.

Although they lost o'er seven hundred Free Warriors and countless Free Dragons, Ariel was the only Sword bearer to Pass, which led to an interesting dilemma. Each Sword was personalized, answering only to the Call of its creator. There had to be a way to hand down one Warrior's Sword to another after they'd Passed, as not only were they a priceless resource, they were extremely dangerous to create and impossible to destroy. Struggling for a solution, in the end 'twas not her knowledge or lack thereof that set its fate. Following Rygyl day after day during the aftermath, 'twas as a stray pup might follow the first person to show him or her any kindness. But Ariel was introverted and her Sword was aloof at best. 'Twas many dawns afore Rygyl could take hold its bejeweled hilt. At first, whenever he tried to reach for it, 'twould simply back away. 'Twas only after his 'Bond, Tegrynn, suggested he win the Sword as he had the heart of his betrothed, that he finally saw the parallel to her personality. Gently, he held out his open hand, standing or sitting patiently alone for marks at a time, and the Sword came to him at last. Laying its polished hilt 'cross his big calloused palm, he firmly embraced it as he would have embraced his love, and for the first time since the battle, the rough fighter openly mourned for his loss. A waterfall of tears spilled o'er his weathered cheeks, and the Sword pulled his hand to nestle firmly against his leather breastplate, as if to offer some comfort.

All Warriors could fight with a dagger or sword in either hand, but there were few who could skillfully wield two swords at once, and Rygyl was no exception. Yet, since he'd claimed Ariel's Sword, he'd been practicing every spare moment and was developing some fascinatingly effective strategies using the second blade defensively in place of his shield. Given the vastly differing personalities and fighting styles 'tween the two Swords he now possessed, 'twas indeed new territory being explored. Even the Trainers were keeping a watchful eye upon his progress and he was doing well in practice. In fact, he was doing so well that he'd withdrawn his place in line for a Thumper. Darque didn't want him to go without, but she knew she'd have to force him to see reason. After all, even if he didn't use the shield on his arm, 'twould be good cover secured against his fairly broad backside, and could prevent serious Flame injury during the battles to come. Only solid rock stood up to the inferno better than Dragon scale. She couldn't help but think 'twas inevitable that such a situation would again present itself, and she hoped to be the one to take up the next Sword, if it found her worthy. But since 'twould mean another Warrior down, she'd rather go without.

Keeping her eyes upon the parchments, Darque waited for just the right moment. The Sword tapped closer and closer in a game it played, sharpening her senses and reflexes beyond even her 'Bond enhancements. Outwardly ignoring the blade, she kept her movements and breathing relaxed. 'Twas good practice for communication during use of the Link as well, for while she did Speak to the Dragons, she must simultaneously speak aloud with her Free Warriors without confusing anything, or having anyone notice. Oddly enough, since her Sword began its teasing, she found she could now Speak through multiple Links (however briefly) while also giving orders and hearing reports.

At just the precise moment the Sword was closest, she snatched it by the tip as it attempted to pull back out of reach once again. Her movements were so fast, 'twould have gone unnoticed by unenhanced eyes. Not that she could move that fast all the time, it took focused effort and consumed much energy. Squeezing tightly, it ceased pulling, and once recovered she sheathed it in the scabbard leaning against the desk beside her knee. If her grasp had been less accurate she could have lost a few fingers, but she'd been playing with sharp objects all her life and thought little of the dangers now. Besides, the Sword wouldn't harm her or allow her to be harmed by its actions, and this most welcome knowledge came in the midst of bloodletting in the heat of battle.

Although the Sword could move despite the scabbard (for nothing would hold it back from answering the Call, even if it might take awhile), 'twould usually remain still for a time once 'twas sheathed. Glancing down to make certain 'twas where she'd just put it like a child in a timeout chair, she went back to staring at the parchments.

After taking her field promotion, she had in turn immediately promoted Storrm from Right to Second, AKA Third Fighter, to her prior status of Second in Command. On the brink of entering their first major battle they had little choice, but the promotions were expected and honorable, and there were no regrets or opposition from the remainder of the Brotherhood. Their arrival shortly after the siege began was the others' first notice that Grifynn was gone and to their credit, and mayhap her own as well, instead of being demoralized they rallied to her Command.

In the aftermath their promotions left Right to Second open, and Storrm made her recommendation. Kydra was an outstanding Warrior and in 'Bond with Ragnyrr, Third Prince of the Highlands behind Gunnarr and Storrm's Mystynn. Darque was not opposed to promoting Kydra; indeed the tall blonde Warrior had been acting as Third since the battle. 'Twas also good sense to have her 'Bond Teams on equal ground, and with Ragnyrr's rank equivalent to Third Fighter, she was pleased that Kydra's qualifications were up to par, as well as confident that if promoted to Second sometime in the future, she'd be worthy of the knowledge of their new Fay alliance.

'Twas something else causing her to delay for so long. Glancing at the quill pen in the ink well upon the corner of the desk, she reached forward and grabbed it firmly. Darque regretted that she'd never had a flourishing longhand and she struggled to make her letters legible, not like her father's elegant script. Although she'd scribbled a few cryptic notes since the battle, this would be her first truly executive act. Somehow, signing this one document acknowledged that he was gone forever, leaving upon her shoulders the enormous responsibility of leadership of Kadoor's largest, most successful, and most respected War Clan. At least, they had been. If her plan worked, they'd be again. Of course, thus far they'd heard nothing about the fate of the other Clans of the realm. 'Twas entirely possible that the Dragon Clan and the Warriors here, were all that was left. She raised her chin and placed pen to parchment, boldly scrawling her signature 'cross the bottom.

Now that she'd finally made the already recognized promotion an official act, she felt the weight of self doubt dissolve and moved on to the rest of the clutter needing to be waded through soonest. As Commander, there was so much more to do than just training. Battle strategy and swordsmanship were her forte, along with the fact that she'd always had the strength, speed, and skill to back her up. After all, a bluff only worked if 'twasn't a bluff. She hated paperwork. But she was getting the hang of this, having o'er a moon of experience. Sticking out her tongue and making a rude noise in the silence of the empty office, she shook her head. Some leader, she thought to herself sarcastically, and added aloud as her father used to say, "Suck it up, buttercup". Still, 'twas amazing that even in their present predicament there was yet paperwork to complete, although 'twas clearly not the same as in the past, for which she was most grateful. "Abba, how did you manage?" She sighed again.

What next? She might as well officially proclaim young Walkyr, the Seer of the Dragon Clan, for he'd been filling that position since Kallyr Passed in the battle. She shuffled through the stack of parchments and found the declaration. Thankful to Warrior Regynn, the Clan Historian, for its creation, she once again set quill to parchment. Regynn was an invaluable resource but he'd been stretched quite thin since taking Sydrayyah in the Second 'Bond. There were just not enough marks in the day to accomplish everything. She knew 'twas truth, as the memories from her own early experiences came flooding back. Among them were accepting and learning to control their enhanced senses, the MindLink, the Healing, and the changes in their speed, strength, and reflexes, which also affected their fighting techniques. Even their sleeping and eating patterns were disrupted 'til they managed to synchronize with their Dragon partners and become proficient with all these new skills. At least the Stable of novice Teams had someone to guide them through the worst, unlike the Warriors of First Flight.

Walkyr would soon see seven winters, and had been in preparation for most of the last five to take o'er for the aging Seer once Kallyr retired, anyway. Despite his youth he was the strongest Seer of all time, having the most frequent and clearest Visions in history, but some had expressed fear 'twould be too much for the boy to handle. Darque wasn't one of them. This was war, and everyone bore pressures. Age meant little. You either stepped up or fell back, and guess which direction would get you killed first? Besides, Walkyr had already proven his battle readiness, having been key to saving most of the Clansmen seeking refuge in the besieged castle. The Dragon's Den was viciously attacked, but thanks to prior planning, some good Spells, tenacious defense, along with the mostly solid rock construction, hadn't been seriously compromised or taken much physical damage, as opposed to the rest of Drekinn Village. And with the quick and fearless assist of Fryya and their bodyguard, Cayell, he helped to save all who made it to the Den. Those who'd not managed to get there afore the battle began, mostly perished in the deadly Flame, with the exception of those who might still be alive in the lower levels of the Port District. Search and rescue continued, and although some had been found and were recovering in the caves, she was optimistic there were many more. Not only would she welcome seeing her friends, neighbors, and fellow Clansmen show up alive and able-bodied, she needed to have precise numbers and familial bloodlines to restore the Clan to its former glory.

When came the forceful knock at the heavy oaken door, her hand was upon her Sword almost afore she glanced up to see the tall young woman pushing past Gunnarr, who sat with a mystified look upon his face while she barged into the room. Passionate about her duties, Tyrza, Master Educator and Director for the youth programs, marched straight in, placed both hands on the desk and leaned forward. Without so much as a 'good morning', she spit forth, "'Tis time we discussed the children."

Darque had difficulty controlling her temper as she replied. "I told you we'd talk when I had time, not when you had time. There are many issues needing my immediate attention. The children are but one."

Raising her hand in disagreement, Tyrza persisted, "There is no issue more important than the children of the Clan."

Darque didn't really want to reprimand the woman, knowing her attitude came from concern and that 'twould have to be faced sooner or later. Still, she felt the need to place some perspective upon the situation. "You didn't lose more than half your charges," she said through clenched jaws, thinking about the three hundred Warriors who survived the battle and now faced the enormous responsibility of rebuilding their ranks, as well as providing adequate defense. "What children we lost were still outside the Den when the strikes began, but relative numbers were few." Holding up her hands to stay the rebuke, she continued, "I do not say that any child lost is acceptable. What I am saying is that I have to protect who is left of the Clan. The children are part of us, and I cannot protect them without their help."

Tyrza stood upright in her rebuke. "The youngest cannot help much in the way of physical labor without using up what resources we have left. Their maintenance is more costly than their output. What I am saying is that 'twill benefit the Clan more to outsource them, free up the space, the food, the supervision and security requirements, for the ones capable of doing the most work, the work you need done, here and now!"

Darque leaned back and crossed her muscled arms. "'Twould appear as if you already have an alternative plan to propose." As Tyrza took a breath and furrowed her brows, she actually looked like she was rethinking her decision. Afraid to speak her mind? Tyrza? She'd never been accused of holding her tongue when she had something to say. 'Twas reminiscent of her father, Regynn. Outspoken, sometimes brash, heedless to what others might think, she would always err on the side of speaking her mind, rather than the opposite.

Tyrza was tall with long straight blonde hair, porcelain skin, a pert nose with high cheekbones, and beautiful green eyes framed by thick dark lashes. Being only half Clan (for Regynn came from the Outlands), she tanned well when she had time to spend in the sun. But 'twas rare since she'd been promoted to Master Educator o'er the youth programs. She'd only seen twenty five winters, which was young for any Master, and she praised Mikkal's Outlander Training program for helping her push through early to achieve her life's ambition. She was rational, intelligent, straightforward, organized, practical, creative, honest, and tolerant of her charges, answering the age old question, 'why', innumerable times without ever growing impatient. When she spoke, they stopped and listened, while at the same time, encouraging them to question everything and seek verification. She was deceptively strong, but not muscular or ruggedly built as most Clansmen were, and she could not run to save her life, which sometimes made her feel out of place. But everyone loved her, and blushing, her eyes would glimmer with their acceptance. Yet regardless of how she felt about herself, her primary focus was the children and she would fight like a War Dog to protect them and to ensure their needs were well met. She'd never backed down from anyone or anything in order to accomplish her mission; she'd even demand the impossible from the Commander.

"I do have a plan," she admitted. Clearing her throat, she stepped back from the desk and blurted forth, "I want to take the children to St Swiftyn's. I want to establish a self sufficient colony there."

Chills ran up Darque's spine. The Keep of St Swiftyn's was within a day's ride of the Bog, where just prior to the battle they'd established the new Training Facility which had become the Lair of the growing Resistance. No one knew about the happenings there. Surely, the Master was ignorant of such.

In response to the pause, Tyrza steeled her resolve, swallowed hard, and took a deep breath. "I know 'tis a long way from home, Sir, but Drekinn will never be 'home' to these children again, nor to any of us, given the way things are proceeding, not to criticize your plan, Sir, but 'tis obvious it involves the passage of much time to rebuild, and our children's lives will be spent underground as 'tis too dangerous to live above as we used to and will be for many winters, so here they're stuck in the darkness and there they'd be free to move about, even our Training schedules have been disrupted, but they'd be safer there in case the Hoard does decide to return to finish us off, and we can become self sufficient, 'twould be an excellent educational opportunity, 'twill stretch their survivalist training establishing our own gardens and such, we could start raising some herd beasts, there has to be a well, and..." If she hadn't needed to take a decent breath, she'd not have stopped long enough for the Commander to get in a word of her own. Darque's expression changed from vexed to amused afore the girl actually took that much needed breath. Hands up in surrender, Darque nodded for a chance to interrupt. The Master shut her mouth and waited with wide eyes. She'd not expected the Commander to agree. She'd come prepared for a fight.

Weaving her fingers together, Darque leaned her elbows upon the desk. "Tyrza. I understand your concerns about the future of the children here, given all the restrictions I've been forced to order." Then with her voice growing cold and calculating, she cocked her head and narrowed her eyes. "Tell me why you chose the Keep."

She hadn't wanted to use Magic against a fellow Clansman. But she'd long been able to lock gazes with another, Pulling the truth from them. Her talents had only grown stronger since the 'Bond, and at this moment she required the truth from the woman standing afore her.

Tyrza felt the Compulsion but didn't understand it, not being aware of the extent of the power wielded by her Commander, nor did she waver. Her ability to sidestep came not from any Magical influence of her own, but from her single minded determination to do what she'd come here to do, which had nothing at all to do with her own needs. Stepping back, dragging her gaze away from Darque's, she had to sit down to avoid falling down from the effort. But she'd managed to break the Compulsion and Darque was impressed. Mayhap 'twould be wise for the time being, not to enlighten the Master on what she'd just accomplished. Sitting heavily in the chair opposite the desk, she seemed to recover well. No damage done, then. Good. Merely a tad befuddled, wondering what had just happened, Tyrza reorganized her thoughts back to the question. 'Twould not be any Compulsion forcing her response. 'Twould simply be the truth.

Tyrza promptly regained her composure. "Because there are only two abandoned villages that I know of, which might sustain being re-colonized. One is Kaddart, the other is the Keep. I harbor no illusions of taking a strong Warrior presence with us, our numbers have been devastated, but our safety is of the upmost importance, as the children are our only future. Therefore, Kaddart is easily dismissed for my needs. 'Twas a farming community, mostly open fields, but 'twas completely destroyed by Flame moons past, with no structure other than the well left intact. 'Twould be most difficult for a crew of children to rebuild sufficiently to start o'er, as well as being near impossible for a miniscule security force to defend."

Darque's brow furrowed as she recalled the Battle of Kaddart. Her fingers strayed to the pouch at her breast. So much had happened since then. Glancing back up, she nodded her head, and clearly and concisely, Tyrza continued, "St Swiftyn's, on the other hand, is not only easily defensible, 'tis impervious to Flame, being made almost entirely of rock, has a history of being habitable, 'tis no known damage other than what any animal presence may have done, and although we know not why 'twas abandoned, I feel 'twould be worthwhile making the attempt. Furthermore, 'tis in the colder regions and the Dragons like not the cold, so the fact that 'twas and remains abandoned gives us an advantage as well, for the Hoard evidently have already dismissed it as useful to them."

Reviewing each point, Darque saw much logic. Tyrza had put a good deal of thought into the plan. 'Twould also be ideal to have the children close enough to the Lair to properly defend them. She'd just been considering more extensive exploration of the Keep anyway, 'twould merely shift the task to the forefront of her priorities.

Sensing the need to further press her point, Tyrza reiterated what she felt was truth, although no one actually knew for certain. "'Tis obvious we cannot rebuild Drekinn within the span of days of these children's lives."

Darque hesitated just long enough to confirm the dire prediction, at least in her own mind, afore stating reluctantly, "'Tis possible."

Tyrza's voice softened in reply. "Then let me take them to St Swiftyn's, where they can grow up feeling the kiss of the sun upon their faces, and not living in the dark of caves as do the Teams. For Dragons and their riders are more suited to the darkness than are human children. Let me take them where they can dance in the rain... "

The Battle Commander cut her off abruptly. "I will consider your petition, Master Tyrza. Return to me in a sennight. I'll give you my decision then. And I don't believe that you need be reminded 'tis not information to be spread about."

Pursing her lips together tightly, she recognized she'd been summarily dismissed, but she also knew the Commander was fair and honest and if she'd said she was going to give her plan consideration, then she would. Reassured and suddenly very drained, for she'd been studying this for many days, she nodded her head in affirmation and took her leave. Darque went back to her mountain of paperwork.

<div align="center">~~~~~LATER~~~~~</div>

Rakkah stood afore his Commander, giving standard report from the Lair. He and Mikkal shared their duties and made report nightly together via the Link, but physically every sennight, first one and then the other. 'Twas his turn to stand in front of Darque, Mikkal having been here the previous night. He looked uncomfortable afore he continued. "Commander, I... as Security Officer... I must report an incident. Or rather, multiple incidents, happening more and more often, which I cannot explain."

Darque had never seen Rakkah in such a state. "What troubles you? You seem quite flustered."

"'Tis Mikkal. He's gone absent at night. Several marks at a time. When I check his rack, he's not there, nor is he anywhere in the facility, and when he shows up 'tis as if he's been drinking. But I've never known him not be able to hold his mead, Sir, and as there's no scent of it about him, 'tis confusing. I've known Mikkal for many winters, we're closer than blood. He's had episodes of sleepwalking along with terrible nightmares in the past, but 'twas easily covered. I admit to doing this frequently 'til he took Daynahmyn. He'd walk outside, visit people. He even dropped by your mother's quarters once, but he never caused any harm. He tells those few who've noticed that he hasn't been anywhere, they must have missed each other in rounds. But since our promotions my duties have kept us apart more often than not, and I just wanted you to be aware, as the behavior seems to be escalating."

Darque thought about their recent visit. Although nothing was mentioned, she'd noted Mikkal seemed more distant than usual. Could he have been Blocking something from her? "And what have your 'Bonds to say? Surely the situation has not gone beyond their notice."

"I believe our 'Bonds are aware, Commander. Daynahmyn and Petrayyah have been in frequent private Conversation and now I begin to wonder. 'Til recently, I'd merely thought they were strategizing for security."

Sensing his uncertainty, she felt the need to reassure him. "The 'Bond cannot be broken, Rakkah, mutual trust is paramount. If something concerns them, 'twould take Flaming good reason to avoid our involvement." Darque paused and considered her next words carefully. "Do you recall how Mikkal's 'Bond process was fraught with disorder?" His face answered her question. "No, of course not. You were deep in trance by then, about to send your own Call. 'Twas Petrayyah o'er whom his Blood Call hovered, but Daynahmyn would not release her edge while they Conferred, 'til she practically yanked the Call along and took Mikkal herself. Mayhap 'tis time to confront Petrayyah. There's something happening for certain, and I believe she may know more than she's Shared with you. And, in case you weren't aware, all Dragons have knowledge of their own futures, even though they may not understand 'til 'tis faced. Find out what you can and report to me at our next meeting. And Rakkah, this is not for Mikkal's knowledge."

Rakkah swallowed hard as he processed his orders and began to face the possibility that his best friend was in real trouble, as well as the fact that he may have unwittingly contributed to the unfolding fiasco.

"Rakkah?"

"Sir?"

"You've done nothing wrong, and I appreciate this report. I know how you feel about Mikkal. And for that reason, you must keep him very close. I don't wish to lose him or you, physically, or spiritually. Now, is there anything else I should know about the security at the Lair?"

Rakkah stood with his eyes narrowed, his jaw set. He'd known about the prophesy all his life, but he'd never figured to be a part of it. He still had his doubts, but things were beginning to come together in a most disturbing pattern. "Yes. 'Tis more. I've been debating whether 'tis important or not, but there be rumors circulating that the True King is amongst the Brotherhood. All Outlanders are being scrutinized, though nothing is said openly. Because of this, I did some research of my own, upon the known records of those Warriors who might qualify as suspicious. I found a handful with potential, none with proof. Nevertheless, 'tis true, both Mikkal and I are on that list. I've always believed I was a bastard son of Bryard. But the prophesy was about a child a winter younger than I, and 'twas why I never told anyone. Besides, no one is proud of having been abandoned. I'm quite certain there are many out there yet, who share my bloodline without benefit. He was a good King, but not a good father."

Darque eyed the Warrior thoughtfully afore responding. "I've often wondered why you felt so driven to excel in all things. 'Twas as if you never felt what you did, or who you were, was good enough. I didn't understand with whom you were comparing yourself. There was an animal inside you, pushing you, and yet, you're one of my best Warriors in all ways. Your skills are unsurpassed, your only match in ferocity and technique is Mikkal. You make a good Team. I appreciate the honesty, and this will be kept private, 'tween us." As her words soaked in, she paused. Known as the 'bad boys' of the Brotherhood, Rakkah and Mikkal had been inseparable since paired in the Pits winters past. Her heart ached for the pain in those green eyes staring back at her, even though no other sign of distress could be seen.

She made her decision. 'Twas time to tell him. "Rakkah, I know all about you and everyone else in the Brotherhood. Make no mistake, what you've disclosed is not entirely news. And while you thought you were born at sea, 'tis not truth. You were birthed in the Port District at the Waterside Inn, and left there by your mother according to an agreement with the Battle Commander to ensure your safety. You were Claimed and brought up Clan as part of that agreement. There's a diary in the safe that was to be given to you when 'twas deemed the appropriate time. I believe that time is now." She stood up and opened the massive safe in the corner of the office. Practically crawling inside on her hands and knees, she shuffled through several stacks of books, boxes, and papers, 'til she found that for which she searched. Pulling the small, leather bound journal from the back of one of the lower shelves, she blew off the dust and handed it to Rakkah, who took it as if 'twould burn his fingers. She'd never seen his hands shake afore, even in full Battle Lust. "You and Mikkal are very much alike. Keep him close. For his sake as well as the sake of the security of the Resistance, do not lose sight of him. This diary may or may not shed some light upon your life and your destiny, but either way, I believe yours and Mikkal's are entwined. Get your 'Bonds to understand I mean Mikkal no harm. But whatever happens, we must keep all others safe as well."

Rakkah clearly understood the insinuation in his Commander's words. His throat was so tight, he had difficulty swallowing, as he tucked the book into the inside pocket of his tunic. Afore he took his leave, Darque secured the list of those other 'potential' Warriors with the blood of the High King running through their veins. Skimming through them, she mentally eliminated all but two. 'Twas Rakkah and then... She let her thoughts go back to the very moment as a child when she'd blurted forth a sudden flash of insight, and Mikkal had inadvertently admitted to the truth. He believed he was sired by Bryard. They'd been quite alone and she was as shocked as he, but she'd never told anyone. Now the information seemed more relevant, and several things came together. The two huge Warriors could be twins, Mikkal was of the right age, and he'd come from King's Gate (also a supposedly well guarded secret, but nothing could be kept from the precocious daughter of the Battle Commander). The revelations made her squint. Mikkal? The True King? Not possible. But there was something happening with the fierce fighter and although he'd always been loyal, she had grave concerns about his stability since the battle. Still, in her heart Rakkah seemed the most likely candidate, but was too old. She wished she'd had the chance to read his diary afore giving it away, but hadn't felt 'twas right to do so. The diary was meant for the woman's son, not for her. Some things were just too personal.

<p style="text-align:center">~~~~~THE LAIR OF THE BLACK~~~~~</p>

The Sorcerer curled his lip in satisfaction. Now he only needed the Dragon's Eye to Call to the Beyond. Along with Grifynn's hair, he could actually use the Battle Commander against his own people, finding a weakness in his daughter, a way to destroy the prophesy. Delicious. How to get it? Use Koryl, of course. She's the one who told him about the Eye in the first place. As a full blood Rashei, her ability to See the future was what kept her alive. But 'twould also be her downfall one day, as she could not keep her knowledge to herself. She had to brag. And, as with them all, evil morphed their abilities, even those not of true Magical origin, so that they were sometimes erratic and became difficult to control, causing the need for more depravity to fuel and strengthen them, thus creating a vicious cycle. Although the changes were subtle, to conjure her Visions took more energy and time than they had in the past, and he did not like risking his life upon their accuracy, nor her truthfulness.

He licked his thin lips and pushed a stray strand of iron gray hair behind one ear. He'd discovered that Gunnarr the Mighty Blue was in possession of at least one Dragon's Eye. 'Twas the first successful scry he'd accomplished, giving him proof of Koryl's assertion, but 'twas exhausting in the effort and had taken him many dawns to recover. How did the Rashei do that all the time? Shaking his head, he realized how long he'd been waiting for just this opportunity to call in the favor she owed him for providing some crucial assistance against her own people many winters past. They'd both been ambitious, she was new to the Hoard and had thoughts of rising to a higher level in the inner circle than he, actually trying to use him as a stepping stone toward that end. She was not pleased the next time they'd met, he at the Black's side, and she a mere subordinate. In order to save face, she'd been hinting at having access to a Warrior. If true, then she could have the Warrior steal the Eye and bring it to him. 'Twould prove her loyalty to the Black and the war effort. If not true, then 'twould prove her to be a liar and would lead to her final ruin. Either way, 'twould be good for him. Another trip to Evanntyr then. Mouth-watering. Thoughts of her luscious body, along with her deca-dence, made him harden in response. He could do whatever he pleased, and she'd come begging for more. An added bonus to make the journey more palatable.

THE FOLLOWING DAWN

~~~~~SCOUTING ST SWIFTYN'S~~~~~

</div>

'Twas eerily quiet as the four massive Dragon brothers and their 'Bonds, High Prince Gunnarr with Darque, Quad Prince Kaygynn and Astraa, Fifth Prince Synddarr and Tannah, and Sixth Prince Shasynn with Tannah's sister, Tiyya, flew in circles under the pink streaks of the dawn skies o'er St Swiftyn's, the home of the Rashei. If Regynn's research was correct, the Rashei and the citizens of the extinct island of Rienne were one and the same. Second in Command was heading the watch at the Den,
~~~~~

while Third Fighter was holding down the Lair. 'Twas the end of fall and the weather was brisk. Fluffy white clouds clustered around the peaks of the mountains. Their exploration would be the first time anyone had set foot inside the Keep for something like thirty winters. 'Twas thought to have been much longer, but Darque believed 'twas Fay Memory Magic at work. She'd been studying the mechanics of such, and even interviewed Shayla, who didn't know anything yet should have known something, and the Dragons, who all appeared to be dumbfounded by her questions about the Keep. Of course they knew who'd lived there, 'twas just that no one had asked. Plus, it seemed few of them had actually ever visited, and only one, Haniyyah, had been there within the past half century, which for a Dragon was a very short time. Biting her tongue, she moved on with her investigation. Since Shayla wouldn't lie, she paid very careful attention to her eyes when questioned, and 'twas clearly something wrong. 'Twould appear once again, that Corbyn had been a busy Raven. When she found him, she'd wring his neck, but the Fay was mysteriously absent again. However, after researching the Archives she'd discovered some interesting discrepancies that went along with the few memories she'd obtained from the Dragons who'd actually been there, and she now believed that instead of having been abandoned o'er sixty winters earlier, St Swiftyn's had been abandoned about the time her mother had seen just ten or eleven winters, making the age difference 'tween her mother and father to be perceived as less than a decade. Although Aalanna's history was beginning to unravel, she was having trouble separating fact from fiction as the inconsistencies mounted. The Keep held secrets that needed to be unlocked.

Then she'd recalled Gunnarr's assertion about Haniyyah. The little Green was rumored to know every Race in existence and had not been affected by the Spell o'er the forests. Gunnarr had begun to gather information, but 'twas an immense task to which they'd had little time to devote, which was one of the reasons she couldn't fault them for not having said anything about the Keep afore. She'd make certain to interview her specifically, as soon as possible. But first and foremost, she needed a safe place for the children now, and St Swiftyn's held the greatest potential. The open ward was easily visible and simply huge, larger than the whole village of Drekinn. But then, 'twould have had to be, in order to sustain an entire thriving population since afore the Last Holocaust. The only visible entry or exit was a natural rock formation bridge spanning the gap, with a rather impressive river at least half a league below. There were multiple waterfalls; some might be accessible, others clearly not, nevertheless 'twould make it easier to supply should there be no well. A very large green region ran along the southern wall where she and Gunnarr had seen the blackberries. Within this area grew multiple trees, bushes, and had what appeared from on high to be places of public enjoyment, resembling a park. As the area didn't seem to have been used for agriculture, she could only surmise 'twas created simply for aesthetics. This gave her pause, as for an isolated society to have enough free time to create areas of beauty for simple enjoyment, spoke volumes of their survival skills. The walls along the southern and western sides were a house thick and several houses in height. The northern and most of the eastern part of the mountain was not readily visible due to the heavy mist from the falls. The living areas within the rock appeared to take up most of the mountain, and probably went down to its very roots. It showed promise to be many times larger than the caves under Drekinn, and could take a lifetime to fully explore. She prayed 'twas not a mistake to make this attempt. She and Gunnarr directed pewter grey Kaygynn and Astraa to land in the middle of the ward flanking them, teal Synddarr and Tannah to stand watch upon the southern wall with all the vegetation, leaving Shasynn and Tiyya flying watch above, his bronze scales glittering.

Darque depended upon their senses to determine their safety, along with the fact that to Haniyyah's knowledge, there was nothing sinister about the Keep. Exploring level after level, the mystery of the disappearance of the inhabitants only deepened. If not for the layers of dust, the stillness, the absolute emptiness, she'd have sworn she was going to run into someone as she stepped around every corner. There was not a living thing about. Not even animal life had taken up permanent residence here, although 'twas evidence of intruders having been in the upper levels and open areas long ago. The exterior gardens were o'er grown, a few wild vegetables attempted to survive, but inside was a different story. 'Twas as if time stood still, the inhabitants going about their daily routines. In the upper levels were mostly community centers for teaching and learning, a wide variety of shops and open markets unseen from above, shielded by o'er hanging rock or the constant high level mist. The Keep was a veritable labyrinth. As they entered the lower levels they found living quarters with plates set out on tables, some beds were made, some not, everything silently awaiting the occupants' return. 'Twas unnatural. No sign of how or why they'd disappeared. No sign of struggle or damage. And the oddest part for the Battle Commander... there were no bodies. The people of St Swiftyn's appeared to have made a mass exodus of incredible timing, practically vanishing all at once and taking nothing with them. It made no sense. What could have happened to a entire society of Mystics? Gunnarr and his brothers could taste no evil or illness, no danger at all. But there was something. "'Tis as a fog blurs my Vision throughout the Keep. Even so, all I sense is... bewilderment." Still, for her purpose they all agreed 'twould be safer here than under Drekinn, at least for the time being.

CHAPTER TWENTY-THREE

Mez Me! or, What History?

THREE DAWNS LATER
~~~~~THE DRAGON'S DEN~~~~~

Darque was o'erwhelmed, weighed down with the burdens she'd inherited, along with those she'd placed upon herself. She'd always been in charge and in control, however, the current events were anything but under control, which made her feel vulnerable. Glancing up from her desk where she'd not been paying attention to her paperwork but had instead been considering the lack of information coming forth from the castle, she declared, "I must journey to Evanntyr. 'Tis time for me to make report to the High King."

Gunnarr choked on his kaafy afore setting down the o'ersized mug. "You will do no such thing."

"I must. 'Twould be expected of the Battle Commander, or anyone who'd be left of rank or file. We can't assume he knows that we know his troops were at the battle."

"You know he's a traitor. I see no reason to fulfill such a commitment. Why do this?"

Darque became more and more animated with her response, rising and walking around the office, her hands flying up in the air to emphasis her points. "If I do not, 'twill invite inspection. He's lost many troops. He has no word back from anyone he finds reliable. He has only the Hoard, who report only to the Black, and the Black fled the battle near afore it began. He wouldn't know if his Agents even arrived, let alone participated, or their fate. If I go, he may stay away, he's too cowardly to do otherwise. I must convince him the Clan has been defeated, wiped out, destroyed. Besides, first and foremost, I'm a Warrior. I need to get into the castle. I need information, and I can see no other way to get what I need. I need to see it with my own eyes, I need to be there."
~~~~~

Despite the fact that the conversation was completely ridiculous in his opinion, Gunnarr felt a familiar stirring 'tween his hind legs with all this talk about her needs. Keeping a straight face was becoming quite a chore, as he tried to think of an appropriate response. "Koryl is a witch. Any doubts would set off her senses like a flare and she'd see through your deception."

Darque knew he was right, but she had no Stealth Teams to send and she must discover if they'd taken any hostages, including Mynx. She'd never shirked performing her own dirty work, and actually preferred the bold approach. At this moment 'twas clear in her mind that all she had to do was play dumb. Still, his assessment irked her in its certainty. No matter her thoughts or needs or wants, Koryl was a witch. "This plan may involve more acting talent than that with which I have been graced, and you're correct. She will see right through me if I falter." Darque snarled, her countenance surly at best, and downright nasty at worst.

Gunnarr was amused but dared not snicker aloud at his feisty lady, he'd not want to hurt her feelings, especially when she was trying so hard to be obtuse. At least, 'twas so in his thinking. Going to Evanntyr was not on the agenda, now, or ever. In any case, not without a full contingent of fighting Teams. And, the Dragon short on acting talent? He'd beg to differ. The only way his woman came up short was in physical stature. As usual, thinking about anything having to do with her physique made his breath stutter and his loins tighten. Slowly exhaling, he willed away the poorly timed reaction. If only they could... but not now. He cleared his throat. There'd be time in the future, after all, she was his lifemate, giving them all of the now as well as the Beyond. His grin was even more difficult to suppress as he realized Darque was giving him 'the look', having been eavesdropping through their Link. Producing an exaggerated sigh, he wrinkled his face into a pained expression that told her he was once again listening.

Narrowing her eyes she continued, "Like I was saying, afore my senses were inundated with sexual fantasies, which I wouldn't really mind were we in any other situation, which we are not..." Her shifting emotions flowed o'er Gunnarr's heart like the ocean waves, and wanting to comfort his beloved, he hugged her close to his leathery chest, enveloping her with his wings, one rough paw wrapped around her narrow waist, the other gently stroking her cheek.

She lifted her chin and stared into his incredibly gorgeous eyes, those eyes whose depths never ended, making her feel so... suddenly her own eyes flew open in triumph as she declared with enthusiasm, "Mez me! Mesmerize me, make me unable to doubt my story as 'tis told; make me an unreadable slate! 'Twill work, I am certain!"

Gunnarr hated to upset her. Hesitantly he growled, "No, my love, 'twill not work. Mesmerizing is dangerous for most Magic bearers. Only the Ice Dragons are truly proficient, and if performed inadequately 'twould cause much harm to the one being mezzed. However, 'twould not work for us in any case, for you and I are in 'Bond and 'twould be as if I were looking in a mirror attempting to mez myself." Shaking his head he continued, "We share our psyches. I can no more mez you, my jewel, than can I lie to you."

Sighing deeply, she dropped her gaze in a flash of disappointment, and huffed. "Well, I know 'tis truth, and even without our 'Bond, I trust your word." The mood passed quickly as she spoke. "Yet, with the exception of the Highlands, all Races can lie. 'Tis an unfortunate side effect of sentience. Makes me wonder how your own Race cannot. I believe I'll find the answer eventually, but I doubt 'twill provide little more than curiosity value to the current efforts." She began to pace the floor as she formulated her next move. "So, no mezzing. No such assistance forthcoming in my need."

Turning about abruptly, she caught the heated look in his eyes, the glistening of intensifying Allure that made it clear his emotions were running high and he'd just been staring at her butt.

Hearing her mention her needs again, pushed him o'er the edge. *"You have only to say the word, my sweet, and I will do all in my power to fulfill your every need."* He raised one brow ridge while his eyes roamed from her muscled thighs to her full breasts, settling there with an expression of desire anyone could clearly see.

With a deep groan, he regained control of the rising heat in the pit of his stomachs, as she waggled her finger in front of his face. "Stop drooling, it's most unbecoming. And don't think I missed that part about 'Ice Dragons', we shall have a long chat on that revelation very soon. They've never been mentioned as more than myth, and that they are is obvious by your statement. We need all the Races with us in this war."

Gunnarr glanced about the room sheepishly, attempting to escape her reprimand. If the Mighty Blue could blush, he'd have been as red as his lady's hair. Letting him off the hook for the time being, she persisted with her plan. "At any rate, I don't want you anywhere close to Evanntyr. I shall ride Konann, you shall fly into the Edge, stay hidden and remain in Contact through our Link." She paused and continued as if talking to herself. "'Twill take much acting on my part to convince Shytin, the Clan is no more. I'll have to avoid Koryl and hide my true emotions as our separation will increase the stress. I have to try to ascertain if the Hoard is truly there or just frequenting, and if there are any prisoners."

The low growl emitted from deep in the back of Gunnarr's throat, signaled his rising disagreement afore he countered slowly in his heavily accented Common Tongue. "I recognize that you are fatigued and we've had no time to gather ourselves since the battle, so let me just say that if we were to go to the castle, you are being excessively protective. And must I remind you that if they know of the 'Bond, of which we have every right to expect them to know, then they simply need kill you to rid themselves of us both? Besides, do you honestly feel I cannot handle a few King's Men? You are a highly skilled Warrior, but if you think I would allow my woman to enter that den of iniquity alone, you need think again."

Darque was taken aback as she listened to the closest thing to irritation directed at her, that had ever come from her mate's mouth. Still, 'twas laced with his true feelings. These were difficult times and his need to protect her was obvious. Yes, he'd warned her of a Dragon's obsessive nature in all things sexual and sensual, but it still warmed her heart and soul when he openly displayed his love. She realized she was one of only a few human females who'd be able to handle such from a life partner, without drowning in the tsunami of sensations. But their raging passions fueled each other's drives, rather than suffocating them. 'Twas wild and raw, and when they made love 'twas incredible. And even though as of yet they'd not fully consummated their union, they never failed to pleasure each other. Gunnarr showed remarkable restraint during these times, which was more than she could say for herself. It helped that they were in 'Bond which allowed her to Share, and thus knowing what he really meant despite what he said aloud, indulgence grew 'tween them, kindling the perfect relationship.

Gunnarr began again. "Sweetness, you try too hard to do everything yourself. Your headstrong conviction and dedication make you a Warrior to be feared in any battle, but leadership requires finesse. Your youth assists you in many ways, but 'tis a detriment in others. Naiveté will get us killed. You really can't just walk in there and expect him to treat you with the respect your position deserves, as his father and his father afore him did with Grifynn. He will not meet that expectation. This time, you must see that I am right."

Embarrassed and frustrated, she replied, "Fine, I understand. I didn't think that out too well, did I? But we do need to get into the castle. We need to talk to Shytin. We need to find out if there are prisoners. We need information we can only get from being there. We have no one to send, our best Stealth Team is missing, and... "

"...and Brannyn can provide this information. Leading is not about being in the front line at all times, little one. You must learn to trust and delegate, send others to do what you need, make wise decisions. Wisdom will keep us all alive to fight again, impatience will likely send us all Past the Veil afore our time."

"Are you trying to tell me that I'm hot headed?"

"I do believe so. After all, you've acknowledged that I am, and we are very much alike. As I recall, when you first met with Brannyn there was something mentioned about my such input."

Blushing, she remembered the moment she'd affirmed Brannyn's comment about her fiery mate. This was one of those times she wished she wasn't as efficient in the Link. Although she could Block her thoughts, she rarely did with Gunnarr, as she felt Sharing all with her mate and war partner was imperative.

Gunnarr's voice became husky with desire. "'Tis good that we Link so efficiently. I didn't bring it up afore because 'tis truth, and it matters not to me because it matters not to you. I would not change our Link, for it allows me to meet your inner most needs and desires. You are very gifted." He marveled at how Magic was Magic, but that each of the Magic bearing Races had drifted apart into their own special talents, each had their forte. Upon this side of the Veil, along with their Memory Magic, the Fay had no match for Shifting. He sighed. If he could Shift as easily, if it wouldn't leave him completely drained and both of them vulnerable, he'd take the chance... just once. He'd do almost anything to take Darque completely, to consume her, to claim her in every sense of the word. Mine, he thought, she is mine, but they could not consummate their love unless he could Shift to Human form. There had to be another way. He had to return to Flight of Fire Keep, research the archives, something must be there. He knew that once there was a very successful Highland-Human match. How had they made that happen? Just thinking about her lying open to him, wanting him as much as he wanted her, made him begin to salivate.

His nostrils flared with the scent of her arousal and his body seemed to take on a mind of its own. His tongue slipped out and he laved the inside of her ankle, then lifted her lovingly and laid her down 'tween his legs, a pillow from the chair tucked under her head. Painstakingly, he used his talons to undress her, leaving her completely exposed afore his hungry gaze. Slowly, teasingly, he licked his way closer to the junction 'tween her thighs, as a moan of desire slipped from her throat in anticipation of his touch. He loved the taste of her, and as the moisture pooled she couldn't help but spread her legs wider, lifting her hips, trying to force his tongue inside her, needing him to take her o'er the edge of ecstasy. He could no longer deny her need and aided by her slippery wetness he pushed inside 'til he could go no further, and then just as slowly, he withdrew. One paw encircled and slid up and down his thickening length, while with the other, he warmed the center of her desire in taut circles, as his tongue continued to invade her core 'til she near wept for relief. Soon, his own climax upon him, he pushed in hard and deep. Pressing firmly into that one place that never failed to please, her head came up off the pillow then fell back in a hard, elongated spasm of sheer rapture that matched his own, the last of his warm seed finally spilling o'er her lush breasts and upon her flat belly.

<p style="text-align:center">~~~~~~~~~~</p>

As their breathing and heart rates normalized, Darque dragged her fingers wickedly through the evidence of his ardor, then leisurely, sensually, licked off the thick amber fluid. His taste was similar to his scent, smoky, like fine aged whiskey, only much more subtle. Her heated gaze still locked on her lover's, he groaned, "Let me help clean you, my love."

Her blue eyes twinkling, she laughed, "I hate to waste it, there should be something it's good for. Other than the obvious, of course."

Gunnarr rolled o'er beside her on his back and stared into space as he pondered a long forgotten memory. "'Twill bring forth life. In the distant past the Rashei added it to their gardens.

'Twas highly prized as fertilizer, stimulating the growth and bearing of the plants."

Darque was intrigued and rolled o'er to her stomach. Propping herself up on her elbows, she replied thoughtfully, "You are certain? How so?"

"I was never certain if 'twas myth or 'twas truth. Still, I should have thought of it earlier and mentioned it to you. 'Twas said that they were exceptional farmers and even on a relatively small island, they managed to produce more than enough for their entire society. When the Rashei settled in the Keep, they came prepared to live off the land, as was their heritage. But their land was now carved from solid rock and what gardens they could create were small in comparison to their needs. Again, they managed. 'Twas said they added the Dragon's semen to the soil when they planted, and 'twould stimulate such enormous and rapid growth, they had plenty and all were well fed."

"Our land has been sterile since the battle. Mayhap 'twould heal the soil?"

"'Twould be worth trying, but even so, I'm curious as to how you plan to present this to your men, my dear."

"Um... well I... I'll think of something. Let's not dive off the cliff yet, first I need to know if it works."

"Simple enough. I'll bring you a bucket of soil from the fields. You'll plant and I will... um... fertilize. Within one dawn, we'll see what... uh... comes up."

"One dawn? You realize if this works we're going to need a lot more... fertilizer?"

"Oh, 'tween you and I, we should have a good handle on that. But, my treasure, there are many Dragons here. Highlands are a lusty Race. A lot more, will not be difficult."

"You were thinking about something while we were making love," Darque Spoke, hoping he would finally tell her what was bothering him so often lately. He seemed distracted during their intimacy, and 'twas unsettling. *"Am I not pleasing you? Is there*

anything more that I can do, to make it better? You keep telling me no, but something is on your mind."

"No, little one, 'tis not... I am not... what I mean," he tried to Explain, but was afraid of hurting her or having her misunderstand. Seeing no way out of the situation, he confided in her at last. She listened attentively, finally realizing that he could Shift. But Gunnarr refused to do so, and his chest constricted with the look of sadness that came o'er his beloved's face. Growling aloud he told her, "The Fay are the strongest Shifters, and I will not pull a Shift that will weaken me to the point I would be rendered incapable of providing your defense, let alone mine."

Hope blossoming anew, she sat upright. "Aw baby, I can provide our defense!"

"Then there's our history," Gunnarr snarled.

With complete innocence and a big smile, she asked, "What history?"

"Must I remind you that quite often our amorous activity is followed by battle?"

Suddenly she couldn't look him in the eye. "That's just happened a couple of times."

He raised one brow ridge. "A couple?"

"Well, mayhap a tad more often," she squirmed.

CHAPTER TWENTY-FOUR
Unwelcome Guests

Simultaneously, Gunnarr and Darque froze at the barely audible sound coming from the south, a sound more felt than heard. 'Twas the resonance of a multitude of beating wings. She cocked her head to Storrm's brusque Voice, *"Commander! We have guests!"* The Hoard had returned at last. Gunnarr helped her wipe away all evidence of their tryst, then she rapidly donned her leathers, grabbed her Sword as it leaped into her reaching hand, and was out the door and down the hallway in a flash, leaving him behind. Rounding the corner, she sprinted to the spiral staircase and raced up the steps three at a time. There was a small landing at the top of the stairs where stood a short ladder to the trap door o'er head. She didn't even recall pushing it open afore she was out on the ramparts, under cover of the eves. Storrm crouched beside her as they peered off to the southwest. She could see the group of Dragons flying toward Drekinn, tried to count the tiny dots in the distance... ten... thirty... seventy five... By all the fires of Hades! What the Flame were they doing? All this time not a single Hoard Dragon had shown up, and now a full contingent. There must be close to a hundred of them. Could the Six Hold under that much pressure? Not to mention that they'd have to kill them all afore they reported the Shield, announcing to the world that 'twas protecting something. They'd be doomed. She searched the sky o'er head, noted the energy begin to snap and sizzle as the Shield was strengthened. 'Twas no doubt. They were under attack. As the swarm came closer, the Six began to stir. Rising to their feet, they bowed their heads and dipped their shoulders toward each other as if pushing against a great weight. The star shimmered, crackled, began to ripple and dance. This was no ordinary flyby. They were coming here to search for survivors, to finish them. Their intent clear to the Six, Darque issued orders to help reduce what was being hidden. *"Gunnarr! Bring in the field teams! Get everyone below,"* she Yelled to the Mighty Blue as he descended o'er the distant fields where the salvage efforts continued, an enormous wicker basket in his talons.

Storrm was already collecting the Warriors working the Port District. Mystynn stretched out his long back legs, latched onto the other basket amongst the debris which had provided it the perfect camouflage, and swooped toward the Warriors scrambling even now for pick up, near where the docks once stood. The devices were a contrivance of Master Craftsman Cathay, inspired by a description Regynn translated of a giant balloon lifting a basket, and could carry six people, give or take, and/or similar weight in supplies, reasonably well by one Dragon. 'Twas safer than the slings, which required at least two Dragons for stabilizing large loads, but the Warriors hadn't really taken to the contraptions, although they had to admit 'twas better than dying. After they'd all rolled in head first while 'twas hovering just above the ground, Mystynn joined Gunnarr as they flew their passengers to the caves via the cliffs along the western border. Gunnarr commanded the Sentries north to the caves in the foothills, sending one to warn the Lair. He Called to the Teams outside to stay hidden, but ready to come if needed.

In the meantime, Darque slid back down the ladder and ran toward the kennels. Although the vast majority of the huge animals were with their Warrior Handlers split 'tween the Den and the Lair, the breeding stock and pups were still housed here. All were secure, Teaka, the Kennel Master, keeping them as calm as possible. She cautioned them to remain so 'til the crisis was o'er. Teaka grit her teeth. "I cannot hide from the enemy, Commander. Every time we do this it feels wrong, and the Dogs don't understand why I don't free them to join the fight."

Darque felt her distress. "We're vastly outnumbered. The Clan will rise again, Teaka. We're not defeated. Shytin is not the True

King, and I'm convinced the Hoard cannot and will not sustain their push without his support. When Evanntyr falls and the Hoard loses focus, we must be ready."

~~~~~~~~~~

The Warrior had been assisting the Master with the pups, unseen 'til now. Hearing his Commander's words, he stood his full height and stepped forward, his Dog on his heels, hackles rising in response to his partner's emotions, as he growled, "Your father would never have stood down."

Gunnarr's Voice was brusque as he flew quickly back to the Den. *"I sense an aggressor. I come."*

"No, 'tis well. I'll explain later." Darque's hesitation to respond aloud, came from her inability to immediately name the one standing menacingly in front of her, but even as she recalled, she sensed he wasn't aware of his posturing. Still, 'twould not do, to let it go. She growled back. "My father is dead. I am Commander here, and you have but two choices. Challenge me, or follow orders and shut the Flame up. Choose now and choose well, for I'll not tolerate anything less than your full allegiance." As she spoke, she stepped threateningly closer to the man, which should have been somewhat comical given that he towered o'er her, however, Darque was no ordinary female. Her very presence inspired awe. Her eyes locked onto his and she spit forth, "Draw your sword Warrior, or back off."

And back off, he did. Bowing his head, breaking eye contact, he replied in a humbled voice, "My apology, Commander, I was wrong." He caught her gaze once more and with an impish smile upon his face and a hearty slap on her shoulder, causing her to step sideways to maintain her balance, he exclaimed, "You do have your father within you! Mayhap the rumors of the Death of the Clan were premature after all." Turning away, he went back to assisting Teaka with the pups.

~~~~~~~~~~

Storrm walked up behind her at that moment, and satisfied in the Warrior's deference, Darque took her sister by the arm and led her back out to the hall. As they walked, she planned. "If they try to force their way inside, the Shield will not hold that many for long. As it begins to collapse, they'll sense the reality around them, and 'twill fail even quicker. At which point they need only besiege us to the caves, to be our final doom." *"And why didn't we receive warning from Brannyn?"*

Storrm didn't hesitate in her Response, her confidence growing, *"I know not, but I suspect 'twas unplanned, or outside the Black's approval. Brannyn has been chipping away at their internal structure, mayhap this is the result. Either way, any spontaneous actions would not allow him time to give warning."* Darque experienced a twinge of shame for doubting the Fay, then shook it off. There were too many other things about which to be concerned.

<div align="center">~~~~~~~~~~</div>

Corbyn was in shock. He'd just returned, drained from his latest foray. Had he Heard them correctly? With Storrm as the Warrior to whom he was tied in this current cycle of his curse, he could Hear her. Were they Speaking of... no, it couldn't be. Hopefulness bloomed in his heart. The Falcon yet lived?

<div align="center">~~~~~~~~~~</div>

Storrm continued aloud, "The Shield has shown itself to ward off a handful of attackers, however, a full contingent will collapse it, I agree. 'Twould be poor tactics to try to fight them here, but we can divert them, take them toward the Lair. They come from the south, 'twould be reasonable to think as they travel northward they'd be too far away to Call to any others. Their Links are not as secure or as strong as ours. And we can defeat them there. Second Stable is Flight ready. No better way to prove them than this." With the spark of uncertainty that shone in Darque's eyes, Storrm felt she needed a reminder of their prowess. "That is, if the recent battle wasn't enough." The Raven sat upon her shoulder, his ebony eyes hard and challenging, an ever present sign of the other Races in their lives, all dependent upon her and the choices she made. Briefly, she thought about her new contact and wondered how the Fay knew each other, for that much was certain. They did know each other.

Darque opened and shut her mouth. 'Twas not the Raven's beady eyes that stayed her response. She simply had no argument against such logic. And this would be a battle in which she'd not participate, for the Clan could not be left unprotected. She and Gunnarr might have to lead their last defense here. *"One of those wise decisions, my love? Delegate the battle to my little sister?"*

"No, my fascination. You are delegating to your Second. You must let go. I have faith in you. You will make good decisions. You will make bad decisions. But you alone, make those decisions, and no one will question them unless you so question."

She continued speaking with Storrm. "I can only add caution. If we divert them to the Lair, there can be no survivors. You know this."

"And so shall it be!" She turned and strode down the hallway. The Second was in Command for this battle. 'Twould be the first time in her life that she'd done anything without her sister. But she'd grown up rapidly o'er the past winter and she and Mystynn were ready to lead, and ready to fight.

"I was referring to them, not us," Darque hissed toward the other's swiftly retreating backside, and was rewarded with a stifled guffaw and a particularly rude gesture flashed o'er her leather and metal plated shoulder, which disrupted the perch of the Raven who flew off into the distant shadows to unruffle his feathers. 'Twas the only farewell they'd have. She smirked, then frowned. If this went wrong 'twas all gone. The Clan, the growing Resistance, the chance of using St Swiftyn's for the children, and her sister.

~~~~~~~~~~
~~~~~~~~~~

Mystynn Called to the troops and all were gathered in the Pits when he and Storrm arrived. Storrm's expression hardened as she counted, strategizing for the ambush. The survivors from First Flight stood afore her in the sands, with the exception of the Commander and General Gunnarr, and Haniyyah and Axyl who were still on the injured list. Counting herself, 'twould be ten Teams. Second Stable, with their surviving ten Teams, would be ready to flank them when they arrived. Her forces would lead the enemy, turning and closing the circle for the battle. She shook her head approvingly. 'Twas far better odds than they'd faced in the last fight. However, beyond the Teams stood five of the seven Free Dragons currently at Drekinn, with Free Warriors already mounted. As they ambled forward, she could see they were all four to a saddle. And that's when she noted the Teams' mounts. Every one of them had at least three extra Free Warriors aboard.

Mystynn Spoke to her with a mix of awe and concern. *"The other two Frees here agreed to stay and protect the Clan should the Shield fail. And I Hear all six at the Lair volunteering for the fight, flying with four Free Warriors each. Storrm, they cannot carry such a load and remain battle ready from this distance, they'll use up their Magic keeping their riders from freezing, let alone fight with them aboard after the long flight."*

Sadly, she Agreed. *"I know. The extra Free Warriors from the Lair can fight on the ground. They won't be heavily taxed on a long flight. But those from here..."* She shook her head then addressed the gathering aloud. "I understand that each and every one of you has the desire and the skill to be here. But as First Fighter, I have to say no. And afore I get too much flack, consider the logistics. Only the Teams have enough experience to fight with more than one armed Warrior per Dragon without beheading our own. And for the Dragons to fly more than two Warriors heavily armed, for as far as this trip will take us, 'twill become a liability. We fly hard, we fly fast, we must not be weary when we arrive, for then the real test of our mettle begins. I don't want to leave anyone out of this, but I have to use appropriate strategies. And although 'tis my hope we all come home successfully, if we do not, those of you left behind may very well be all that's left to carry on the Resistance. Now, I'll let you choose 'tween each other but do so quickly, leaving only two per Dragon. I need volunteers to stay and protect the Clan, as much as I need volunteers to ride this day."

They understood, but weren't happy. Amidst much grumbling the extra Warriors all dismounted. But the two brothers sitting behind Yanais on Shykiyyah, stood firm, neither one giving up their seat. "If you make me decide," she began, but was interrupted.

"You must, or we both fly with Yanais."

"Then I say 'twill be you, Courtney. Shallyn is not as adept at the sign language as are you, and I will not have both brothers Pass in the same battle, if this can be avoided. The Clan needs your bloodline."

Courtney and his little brother clasped arms and hugged afore the young man reluctantly dismounted and joined the rest of the disappointed Warriors unable to get to the fight.

All eyes and ears were upon the Second as she gave her orders. "As soon as possible after arrival I want one rider per Dragon aerial, Free Warriors are to land and join the others. Courtney, you are First Fighter of the ground assault. Now launch! We ride!"

~~~~~THE ARCHIVES OF THE CLAN LIBRARY~~~~~

Fryya was yet again where she shouldn't be, doing what she shouldn't be doing. The youngest of the Aalanna Grifynn siblings had grown like a weed o'er the past winter since she'd come to live with the Clan. Highly precocious, curiosity ruled her behavior, practically forcing her to seek out anything she didn't already know and understand, regardless of the consequences. With her enhanced senses, excellent hearing and vision at the forefront, she rarely got caught in her forays, which only seemed to fuel the
~~~~~

need to push her boundaries further. At just eight winters, she could teach the Stealth Teams some very useful techniques, however, she was still small in stature and the other children teased her that a stiff breeze would knock her off her feet. Given 'twas close to truth, 'twas her belief that she required wearing sufficient weaponry, and/or ill gotten gains, in order to weigh her down. 'Twas how she justified obtaining that which she felt was necessary.

Since she was one of only three humans, albeit hybrids, who could walk through the Spell door in the dungeons, she made frequent visits to the Den alone, against the Battle Commander's orders. Her need to satisfy her curiosity compelled her to shadow Regynn, keeper of the vast library which housed innumerable secrets of unimaginable attraction. Regynn was one of those people who also seemed preoccupied with his learning and she felt a kind of kindred spirit when she watched him. The Elder Warrior, in 'Bond with Sydrayyah, a close friend of the Last Dragon Matriarch, would study for marks, talking to himself, puttering about, tinkering, and constructing many intriguing things. A few were strictly for fun or beauty, and 'twas obvious he and Master Craftsman Cathay liked each other, as they often worked together. But since most of his projects were directly related to their survival, 'twas odd that lately he'd been making black powder, the kind they used in fireworks during the Faires. She loved them, but they'd not had a Faire since the war began o'er a winter past. So, why was Regynn making fresh powder? When he'd stepped out for a moment she'd seen her chance, and racing to the table she'd grabbed one of the 'hot candles' he'd made and tucked it into her pouch. Then she'd vacated rapidly, raced toward the other side of the Den, and disappeared down the stairs to the dungeons, quite certain her retreat went unseen.

~~~~~~~~~~

Regynn stood watching the girl from the shadows of the alcove. When he thought she'd probably had time to get back to the
~~~~~~~~~~

caves, he returned to the library and counted his latest projects. The normal ones would simply explode high in the air in multiple colors with loud screams and bangs causing little to no damage, except mayhap a burned finger. But he'd been working on more than that. He'd created an explosive device no bigger than a hot candle, that should be able to break down huge rocks, help build roads, clear fields and ruined structures for rebuilding, and he'd been especially interested in trying them as a weapon. He didn't know how to deliver such, but he was quite certain 'twould kill a Dragon. He just wasn't certain 'twould penetrate the scales, and how would you test it anyway? They couldn't afford to waste a Thumper, and 'twas not likely any of the Dragons would volunteer, after all. And if it didn't work, trying to use it in the thick of battle could get a Warrior killed. His thoughts returned to the table. One missing. He wasn't too concerned. She wouldn't be able to use it, as he'd built in a safety feature. 'Twould take the heat of Flame itself, to light the wick. He grinned. He rather liked that child. She was going to make a good Warrior one day.

~~~~~~~~~~~

Darque ran back down the hallway, mentally strategizing. Storrm would provide the diversion by leading the enemy toward the Bog, who'd be forewarned of the arrivals and were even now prepping. She envisioned the positions to be taken, including hers and Gunnarr's. The Second's orders were Heard and she knew the Teams of First Flight were already 'running' outside the Shield. Mystynn Brewed a Spell of Allusion to make the Hoard think they could not catch them, always just ahead, in order to help fuel their passion to keep following. So close and flying in fast, she didn't have to watch from the ramparts this time, to see the incoming swarm. They were less than a quarter mark away she'd wager, but when she checked 'twas clear the enemy was splitting up. That wasn't good. Some chased Storrm and the Teams, but not all. Calling to her Free Warriors, she had Gunnarr relay her orders to lay in, prepare for siege, and to stay under-
~~~~~~~~~~~

ground. If the Hoard attempted to get to them they'd be greatly hindered, giving her Warriors the advantage as long as they didn't come topside and fight openly. She'd already had them set up stone barriers at all the entrances to protect them from Flame should the need arise. She hoped 'twould not.

Abruptly she Heard another voice, deep and ominous, stopping her thoughts as surely as it stopped her movement. If she hadn't heard it afore, she might have been slightly intimidated, however, 'twas Brannyn. She stood very still and listened carefully, but the message was not repeated. Just three words. Surely she was mistaken. She shook her head. No. There could be no doubt. The message he Sent was, 'they seek Fryya.' But why? He'd already explained how the blood of children had the most intoxicating effect, but his message clearly wasn't about just any child. And why would they think any child had survived anyway? No, he specifically stated that they wanted her little sister. As a warning, she wasn't quite sure what to make of it, but she'd not look that gift horse in the mouth.

"Gunnarr? Get hold of Shayla, I need her topside, now."

"What say you, Flame Spitter?"

"I've Heard from Brannyn. I want Fryya with me. It appears we may be entering this fight after all." 'Twould take merely a few moments afore...

"She comes now."

"Fryya needs her weapons."

"She's never without them; Ragnyrr has been tutoring her."

Despite the gravity of the situation, she chuckled. *"Is that good or bad?"*

"Pfffft."

WALKYR'S QUARTERS

~~~~~THE CAVES BENEATH THE DEN~~~~~

</div>

At just seven winters, Walkyr's Visions were legendary. His life's story was short but complicated, and as the strongest Seer in
~~~~~

the history of Kadoor (as well as the youngest), his safety was considered a priority to the Battle Commander. He was born in the Outlands, the thirteenth child of subsistence farmers, who were happy to have the Seer of the Dragon Clan and his mate, Claim the toddler based on Kallyr's Vision. They'd never see him again, but 'twas a guarantee he'd be well cared for and would have a profession, more than they could say about the rest of their brood. When Kallyr died in the battle Shayla was left alone, but her duties as Clan Healer had her unable to provide the two things a growing boy needed most; a strong male influence, and time.

Cayell, Walkyr's bodyguard afore the battle, stepped up to Claim him as his son, as they'd grown very close. Normally Claim parents were mated to each other, however no one saw this unusual situation as reason to deny either the boy or the Warrior. Shayla provided all the time and energy she could, given her massive restraints, and Walkyr was acting as Clan Seer now, his own restraints resulting. Having accepted a lifelong duty station commitment, Cayell's primary responsibility was to continue as Walkyr's bodyguard, and they shared quarters. All were pleased at how things were working out. With his War Dog always at his side, for all intents and purposes the boy was being raised by the entire Clan.

Sitting opposite and enjoying the antics of Horace at play, Cayell was quick to take heed of the Dog's reactions and reached forward just in time to keep Walkyr from falling on the floor as he came out of a fierce Vision. Cayell had much experience with the boy's Sight and when Walkyr jumped up and darted out, saying not a word, the Warrior quickly followed. Sword in hand, Cayell raced after the boy and Horace, never losing sight of either.

Walkyr ran through the caves toward his best friend's quarters. His own safety wasn't in question as he was positive he'd See danger to himself, and such a Vision had yet to occur. He'd been in dangerous situations, but thus far had never been seriously injured. Even as horrible as 'twas, he was excited to see Fryya again. Training Horace, along with his duties as Seer, kept him extremely busy, and the two hadn't even had time to talk since just after the battle. Still, he had to tell her about his Vision. Running around the corner he bumped into Shayla just requesting to be taken above. He couldn't let her leave without his warning, but he didn't want to give away her recent excursion, for he'd Seen that was well. Nor did he want to get her into trouble with Darque, but her life would soon be in much danger. Even so, at this particular moment he needed an excuse for being there, and in such a hurry, or Shayla would be suspicious. With wide eyes, he blurted, "Have you seen my father? I seem to have misplaced him again." Walkyr was not supposed to be without Cayell, but 'twas well known throughout the caves that he frequently 'lost' the Warrior. Shayla smirked.

Fryya's pup, Drys, along with her guide duties, kept her just as busy as was her friend, so she was very happy to see him. "I believe he's just behind you," she laughed. "I'm sorry Walkyr, I have to take Shayla topside quickly. I shan't be long, mayhap we can talk then. Drys would love the company."

Fryya grinned and reached out eagerly for a hug as he entered the room, but he pushed past them and picked up her pouch from the other side of the bed. Shoving it toward her, he stated firmly, "Here, you forgot this." Staring at her with that look that said he knew exactly what it contained, she was initially upset. She'd not planned on taking it with her, and had barely had time to toss it o'er there afore Shayla saw it. But his expression gave her goose flesh and she took the pouch, carefully securing it to her belt. A bewildered, "Thanks," was the best she could manage in reply. Then he pulled her close and touched the base of her throat with one finger. Kissing her on the cheek to cover his actions, he whispered in her ear, "'Twill come from here, what's required."

Puzzled by the obscure message, but understanding he was trying to protect her, they shared a hug afore she left. Repeating his warning in her mind, she was certain 'twould be necessary as Walkyr's Visions were never wrong. But just what had he Seen?

~~~~~~~~~~
~~~~~~~~~~

Her original intent to protect the child, she'd not imagined how twisted the Fates would become as Darque quickly accepted she'd have to risk her own sister's life in order to protect the Clan. Taking the short cut through the Pits, around the Tower, back inside and then to the dungeons, she caught Fryya's hand as she was jumping up the stairs two at a time, Shayla in tow.

"Who's bringing who here?" Darque said with a wide grin trying to lighten the mood, rather successfully at first. But the brief smile upon the Healer's lips faded into a frown of unease. Pulling her niece to the side and keeping her voice low, she asked, "What's happening? Can I send Fryya back now? What did you need me for?"

"Actually, I need both of you. But try not to get into trouble, you may have to stay topside for awhile, and I believe we shall want your services very soon."

"Translation: Storrm is currently outside the Shield, neither you or Fryya may be available in the near future to walk anyone back through the Spell door, and we're expecting a fight?"

"Precisely. Aunt Shayla, I know you're concerned, but we can't shelter her any longer. She must stand with us and shoulder her load."

"I shiver when you call me that. It means you're about to do something you'd rather not. And we haven't sheltered her, she helped secure the safety of the refugees during the battle..." She gasped. "The Ancients preserve me! You mean to have her actually fight!"

Darque ignored the outburst and after glancing at Fryya she stated quietly, "I realize I've been somewhat out of touch of late. Thank you for dressing her appropriately."

Fryya was uncomfortable by the reference to her apparel, hoping she wasn't going to be caught. She'd meant to leave her new 'toy' in her room. She'd not intended to keep it, just study it and then return it to Regynn's stash afore anyone was the wiser. 'Twas intriguing, she was certain he'd altered the recipe, and the casing was unlike anything she'd ever seen afore. But Aunt Shayla came running through the cave, and she just barely had time to conceal her pouch. And then Walkyr made sure she took it with her, but she'd no idea why. Suddenly, she realized what Shayla had just said and her eyes grew wide, not in fear, but in anticipation. Did Darque truly intend to allow her to fight?

"She's just a baby, you can't possibly expect her to take up the sword!"

Darque locked her gaze to the Healer's but said not a word. Shayla felt the rebuke like a battering ram to the chest and as soon as the Commander released her, she physically stepped back, staring at the floor. She'd allowed the initial affront, but family or not, true blood or no, the word of the Battle Commander was law and what she had to do would not be questioned. "Fryya, show me your weapon."

"Yes Sir!"

Darque was pleased as she tested the sharpness of the blade with her thumb. "'Tis a good edge upon this sword, did someone assist you?"

"No Sir, 'twas my own labor."

"You did well. I've heard that Ragnyrr has been tutoring you. I'd like to see what you've accomplished."

Fryya retrieved her weapon, stepped back, and began to swing her cadence. Using precise technique, she circled side to side, in front, and o'er head with increasing speed. Ducking down and side stepping, thrusting forward, sideways, and behind, she chewed her bottom lip in the tell tale idiosyncrasy of her lineage. Her face was a mask of concentration as she didn't want to disappoint her elder sister in the performance of the advanced kata.

"Excellent. Your swing has improved, impact will be much more effective. How about your boot blade?"

"I carry two of them," she beamed.

Darque had to smile, she was so much like her sisters. After quickly inspecting the blades, she pulled one of the special ones their father had given her when she and Gunnarr had taken the

'Bond. Originally a matched set of four, she had but two left. Hopefully, the lost ones would one day find their way home. She'd always known they were extraordinary, and although they seemed older than she'd been led to believe, thus far she'd found no history, no legend, nothing but her own senses to guide her. Strikingly beautiful, with intricately carved bone hilts and guards inlaid and encrusted with Mother of Pearl and Fire Opals, the flats were etched with Dragons, each depicting a different fight scene. Upon one side of each of the blades the Dragon was streaming Flame, upon the other, roaring his defiance.

Darque was no longer surprised when her hand touched the steel, for 'twas warm as if with recent use. While her heart told her they should be kept together, she wasn't certain 'twas not sheer vanity, and since she was about to place her own blood kin into the midst of the heat of Dragon warfare, she made her decision. Challenging Fryya, she was impressed with how she handled herself as they mock fought their way down the hall and up the flights of stairs to the top floor, where she grabbed a fistful of the unruly mop of flying copper curls and steered the child toward the ladders leading to the ramparts. "You should be warmed up by now, how do you feel?"

"Ready for your orders, Commander!"

Leaning down to face her, which wasn't all that far, she stated respectfully as she handed o'er the blade, "This is for you. 'Tis blessed, and you must promise to keep it always close. Use it well and 'twill keep you safe." She swallowed hard. She prayed she was correct for otherwise she might be taking her sister to her death this day.

Fryya nodded her head solemnly, and trading blades, she slipped the new one into her boot with wide eyes and a tight smile. After climbing the ladder and pushing out onto the wall, Darque tucked her under her shoulder while they half kneeled and fixed their eyes upon the incoming attackers, arriving at the perimeter.

The slight girl looked first to the Dragons and then to her sister. With maturity far above her winters, she stated, "Darque. I know you called me for a reason, for something only I can do. You aren't trying to protect me here, I'd be more protected in the caves. Topside, I'm fodder. Spill it."

Although she'd struggled with the decision, Darque did not waver in her plan. But having Fryya volunteer to be a part of that plan, relieved her conscious. Slightly.

She pointed. "See all those Dragons?"

"Yes, Sir."

"They should all be following Storrm."

Innocent eyes probed hers for conclusions. "They aren't."

Darque provided the answers. "They're trying to push through. They're going to compromise the Shield."

Fryya was appalled. "Where are the others? Will they hurt the Six? What do we do?"

"They follow orders." She wasn't ready to tell the child everything at this moment. This mission was all or nothing and they had to hit the enemy with everything they had. Having only half the surviving Free Warriors stationed here and the rest at the Lair, there were few fighters left in the caves below. "Come with me. We are the final protectors of the Clan."

Fryya's huge eyes were bright, but not fearful. Quickly, Darque braided her hair into a thick rope, tying it in a knot at the back of her neck afore helping her slide down the ladder. Hand in hand, they hurried through the cavernous hallway. Fryya was saddened by the eerie silence, the echoes of their boots the only sound. 'Twas wrong, and 'twas because of the Hoard. She wanted to strike back at them, to avenge her friends and family, all those she used to see bustling about in these very halls, now empty. She sensed hesitancy in her sister, a struggle that she felt in her own heart. But 'twas a burden shared, and as they neared the Pits she became determined to make a difference, to take her place beside her fellow Clansmen, to earn her right to become a Warrior one day.

Strengthening each other, they traveled a bit faster and soon arrived at the Pits where Gunnarr was waiting. Hoisting the little girl onto his broad back, Darque stated, "Your heart is that of a Warrior, just as I told you a winter past, when I knew not that you were my own flesh and blood. I am very proud of you. And here's the spill. We have to kill those Dragons, every one of them. We can't stand and fight them here, there are too many. Furthermore, we're too close to possible reinforcements, should they attempt to Call. We must bait them to the Bog. Half of them are already on their way; they follow Storrm and the other Teams of First Flight. We shall bring the other half. They want you, specifically. That's why these stayed and are trying to force their way through. Somehow, they know you're still alive. They'll follow us, to get you."

Calm surrounded Fryya. "Being 'protected' from the truth has always been more frightening to me than knowing the worst. Don't forget that I was raised at Evanntyr. I may only have eight winters, but I grew up surrounded by wickedness, and have defended my honor many times. The Evil One frightens me not, nor do his minions. I will kill them with my new blade."

Darque could sense the sincerity in her words, and what the child had already been through, made her angry. Nevertheless, killing was not wished upon the young, even the young of a War Clan. "'Tis my hope you won't be forced to such, but truth is, you may very well get your chance." Darque mounted and settled in front of her little sister after ensuring the girl was properly secured. Fryya snuggled up and wrapped her arms tightly around her sister to share the warmth. The Commander Pushed her thoughts outward through the Shield as they went about the charade. To ensure the ruse worked, the enemy must Hear them, and they did. They near drooled with expectation after she let their need to take flight 'slip' to Gunnarr, making it appear there was no one left but the three of them, that she had Fryya and they were on the run, abandoning Drekinn. O'er head, the ribbons of energy danced and shimmered while the Six continued to Hold.

Once outside the Shield, Darque was exhilarated. Not only did she welcome full Battle Lust, but she was extremely relieved that the Shield hadn't failed with the added assault of her Push to allow the Hoard to Hear them, followed by the extra burden of them slipping through, considering so many were trying to get in at the same time. So dull were they, although the Dragons caught their scent quickly, Darque had to 'help' them catch a visual by slowing down and appearing confused about which direction to run, finally getting their attention. The chase began.

<center>~~~~~EVANNTYR~~~~~</center>

The Sorcerer was infuriated with the witch's failure to produce that which he desired. "Call to him! Draw Mikkal here, make him bring me the Eye!"

Sweating profusely, Koryl had already Seen Mikkal stealing the Eye but wasn't certain how long he'd had the precious gem, or even if 'twas an event of the future, therefore, she'd not revealed her knowledge. Staring into the bowl, waving her hands o'er the churning waters, she attempted to settle them once again. O'er the past few moons the Sorcerer's presence had grown to have a most unsettling effect upon her, making her decision a simple one. After she completed this task, she was leaving. The Flame with all of them. She was losing control o'er Shytin and he no longer sought out her favors anyway. 'Twas odd that after forcing him to give up Aalanna, the Sorcerer had actually managed to make her son believe 'twas her fault, the rift 'tween them growing wider by the day. Shytin was, in fact, making some rather disturbing demands lately and 'twas directly related to the increasing influence of his new 'advisor'. Let him try to remain on the throne without her. Even with the Sorcerer's help, their failure was inevitable. She'd just back away, go into hiding and rebuild, while Shytin fell flat on his scrawny ass, possibly dragging the

Sorcerer with him. In the meantime however, she found herself in real peril. 'Twas just a matter of time afore she'd be cast out, or mayhap even sentenced to death. She turned her head and looked at him in anger. "Be still! I can't See with the waters like this! And if I can't See him, I can't Call him!"

Rolling his eyes with contempt, he said, "Here, this should help." The Sorcerer casually pulled his dagger and slashed his palm. A small but steady stream of blood dripped upon the floor as he watched it in fascination. Making a fist, he held the welling pool momentarily, then reached forth and let it drip into the water with outstretched fingers. Afore she could stop him, he slapped his bloody palm upon her chest. The power transfer was too much. Throwing her arms wide and her head back, she struggled to breathe. Removing his hand, she dropped to the stone, ashen but alive. "Humans," he sneered. What had he seen in her for so long? He shook his head and then kicked her limp body out of the way as he took her place, peering into the bowl. When next he glanced up, Koryl was nowhere to be seen. 'Twould be several dawns afore he'd realize she was not in the castle, nor anywhere in King's Gate. After which he simply had Shytin sign an Order of Detention for suspected treason, which meant she had a bounty on her head and 'twould be paid dead or alive. He cared not which. Little did he know that Koryl had been planning her escape for a very long time, and was no man's fool. She'd never be found by the likes of him or anyone he might send. Never.

CHAPTER TWENTY-FIVE

The Battle of Ice Mist Falls

~~~~~THE BOG~~~~~

"No! Leave me alone!" Spasms of pain and nausea racked Mikkal's body as he slowly regained consciousness, lying half naked in the frost covered grass. Daynahmyn's long rough tongue was licking his bare chest, desperate to wake him.

"I've been with you for marks, you tried to go back to Drekinn again, you wanted to take the Eye. I kept you here in the clearing, but 'twas more difficult than ever afore. I couldn't let you go."

She helped him sit up, then gathered his leathers from the surrounding meadow where they'd been ripped off in the struggle. Unsteady on his feet, he dressed with one hand leaning against her for support. As his head stopped spinning and the nausea subsided, he checked his weapons, mounting with her proffered knee. Originally thinking they'd just be trying to return without having to answer too many questions, he suddenly realized they were about to enter a battle and Rakkah was searching for him even now.

Mikkal already had the Eye. He'd taken it from Darque's quarters that night he'd made report. Ashamed, he'd not Shared with his 'Bond nor anyone, Blocking all thoughts of the transgression. Apparently the stress of this had caused the latest episode to be explosive, as well as revealing. *"Day, I finally saw her. 'Twas Koryl, the Queen Mother. Make no mistake, she Calls to me even now, her hold ever strengthening. If I cannot control my own actions, I pray for death, but 'twould take you as well. 'Twas my fault, I did this winters past. I opened myself to evil and she's bound me to her will. How do we fight such power? What do I do? Day, what do I do?"*
~~~~~

"Koryl? She's just Human. She couldn't have gained such a hold without aid, whether you opened to her or not. She has no true Magic. 'Tis not your fault, think no more of that. And I'd welcome the Veil if it meant your spirit would finally be at peace. But do not hasten such, for I've controlled your physical actions thus far, taking you away from the eyes of others while in her grip. 'Tis only how you respond that I cannot control. And Rakkah helps."

"You're closer to me than even Rakkah. I can handle the pain, as long as you can keep me from committing some atrocity while I'm lost. Don't allow me to bring harm to the Resistance. Did you know this afore you took my 'Bond? Did you know what was in store?"

"I knew some, but not everything. 'Twas why there was such confusion with your Call. It settled o'er both Petrayyah and I, because you and Rakkah share the same bloodline and your destinies are tightly interwoven. I reasoned with her, then pushed her aside, for I'd Seen all of us in the future. 'Twas you and I together, with Petrayyah comforting Rakkah upon your death. She didn't want this for me and tried to take it upon herself. 'Tis tangled and unclear, however, I know your death will occur by your own choice, yet not by your own hand."

"Then let it be in battle, and let us take many with us afore we Pass."

"Do not fear, our Legend Song will be one of heroic battles and valiant deeds. We shall make a difference, and neither of us shall Pass afore our time."

As the pair approached the Bog, they settled into formation behind Rakkah and Petrayyah.

"I'm here, my brother."

"Mikkal! Where have you been?"

"I... I don't know."

"Again? 'Twas as bad as afore?

"Worse. If not for Day... does Darque know?"

Rakkah couldn't bring himself to lie to his brother. Vaguely, he Responded, hoping Mikkal wouldn't notice. *"I've always covered for you, haven't I? Forget it. Can you two fight?"*

Mikkal didn't question the response, Answering, *"We're ready. I welcome the Lust even now. Let the Hoard come. But I step down from my position as Security Officer. Rakkah, you can no longer cover for my lapses, you must take o'er. I will not issue orders under another's influence. I could be used to harm the Resistance."*

"We'll work this out later, but know that I stand with you, shoulder to shoulder through whatever the Fates have in store, as have I always. Draw your sword, brother, 'tis you and I, here to the Veil!"

"For brother and Clan, here to the Veil!"

Given the efficiency of the Link and the propensity of the Highlands for telepathy, the two Dragons carried on their own Exchange while simultaneously relaying for their riders.

"Daynahmyn, are you recovered? Does he yet understand?"

"I can't thank you enough Petrayyah, for supporting me once again. 'Tis getting worse with each episode, and although I fear I shall lose him to her soon, we can fight. And yes, he's breaking through; he saw her, he knows. He's beginning to accept his destiny, although he doesn't fully understand what 'tis."

"I suspect Rakkah also begins to understand. I cannot keep my Thoughts to myself. Helping you has opened me up to my 'Bond more than I can Block. In the meantime, I've researched every possible way to break her hold upon him, my sister. I've found nothing other than her death that would make a difference. Her hold is strengthened by pain and blood and 'twill only lessen with her Passing. Or his."

"As I thought 'twould be. One thinks to modify what has been prophesied, but in the end, 'twill only be our interpretation of such, which can be altered. Prophesy shan't be denied, it can

only be delayed or assisted to fulfillment, and 'tis our solemn duty to do just that. I know I am to keep Mikkal alive as long as possible, and fight the evil that burns to take o'er, 'til 'tis clearly our time. Still, I'm puzzled about my own destiny. I'll welcome the Veil to relieve Mikkal's suffering, 'tis not his fault. Yet, I've Seen myself with him long after his demise, and I cannot See the actual moment of his Passing, as if it happens, but doesn't. 'Tis a quandary, as through the 'Bond our fates should match."

"We cannot ponder such puzzles now, I only know 'tis not our time, and the battle begins. Fight well, my sister!"

~~~~~LEAVING THE LAIR~~~~~

Raynah's knees squeezed tight as she leaned o'er, clutching onto a Dragon's shoulders for the third time in near as many moons. Just a winter past she'd only dreamed of flying. A different Dragon had taken her to the new Training Facility and yet another had transported her to the big battle. She'd been disappointed when the first was taken in the 'Bond and then the second was lost to the Veil. She'd been one of thirty handpicked candidates flown in to carve out the new Lair as well as stand for the LifeBond ceremonies, but she'd not had the chance to release her Blood Call during the second, and the third had yet to be held. Ending abruptly, they'd come close to losing Daayn and Kashiyann, but fortunately all had survived. Raynah wasn't the only one who'd ended up disappointed that night. Out of all the Warriors prepared to take the Cut, only thirteen had. However, all participated in the epic battle either as Free Warriors and Dragons or as part of the new Stable. Both had about as much chance as the new Teams were still working on their skills together, giving them only a slight advantage, the Link being the most important. But all Warriors were duty bound to enter the fight.

The battle had been the most vicious she'd ever imagined, but she'd not only managed to survive, she'd taken out a full company of the enemy a'foot, as well as assisting in the demise of several (she'd lost count after the first three) of the Hoard Dragons. She was a Warrior, and Warriors were well trained and highly skilled, prepared to do battle anywhere, anytime, under any conditions. She relished the Lust as did they all, but only for how it helped them during the fight, and as the passionate reward of a job well done. They did not seek conflict, however 'twas a reality they faced daily and what would be, would be. Fear was a misplaced emotion that hindered success. She only hoped that if today was to be her last upon Kadoor, that she'd take many of the enemy with her. Her only regret was that she'd not have the chance to 'Bond with one of these mighty Dragons. That and mayhap, not being able to explore a budding relationship with her fellow Warrior, Torstynn.

'Her' Dragon was following several others, circling around from the west and east to flank the incoming. Communication was much enhanced with the sign language and the Dragons had near 360 degrees of clear vision. As long as she had his attention, and wasn't in one of his two narrow blind spots, he'd see her signals. Sadly, she considered the similarities to the recent battle. She'd watched her best friend Haleeyah, die by Flame, a particularly gruesome and painful ending to a short career. Then there was Flynn, along with the Dragon, Shanndynn. The un'Bonded duo had single handedly ensured the new Lair was not compromised by diverting the enemy's attention and taking them away from the Bog, comparable enough to the current situation that she hoped 'twas not a bad omen. Haleeyah, Flynn, Shanndynn, hundreds more. They'd all known the dangers. They'd become heroes by that nightfall, something to be envied. What was to be her fate this day?

~~~~~~~~~~

Storrm checked all her weapons for the tenth time. Mystynn's wings beat long smooth strokes in rhythm to the heartbeat pounding in her ears, fueling her Battle Lust. Calling for her Security Officers, Rakkah delayed, then Sent his message.
~~~~~~~~~~

"Mikkal is on patrol, but we'll be ready when you arrive." Something was amiss, but they'd have to deal with it later.

A few leagues from the Lair, the Bog became a system of many branching streams and rivers ending in multiple waterfalls on their long journey to the Sea of Dreams. Although difficult, one could still traverse afoot or a'horseback this time of winter, however during the Spring Melts one could only fly 'cross. The incoming enemy would not be able to see those in hiding within the surrounding landscape, and they'd not expect the ones running, to turn and fight with no obvious escape. Ice Mist Falls was aptly named, as during the deep winter the very mist froze, creating both sinister and breathtaking 'sculptures', appearing alive as they slowly floated ever downward throughout the region to their final resting places below. Although not that cold as yet, the icy water would stop one from bleeding. Of course, it could stop one from breathing as well.

She considered her strategy along with her choice for the ambush. Originally not concerned with ground forces, the uneven terrain meant little, 'twas the lack of heavy forestation that set the site. And 'twas the only large enough clearing in the area for so many combatants to allow sufficient room for fighting a'Dragonback. But, she felt 'twould work for their Frees on the ground as well, as their mission was to finish any who fell disabled, to harass the enemy to keep them from resting 'tween strikes, as well as joining the Teams midflight to skip scales, slow the Healing, and set up the kills. The Aversion Spell o'er the forest, although somehow diminished for the Teams since they'd taken up residence here, was still an irritation, and Storrm wanted no disadvantages for her troops. 'Twas also closer to Drekinn and therefore 'twould take less time to get there and get the job done. Even so, 'twould be marks. The chase continued.

~~~~~~~~~~

Ragnyrr beat his long wings steadily, lifting them to the highest level of the incoming Hoard. He and Kydra were stationed
~~~~~~~~~~

at the Bog, with the Battle Commander holding down Drekinn and the Second skipping 'tween. The first to Hear of the swarm, a mix of anger and regret fueled his Battle Lust. He didn't want to think about more bloodshed so soon, he hated warfare. So many innocents slaughtered, so many more left injured, but 'twould have been much worse had not the Clan been prepared. As the Prince with the kindest heart, 'twas only his fierce determination to keep Kydra safe and not fail his family or his Race, that fueled his considerable fighting prowess. Make no mistake, if necessary, the Third Prince was ferocity personified. But if a fight could be avoided without loss of freedom or life, he'd do everything in his power to forge that path. In point of fact, he'd become teasingly known to his brothers as the Highland Ambassador, and he could think of no better way to spend his spare time than with the young of any Race, enjoying life, playing, learning, experiencing all that Kadoor had to offer. But that was afore the return of the Black, who gave them no option. 'Twas kill or be killed, and then there'd be no one to protect those innocents. Now, he held a rank in his society equal to his lovely rider, at Third Commander. A rank he'd earned during the last battle; a rank in which he took great pride. They flew onward.

<div align="center">~~~~~~~~~~</div>

Every Team, Free Dragon, and Warrior trembled with Battle Lust. This wasn't going to be a fight. This was going to be a slaughter. Soon 'twould come sweet revenge for all their friends and families, Clan and Highland alike, so recently forced Beyond. These very Hoard Dragons may have participated in that battle and the need to exact retribution burned in all hearts. Pounding its rhythm, they prepared to annihilate the incoming enemy. There'd be no mercy. They'd take no prisoners. Fighting under those orders made it much easier to do what they had to do, and they didn't even try to contain the Lust. Let it rise, let their vision turn crimson, their hearts racing to pump much needed blood and adrenaline to muscles to increase their reflexes and mask any sensation of pain. These were all Warriors, all ready and eager to tear the enemy apart limb by limb, spill their blood, rip out their hearts, force them Past the Veil without remorse. Each and every one of them mouthed the names of known fallen, hundreds of them, as they waited for the arrival of the enemy. This time, the advantage was to the Clan. 'Twas a hundred incoming against ten each from First Flight and Second Stable, plus the added un'Bonded Frees of both Races who'd joined in for the blood bath. Although Free Warriors were not as effective against a full grown Highland in the Lust, 'twould be unwise to count them out, given such motivation. Nevertheless, for all practical intent and purpose 'twould be roughly one against three or four of the enemy. Expecting to fight against odds, 'twould make little difference, however, 'twould be a veritable picnic in Far Meadow as compared to the last battle. And unless you were in the Stealth profession (the smallest elite profession within the Brotherhood), you never ambushed your rivals, however, they now fought against inconceivable malice, and the future of the Resistance lay in their hands and talons. Not one of them harbored a feather's weight of guilt.

~~~~~~~~~~

Ragnyrr was restless, hovering behind the largest of the falls in the area, Kydra helping to contain his Lust. Both of them considered what they'd soon face. Thus far, they'd discovered all of the Hoard Dragons were Highlands under allegiance to the Black. They were young, strong, and depraved beyond belief. Highlands were the hardest of the Dragon Races to kill, and they were particularly adept with the Healing. The Battle for the Dragon Clan gave them practical experience, but they'd been working on perfecting their strategies since that time. Confidence building and rage controlled, the Lust kept them fueled and battle ready as they waited for the ambush.

Abruptly, their enemy appeared o'er the trees. Ragnyrr was concerned. *"There are not as many as was anticipated. Where are they? Did they see through the feint?"* He was fully aware of
~~~~~~~~~~

the parameters of this mission. 'Twas supposed to be an ambush and it appeared they might be on the wrong side of the 'bush. Suddenly he Heard Gunnarr's booming Voice echoing through their Link, *"We are incoming, being chased by the rest of the Hoard contingent. We have Fryya aboard. We will explain further later. Do not fail me, my brother."*

Gunnarr knew the impact of hearing that a child was involved, especially this child, would have upon his brother, but 'twas necessary. Ragnyrr Spoke with Kydra, his massive heart pounding, *"There is much more at stake here, than our own lives. I must not fail you or them."*

Kydra was the perfect match for Ragnyrr. She had him wrapped around her little finger. Able to redirect his misgivings and focus his strengths to the mission at hand, no matter the odds, his feisty blonde Replied with exuberance, *"Of course you won't. You are a mighty warrior ranked equal to my own, and we are battle hardened. Do not worry so, my fearsome friend, we shall fail no one. Besides, my curiosity is peaked, I wish to learn the tale behind this development."*

~~~~~~~~~~~

The Hoard Dragons were beginning to wonder if their prey planned to keep running forever. They'd begun to fly o'er heavier forestation and there was nowhere for them to land, causing a bit of rising panic in some. And how in Hades had they managed to keep ahead of them? Several times they'd attempted to catch up and end this fight, the odds were with them and 'twould be a simple mission to complete, but somehow their enemy remained just out of reach. The last of the Clan, the last of the Warrior Brotherhood, running like cowards just a few leagues ahead of them, kept them chasing with insane fury. 'Twas easily discovered the girl child was not amongst them, given the Sorcerer's Spell allowing them to scent the half breed. Splitting up, they'd left the rest of their contingent to break through the Shield. Also tasked with the return of the True King, how they were supposed
~~~~~~~~~~~

to find him, they knew not, nor did they care. However, the Shield o'er their former battlegrounds protected something, and 'twas likely the child or the man their master wanted. Nevertheless, he'd also made it clear they were to finish what they'd started at the battle. All of the Teams and the remaining Clan were to die by this dusk. The Sorcerer would know if any abandoned the mission afore 'twas completed as ordered this time, and they'd be cruelly punished. 'Twas an unstated promise of brutal torture that gave each and every one of them the drive to follow his instructions. Once in allegiance with the Hoard, you could not depart. At least, not alive.

Inhaling deeply, they could scent water close by.

Suddenly they lost sight of their prey as all of the Teams dipped below the treetops just a quarter mark ahead. Why would they go into the forest? Confused, they flew faster thinking they'd lost their chance, when they suddenly arrived o'er a massive open region of falls and waterways. They'd been so focused on the chase, they'd not heard it coming. After so long traveling 'twas difficult to stop their forward momentum and they were in the middle of the area afore they could slow to hover. Frantically they searched for their prey. There was nowhere to go. How had they lost them?

~~~~~~~~~~

Storrm and her Teams arrived at Ice Mist far enough ahead of their pursuers to drop off the extra Warriors, who immediately made their way under cover to the namesake falls of the region to hook up with the Frees from the Lair, already in place. Courtney took command and quickly gave his orders, then they spread out to increase their effectiveness in the coming battle. He signaled Mystynn who Told his rider all was ready.

Storrm Spoke to the Teams. *"The Battle Commander is incoming and will be sandwiched 'tween these and the ones following them. We must break up this group to allow General Gunnarr to fly through in relative safety afore the rest of the Hoard arrive. First Flight, Daxx and Linayyah, Yanais and*
~~~~~~~~~~

Shykiyyah, Rolf and Nalwynn, Rygyl and Tegrynn, Tyndall and Fyndarr, Apryya and Kyrlayyn, and Ethynn and Makayyd, take the north and east. Second Stable, Astraa and Captain Kaygynn, Tannah and Captain Synddarr, Daylyn and Makyyan, Tiyya and Captain Shasynn, Thorrn and Taniyyah, Hannah and Izayyah, Daayn and Kashiyann, go west. Position yourselves to close the circle around them after the Commander arrives. Rakkah and Petrayyah, and Mikkal and Daynahmyn, you ram straight through the Flaming middle of these bastards. I want you to split their ranks into multiple smaller groups, make them lose their focus. I want them to piss themselves. Frees, back us up, help us keep the enemy separated, take down any who fall."

Her hand raised high, she simultaneously signaled the plan to the Frees, who passed their orders to the others. Then they watched with gratification as the confusion mounted in the eyes of the enemy, just now appearing o'er the trees.

~~~~~~~~~~

Rygyl and Tegrynn waited anxiously for the signal to attack. They were ready as they'd never been ready afore. The Hoard took his woman and he was determined to settle the score this day. The brawny Warrior always wondered why his 'Bond and Zayddarr, the 'Bond of his betrothed, kept them from consummating their relationship by their actions, effectively keeping them apart for moons. After the battle, Tegrynn finally revealed that Zayddarr had a lifemate who was killed by the Black during the Last Holocaust and he was stressed with Sharing their emotions. Since Highlands mate for life, he'd been in a quandary as to how to handle the increasingly uncomfortable situation. The LifeBond had not been called upon for eons and they had no idea how to resolve the issue, or the possible consequences thereof, and Tegrynn did all she could to help. But afore they had their answers, they'd Passed in the battle, allowing Zayddarr his reunion with his beloved, and actually allowing Ariel to discover her true lifemate was already Beyond, awaiting her arrival. Knowing that
~~~~~~~~~~

Ariel was happy helped the big man to cope but 'twas a double edged sword, as he was left alone with a broken heart. Tegrynn, feeling she'd made things worse for her 'Bond, decided to keep to herself the fact that his true lifemate was still this side of the Veil. As Tegrynn was not yet mated either, she expected much excitement in their future. Rygyl just wanted to get through this battle, raining terror upon the enemy. And when all was done, mayhap he could let go the past. But he would never forget.

~~~~~~~~~~

Storrm saw her sister and the Mighty Blue break o'er the trees. *"Wait for the visual. Here they come!"* At her signal, Mikkal and Daynahmyn, and Rakkah and Petrayyah flew straight at the Hoard, splitting their ranks and causing total chaos, allowing Darque and Gunnarr to pass under their wings. The rest of the Hoard followed them closely, never expecting an ambush, and breaking up in confusion they turned and faced their enemy coming at them from all directions. The gap closed, and the battle began.

~~~~~~~~~~

Raynah jumped to the ground to finish the creature they just dropped with a well placed talon to the eye. She had to be fast, the injury wasn't as deep or severe as they wanted, and his Healing would take o'er quickly. As she ran closer, sword in one hand, dagger in the other, she watched in frustration as he dragged himself upright, shaking his head. He tried to beat his great wings to slow down her approach, but she was already all o'er him. Stabbing again and again, she targeted the eyes, slowing him down once more. Tyrrsyn watched in horror as his twin brother's girlfriend placed herself time and again in the way of wicked fangs and slashing talons. Ducking and dodging, she tucked under his chest and drove her sword upward, but hit the heavy ribcage. His Healing was too slow to keep her from pulling her sword and trying again and this she did as he attempted to brush off the annoyance. Continued attacks kept him from Healing his vision or producing Flame, and for some reason they didn't understand, he was unable to recover as quickly as he should from the simple wounds. Raynah didn't even stop to consider the phenomenon, taking advantage of the beast's vulnerability to keep stabbing, trying to get an angle of entry that would allow her to do more damage to the heart. She worked as fast as she could.

~~~~~~~~~~

Tyrrsyn just finished his opponent, losing his Thumper in the process. But with that sixth sense of a Warrior he saw the inevitable in slow motion; the incoming enemy reinforcement, Raynah having trouble ending her target, Torstynn still battling 'cross the grounds. He left the precious shield where it fell. Skipping scales, leaving his Dragon to fight alone, he leaped 'cross three of the Hoard to get within range as the tragedy unfolded. Neither Raynah nor her Dragon, both in standoffs against their attackers, saw what was coming at their backs. Torstynn, having finally won his fight, was horrified to discover both his girlfriend and his twin were in serious trouble. Signing to his Dragon, they flew 'cross the battleground with all haste. Raynah plunged her sword deeply into the creature's heart yet again, cutting upward and 'cross afore yanking it out for another strike. Torstynn was flying as fast as he could to get to her afore the Dragon sneaking in behind, Flamed her to oblivion. Tyrrsyn was almost atop them, leaping off to push Raynah out of the way of the incoming stream. Still too high, Torstynn dove head first, hitting the ground and rolling, his Thumper in his hands, just in time to cover his twin. Their Dragons engaged the beast and cut short his Flame, but not quickly enough to prevent a direct stream from hitting Tor. Raynah finished the beast on the ground afore she realized who'd pushed her out of the way, and that 'twas one Warrior down. The twins' Dragons warred with the enemy in the air, viciously beheading him. The blood bath cooled Tor's burns, and the addition of Dragon spit laved on generously was all that kept him alive.
~~~~~~~~~~

<div align="center">~~~~~MEANWHILE, 'CROSS THE BATTLEGROUNDS~~~~~</div>

"Darque! Behind us!" Fryya screamed her warning, but Darque had her hands full with one Dragon below them and one attacking head on. 'Twas time Fryya took matters into her own hands. 'Twas obvious she was attempting defense only, and Fryya knew her sister's strength in battle was her full Lust, offensive approach. Without her, Darque and Gunnarr would have no restraints. Freeing herself from the saddle, she stood up carefully against the bucking of the battle a'Dragonback, one hand on Darque's shoulder to help her balance. She remembered to duck to avoid a beheading as her sister swung to keep the enemy at bay.

Darque shouted, "What the Flame are you doing back there? Get down!"

"I'm giving you a decent chance! Do what you do best! Stop playing with them and kill them," she yelled. And then she was gone.

Too high to leap safely to the ground, Fryya had watched mesmerized while the other Warriors skipped scales, leaping 'cross Dragon backs, friend or foe, to get where they were most needed. They were protected for a moment, as when flying, the Dragon was unable to turn his massive head around far enough to reach between his shoulders and he could not use his claws to reach his back or neck without losing altitude and focus, therefore, they were unwilling chauffeurs as the Warriors hopped from one to another, causing much damage while there. She'd be relatively safe for a brief instant or three, as long as she didn't fall off, for they could easily fly upside down if they noticed her slight weight in the heat of battle.

The Dragon approaching them from behind dropped his head to increase his speed, and she jumped. Although her distance was accurate, her timing was a tad off, and she slipped and fell on her butt mid-back of the beast, with no way to hold on as she continued to slide off the side. His massive wings upbeat just as she reached the edge of his ribcage and tossed her battered body back up, but still she had no grasp and she found herself in a repeat performance. Getting hit by the wing was worse than falling off a War Horse, and she didn't want to do that again. Her sister's words that her blade was 'blessed', had her reaching frantically for her boot. Grabbing it, she thrust it out beside her as a drag line just as she ran out of backside once more. The blade seemed to catch in the scales, and if she'd had time to think about it, 'twould have been remarkable. But she was not her sister and she hadn't stabbed deeply enough to secure her sliding weight. The blade pulled out as she slipped further off to one side, and then her journey slowed a bit as it began to cut deeply into the leathery wing, causing the creature to cringe and roll away from the accursed pain, tossing the child o'er to the other side. Unfortunately for him, this tactic merely deepened the cut, and Fryya held on with both hands as the blade hit bone while slicing its way through the wing. Fleetingly she hung suspended, and then with one great stroke he flipped her off like a scorpion fly, sending her into free fall.

<center>~~~~~~~~~~~</center>

From 'cross the bloody grounds, Kydra looked up and witnessed the unthinkable. They'd just put down one of the last of the Hoard, and her head spun to see where they were needed next. Her ears picked up the shouts of her Commander but 'twasn't a battle cry, although she was still engaged. However, afore she could direct Ragnyrr to change course, she gasped as Darque screamed, "Fryya!"

Ragnyrr almost bucked Kydra out of the saddle as he shot forward and raced toward the opposite end of the battlegrounds, bellowing, "We come!"

<center>~~~~~~~~~~~</center>

The Dragon flew far 'cross the clearing in his efforts to be rid of her, and unbeknownst to either, beneath them was the last unengaged Dragon of the Hoard contingent. The handful left were 'cross the clearing and in the process of being butchered, but this one had attempted to sneak away and might have been successful if not for happenstance and a brave little Warrior-to-be. Deserting his companions while they fought in vain for their lives, he was almost out of sight when something landed upon him from above. He missed a few beats of his massive wings, making his wounds ache. He'd not been able to Heal himself, his Magic was severely compromised and could not be adequately explained by battle fatigue. He only knew he had to get out of this region, 'twas possessed.

Fryya actually managed to land on her feet this time, but just long enough to grab on tightly, using her blade once again to lodge a stake into the hide. Looking up, she saw Ragnyrr and Kydra almost on top of them, as the Hoard Dragon reared up to face his attacker. Again, she was sliding down the length of yet another one, when a flash memory of Darque telling her a story about pulling a Dragon's tail causing him to roll uncontrollably, gave her an idea of how she could make this kill. When she felt the base of the tail under her hip, she arched and reached backward, sliding around and twisting so that she was holding on beneath him. With lightning like reflexes, she stabbed with all her might into the sensitive region thus presented. She'd skinned her own meals in the past, but her young mind cringed when she realized that she'd just begun that process on a living being. The Dragon screeched in pain, the pitch hurting her ears. In the span of a heartbeat he rolled into a ball of agony, falling like a lead weight through the air. But she was in the Lust now, protecting Clan, Darque, and herself, and she'd not fail. She stabbed again, this time harder and deeper than afore, and found herself no longer hanging freely but actually standing on the creature's belly. She had to keep up the offensive or she'd be eaten, as his great jaws came around, his eyes wild, searching for the cause of his pain. He was also confused, as he'd suddenly Felt the source of the interference with his Magic as coming from... the Bog? His confusion gave Fryya a moment of stability, and taking the blade with both hands, she made a long slash from the base of his tail toward his chest, Darque's blade slicing through the hide like butter in her tiny hands. 'Twas the easiest skinning she'd ever attempted, but she rationalized it to the Lust giving her more strength, ambitiously focused on cutting out the heart.

~~~~~~~~~~

Ragnyrr was ducking and dodging by now, trying to reach in and pluck her out of harm's way, but he could gain no ground toward his goal, for which he was furious. Watching helplessly, he stayed close to the Dragon to try to keep her or him from falling to their deaths below, waiting for his moment to arrive. Then they saw the girl pull something out of her pouch.

~~~~~~~~~~

Unexpectedly 'twas not her sister's words that came to mind, but those of Walkyr. Of course! Now she understood his Vision. Fryya used her size, speed, and reflexes to her advantage, swiftly pulling the hot candle out of her pouch. Slamming her blade into the base of his throat, the Dragon choked and coughed up a ball of Flame. Then she shoved the hot candle into the tiny glowing mass and swiftly plunged the now lit explosive device deep into the open chest cavity. Stretching her arms wide, she stepped backwards.

~~~~~~~~~~

Ragnyrr and Kydra watched for their chance. Engaging the beast with his talons, Kydra leaned o'er as far as her straps would take her, but was still unable to reach the child. After yet another failed attempt, she watched in spellbound horror as Fryya fell backwards off the creature into free fall yet again. Cutting her straps, she leaped off Ragnyrr in a calculated effort to secure a hold and push them both further away from the falling Dragon, giving Ragnyrr enough clearance to safely catch them afore they hit the ground. And then her eardrums burst.
~~~~~~~~~~

~~~~~BACK AT THE BOG~~~~~

Bryynn didn't open his eyes anymore. 'Twas pointless. He'd not even seen a shadow for moons. He could sense personal danger lay outside his shell, and he knew he needed to keep from hatching, but 'twas getting harder lately. He was first laid after all, long afore the Last Holocaust, but he'd now be 7th hatched. If he ever hatched. 'Twould be a shame, really, the 7th Prince of a 7th Prince was supposed to have special Magic, and during his long, unintended confinement, he pondered just what that might be. The Magic of all the 7th Princes ahead of him had been unique and powerful, completely out of the ordinary, something they were particularly good at and no other could effectively accomplish. Of course, 'twas also a given that the Black and the Hoard would want him dead, as his strength might very well mean their end.

Saddened, he wasn't certain he had what it took to be a 7th Prince. Again he recalled that he should have been High Prince. How had that happened anyway? And was his eldest brother, Gunnarr, showing signs of special talents? For 'twas Gunnarr who'd been last laid. The Mighty Blue should have been 7th Prince. 'Twas confusing, honestly, it made his head hurt and then he lost concentration. He needed to go back into stasis. 'Twas what kept him from hatching afore his time. But when was his time? All he knew for certain was that 'twasn't now. And if he hatched now, he'd die afore he took his first breath, for he was not where he'd been since Gunnarr tossed him 'cross the Sea of Dreams to the Water Dragons to protect him during the Last Holocaust. As a matter of fact, instead of sitting in a pampered place of royalty, he seemed to be in... a Bog. And one of the last things he recalled afore he awoke to this, was protecting the Sprite heir apparent, Kevon, from a most vile Magic. He was a nice boy. They'd had many good conversations through the past few winters. Then, the Spell which protected his perch dissolved and he'd been carried off to... a Bog.
~~~~~

Since his 'burial' in the muck, he'd Felt a slight irritation about, which made it quite uncomfortable, so he studied the problem for awhile. Realizing he was in a forest, and that 'twas some kind of odd Aversion Spell causing the irritation, he simply Brewed a 'blanket' to toss o'er it, which was as if one applied lotion to dry skin. A simple task, even though broadly applied.

'Twas almost a winter later when he Felt a presence that made his heart beat faster. The Vision was clear, the little green female stirred his senses and his loins, and he struggled to keep from hatching, as the danger to this one enraged him. She and her 'Bond were ambushed in the surrounding forest, and both would soon be forced Past the Veil if he didn't help. She was suffering great pain from horrible injuries, but she battled bravely and fiercely to protect her 'Bond, refusing to surrender. She inhaled one last time and he Reached out to help her. Suddenly she belched the longest and hottest stream of Flame any Dragon had ever spit forth, and the three Hoard Dragons attacking them were as good as charcoal. After which, he was exhausted and fell asleep. 'Twasn't long later, that he Felt the presence of his brother, Gunnarr, but he couldn't Call out to him, barely able to Send a sensation, which he wasn't even certain Gunnarr noted.

But just now, he was trying to prevent the Healing in many of the Hoard. 'Twas a wicked battle raging nearby and he had to help, his brothers were there! But he'd not ever attempted to Reach more than one at a time (other than easing the Aversion Spell a tad, but that was originally for his own comfort, now extended for the residents beneath him), and 'twas traumatic. It stretched him too thin. He felt his surroundings tighten. Then he heard a crack.

<center>~~~~~BACK AT ICE MIST FALLS~~~~~</center>

As Ragnyrr watched his beloved rider hurl herself to push the little girl into clear space for pickup, he didn't even have time to register shock afore the Dragon literally exploded, flinging the two apart. He only had a few heartbeats to choose. Unable to catch them both, he accepted that when Kydra hit the ground they'd Pass, but he knew what she'd want. Banking hard, he made his urgent Call for assistance and without missing a wing beat, he tucked and dove to catch Fryya, his talons grabbing the knot of her long hair and swinging her back up into the air, literally just afore she would've hit the rocks below. 'Twould have killed her instantly. In less than a candle drip, Storrm and Mystynn were there, taking Fryya from his clutches, as he turned to try to locate Kydra, happy that the girl was safe, confused that he yet breathed this side of the Veil, for she should've hit the ground by now.

His original thought that mayhap she landed in deep water was dashed by what he faced. His stomachs near turned afore the fury took o'er. The Hoard Dragon was utterly unrecognizable, but although Kydra was nowhere to be seen, he could Feel her Life Force and 'twas slipping away. The Third Fighter had fallen atop the beast after he'd exploded, and apparently this created some kind of pillowing effect. She should be close, but if she were under this mess, she'd soon suffocate. Grounding, he practically dove in head first afore frantically wading through the carcass, an endless sea of blood and body parts, feeling for his 'Bond with all fours. Pushing his way through the slop, he slung broken limbs and entrails in all directions as he searched. Racing against time, he opened every sense and shoved his huge head under. 'Twas as if he were swimming in a cesspool. Then he felt her. Hauling her body up and out of the garbage, he held her in front of his face, inspecting her from head to toe. But all he could see past the grime was that she still wasn't breathing. If she wasn't bloody all o'er, her normally pale skin would be blue. If she'd been underwater and brought back to the surface, she'd be able to breathe now, but she was still dying. Her long blonde hair was plastered to her body and he couldn't even discern her injuries. Although her mouth was open there was no air exchange, and if he couldn't correct that, they were lost. With gritty determination he held her limp body o'er his knee, tried to sweep her mouth out with his talon, and when the obstruction became visible as deeper, he thrust his long tongue down her throat, dragging out large amounts of bloody grunge, slinging it everywhere in his anguish and rising panic. Three times did he do this afore she coughed violently, her entire body wracked in spasms, tears streaking down her filthy face. Taking a long stuttering gasp, she opened those impossibly green eyes and glared at Ragnyrr, trying to focus. Laboriously she lifted one hand and slapped him feebly 'cross his great snout, grumbling, "Took you long enough." He hugged her to his chest, rocking back and forth in gratitude. Kydra tried to ask about the welfare of Fryya when she went into a coughing fit, hacking up bloody sputum, grimacing with the pain of multiple fractures and severe aspiration. "She lives. She's been taken to the Den for treatment." Gathering her frail body, he held her tightly and took flight back to the Bog to seek Lowah. Shayla was the best but was at the Den, and Kydra would not survive the flight. The Bog was closest and Lowah's skills were very good, however she'd just been promoted to Senior Healer. He prayed to his ancestors 'twould not be a mistake, for without immediate and adequate care, he and his partner could still Pass this night.

CHAPTER TWENTY-SIX

A New Ally

~~~~~THE GREAT PLAINS OF DREKINN~~~~~

</div>

Aalanna's increasing ability to See not only indicated the Magic surrounding their goal but kept them safe on the journey, and verified that Darque yet lived, if no other. Gheryh crouched amongst the rocks and sparse vegetation wondering if enhanced eyes could see her from Drekinn. The foliage was brittle and sparse with the wintery bluster, the grass was yellow and dry. She pulled her furs closer around her neck when she shivered, but wasn't certain if 'twas from the chill winds or the effects of the Magic. If she'd not been warned of what to expect, she'd not even dared to approach.

Traveling hard and fast, they'd arrived at the edge of the Great Plains in time to observe the incoming Hoard. She'd watched as a few of the great Dragons suddenly appeared in the skies at the outskirts of the plateau as if they'd been uncloaked, and then they flew northward, chased by half their enemy. They'd apparently emerged from the Magic, but why had they run? There must be something she was missing. Mayhap there were more in hiding? There had to be survivors. 'Twas rumored the battle totally devastated the Clan, but she refused to believe such. Yet, the Den itself was all she could see, no other structure blocked her view. In the distance the remaining Hoard Dragons hovered as if standing still, unable to move further into the village, obviously repelled by the Magic. 'Twas there for a reason. But with nothing left, what was it protecting? She shook her head. 'Twas beyond anything of which she'd ever seen or even heard.

When night fell, she'd send Ryygg to reconnoiter. He'd have to be careful, for there was little behind which to hide 'tween here and the castle. The plateau, all that remained of the oldest moun-

<div align="right">

355

</div>
~~~~~

tain in all Kadoor, rose up from the Plains about a league ahead, then 'twas another league to the Den. Normally, 'twould be farm and then village buildings in abundance with the fields close to winter harvest, but now 'twas completely razed. The only clear landmark was the North Tower, where the legendary Shyffah was housed. In her mind, she imagined the thunderous voice of the massive curled horn, warning the Clan that the enemy was incoming. The Call to Arms for the Warriors had never been heard afore, and now, might never be heard again. She grit her teeth and fingered her bow to clear her mind of such negative thoughts. The prophesy told that Darque would return by the will of the One True Liege, and would lead them all against the Hoard for victory. She'd returned. If all the Clan were now dead, Darque would need the People to help fulfill the prophesy.

She turned and studied her Hunters. Out of their element upon the Plains, they were used to closed environments, rugged, high, and dangerous terrain, with an abundance of trees. And although the People knew of the Clan, following their actions for winters upon winters through multiple generations, to her knowledge the Clan did not know of the People. How to approach and join forces? 'Twas a dilemma she'd not had time to consider.

"Ryygg? Can you make it there unseen?" Her voice betrayed her skepticism.

With a look of chastisement, he replied, "With ease. Should be no different than hunting the Breath."

Now she felt dense. The Dragon's Breath was the great desert of Kadoor, and the People living in the far southeast whose lands shared borders, actually ventured there to hunt, for many delicacies were to be found in the vast sands. Gheryh had never done such, her position keeping her travels north and west, the Razor's Edge covering thousands of square leagues. "I didn't know that you'd ever been to the Breath, Ryygg. When were you there?" She was more than confused by this revelation, as she'd known her partner since her birth.

"Not I."

She wrinkled her nose. "Huh?"

"I've never been to the Breath. But there is one amongst us, who has been there often. She has taught me much."

"And that would be… ?"

"Traddya."

<p align="center">~~~~~MIDNIGHT O'ER THE PLAINS~~~~~</p>

Bayl clung to the shoulders of the big Kahyah. Even Kyrag couldn't convince the Night Wing to leave her. Traddya told them that it wouldn't make any difference, and in truth, if she was spotted with the Wing upon her back she'd not be recognized. 'Twas entirely possible she'd be mistaken for a young rogue Dragon, and mayhap ignored. That is, if anyone was out there watching. Moving forward, she was patience incarnate. The key to the hunt was audacious serenity, slowly gaining ground upon the prey, in this case, the Magic and the Den beyond. As they approached she was flooded with a warm tingling sensation and felt the Push, a sinister rising panic, which Bayl calmly ignored. His calm helped rein in her emotions. As long as he didn't react, she shouldn't, either. Closer and closer she came, 'til o'er a mark later she walked head first into a firm but giving barrier. 'Twas warm. 'Twas painful. Bayl did as she asked, reaching out his clawed wingtip and jerking it back sharply with a squeak, afore tucking his head firmly into her thick mane to cover his eyes. So, 'twas a shield of some kind. She walked a distance in either direction, mapping it in her head, but 'twas solid. She attempted to dig under, but the pain and sense of panic were too much to bear. She could see the ruins of Drekinn beyond, appearing as if just destroyed, but as she stared, she noted something was wrong and quickly recognized 'twas as a mirage. Insects, a pair of mice, and at least one bird, passed through the invisible barrier with ease during the time she was there, leaving her bewildered as she sat and pondered her next move. Hearing the wings of a Dragon coming from the north, she peered into the darkness and noted two more coming into view behind the first. 'Twas now or never, she had to try to rush the barrier. Just as she began to turn, Bayl screeched and her world went black.

<center>~~~~~A MARK LATER~~~~~</center>

Traddya awakened lying upon a makeshift bed of blankets and pillows. The Night Wing was crouched o'er the carcass of a deer, drinking his fill, his injured wings spread upon the stone flooring for balance. A pretty, middle aged woman with a wild mop of auburn curls hanging just past her shoulders, stepped into view and stated warmly, "Hello. My name is Shayla. I'm the Clan Healer. I thought your friend could use some meat. Seems he prefers the blood. We tried not to harm you when we brought you inside, I hope we succeeded. Haniyyah tells me you don't have access to the Link, therefore she can't really Hear you, but she also knows you're more intelligent than other animals, including your friend." Shayla nodded toward the Wing.

Traddya wasn't sure what to think. No one but Gheryh had ever actually tried to speak with them. And 'twas true, the Kahyah had no ability to use the Link. They only spoke with the Word Sayer. She had no idea how to communicate with this one. Shayla began again. "I've never seen anything like this winged creature afore. I would've thought he was kin to the Highlands, but Han says they share only a very distant relationship." Now Traddya was totally stunned. One of their Kind, knew of hers? 'Twould mean a traveler, and there were no travelers into their depths. The People had always been very careful to avoid any who ventured into the mountains, but if they came into their territories they were no longer travelers, they were trespassers or worse, spies, and they were killed. The People did not want to be found. They'd been avoiding others for ages. Just who was this Haniyyah?

"I am Haniyyah." Traddya jerked in surprise at the new voice seemingly answering her unspoken question, but she promptly realized 'twas merely coincidence. As her jaw dropped slightly in amazement, the smallest Dragon she'd ever laid eyes upon, ambled into the room just behind a massive Human male wearing a vast array of metal, weaponry, and leather. 'Twas quite obvious that he protected her and that they were in the legendary 'Bond. He stood aside, pointedly staring at her after watching Bayl finish his meal, afore allowing the little Green to step past. She moved as one who'd recently recovered from severe injury, slowly and carefully. She winked at Traddya, then spoke again. "I've traveled everywhere. I know of the People, of the Beasts and the Wings, although you're much bigger than you used to be, and you're all very far from home. Also, I must think that you come with a hunting party and if they're waiting for you, they're in danger and need to come inside the Shield, particularly this night. Things have been a bit chaotic up north, and we're watching for more trouble to follow soon. Do you understand? If yes, please nod your head up and down." Traddya was afraid that she was going to be asked to do something silly, like paw the ground or turn circles, 'once for yes, twice for no'. How many times had they tried those ridiculous techniques? Always an exercise in futility. But this one was treating her with respect. Striding calmly to the Dragon, she nodded her head up and down in a dignified manner. They stared into each other's eyes. Haniyyah wrinkled her nose apologetically, and continued, "So, for lack of a better system, and if 'tis acceptable to you, nod up and down for yes, side to side for no?" Traddya nodded yes again. This system was tolerable. 'Twas the same one used by the People for silent, simplistic communication, and she was not insulted. "Are you hungry?" Traddya nodded no, although she was, she didn't want to waste time. "Are you injured?" Again, no. "You're in the Dragon's Den of Drekinn. You were trying to get through the Shield. Did you want to see someone here?" She nodded yes. "Are there others with you?" Traddya froze. She wasn't sure what to do now. Suddenly remembering she didn't know how she'd gotten here, and didn't know for certain who's side these Dragons were on, she needed more information. She had no idea if Haniyyah was being truthful. Would she betray her own by telling them who and where they were? She wished Ryygg was here, he'd know what to do. She was not a fighter, she was a hunter. In the quiet space of time she hesitated to answer, Bayl belched loudly and her head spun toward the sound. Then he crawled awkwardly toward her 'cross the flooring. She laid down so that he wouldn't have to pull up her leg, and when he was settled, she sat back up in front of the Dragon, who continued in a quiet voice. "I see. Let me tell you what I think. The People have been attacked, your friend was injured, and now you and your entourage are in retreat. You came here looking for Darque, wanting to join with the Clan against the Hoard, but are unsure whom to trust. How did I do?"

~~~~~~~~~~

As soon as Gheryh and Ryygg saw that Traddya's position was compromised, they armed up in preparation for a rescue. Watching helplessly, she was dragged through the Magical barrier with Bayl clinging to her fur as if stuck there. Neither did they have any idea who were those Dragons flying in from the north, since they couldn't tell one from another. Were these the ones who'd left Drekinn earlier to be chased, or the ones doing the chasing?

"Aalanna, you stay here with Matana and Gabriel. Kytarg, you are their protector. Guide them to St Swiftyn's if we do not return."

"Yes, Danah. 'Twill be done as you say."

Aalanna quickly protested. "I have to go with you, Darque is there, and she... "

Gabriel's own protest rang out o'er Aalanna's. "I'm going, she's my partner!"

Kyrag raised his hands to silence them both and the look on his face brooked no argument. Shifting his gaze from one to the other he stated clearly, "No. Gabriel, we need someone who can
~~~~~~~~~~

get back to the People, find out how they fare, and mount a potential rescue on us, if this goes awry. You're the man for that mission, should the need arise." He dared him to protest further, as his behavior was not like a true Hunter, but Aalanna hadn't noticed. He glanced at Gheryh who nodded her approval afore he continued. "Aalanna, I will not put you in any more danger than necessary. You barely got out of Wyndsyr Forest alive, we don't want to lose you again. The Hoard would simply kill you now, or worse yet, torture you to get to your daughter. And, you must conjure Grifynn afore the Sorcerer does. Your destiny lies at St Swiftyn's, whether you find your daughter or not."

"But, I must talk to Darque!"

Gheryh's patience was gone, and she pushed past her mate. "There has to be another way. Find it."

Aalanna recognized the Danah's irritation and although she was not of the People, she bowed to their leadership. "I will. But you know I've Seen that Darque yet lives."

Gheryh had begun to feel true kinship with the woman in the short time they'd traveled together, and tolerantly replied, "Even if Darque is here, our success is not a given. Use the knowledge of those available to you. Artemis is a gifted Healer and Matana was her assistant. Surely something good can come of your work together." Turning to include Gabriel again, she continued, "You comprise our base team. You must not reveal your location or your identities to anyone 'til we, or one of the Beasts, return for you. Promise me this." She stared meaningfully at Gabriel. Aalanna's senses told her there was more going on 'tween the two, than was clearly stated.

Kytarg gathered his charges and retreated into the thicker woods while Gheryh, Kyrag and the Hunters, along with their Beasts and Wings, began the crossing. Instead of traveling covertly, they made the journey as quickly as possible. Once the party hit the barrier they attempted to push through, and when that didn't work they tried to dig under. The pain made them angry and instead of withdrawing as any other would've done, the Hunters attacked the barrier with their weapons. After a few unsuccessful attempts, Gheryh tried to order the others to go back, but they wouldn't leave her side. "We'll all leave, including Traddya and Bayl, or we'll all stay," was the general consensus. O'er head, the Dragons from the north were much closer. They renewed their efforts to get inside, as 'twas the only safe zone within any visible distance. There were places to effect a defense inside, but they were doomed out here if caught. They could barely see in the darkness but 'twas no sign of life past the invisible wall. Had their journey been futile?

<div align="center">~~~~~~~~~~</div>

'Twas long past dusk when the Teams split up at Ice Mist Falls, those returning to the Den and those to the Lair. Several marks of hard travel later 'twas still dark in the early pre-dawn skies. Gunnarr inhaled deeply, readying his Flame once again. He was in no mood for this crap. Haniyyah Told him about the Night Beast and her belief that they were here as allies, but the Humans were not reacting to his attempts to communicate, and may or may not be working with the Hoard, in his opinion. Regardless, things were too risky to put up with much, after having just survived a harrowing battle. Darque needed Shayla to help her tend her wounds or the Healing would set her fractures wrong, and they'd have to go through the whole process again, after re-breaking everything. She was in pain, and although she protested him trying to Flame these strangers, he was responsible for her life as well as for the rest of the Highlands, and he'd do what was necessary.

"NO! Wait! Haniyyah Says they're not King's Men, they didn't come with the Hoard. They come to ally themselves with the Clan. They may not have Heard you. At least let us try another." Ignoring his grumbling Reply, she sent out a Call. *"Nalwynn! Rolf!"*

Nalwynn hesitated. She remembered the horrifying result of the last time she and her rider tried to use the Link to communicate with Humans. Refugees, they'd not understood her and thought they'd be tortured and killed as had all the others in their village afore them. Rather than face such a grisly end, they all willingly perished by the hand of their leader. Nalwynn and Rolf could not stop them, and they were devastated. She'd vowed never to try again. Darque understood her turmoil. *"Nalwynn, the 'Bonded have had difficulty with the Link outside of their own partners. You've been the most successful of us all, in getting humans to Hear you. Regardless of how they interpreted what you Sent, 'twas successful. They were not fighters, they were severely traumatized, and you weren't responsible for what they did with the information. You tried to save them. If we can't reach these, we may have to end them ourselves, and I don't believe they're evil. But we cannot risk the Shield."*

Nalwynn Spoke to her 'Bond. *"Rolf, I don't know what to do. I swore I'd not cause harm to innocents again. 'Twas my fault those Humans died."*

"No, Nalwynn, 'twas not your fault. Darque is right. You were not responsible. You did not wield the weapon of their destruction. You Sent only good thoughts. Like Darque said, they were not fighters. These are! And, they may be a good addition to the Clan. We need allies, Nal, and there's been enough bloodshed for this day. Please try. For me."

The great Dragon circled high o'erhead, spreading her wings wide, and focused her Thoughts toward the band of Humans and their animals. She tried to See into their minds, find a receptive individual, someone who'd not be harmed by the Link, as it could be painful. She closed her eyes as Rolf silently encouraged her, Sharing his strength with her, reinforcing the Link to direct the flow of energy toward the tall young woman standing beside the biggest cat or dog like animal she'd ever laid eyes upon. She Sent images of them greeting the others in friendship. Suddenly, the woman stopped, gasped, threw up her hands and froze in place as if just doused with a barrel of ice water. Her breathing stuttered, her heart raced, and Nalwynn was afraid she'd gone too far. *"Don't stop yet, Nal, we've got to make her understand. Keep Sending! Try words, not just pictures."*

"Words are harder for them to handle, what if I hurt her irreparably?"

"They all die if you cannot reach them. 'Tis up to you."

She made up her mind and with Rolf's encouragement, she banked hard and flew straight at them. The rest of the party stopped and backed up to the young woman, who was now facing the pair, weapons in hand, held ready at her side. Nervously they watched them approach. Nalwynn and Rolf landed several lengths away. Gunnarr huffed as they hovered o'erhead, ready to Flame them at a moment's notice. If anything happened to Nal and Rolf...

Nalwynn Spoke to the woman, hesitantly at first, then with increased enthusiasm, trying to convey they were friends, not enemies, and their Beast was safe. At the same time, she Sent word to Gunnarr, *"Bring the female Night Beast to the edge of the Shield. Let them see her come, we'll bring her through."*

Rolf encouraged her efforts. *"Hurry Nal, we've little time afore we may be spotted. We must end this quickly."*

"I am Nalwynn of the Resistance." Rolf snorted and coughed. Nalwynn tried to ignore him. She had to say something, and 'twas the first thing that came to her. Shrugging her shoulders, she Continued, *"In partnership with the Warriors of the Dragon Clan, we are the defenders of Kadoor and the sworn enemies of the Hoard. There are some Humans who can Speak with Dragons, Seers, those with the Sight. If you are trying to Speak with me I Hear you not, but if you Hear me, let me know."*

The woman stood very still for a moment, then put one hand to her head as if in pain and crouched down, sitting on her heels. With the other hand she waved toward them in circles as if bringing the sounds to her ear, indicating she Heard and to continue.

"I sent for your female Beast. We've not held her against her will. She too, was compromising the Shield and our security. We took her inside, but she's free to go."

Traddya approached the barrier and Rolf walked to her, bringing her through. She loped to the group, nosing and licking her mate enthusiastically, talking to Gheryh. Bayl barely held onto her fur, frantically flapping about for balance, making her look like some winged griffin of myth. 'Twas a challenge, but Kyrag eventually latched onto the creature, and swung him to his own back where he settled peevishly into his usual position. Holding himself tightly in place, he appeared to melt into the man's body, his head o'er the Hunter's shoulder and chin resting on his chest, hind legs perched upon his hips, long tail wrapped around his waist upon which he actually sat, making the position one of comfort. Swiftly, he closed his black eyes and fell asleep. Now, instead of a griffin in their midst, they had a two-headed, hump-backed, winged and tailed humanoid figure who'd strike fear into anyone who didn't know at what they were looking.

Several moments passed, and Nalwynn held her breath. Rolf remounted and waited.

Gheryh conferred with the others, then all turned toward the pair.

Nalwynn stepped forward, hope blooming in her heart. She glanced meaningfully toward the east and the first rays of light breaking o'er the distant horizon. *"Do you wish to enter? Do you wish to join with us in our fight against the Evil One?"*

Gheryh slowly and deliberately pulled her bow off her shoulder and leaning o'er, she laid it ceremoniously upon the ground at her feet, while she brought her right fist 'cross her chest. Kyrag and the Gordatch, along with all the Hunters, followed their Danah's lead. "Tis why we came," she stated clearly. The Kahyah all sat down and grunted. The Night Wings snored upon their Handlers' backs. After all, 'twas dawning.

~~~~~~~~~~
~~~~~~~~~~

As soon as Gheryh made her declaration, Darque and Gunnarr helped Nalwynn and Rolf to get the People inside the Shield, then Gheryh went with them to retrieve the others. "Ama!" Darque cried aloud as she leaped from Gunnarr's back afore he even landed, and ran toward the tiny red haired woman, rushing out to meet her. Tears of joy flowed from almost all eyes present, with the exception of Kytarg, who was completely surrounded by females pushing past his attempts to be cautious. Gheryh took advantage of the family reunion to avoid formal introductions, and all else was delayed for after they were inside the Shield. Transport complete, most of the People and their animal partners were given accommodations in the caves, with Gheryh, Kyrag, Gabriel and Aalanna set up inside the Den. The Night Wings were ecstatic, despite the dawning of the sun outside. The caves were huge and comparable to their home lands, and all but Bayl flew off to explore.

~~~~~THE OFFICE OF THE BATTLE COMMANDER~~~~~

Darque was elated to see her mother again. 'Twas so much to say, so much to share, so much to learn, but only so much time in which to do all this. The Commander needed information now. The rest would have to wait. Without preamble, she began, "I move the children to St Swiftyn's as soon as possible."

Aalanna was used to this. She'd been Grifynn's mate long enough to understand the art of war. She dove head first into the discussion. "The Sorcerer has his hair, Darque. I have no idea how he obtained such. In order to complete the conjure all he needs is some kind of eye, whatever that means."

"He does not have the Eye, nor will he get it. As for Grifynn's hair, 'twas here in this office, stuck to his necklace, the tag he always wore. I Saw it happen. 'Twas after he'd left for your rescue. I'm sorry, Ama, I already gave the tag to Shayla, but I will retrieve it if 'twould complete the conjure."
~~~~~

"'Tis fine, I don't begrudge his sister such a keepsake. But I need something of Grifynn himself, something more personal than clothing or jewelry."

Darque thought for a moment, then remembered. "Will his tears suffice?"

"You have his tears?"

"Dried, but sealed with my own." She moved the platform under the desk, revealing the stain. Sharply, the Vision returned. His tears had fallen freely, pooling on the floor, soaking into the dry wood. She'd cried for his anguish, for his loss in her life, for the past, for the future, and her tears sealed o'er his. "I'll have this piece cut from the floor. We can determine how to use it later. In the meantime, we have much to accomplish in a few short marks, and I need to speak with Gheryh and Kyrag. 'Twould be wise to rest for awhile, then gather your belongings from your old quarters and transfer them to the caves below. There are an abundance of sleeping areas still open, many private and quite comfortable. We can increase the lighting wherever you choose to stay, with Magic, otherwise, 'tis aglow throughout but may not be enough for you. Let me know. Rest, and then begin your research on how to complete the conjure. Let Regynn know what you need, and he'll help you as much as he can."

Aalanna sat still, with a look on her face that clearly conveyed she was trying to remember something important. Absently, she stated, "You know, I only saw him cry twice. 'Twas upon your birth, and that of Storrm. He would've done so again with Fryya's birth, if he'd been there."

"Abba cried when I was born?"

"He loved you more than he could ever show. I wish you'd known."

"As do I." Darque fell silent. Her mother sat in the chair and stared into space as she continued to ponder. Trying to jog her memory, Darque asked, "Is there anything else you know, that I should? Think, Ama. Even the smallest detail may have significance."

Abruptly, Aalanna's eyes shone with the near forgotten memory. "Oh, by the 7th Egg, as a matter of fact, there is. Afore Grifynn Passed, he made me memorize a poem." Her brows furrowed in concentration. "'I will journey to St Swiftyn's for the shortest day of the sun. The path will shine through the eye made wet with your tears, and you will come. Thus shall be restored my heart, for even the Veil cannot keep us apart'. For many moons I've tried to decipher some hidden meaning in the words but nothing made much sense 'til now. Obviously, I'm supposed to do the conjure at the Keep, and use his tears."

Darque completed the meaning. "The shortest day of the sun is the winter solstice. 'Tis nigh upon us. And the Eye is my Dragon's Eye."

"But what path will shine? And my heart has been broken since he Passed, it cannot be restored, for the Veil is evermore. Darque, what did he mean by that?"

She stood up and led her mother to the doorway. "This is very important information, for surely the Sorcerer will also try at the solstice. If we don't complete the conjure first, Abba's spirit will be enslaved and the Clan will be in even more danger than we are already. We have little time, and you will, you must, discover what he meant, at the Keep. Don't get comfortable here, you go tonight with the relocation." She recalled her research, how her mother's history hadn't made sense, and suddenly she remembered what Brannyn said. "There is more to you than even you know, Ama. Many secrets await us there."

<center>~~~~~~~~~~</center>

Darque stood at the open doorway and watched as Aalanna disappeared down the corridor toward her quarters to pack her belongings. The winter solstice was very soon, and 'twas much to accomplish. From the opposite direction, walked a young Hunter of the Daggogh, the Beast known as Traddya striding beside him almost shoulder to shoulder. Her head turned to the sound of the padding of huge furred feet coming down the hallway, and time seemed to slow as she caught his gaze. The tall, ruggedly built man didn't even blink when their eyes met, his sea green eyes intent as they stared at each other. But then the Beast nudged his thigh as he passed and he dropped his gaze and continued walking out of sight down the hallway. Despite his appearance, dressed and painted as were the rest, there was something very familiar about that Hunter. She bit her lower lip. 'Twas most peculiar. Although she'd never seen him afore, 'twas as if she'd known him all her life.

<p style="text-align:center">~~~~~A SHORT TIME LATER~~~~~</p>

Gheryh sat on the edge of the chair opposite the Commander while they discussed battle tactics. Kyrag had stayed with the Hunters below, ensuring all was well. She'd already explained that Mynx, Artemis, and the Highland Princess were in the dungeons of Evanntyr, information Darque wasn't quite sure what to do with. She had no resources to spare. Gunnarr had tried several times to contact Maahayyel via their Link, but hadn't received a response to his queries as of yet. As far as she was concerned, although grateful that the Warrior and Artemis were safe, and the Princess was alive, they sat squarely at the bottom of her list of importance for now.

Darque's attention returned to Gheryh as she spoke. "The reason the Highlands are so Flaming hard to kill is twofold. One has to penetrate the hides, already extremely difficult, but 'tis made even more difficult by the Healing. Our weapons mostly bounce off or break on those accursed scales. We've killed individuals, but it takes too many lives and weapons. We can injure them by shooting through the eyes and when they hit the ground, we can get close enough to hack through their chests to the heart via the sweet spots. We do everything we can to slow the Healing during this process. Usually keeping a spear through the eye does the trick. Of course that's proven erratic and doesn't work forever, and then some are stronger or quicker than others. We've found a fairly effective poison, if delivered in sufficient quantity directly to the heart. 'Tis showing great promise. 'Tis from a natural source, as are all of our medicines, but our Healers have worked on modifications to make it even stronger and faster acting. Thus far, we've only been able to deliver it by hand. We do know they don't like the forests, so we stay in the trees. They fly o'er, but seldom ground except in the largest clearings, and they won't Flame."

Darque spun the tooth upon the desktop as she spoke. "You use mostly thrown weapons, bolos, darts, the Star Wings and such, but 'tis your bows that deliver with the greatest force and from the greatest distance, are they not? From what do you make your arrowheads?"

"We've taken what outsiders have brought us, but 'tis not often, or in sufficient quantity to provide all our needs. We cast our own from iron and other metals found in abundance in the mountains. The most freely available material is bone, flint, or obsidian, that we flake or carve to a sharp edge. But, I must admit, I was hoping to get Clan steel."
"I can supply you that. But I believe I have something harder, which will greatly increase our odds."

"Harder than Clan steel? 'Tis legendary."

Darque nodded. "'Twould rival my Sword." She spun another one of the glistening white objects sitting in the pile on her desk and smiled as it clattered to a stop falling o'er onto its relatively flat side.

Gheryh stared at the pile. "What are those?"

"Dragon teeth. I hadn't figured out what to do with them 'til now. I have baskets and baskets of them."

Gheryh's eyes grew wide as she quickly grasped the concept. "Yes! Their teeth can slice through scales and pierce hide. Not only could we impede the Healing, we could dip them in the poison and mayhap deliver the killing blow directly to the heart." She stopped for a moment and her eyes grew ever wider in sheer triumph afore she continued. "With the poison upon their tips, we may be able to kill them from afar, mayhap even still a'wing. 'Twould be a most effective weapon in our arsenal, Commander."

"Would you be willing to teach my Warriors your skills in archery and the construction of your bows and arrows?"

"'Twould give the Daggogh and the Gordatch much satisfaction to offer whatever assistance you require."

"Danah, 'tis a pleasure to be working with the People."

~~~~~~~~~~

After a brief discussion, 'twas decided to have the Danah and Danoh, along with their entourage, conduct a series of continuous teaching sessions, allowing every Warrior, Dragon, and child to learn and then share their learning, and to help craft the weapons they'd soon require. Bows, quivers, and arrows tipped with Dragon teeth would be produced for all, and all would learn how to shoot, keeping their new weapons close to them, as did they their blades. Cathay and Regynn led the efforts to not only inform and supervise, but also to start stockpiling, distributing, and constructing the quivers required. Several of the older children and one of the youngest seemed quite adept and they were singled out to assist.
~~~~~~~~~~

CHAPTER TWENTY-SEVEN

A Most Unusual Duty Station

IMMEDIATELY FOLLOWING THE AMBUSH
~~~~~THE LAIR OF THE RESISTANCE~~~~~

Lowah had her hands full, literally and figuratively. The new Senior Healer had just been appointed head o'er the Apprentice Healers at the Lair, but she was no virgin to battle. As one of the earliest refugees to arrive in Drekinn, she'd been training with Shayla since the war began, and she'd immersed herself in the Healing arts. She didn't want to lose anyone, but she knew 'twas a fantasy to say none would die under her care. She couldn't save them all, but she didn't have to like it, and she worked very hard to try to avoid the inevitable. 'Til now she'd won most often, but there was no time to be proud. Especially tonight.

The ambush was vicious, both sides out for vengeance, and in this war there were no rules of engagement. 'Twas kill or be killed, any way it could be accomplished. All of them returned with serious injuries, and organizing her staff, they cleaned, stitched, set fractures, managed more than a few dislocations, and bandaged burns and lacerations. But thus far, no one was as severely injured as Torstynn, and Lowah was worried he might not live to see the dawn. The others had suffered one or two of the injuries, but Tor had suffered them all, and the Flame wound was the worst she'd seen upon a still living being. 'Twas the un'Bonded humans at the most risk. They didn't Share the Healing, and what injuries they sustained were more likely to be fatal. Torstynn had a dislocated left shoulder, fractured left femur and tibia and multiple ribs on both sides, as well as deep lacerations with imbedded dirt and leaf litter from hitting the ground afore covering his brother, along with major Flame wounds o'er most of his right side, his shoulder, back, and down his right leg. Granted, 'twould have been much worse had not both their Dragons engaged the enemy afore he could finish their Human partners. Fortunately, his wounds had actually been sealed by blood and saliva as some kind of field bandage, preventing worsening of the acidic Flame. 'Twas well known that the saliva of Dragons prevented infection and hastened healing even outside the 'Bond. Although there were many injuries, the ambush was successful, all the Hoard were destroyed, and thus far there were no casualties for the Resistance. Thus far.

She looked up from cleaning his wounds when she heard the running steps coming closer. "Lowah? Ragnyrr is bringing in the Third Fighter," exclaimed Chynnar, trying to catch her breath.

"Oh by the One, tell me she's alive!" They couldn't lose their Rank. Lowah was so alarmed, she'd forgotten the fact that if half a 'Bonded Team yet lived, so did the other.

"Sounds bad. Something about aspiration. I don't know how that could've happened, but I don't question much the Sentries tell me anymore."

Chynnar was an upcoming Junior Apprentice Healer with very good potential. Young and skinny, with straggly shoulder length brown hair and unremarkable matching eyes, she'd also been a refugee of the war in the early days, o'er a full winter past. Lowah took a moment to think. The girl hadn't seen thirteen winters when she'd arrived, not long after Lowah herself. The child lost all her family and had nothing. Yet instead of allowing her rescuers to take care of her, she'd volunteered to learn the trade and help the Resistance. She was a quick study, intelligent, a hard worker, reliable, never complained, always asking questions, and with the last two battles under her belt, she was anything but inexperienced. Lowah weighed her options and made her decision. They were stretched thin, but she'd still be available to the girl, and Chynnar could be trusted to do her best. "Neither do I. Take o'er for me here. I've already set this Warrior's left shoulder and leg, but he'll need more sutures in these deep lacerations, and that arm strapped down for awhile, and a rib wrap. Get a strip of leather and cloth from the storeroom and I'll help you tie it, then I'll prepare for the Third."

The girl did as she was told and soon the task was finished. 'Twas wrapped all around his waist and would support his ribs while immobilizing his left arm, his hand on his chest. 'Twas now just loose enough to finish cleaning and dressing the Flame wounds 'twould cover. Lowah grabbed her bag and gave her directions. "She's here! Clean, salve, finish those sutures and cover the burns, then tighten that wrap afore he regains consciousness. And if he wakes, keep cleaning! Clean very well, and don't spare the salve! Quickly now!" Spinning around, she darted away as Chynnar nodded her understanding, then set her jaw and went to work.

<center>~~~~~DAWN~~~~~</center>

'Twas a very long night, but even though both the Third Fighter and the Warrior made it through, in Lowah's opinion they were still not out of the woods. Shayla's assistance would have been appreciated, but she was busy at the Den. There'd been some unexpected guests when all had returned to Drekinn and speculation ran rampant.

Because Kydra Shared the Healing with Ragnyrr, she was likely to improve shortly. However, it hadn't been a picnic. The Healing didn't spare the one being Healed, and with moderate to severe wounds 'twas excruciating as the Magic compacted the majority of the process into a relatively short period of time. She'd spent most of the night in the grip of extreme pain and nausea, throwing up blood, coughing, wheezing, moaning, and with a high fever. She actually vied with Torstynn as the most seriously injured. Still, Ragnyrr was even more concerned than was Lowah, and the huge reddish bronze Dragon had stayed beside his partner throughout the long night, sticking his big nose into every little thing they tried to do, 'til finally the Healer had enough and threatened him with banishment to the Bog above, if he didn't behave. In the meantime, Tor had his own troubles. His brother and girlfriend never left his side, and Lowah likened them to Ragnyrr in their ability to get under foot. If they hadn't been there to be treated themselves, she'd have definitely sent them topside.

She didn't know if Tor could survive, but she'd not give up on him. Chynnar had done an excellent job with her treatment, and given the Warrior was awake during most of it, Lowah was proud of the girl's tenacity. While the Third Fighter was left to the Healing after they'd done all they could for her, making their rounds every mark or so, Torstynn had Chynnar's constant supervision and care. She'd just sent the girl to her own rack for some much needed sleep. For Lowah, 'twas all too clear what must be done. 'Twould be her loss, but the gain of the relocation, and the children needed a good Healer. After making her patients as comfortable as she could, she prepared to report to Storrm.

<div style="text-align:center">~~~~~LATER THAT MORNING~~~~~</div>

Tyrrsyn faced his Second and cleared his throat. He wasn't sure how well this would be taken, given the state of affairs, but he had to do what he had to do. "Sir, Torstynn cannot be ready for the 'Bond for some time to come, if ever, and may not even be able to return to active duty. 'Tis clear that he'll require care for many moons, mayhap longer, and we have little staff to spare for such. Therefore, I wish to withdraw from the next 'Bond, and I seek permission to care for him myself."

Although their Dragon Swords required no such maintenance, the Second glanced up from the whetstone upon which she was refining the edge of one of her boot blades. "While we'll need every Warrior we can get for the next 'Bond, 'tis not scheduled for some time, so I believe you can be spared. However, as for taking care of Torstynn, you're too late." Storrm immediately regretted her choice of words as the shocked look on the young man's face made it clear that he thought she was trying to say that his brother had died. She added quickly, "No! I mean, someone has already volunteered for the duty."

His mouth fell open, and then he asked incredulously, "Who?"

"Raynah. She's pulled herself off the list for the next 'Bond as well, and has accepted a duty station offered by the Commander which includes caring for Tor. 'Tis a deployment situation for which we'll require one more able-bodied Warrior, if you're interested."

"Yes Sir! I'm in!"

<center>~~~~~LATER THAT EVENING~~~~~</center>

Tyr was not quite as pleased now, as he'd been when he'd accepted his new position. Leaning against the rock wall entry to Raynah's quarters, he crossed his leather clad arms and asked dubiously, "Children? We're the only Warriors to care for and protect the entire surviving population of the Clan's children?"

Raynah was bustling about the tiny living space, gathering her few belongings into a pile upon the rack, and didn't even face him as she replied with excitement. "And the best part is that we care for Tor as well! 'Tis a challenge, 'tis it not? I'm well pleased. 'Twill be my first deployment, you know. 'Tis not really a deployment, 'tis more of a... well, I don't know, but I'm very excited. We're given the opportunity to help the Clan in a huge way. 'Til we get Tor up to par, the two of us will have o'er three hundred in our care, all under the age of thirteen winters, with just one other adult, the Master Educator."

Tyrrsyn was skeptical. "That's an enormous responsibility, Raynah. Did you really think about what we're getting ourselves into? There won't be a Healer, and the Educator is not a Warrior. She's probably not even a decent fighter. I'd wager she hasn't lifted a sword since Early Training."

But Raynah's enthusiasm could not be dampened. "Well, I understand we'll be getting a very capable young Junior Apprentice Healer, which will ease our burden by much. And afore you judge the book by the cover, I've seen the Master Educator in the Pits on occasion. She may not be a Warrior but she's quite talented with a dagger, and if we get any chance at all, I'll be asking her for some pointers on her throwing techniques. Besides, we aren't going to be more than a day's ride from the Lair."

"A day's ride? We won't be taking War Horses."

"I was referring to them coming to us."

"Oh yeah, right. And just what are we going to do about water? We don't know if there's a well, they didn't mention having found one."

"Of course there's a well, all villages have a well, there has to be a well, and if not, there must be springs, the place was inhabited for centuries, after all."

He stepped away from the entry and began to follow her from place to place while he continued to ask his questions. "How will we get supplies? Food?"

Raynah turned abruptly and pushed past him, still working as she replied. "I heard we'll get drops directly into the ward 'til we get on our feet."

"Could be dangerous. We don't know why 'twas abandoned."

"The scouting party found no threats, remember? Besides, we'll discover soon enough for ourselves."

"Raynah, we don't have our own Dragons, and we don't have the benefits of the 'Bond.'"

Sorting through her things, she separated what she'd need immediately, and what could be delivered later. "Well, there is that. But we're going to be watched from afar. They're setting up some kind of communication system, I haven't heard what 'tis yet, but I'm sure everything will be fine."

Tyr threw up his hands, his volume rising in frustration. "So much speculation on your part, so much yet to be determined! All we know for certain is that we're the only Warriors, and we'll be responsible for the entire population of the children of the Clan, as well as nursing Tor back to health!"

She stood still briefly and scowled. "Stop repeating yourself and listing all the problems without suggesting some solutions. And get your gear packed, we leave in less than three marks, we're to be there ahead of the children and Tor." Then she pushed him aside again, as she continued sorting her belongings and packing her duffle bags.

Tyr stood in the middle of the room, staring at the young woman. Softly he said, "I can see why my brother loves you so much."

She froze. Her eyes riveted to the leathers in her hands, she asked, "He loves me?"

Now the Warrior was truly surprised. "Of course, hasn't he ever told you?"

Regaining her focus, she returned to packing, responding cryptically in order not to show her true emotions. "No. He has not."

Tyrrsyn was amazed. His brother was an idiot. "And you're still doing all this? Yeah, I can definitely see why he loves you so much."

<center>~~~~~THE DEN~~~~~</center>

'Twasn't long afore they realized the logistics of using the teeth as arrowheads. Although the smaller ones could be used on any shaft with any bow, most of them were larger than normal and required a stronger shaft and bow, therefore requiring a stronger bowman to shoot. To help alleviate this problem they began to make crossbows, Regynn redesigning his original trial bow that was lost with Graasyn and Bastyen when they failed to return from Kaddart. The new design incorporated elements from a combination of the Warrior's ideas, the expertise of the People, and of Weapon's Master Alric, leaving all but the lightest weight of them (mostly the youngest children) able to nock and shoot the special arrows much further and with greater accuracy than with a long or recurve bow. Some of them had to steady the crossbow upon a wall or a special portable frame, but most could shoot without such assistance.

The second problem was, regardless of how many teeth she had, 'twas not an endless supply and given their targets, there'd be losses that could not be recovered. Therefore, Darque issued orders to supply ten full quivers to every 'Bonded Team first, as they could pull and shoot very quickly regardless of the bow. Then they'd supply the Free Warriors with one full quiver of the special arrows and all the regular ones they could carry, and after the Frees, what was left went to the Clansmen and the children. Everyone ended up with at least a limited number of the precious arrows, along with both a recurve and crossbow. Instructions were provided with archery lessons to aim for the eyes, and especially up through the soft pallet, the second way to reach the brain. Either of these shots would slow the Healing. Another good target was considered at the base of, or down, their throats, as 'twas hoped 'twould interfere with their efforts to stream Flame (suggested by Fryya's experience in her recent battle). And then if possible, they were to aim for the hearts. If the arrows worked, they might be able to pierce the hide and hit the heart with a poison tipped one, and actually take them down. Even if they couldn't kill the creature, 'twould surely drop them for any Frees to finish. Suddenly, teeth became one of the most sought after salvage items, and afore they left, the children were sent back out to the battlefield to sift for any that might have been missed.

~~~~~~~~~~

Darque and Shayla gathered Aalanna, Raynah, Tyrrsyn, and the Master, into her office to discuss their findings afore their relocation. Tor was being kept in a drug induced stupor due to the pain, and couldn't have made a decision in his state of being anyway. The two Warriors and Aalanna, along with their most important belongings and weapons, were taken to the Keep just afore dawn and left with sufficient supplies to begin preparing for the arrival of the children.

The following night, the mass exodus of the pride of the Clan commenced. Sentries posted, several Dragons at a time
~~~~~~~~~~

exited the Shield with precious cargo aboard their broad backs and within slings carried 'tween two. This scenario was repeated o'er and o'er, 'til just afore dawn each morning. Cloaked in black wool, 'twould have been impossible for any unwanted eyes to know they carried anything, let alone just what they carried, but Darque had Free Dragons patrolling to ensure they had no watchers. Included in the second night's load were Torstynn and Master Tyrza, along with all their personal weapons and belongings, the rest of Tyrrsyn and Raynah's weapons, some of Aalanna's personal items, as well as more general supplies. The eldest children were the first to make the journey, for they would assist the adults to ready for the littlest of them. If everything went as planned, all would be ensconced at the Keep within three nights. Darque was still considering the suggestion of Lowah about her protégé, Chynnar. 'Twould solve some major concerns, but she wanted to discuss it with Shayla first. The quick relocation was considered essential, due to the notion that they'd be under more scrutiny once the ambushed Hoard contingent failed to report. Darque gave that about a sennight afore the King began to suspect that something was wrong, a fortnight to know for certain, and mayhap launch another attack, or at the very least, send an expeditionary force to reconnoiter.

CHAPTER TWENTY-EIGHT

Recognition

Brannyn Demanded an answer. *"Is she safe?"* His Voice was tense, as if he'd thought the worst.

Darque Responded immediately. She had no idea how much time they had, or how much he could Tell her. *"Yes."*

She actually Heard a sigh of relief. *"We do what we must. Beware."*

She paused. He'd just thrown her own words back at her. Had he betrayed them? Fleetingly, she wondered again how the Hoard had known that Fryya yet lived. *"'Tis more to tell?"*

She was somewhat shocked at his instant reply and the urgency in his Voice, but 'twas not the admission she'd expected. *"They come again soon for the True King. Prepare yourselves. Shytin's deeds are for his own gain and 'twill return to haunt him. Thus far, the Black remains silent. He's not shown himself since the battle but I..."*

The Link was abruptly broken. Several heartbeats passed afore she shook her head and took a deep breath. 'Twould do no good to wonder about the Fay. She had enough to handle. But...'the True King'? And, 'again'? Had they wanted more than Fryya when they'd attacked? What made them think he was here? And how had her father managed all his contacts and their information exchanges? She had no room for mistakes or misjudging others. Once again she reminded herself that misplaced trust would get them all killed. She wrinkled her nose as if she smelled something noxious. By the Ancients, she was a Warrior and a Flaming good one, not a diplomat.

<center>~~~~~WYNDSYR FOREST~~~~~</center>

Brannyn dropped the Link and side stepped just in time to avoid the incoming blade as it sped past his ear to lodge in the tree trunk behind him with a solid 'thock'. His blade returning along the same path almost afore the other struck wood, the prospective assassin dropped to the dried grass, his Life Source pouring from the severed carotid. All that could be heard was the strangled gurgling of his death throes. A dull brown Dragon he'd seen frequently since taking his new rank, came out of the underbrush and ambled closer to sniff at the dying man. Brannyn pulled his blade, which caused the blood to flow ever more freely, but his eyes were upon another Dragon, a female with amber hues to her scales, who appeared from 'cross the tiny clearing as if she'd been out taking a stroll and just happened upon them. He wiped the blade upon his trousers, his lip quivering in disgust. Could he not get any freedom from the stench of Evil? Could there not be just one, just one other from whom he could derive support? The anger he still felt at losing Dyrrk, made him misinterpret the barely disguised resentment in the eyes of the Brown. Assuming 'twas directed toward the Human for attacking his Third, the Dragon appeared uncomfortable afore shifting his gaze away from him to stare intently at the female. Something was being Said, and Brannyn was having trouble Hearing. 'Twas something about a heart wound, something about a death upon the battlefields, which the female adamantly denied. His frustration slowed his thinking and his reaction would've been too late, if not for her. Without any warning, the Brown spun and lunged at the Predator, decapitation his intent. Long fangs flashed and his foul breath blanketed Brannyn as he attempted to duck. And then, the female Flamed him. To a char. In the forest. What, by the 7th Egg, just happened?

"That one," she calmly pointed to the Brown, "has been starved into weakness. His Allure was dull, making him fairly easy to kill. His services had been bought and paid for. He came along as the Human's backup, to take him away after the deed was done. They were here to assassinate you. You have many enemies in the Hoard... Fay." She stared into his dark eyes, willing him to deny her assertion.

Brannyn was thunderstruck. He couldn't breathe. If this Dragon knew what he was, others might, too. He was a dead man walking. But then, why had she helped him? Or had she merely helped herself by killing one who'd been trying to expose her? "I don't know what you're talking about. And for making such an accusation, I should simply kill you. But I find myself bored and curious."

"Do not bother denying, our time is limited and I know the truth, because I know you. We're safe for the moment, I scouted after I followed these two here. But we both know how strays can suddenly appear and truly mess up our plans in the blink of an eye, the beat of a heart, the drip of one's Life Source. I know you're not who you pretend to be to the others, but rest assured, I'm the only one who knows, and I shall take your secret to the Veil."

Brannyn chose to listen and not partake in an exchange. She was right. She had him. And they had no idea how much time was safe. Her barely concealed reference to losing Dyrrk made his heart skip a beat. She continued. "I too, am not whom I pretend to be. I Heard you, Fay. I Heard the longing and the need of another. I've had those same thoughts and needs through many winters. Our load is solitary, thankless, profound, and never ending. I propose a truce, and an alliance."

A truce? He sighed. She'd recognized his wavering decision to kill her anyway. "How do you Hear me when I don't project my thoughts? I am good. But you Hear more than you ought. And there is nothing that can make me trust you, or anyone in the Hoard."

"Quickly then. I have four points to make, which should prove that I can be trusted. One, you've recently embraced strong emotion. This makes you more vulnerable 'til you can learn to alter your control. I have thus far, been able to contain your leaks. And, I will continue to do so, for the Resistance cannot afford to lose you. 'Tis also why you're having more difficulty Hearing others. Both shall improve as you gain control. Two, at the time of the Last Holocaust, I was heart struck upon the battlefield and should have died. 'Twas one still living today, who saved me. For many marks through the night, I drifted from this side to the next of the Veil, and finally, I was able to Heal myself. Once started, 'twas more rapid and complete than I'd ever experienced, and since that day I've had extraordinary Hearing, among some other benefits." She puffed a tiny Flame to emphasize her point, afore she continued. "The Brown recognized me. I would have had to kill him anyway. Three, I left afore dawn. I never thanked her. I could've been the enemy and she did everything she could to save my life. I've followed her since that time and have done everything I could to repay her, albeit without her knowledge. 'Twould not have gone well, had her brother known of her actions. I wanted to protect us both. Through the winters I've found a few ways to do so, without repercussions."

Brannyn was nervous. But even though she knew he was Fay, it didn't mean she knew who he was, and there were many Races in the Hoard. Being heart struck doesn't always kill a Dragon, but she should know if 'twas a death wound. And 'one still living today' would have had to have been a Magic bearer to still be around. Odd. He was of a position to know if any of the Races had ever done such a thing for a Dragon. Mayhap he could pretend to be ferreting out a spy, and have her prove her claims. Then he noticed the silence. He caught the look in her eyes. He remembered. "And the fourth?"

Her lips curved into a smile, and she stretched out her long neck coming face to face with the Fay, who near stepped back a few paces. "Do you not recognize me... Bronna?"

All the color drained from his face as his eyes widened and his jaw dropped. The name was from his childhood, a simple nickname from his past. 'Twas long afore the Last Holocaust. Only his family dared to use such a familiar name. And one other. His nanny. 'Twas no way that anyone could have learned of this. She knew him, had cared for him as a child, recognized him. And he finally recognized her. He even remembered her loss in the battle of which she spoke. She'd never returned. She was who she said she was. But that still didn't prove her position.

Abruptly she cocked her ear toward the north, and then turned back to him. "I must go. You should also, and be careful. You're still having a difficult time with trust. I wish to join with you, if you'll have me. Inquire of Shayla, the Healer of the Dragon Clan, about the heart struck Dragon in the battle field. She used a salve upon me. 'Twas red. Inquire of Darque about her father's horse, Konann. His saddle was ripped from him, he suffered severe lacerations and had claw marks upon his sides and flanks. He recognized my scent was not Evil and allowed me to use my saliva to assist him to Heal after the battle, or he would've Passed. And one other thing! Ask her about the Sentinel, the Dragon she and her sister heard Singing from Far Meadow when they were but children. They climbed to the timberline to confirm, then ran all the way home to stand afore the Elders. 'Twas the first real Dragon they'd ever seen. 'Twas me. There's more, but I have no time. Trust is a faith issue, Bronna, but at least you'll know I'm telling the truth!" Afore he could respond she spun around, spread her great wings, and flew away.

<p style="text-align:center">~~~~~THE KEEP~~~~~</p>

Corbyn was careful not to let anyone see him as he was in a hurry, but had to take care of a slight snag from the past. Aalanna slept fitfully. Her memory had not been easily altered as a child, for the Rashei had certain defenses that ordinary Humans lacked. Similar to Seers but much stronger on average, they were Mystics, as close to Magical as it gets without actually crossing that line, and Aalanna was one of the strongest Rashei he'd known since her distant ancestor. But that one hadn't been successfully Called back, and now their hopes lay elsewhere.

With no time to ponder the past, he turned his focus to the chore at hand. The Magic involved was a problematic Brew.

Despite his skill, altering memories required a refined and multi-layered technique, so intricately executed it left a brand upon the altered one, much like a fingerprint. Most Fay could 'read' this print and know who'd created the alteration, with the exception of what was done by the royal family. Of course, if one had sufficient evidence of a suppressed memory and there was no trace, 'twould lead one to suspect 'twas a Fay royal who'd done the deed.

Nevertheless, there were two sides to the process and many factors to consider. On the suppression side, how long and how deeply did one need to suppress memories, how many highly emotional events had occurred during the time being suppressed, and what affect had they upon them during this period. Then there were the supplemental memories to add, if any, and when altering an already altered memory, well, the complications rose and could be a recipe for disaster. Corbyn was the best of the best when it came to Memory Magic, even surpassing his father, Bardyn the Bear, and he'd had plenty of experience o'er the past several ages. All the same, he didn't take unnecessary chances that might adversely affect the prophesies, and therefore he chose to simply open, or unleash the tethers he'd placed in her mind, to allow her to bring forth her old memories as people and events elicited them, now that she was back in the Keep. The supplemental ones would fade as those recovered came to the surface. He didn't think 'twould take long, he only hoped 'twould not be too traumatic.

Just afore he left, he sensed something abnormal. 'Twas a trace of the very thing he'd pondered earlier. Someone had altered her memory again, and after his original work. He touched both her temples with his fingertips. His cursory search provided little. Surely his brother wouldn't have done such. She knew not, what? He stopped and took a deep breath. Did he have time for this? Shaking his head, he went deeper into her thoughts, and finally, he opened her to what had been blocked so long ago. 'Twas a dual memory of Mikkal asking her to meet him and then actually meeting her outside the Den, within a fortnight of having birthed Storrm. He'd betrayed her, he'd orchestrated her abduction. Corbyn was furious. He had to leave. He had to find out what really happened. Knowing it couldn't have been the Warrior, 'twas certainly the one who'd erased the memory, which meant 'twas Fay. But he didn't want to cause undue harm and the memory would surface now, so he arranged for her to make the revelation later with some unnamed trigger, otherwise she'd feel like she'd been struck by lightning when she woke.

~~~~~~~~~~

The mother of the Battle Commander had been awake o'er three days, working nonstop helping the incoming, organizing sleeping arrangements in the ward region, and directing work teams with all but the youngest because they couldn't sleep from the excitement anyway. The Warriors were mainly concerned with their security and the exploration of the heart of the Keep, so she and Master Tyrza worked together to prepare for the children's arrival. Finally, she'd dozed off for a short while when they'd been assured there'd be no more incoming for a few days. She'd made certain Tor was comfortable, performing his daily wound care and giving him the medications Shayla sent with them, and then her eyes refused to stay open any longer. She closed them for just a moment and discovered she'd fallen asleep when next she opened them. She was certain 'twas less than a mark as the stars shone brightly, still close to their original positions, but she felt energized. And curious. She looked around. 'Twas familiar in a way that the last three dawns could not explain. Standing up, she carefully stepped away from Tor and the sleeping children, noting Raynah snuggled up close to the Warrior, sharing her warmth. Gazing around the ward, her eyes adjusted to the darkness and she could see the shadows of the multiple tents they'd all helped to pitch. They had no fire pits. Along the walls were perched several Free Dragons, so still she could barely see their outlines. They'd have to return to the Lair
~~~~~~~~~~

soon, but not only were they here to help protect them, they were providing heat through the very rock itself. Using a united, wide spread and low level Magic, they were able to keep the effort from being seen from the skies above. Tyrrsyn was on watch and she found him by one of the supply tents.

"You should be sleeping, m'lady. We'll all need our strength in the coming days."

"I did sleep, for a short while. I feel the need to..."

"What?"

"I'm not exactly sure. I feel like I've been here afore."

"No disrespect m'lady, but if you've been here afore, then find the well. 'Twill be our first concern."

She hesitated more from thinking he'd not believe her, than for knowing not where to go. Then she stared at him with an strange look on her face. "Follow me."

"Seriously?"

"Yes. I know it sounds peculiar, but 'tis as if I've been there many times in the past."

He grabbed her arm as she turned away. "Wait, m'lady. 'Tis too dangerous in the dark, and we don't want to use a torch just yet. Come the dawn, we shall see." Aalanna shook her head in agreement, then returned to her bedroll. Lying there, unable to settle, she thought about the Keep, the well, the children, the poem, the conjure of her mate. Her fingers strayed to the Eye Darque had given her, hanging 'tween her breasts in the green suede pouch. If all went well... she squeezed her eyes shut tight to avoid the falling tears. Soon she was once again, fast asleep.

<p style="text-align:center">~~~~~~~~~~~</p>

The children stayed close to their siblings if they had any, and everyone at least knew each other, having been in the caves collectively for so long. Chores became routine, the elder ones keeping the younger ones in line. Expectations were similar to what they'd known, and even though some were homesick 'twas not as bad as 'twould have been, since they'd lost everything in the battle, not with this relocation. Still, new rules were to keep out of the open to avoid any potential flybys, go nowhere without your partner, and immediately obey orders to seek cover.

The ward was surrounded by a massive wall carved under to provide a wide hang o'er giving them plenty of room to move about without being seen from the skies, and 'twas where the tents were currently pitched. Master Tyrza divided the children into small and large groups of various ages, each group and each person within the group, having specific duties to perform. Amazingly, the Educator knew every one of them, first names, parents' names, and was even familiar with their inclinations. She quickly drew together two groups for the Warriors to assist with the care of Torstynn 'til the Healer arrived, and a third and fourth group to help with the watch. The children who'd worked with the 'Gogh and the 'Datch on the archery project were grouped to continue this, as well as to set up a schedule for practice. Temporary sleeping arrangements were organized after everyone had a hand in pitching the tents, along with kitchen and cleanup crews, and salvage patrols to begin explorations upon the first morning. Training and school assignments wouldn't be neglected for long, and her list of items they'd need brought to them soon, kept getting ever longer.

The construction and layout of the Keep was amazing, the more they explored, the more fascinating it became, and treasures of all kinds were discovered. 'Twas a highly sophisticated and wealthy society who once lived here. Within days the Dragons vacated and then Chynnar arrived from the Lair of the Bog along with more supplies. Although scarcely a few moons elder of the eldest of the children for whom she now cared, she quickly took responsibility for setting up a clinic, complete with her own volunteer assistants. Chynnar had a way about her that garnered respect and no one questioned her expertise except Chynnar herself. She brought along much reading material and spent a great deal of time in her combination study and laboratory. When she wasn't studying she was checking out every single child, getting to know them and their history as well as caring for Tor, which freed time for the Warriors and Aalanna, leaving him in very good hands.

CHAPTER TWENTY-NINE

Beware the Bastard Fay

Tyrza knew what she'd seen. Although not clearly visible, the spirit child was clearly in her room, gazing through her as if unaware of her existence afore he simply vanished. She wasn't certain if she should say anything initially, unsure of the Warriors' reactions. But after it happened for the second time, she divulged her thoughts o'er supper with Raynah, to gauge their support. "'Tis possible the Keep is haunted?"

The Warrior answered without missing a single bite of stew. "'Tis possible you've lost your mind?"

Well, that made their position plain and she didn't say another word all evening. 'Twas good they didn't spend much time together, for Tyrza would probably have said something she should regret.

Nevertheless, 'twas not long afore the children also began to see things. At least, 'twas so in the eyes of the Warriors. Torstynn was still under heavy medication, so his 'hallucinations' were easily explained away, but Tyrza was actually listening to their stories of ghostly images of men and women and even children, moving about in slow motion, living in another time, ignoring the intruders to their domain as well as seemingly ignorant of the other spirits. Apparently the children weren't frightened, however 'twas becoming a distraction as the littlest ones saw them most frequently and everyone wanted to see what they saw. Dropping their tasks they rushed off to try to catch sight of the latest claims, usually disappointed by empty space. In the opinion of the Warriors, Tyrza's attitude was encouraging of the distractions and they had much to do in order to make the Keep safe and livable again. They couldn't depend on supply drops forever, they needed to get organized with the children becoming a united work force. On top of that, true winter had already begun this far north, a light snow falling near daily.

They reinstated the katas and began limited training schedules, but most of their time was spent in finding appropriate living quarters, mapping the Keep, and exploring for whatever supplies were left behind, of which they'd found much, most in good condition simply in need of cleaning. However, to no one's surprise, they found no food that had survived the long winters of abandonment. The most unsettling part was they also found no evidence of gardens with sufficient capacity, even with the enhancement of the Dragon 'fertilizer', to have sustained such a large population. There were many open areas which acted as balconies for personal use, and there were much larger ones (none as large as the main ward in which they landed) outside of public enclosures such as the markets and reading rooms, as well as multiple small, well landscaped gardens for flowers or herbs (all full of dead weeds and o'er grown), but nothing that would sustain an entire family, let alone an entire civilization. Even these were obviously more for personal enjoyment than survival. How had they lived?

<center>~~~~~~~~~~</center>

Aalanna found the well on the morning after the last children arrived. Calmly leading Tyrrsyn and Tyrza deep into the mountain this way and that, through a maze of tunnels both manmade and natural, she walked with the confidence that came from lifelong familiarity. Released from all other duties, her primary task was also a solitary one, but 'twas just as important as was their survival. Her memories were returning with every room she entered, every tapestry she saw, every book she opened, every new discovery leading to yet another. Learning what she could about the Keep, the inhabitants, and what might have happened, she also had to learn where and how to conjure Grifynn, which information she was hoping would be available through one of the libraries. It seemed highly likely that there'd be some special section for this type of information, since everything pointed to a very sophisticated and organized people, as well as extremely gifted in the Mystic realm.

'Twas for certain this had been her home at one time. She was Rashei, but was baffled about what had happened. She could almost feel her mother, Myriam, close to her, urging her on, and within a few dawns of the upcoming solstice she found that which they so desperately needed. The reason she was here. The altar room. Among other items, sitting half imbedded on a stone platform along the far wall was a huge basin arranged at the bottom of a series of progressively smaller bowls seemingly carved from the wall up to the ceiling, each filling the other with water originating from a small opening at the top, giving it the look of a natural and winding waterfall. The water was flowing very gently, the basin remaining smooth and crystal clear as it spilled o'er the edges into a well disguised drain. 'Twas no more than knee deep if one stood in the middle, and although round, could be used as a bathtub for several. 'Twas beautifully decorated, as was the entire room, in an intricate and colorful mosaic pattern that depicted some kind of story which she vowed to study when she could.

But first and foremost, 'twas in this room, using this altar bowl, that she'd conjure Grifynn's spirit. Mayhap his knowledge would help fill the gaps in her memories. There appeared to be so much missing. Darque had given her the section of wood with Grifynn's tears and she'd soaked it, straining them through a piece of finely woven fabric to remove the debris. She then dried the liquid and placed the powder within the pouch with the Eye. She climbed the steps to the altar bowl and stared into the clear water. Mesmerized, she knelt beside it and felt compelled to reach in, as if taking hold of someone's hand. His name upon her lips, she mouthed the poem and proclaimed her love. Leaning o'er, the pouch dragged 'cross the surface while tears rolled down her cheeks, falling into the basin, the ripples clouding the water.

She'd felt something, or someone, touch her face. All night she knelt there, trying to repeat the experience, to no avail. Upon the dawning of the new day she sighed, 'twas nothing to do now but find the library. Try as she might, she couldn't remember how to perform such a conjure properly. Mayhap she'd never known. But she had to learn fast, for the solstice was just dawns away.

<center>~~~~~EVANNTYR~~~~~</center>

The Sorcerer wiped sweat from his brow. Fatigued and incensed, he'd spent most of the night attempting to conjure the Battle Commander. But without the Eye, without Koryl, and without the blood of the child, he did little more than trace Grifynn's spirit, sensing initial excitement rapidly followed by confusion, then angry defiance. Relatively easy to find as if awaiting him, something happened and the session turned into a spiritual tug of war. 'Twas infuriating. Damn the Fates. Still, why wasn't it working? Abruptly, a new thought occurred to him. 'Twould thwart his efforts if another Called. Was it possible Aalanna managed to survive? 'Twould explain the Commander's initial eagerness and ease of location. If still alive, she'd have traveled to St Swiftyn's and 'twould be there that she'd attempt to conjure her mate. Their love alone might be strong enough to pull Grifynn to such a site, but if she'd gained access to the Eye, he might not be able to stop her. He'd have to rest and try again when recovered, hopefully in time for the solstice to boost his efforts. If he didn't complete his task afore the Black discovered his duplicity, no amount of groveling this time, would appease his wrath.

<center>~~~~~THE KEEP OF ST SWIFTYN'S~~~~~</center>

After much research, Aalanna uncovered information that made her confident of success. Upon the solstice she tried again, this time fully prepared to use everything to her advantage. Darque stood present, as did Storrm, their hands resting upon the grips of their Swords, biting their lower lips in concentration.

Prepared for anything, neither was sure what to expect. Striding barefoot into the room, Aalanna wore a gown she discovered in Myriam's chambers. The fabric was a double layer of shimmering sheer white with gold threads woven in knotted patterns. With elongated bell sleeves, a 'V' neck open to her navel and cinched with a golden rope ending in tassels. 'Twas ankle length in the front, the back long and seemingly floating 'cross the tile floor. Her long red hair was pulled back from her face and she wore a golden circlet with pearls dropping at various lengths giving the effect of rain down her back. She was stunning and even her daughters smiled in admiration. Aalanna climbed atop the platform and stepped gracefully into the bowl, kneeling in the middle, the water up to her breast. Bowing her head, she removed the Eye from the pouch. Grifynn's tears rehydrated during her last attempt, drying again on the Eye. She held it in her hand under the stilled waters, as she began to chant the words she found in the library. Holding it in both hands, she lifted it and stared at the light seemingly coming from deep within. At first she felt stilted, but soon the foreign words rolled fluently off her tongue and raising her hands o'er head, asking for help to reach the Beyond, to bring forth her mate's spirit. Soon the waters began to swirl, a heavy mist entwining her legs and rising up her body as she felt drawn to her feet. Great clouds actually formed above their heads, obscuring the murals on the walls and ceiling. As she continued chanting, the clouds parted to reveal a night sky with a multitude of stars, sparkling as diamonds scattered 'cross black sands. The light from within the Eye suddenly shot straight into the heavens like a flaming arrow and when she felt someone rising in the bowl to stand behind her, she stopped chanting. The mists melted back into the bowl as she turned eagerly. She was in the arms of her lover once again, his embrace as a breeze against her body. Tears rolled down her cheeks as he kissed her forehead, the soft brush of his lips barely noticeable against her skin.

~~~~~~~~~~
~~~~~~~~~~

Darque helped her mother step out of the bowl and handed her to Storrm who gave her fresh clothing, all the while keeping her eyes upon the spirit thing that looked so much like her father. Amazingly, Aalanna was dry and as the room returned to its normal appearance, the spirit remained in place, unable or unwilling to leave the bowl. Yet he seemed not to be standing in the water either, as if he was only a reflection coming from another place. While Aalanna changed clothes, the spirit spoke. "You've done well, my love. You remembered. Did I not tell you that even the Veil could not keep us apart?" Then he looked to his daughters but 'twas no smile upon his face, his voice now gruff. "Warrior, report. Tell me what's happened since we last saw each other." 'Twas as if the Battle Commander was back. All doubt left Darque's mind. Efficiently, as of times long past, she made her report on everything that had occurred since she escaped the tower at Evanntyr. Sadness enveloped him when she was finished. "You, too, have done well, and I'm very proud of you both. But I have nothing to offer, except that I would've made the same decisions. Have no doubts about my presence here. I cannot help other than what I can impart to you, and I am no longer the Battle Commander. I'm from Beyond, but Aalanna has anchored my spirit safely here, as another is actively seeking to snatch me away. This must be avoided at all costs. I must remain here, in this room. If I leave or return Beyond, I am vulnerable. 'Twill be so as long as he lives."

Darque nodded her understanding. That 'someone' would be the Sorcerer. "Abba, I shall do all in my power to ensure your safety here." Her gaze shifted to Aalanna afore she left the room. "Find out what you can, Ama. Report to me later."

~~~~~~~~~~

For several marks, Aalanna and Grifynn talked. She'd felt guilty for dragging his spirit away from the Beyond, but once he'd made it clear they had no choice, she accepted her role. "What happened here, Grifynn? Who am I, and even more important, who are you?"
~~~~~~~~~~

He thought for just a heartbeat afore he resolutely replied. "I was known by many names, the most recent, Baadyyn. 'Twas during the time I carried both mantles, Grifynn as the son of Baadyyn, that I discovered the Keep and became involved with the Rashei, visiting St Swiftyn's regularly. Early on, I befriended a gifted Mystic named Myriam who became my contact within their community. She was mated to a fellow Mystic named Treygyn and they had a little girl. 'Twas you, Aalanna. As you grew up, I was drawn to your intelligence, fortitude, quiet strength, and beauty. I knew you were the woman I'd been waiting for, the answer to the prophesy. I became obsessed with the belief that I had to make you mine once you were of age. Myriam approved of my desire, though it meant you'd leave St Swiftyn's. Just prior to when I was to shed my 'father's' image and Grifynn was to become Battle Commander, Myriam confided that she believed the Evil One had infiltrated the Rashei. At that time she knew not who was working with the Hoard, but 'twas becoming more apparent that they were in trouble. She wanted my promise to return if things became dangerous, to rescue you and keep you safe by making you ignorant of your past. Although I was surprised that she appeared to know what my life entailed to some degree, after discussing the situation with Corbyn, I did so swear. Corbyn was fascinated with her knowledge and vowed to keep tabs on the situation. In the meantime, you were still quite young when I returned just afore I took my promotion to Commander, warned by the Fay that the circumstances were becoming dire and disturbing events were increasing. 'Twas worse than I could imagine by the time I arrived, and with the Fay's assistance I managed to sneak into the Keep. In effect, I kidnapped you. Alerting Myriam was out of the question, but the promise of getting you to safety was kept; my plan to return as soon as possible to assist the Rashei. When I did return three moons later, the Keep was empty. I found no trace of the inhabitants, of where they'd gone, or any indication of what occurred. There was no structural damage, no sign of a battle. Plates were laid out on tables with food partially eaten, beds unmade, multiple indications of life having been as usual. 'Twas an eerie cast to the Keep that made me jump at my own shadow and gave me gooseflesh. The only physical clue was a note, scrawled in blood 'cross a torn piece of linen, rolled up tightly and stuffed into a crack in the floor under the side table of Myriam's bedchamber. The note read, 'Betrayed from within but works not alone. Keep your promises. Beware the bastard Fay.' 'Twas all I could do to continue to work with Corbyn, as I'd seen all the Fay as bastards. But, as Commander I knew 'twas more to the message than what lay upon the surface. Nevertheless, I never mentioned the note. Mayhap 'twas a mistake but time ran out, my presence was required at the Den, and with the exchange of lifespans, my hands were full. 'Twas soon forgotten. 'Twas then that I took your mother's name as mine, to honor her life and our friendship the only way I could. For several winters after, I sent Teams to investigate, however, they returned terrified of nothing and of everything, and could not voice what troubled them. Ultimately, I had Corbyn erase the memories of what they experienced, as well as all memory of who went on these expeditions, causing the rumors that they never returned, as well as lengthening the memory of the time the Keep was abandoned. After this, I declared the entire region a forbidden zone. To protect you, Corbyn made you believe you were born and bred a Clansman. 'Twas not too difficult, as although the Rashei had all skin, hair, and eye colors represented, a true mix of Kadoor, your coloring was similar to those of the Clan. No one ever questioned, as the Raven wove your existence into our lives. And then in the fullness of time, I courted you and you accepted me as your lifemate. Now I realize I should've told you who and what you are, should've told you the truth. You need your heritage, knowledge, skills, to survive against Koryl, as I now believe 'twas she who betrayed her own people. I can only wonder if one of the Fay assisted in her scheme. 'Twould be the only way Myriam's note made sense."

Aalanna considered all that she'd heard o'er the past marks. "Are you sure of the wording? 'Keep your promises', plural? My safety was but one. What others had you made?"

"Others? Yes, I'm certain of the wording, 'twas plural. I hadn't considered that. I can't remember." The Commander stood deep in thought for awhile. Finally, he stated, "Wait. I do recall one other. Myriam once told me of an ancient book held in a special vault under heavy security. 'Twas the only one of its kind and 'twould be fought o'er, if taken. 'Keep safe the book', she'd made me promise. 'Twas forgotten in the search for what happened. I regret a broken promise, but, a book? Your safety came afore a treasure hunt, my love."

Aalanna stood beside the bowl and reached forth her hand, Grifynn taking it. She could almost imagine the strength of his grip, but 'twas not solid. She bit her bottom lip to avoid the tears, happy for what they had, but somber for what they'd lost. "Do you recall the vault's location? I have no memory of such a place. If I see the book or where 'tis kept, I might remember, and we'll know why 'tis so important. Mayhap it has something to do with their disappearance. I can only think 'tis so, as 'twas obviously of grave significance for her to make you promise."

Grifynn knew his presence, such as 'twas, distressed his woman, whom he loved with all his heart. Sorrowfully, he accepted that he could do nothing to ease the pain. "I have only the memory of what she said. 'Twas kept in the bowels of the Keep."

Aalanna put up a bold front for her mate, understanding from whence his sorrow came. "Fear not, my love, all will be well and we shall find both the vault and the book."

"The note wasn't the only thing I found in Myriam's room that day."

She stared at him uncertainly at the ominous statement, waiting for him to proceed. Her chest tightened, making it difficult to breathe, as her senses picked up the Vision of what he'd found.

Tied beneath the bed frame, wrapped tightly in gold threaded cloth and sealed with blood wax, was a package.

"Four superbly forged blades of the highest quality, with exquisite designs carved into the steel. Myriam told me about them, and finding them in her room I thought she'd wanted you to have them. Mayhap as a dowry. But even if they weren't, I could but wonder why they were in her room, and why she'd felt the need to hide them in such a manner. I didn't feel right about leaving such Rashei treasures. They'd be safer with the Clan. I could never bring myself to show you, but on impulse I took them out of hiding with the return of the Dragons. I gave them to Darque upon her LifeBond."

<div align="center">~~~~~~~~~~</div>

Corbyn was the strongest of the Fay, and Memory Magic to the Fay was like making a daisy chain. Easy if you knew how, but not to be rushed or spread too thin and still required skill and careful weaving, as something could fall apart and then there'd be Flame to pay. So, he was careful upon whom he applied his Magic. He'd never attempted to alter the memories of the entire village en mass, 'twas far safer if he just planted fleeting recollections in a select few of them, relying on Human nature to seek inclusion, ignore what they didn't remember and what didn't attract their attention, to believe what they were told, to accept what they thought they saw, and to rarely question details. He'd orchestrated multiple lifespans for Grifynn and Shayla, and they'd all gone quite smoothly for the most part. There'd been a few blunders beyond the Fay's control, but they never amounted to much and all was forgotten with time.

'Twas during the last few winters of the approaching exchange of lives, Corbyn would suggest to a villager here and there that they'd seen Grifynn as a child, watched him grow up. Different villagers would have different memories and they'd share them, as would be in any village. After a time, any of them would swear 'twas truth, for surely their neighbors wouldn't lie about the child. Sometimes they'd embellish the memories, and sometimes the villagers, without his 'assistance', would find their own stories to tell, which all served his purpose. 'Twas no harm done, after all. He'd plant memories in the Warriors' minds of Grifynn learning how to fight as a young man, going through Training, taking the Oath, being in different places at different times. Using their actual memories of Baadyyn, the altered ones weren't far off the truth. Not all Warriors would've been home long enough to see the youth born and grow anyway, most were deployed or in and out and therefore, only a few would require memories of having actually worked with him in the Pits. Drekinn was a very large village, and there were many Warriors. With Corbyn's suggestions of different aging, Grifynn would begin to do things as Grifynn instead of as his father, and the split in their identities would grow wider and more solid 'til the time for the full exchange, the 'elder' to 'Pass' and the 'younger' to take o'er as Battle Commander. 'Twould be orchestrated as an accident, away from the Den and away from a large group, so that fewer memories need be altered with the event. Timing was also critical, as there had to be no one left this side of the Veil who'd been present and/or altered at the last exchange event, for that would cause a ripple in the memory timeline and again, 'twould lead to ultimate failure. Therefore, the Commander had to literally outlive them afore he could 'Pass' once more. And, due to prophesy the Raven had not shared with Grifynn, the lifespan in which he sired Darque would herald the end of his days.

The last exchange occurred while Baadyyn had supposedly gone on a hunting trip (they'd journeyed to the Keep to take Aalanna), 'leaving' Grifynn behind as acting Commander (he'd taken o'er as Second a few winters past). Right to Second was on the hunting trip with Baadyyn and had actually gotten himself killed in a freak accident during their solitary rescue of Aalanna, leaving Baadyyn to return to the campsite with the girl and the badly mutilated body of his Third. Corbyn orchestrated the memories of the rest of the party to recall being in a different locale and returning home with their Commander in shroud after his terrible accident. The real dead man was of course, in the shroud, and the funeral pyre was successful in eliminating any evidence of true identity. Corbyn's work was greatly diminished, merely required to alter the memory of the team not seeing Aalanna at all, seeing the dead man as Baadyyn, while Baadyyn was viewed as the Third Fighter and then was 'deployed', never to be heard from again. Since the man had no kin, 'twas easy enough to misplace him. Eventually, even his references in the archives became obscure.

Aalanna was left in a daze from the entire traumatic experience, during which time she was made to forget her past and believe she was Clan. A couple in the farming community took her in, literally thinking she was their own. What was one more mouth to feed when you had o'er a dozen? Corbyn was ever dumbfounded at how easy 'twas to manipulate the memory of most Humans. He also understood all too well, the urge to do more than just what he did. But he rationalized, and rightly so, 'twas to further the prophesy, for 'twould be Aalanna who would at last, stir Grifynn's loins. She was the one woman who'd finally bring forth the seed that would become the reincarnation of Darque Abriya D'Rienne, the fulfillment of prophesy. Chills ran up his arms as he recalled the funeral pyre and the words of the Rashei Sage as Darque's body succumbed to the flames and her spirit drifted toward the heavens. In a deep, staid voice, she declared for all to hear, "You have given all to your duty and your people, and have earned your final sleep, my sister. Go in peace. But your duty is not ended here, for the Evil One will return. When we are in our greatest need, with the help of our brethren so shall you rise again, Darque of Man." Corbyn was young, too young to have known her in her prime, but as a child sent to the island of Rienne often afore 'twas destroyed, he'd spent many moons with her. And although her soul harbored a deep sense of loneliness, her presence was most powerful. He'd felt grief with her Passing. She'd told him the most fantastic tales of adventure and of war, and he sometimes wondered if 'twas her influence that led him to defy his father and attempt to fight for their realm. Of course, that was another story, ultimately culminating in the curse under which he was now chained. Would he alter anything of the past? He'd wish that his woman and his unborn son had survived. Mayhap Grifynn was right. Our past did not orchestrate our present, it merely prepared us for it. 'Twas inevitable, the events leading us to the here and now. No, he'd not change who he was, he'd not alter his actions, except for that one thing. He wouldn't have left her alone that night. Not that night. If he'd waited 'til morning mayhap 'twould have been a different story. But he was who he was and he was duty bound. And 'twas no knowing if he would've been able to prevent what happened, anyway. Yes, mayhap 'twas the way 'twas meant to be. One could not circumvent the Fates.

<center>~~~~~THE ALTAR ROOM~~~~~</center>

As Aalanna stood chanting, a second spirit form coalesced unseen, within the room outside the bowl. Nor did the one they actually Called, notice her when she joined him along the path through the Veil. His Draw should not have transported another, but those tears called to her as loudly as did the ones in which they were mixed, call to him. Mystified, she looked at her hands once more, or rather, through her hands. Holding up the pearled gown, she gazed at her bare feet, long red hair spilling o'er her shoulders as she tucked her chin. She couldn't remember ever seeing herself in this gown afore and 'twas initially puzzling, as 'twas a funeral gown. But even more puzzling was that she could somehow see through herself, as if she didn't truly exist, yet she could think, feel, see, hear, even move freely about.

Drawn with the same conjure as a completely different individual, she didn't believe 'twas a mistake, yet if she'd been Called, why was she being ignored? 'Twas confusing. She was not to be Called unless the Evil One returned. The Sage had everything she'd require when the time was right, and 'twould have been in the High Spire, ready for battle. Yet, this was not the High Spire, and she saw not her Sword. Ever more questions invaded her growing consciousness. How long was she away, why Call her in this manner, how had her tears come to be mixed with the tears of that man, and who the Flame were these people?

She was at the Keep. Although she'd not lived here long afore her Passing, 'twas easily recognized. The Rashei made this their home after the Island of Rienne was destroyed. 'Twas betrayal from within, and the culprit was not adequately punished, in her opinion. She rendered her judgment in support of banishment from their midst, but 'twas blocked by her peers. The others could not be convinced that the destruction of Rienne was directly related to Beryl's activities. Too tolerant, they'd not been in the thick of the fighting during the time of chaos, even to the point that some doubted the reality of such. She was the only one who'd seen battle. 'Twas a mistake to allow Beryl to walk free with only an apology and her promise of never attempting to use the Book again. She left the altar room and floated through the Keep. 'Twas so empty. Trying to make sense of things, she felt a growing disquiet that letting Beryl go free had been a mistake for which they ended up paying dearly.

<div align="center">~~~~~A FEW DAWNS LATER~~~~~</div>

She was back. She'd been Drawn forth from the Beyond recently, but was pulled away again. She shook her head. She deduced that she'd Passed the Veil, but was unable to determine when. How long had she been here and how come she couldn't seem to stay here for more than a short while afore she went somewhere else yet again? And she couldn't remember where. 'Twas just blank. She was beginning to feel like a fish bobber. Try as she might, there was no time reference. Her memory seemed to clear and her form become more solid each time she was noticed, as well as lengthening the time she was here. Talk about a vicious circle. To become easier to see, she had to get them to see her. Her form ethereal, apparently invisible to most eyes, the youngest children were the first to notice her amongst them, usually when she was in the light of day or fire, and she had to smile as they pointed their fingers and stared in awe, open mouthed and wide eyed. They talked about her, calling her 'the pretty lady' or 'the fair one', the older children referring to her as 'the First Warrior', even going so far as to liken her appearance to the Battle Commander. 'First Warrior' could refer to them recognizing her, which she couldn't decide whether 'twas good or bad. But that last was a bit confusing, since the only Battle Commander of whom she'd been aware, was male. However she'd been 'here' just long enough to have heard a few discussions leading her to believe the current Commander was female. Perplexing.

Some of the children bowed in her presence and she obliged them with a courtly nod and a wink which elicited animated giggles and gasps in response. She was quite powerful once, but 'twas long ago. The past faded slightly with their attentions, their innocence flooding her mind with pleasant memories. 'Twas the first time she'd felt anything akin to happiness in countless long winters. She frowned once more, her heart heavy. The loneliness was unbearable, 'twas as if her body and soul were torn asunder. 'Twas just as bad Beyond as 'twas on this side of the Veil. Ever since she and Solvyngarr... She dropped her head again and closed her blue eyes. If she was more than a spirit thing, she'd sigh, but although she no longer breathed, her heart no longer beat, and her memories were still a bit clouded, her senses were as sharp as ever and she wondered if this pain would ever end.

They were desperate, the war had taken a turn for the worse, and they attempted something brash, something no one could or should have tried to accomplish. Everything had gone according to plan, they'd depended upon the shock of their results, and their mission was an ultimate success. With the Evil One in full retreat they'd managed to save Kadoor once again. But, there was a reason the LifeBond took both partners Beyond, as one. Afterwards, she forged the four blades, Magically disguising them, doing everything within her power as per their research and preparation, but the 'shearing' of the 'Bond had caused more damage than either of them realized would occur, and she failed to affect his rescue. Powerless to use the blades as intended, she lived and yet not lived, winter after winter, unable to Pass by her own hand or in battle, unable to do anything but pine away, aging but not aging, ever alone, with Solvyngarr imprisoned for eternity, neither of them whole. No one truly understood, their 'Bond was the only one of its kind, and she became a recluse even amongst her own people. Her elongated span of days drew the sorrow into an everlasting torment, 'til she finally succumbed, and then she found no relief from what she'd endured, and no way to join her partner, still trapped. She bowed her ghostly head, her long flowing mane brushing the stone floor as she stepped away from the children. She didn't want to bring her own sorrow to them, didn't want to taint their innocence. What she did want was to discover who they were, why they were here, and what had happened to her own people.

She was in St Swiftyn's, that much was certain, alone and yet not alone. The Keep had not been empty since the Rashei took up residence here after a devastating combination of volcanic eruption, tsunami, and quake, caused their island to sink beneath the waves of the Ocean of Fears ages past, and yet now there were only three adults with o'er three hundred children, all foreigners. Her existence had been altered, she was not where she'd been spending all her time since she'd Passed, she was not in the Fade, but still not quite this side of the Veil. What had happened? With purpose in her thoughts, her jaw set, she made her way to the Hall of Life, which housed the diaries of every Rashei who ever lived at the Keep, literally thousands and thousands of leather bound volumes of hand written accumulated observances, feelings and knowledge. She smiled slightly. Without a bit of conceit, she was fully aware she'd been something of an icon. Certainly someone would have written about her Passing. And she wouldn't have to actually read them all, although she had nothing but time, she merely had to 'sense' them to locate that for which she searched. Something horrible had happened since the time of her Passing, and her own obituary was the best place to start. Floating along, she thought of another question. 'Twas evident the children saw more ghostly images cloaked somehow to her vision, but her other senses told a different story. Who were they?

Chapter Thirty

Vital Information

~~~~~THE DEN~~~~~

Gunnarr had just returned from his hunt, bringing much needed supplies from the mountains. Walking into their private rooms, Darque was livid. "Someone raided our quarters."

"When?"

"I'm not sure, but could've been at least a moon. Mayhap more. I haven't actually been here for quite some time, and neither have you."

Gunnarr inhaled, his nostrils flaring, afore he snorted with a puff of smoke in disgust. "'Twas Mikkal, I can smell him. The Eye?"

"'Tis safe. I was expecting this. Aalanna wears the real Eye. But..."

"He has taken the fake? This pleases me, little one. But Mikkal has gone too far. Koryl's hold upon him has reached its apex. Regardless of the Oath, we can wait no longer."

Darque grit her teeth in a combination of anger, resolve, and heartbreaking acceptance. "Agreed."

~~~~~THE WITCH'S DUNGEONS~~~~~

Artemis was healed of her injuries, still sore and not quite up to par, but close enough. Striking up a conversation while preparing some medications and supplements for the Warrior to give to the Dragon, she said, "You could have escaped, returned to the Brotherhood."

"'Twas my sworn duty," Mynx answered without emotion.

"Yet you did not. You stayed."

"I could not leave Synahmarr."

Now Artemis was truly curious. "You didn't even know who she was, you had no idea whom you were protecting."

"The Highlands are our allies. 'Twas simply the right thing to do."

"So now what? If you return to the Clan, you've broken your Oath."

Mynx didn't hesitate, her response born of new confidence. "The Oath also states I am to protect those who cannot fend for themselves, although the war has shifted our priorities. Still, I will face my Commander with a clear conscience. In the meantime Healer, you are now able to take your leave, and I ask you to get word to Maahayyel as soon as possible. She must know of the plight of the Princess. She must come. We need her assistance."

"Not to the Clan first?"

"I sent Larken and the rest, to the Clan, but we know not if they will be, or have been, successful. Believe me when I say that I've struggled with this decision for many moons. Syn is still in imminent danger of Passing and she will be killed outright, if found. She must escape soon and I feel the only way to do that, is to get word directly to Maahayyel. Syn can feel her aunt. She says she is home at Fire Heart in the Dragon's Tears."

Artemis was astounded. "'Twould take me o'er a winter to get there a'foot."

Mynx shook her head. "You won't have to travel a'foot. If the arrangements can be completed, you'll not be traveling above ground at all."

Comprehension bloomed. "I've never traveled by Water Dragon afore."

"She's been a valuable asset to our survival. However, time is running out, consequently Syn and I have discussed our options. There are none, at least nothing feasible. Therefore, the next time Islyth comes, barring complications, she will take you with her. That is, should you choose to go."

Surprised at having been given such an option, she blurted, "What else would I do?"

Mynx stared at the Healer, gauging her fortitude. "You can easily escape the castle, as can I. Still, if you so choose, I'll assist you in any way possible, without repercussion. You have no duty to help us, your duty lies with the People. Per my resources, they've scattered, but some have reportedly attempted to join with the Clan. You'd be accepted there, regardless. Your skills would be appreciated."

"'Twould not be my home. I have no home now. We know not the reality of the circumstances on the outside, although your information is most likely correct. If I waste time going to find the People, Syn may Pass or be discovered. 'Tis my first duty to assist my Vision to fruition, and time is short indeed. I will go with Islyth, if she'll take me."

"And I will protect the Princess to the Veil, as we await your return."

~~~~~LATER~~~~~

Synahmarr was getting a little stronger by the day, but 'twas unlikely she'd ever be strong enough to escape the dungeon by herself. With regal poise, she asked, "You are certain you can make such a long journey with a passenger? I want not to be the cause of harm, my sweet cousin. You've been very helpful already."

Islyth's eyes sparkled with the concern, however, she was a tad miffed. Did the Princess think she was so frail? Did she not think she was capable of completing such an essential voyage? However, she wasn't happy about having to take the Human. She'd been wanting to find Maahayyel for moons now, to tell her about the Princess. Knowing the Matriarch was at their ancestral home would bypass the need to travel the Fears in search of Myrrdin, and 'twould merely require her to swim 'cross country to the Dragon's Tears through the Raptor's Talons, beyond Darkling Forest. Standing up on her hind legs bringing her eye to eye with the Highland, her paws tucked under her armpits
~~~~~

and shoulders elevated, Islyth cocked her head and declared, "Pffffft!"

Synahmarr laughed while wiping the spray of spit from her muzzle. "I believe I've been properly chastised, brave one."

Drooling in her efforts, Islyth spit, "Can this one at least be taught how to ride?"

Syn was stunned, 'twas the longest sentence she could recall being spewed forth from any Water Dragon. Apparently 'twas of some importance, and she could only speculate as to the reason. "I take it the last one was a bit of a nuisance?"

"Last two," Islyth corrected with her heavy lisp, throwing up both paws into the air. Just afore she added her earlier response, Syn stopped her with one paw gently laid 'cross her muzzle. She'd been sprayed quite enough for the moment. "Ahhh, I see. So you're the one who woke me, bringing in the Commander. Now it all makes sense." Nodding her head as the sequence of events fell into place, she went on, "I'll see that she is educated on the proper handling. But keep in mind, Humans are not Sprites, and they have no Tie with you. Therefore, they'll never achieve the same riding proficiency."

"They stiff. Hurt Islyth's neck. 'Tis distress. Humans breathe not in water! No Magic!" She finished with her paws up in the air again, as she shrugged.

The can-you-believe-that look on her face tickled Synahmarr and she tried not to laugh. "Well, to be precise, neither can Sprites, they're just able to hold their breath a bit longer than Humans." Syn noted the expression crossing Islyth's face and hurried to add, "But still not long enough to travel 'cross the seas and through the underground river system without a Water Dragon. You are much needed by us all. Especially now."

Again, Islyth beamed with the praise heaped upon her and stood up even straighter. "Need Maahayyel. Islyth tell."

'Twas clear the Dragon wanted to accomplish the task alone. Syn had to impress her with the need to take Artemis without hurting her feelings, or she'd lose interest and mayhap disappear. There was no telling how long 'twould take for her to return, ready to talk again. She chose her next words carefully. "Yes, you will tell her. And Artemis has vital information for her as well. She must go with you to Flight of Fire to speak with the Matriarch."

"'Tis very important?" Islyth furrowed her brows and pouted. Synahmarr held her breath. "'Tis."

Suddenly the Dragon's entire expression brightened, and with excitement and commitment, she responded. "Islyth do! Easy."

A SENNIGHT LATER

~~~~~THE TOWER OF FLIGHT OF FIRE KEEP~~~~~

</div>

Maahayyel had listened to Artemis closely, considering the implications of the Vision. The Matriarch knew that Visions were not always to be taken at face value. Sometimes, 'twas difficult to discern their true intent. "Two Warriors clashed? Two Dragons in the air? You are certain? Only two?"

'Twas now the turn of Artemis, to consider carefully what she'd just described. "I am not certain of the numbers. I was very young and at the time of the Vision, I'd never actually seen Evanntyr, let alone a Dragon. The edges were blurred, the focus upon the two Warriors battling each other on the ramparts. When one was stabbed, a Dragon faltered. Then shortly after, I Saw a Dragon Pass the Veil."

The Matriarch stared at her. "And were they the same Dragon?"

The Painted One hesitated for a moment afore answering. "I'd never really thought about it 'til Dragons began to visit Evanntyr again. I'd always assumed they were one and the same. But although the Warriors looked very much alike, not so the Dragons. No, Matriarch, they were not the same, nevertheless I am certain of the identity of the one who Passed." Her voice faded and 'twas difficult to meet the gaze of the great Dragon, afore she contin-
~~~~~

ued. "But why would I not See the other one Pass? I know that the Warrior died. I know that 'twas his Dragon fighting. Why would I then see... Surely this was a Vision still in the future, for you are not in 'Bond, and 'twas his Dragon who fell with him."

Maahayyel nodded absently, and looked out upon the balcony, toward the west. "You know who the Warriors are, do you not?"

Hesitating once again, she tried to avoid choking as her throat constricted. "Yes. I now believe that one of them was my Claim Son, Mikkal, although he was not fully grown when last we parted, and 'twas from a great distance. I did not make this connection 'til most recently, however. And the one he fought against looked like his twin, Gabriel. 'Twas difficult to see him clearly."

"Gabriel is the First Born, the True King?"

"Yes, Matriarch. But we cannot prove this without the documents, and we cannot get to them now. Besides, paper can be forged or destroyed. I doubt Shytin will so easily step aside for his half brother to take the throne upon the presentation of such evidence. We need something more notable. Something that would leave no doubt."

"Gabriel did not live with the Clan. He has not taken the 'Bond." Maahayyel voiced her thoughts aloud. Since 'twas not a question, Artemis remained silent as the Dragon continued to ponder. Finally, she spoke again. This time, 'twas a question. "And where is Gabriel now?"

"He traveled with the People to Drekinn, while I stayed behind to heal and help with Synahmarr in the dungeons."

Maahayyel shook her great head again, as she concentrated. Artemis said she'd not been to Drekinn or the Lair, coming straight to Fire Heart, which would have eliminated any chance of her meeting the ones she'd Seen so long ago, therefore, her inability to positively identify them was understandable. And there was something on the edge of her perception, pointing to the importance of Gabriel being the eldest twin. What was it? "Is there anything else you remember about the Vision? Anything at all?"

"I do recall one more thing. I Heard a voice, or mayhap several repeating, 'With the Passing of the one, the other is proven.' Do you know what it means?"

Maahayyel pondered the words, and as the sun dawned upon her, she not only knew all the players of the Vision, she understood the time was now and she held a dual role. She'd been shocked to learn that Synahmarr was, and had been, at Evanntyr all this time. But after hearing of what she'd endured through the ages, and of her stasis, 'twas a wonder she yet lived. Nonetheless, her niece's efforts would've been in vain if she didn't get to her in time. 'Twould take an incredible amount of energy in order for her to Brew the Greater Magic she'd require for saving the life of her niece as well as passing her rule. And could she orchestrate the Vision to prove the True King? But given the sequence of events apparently about to unfold, that energy would surpass anything she'd experienced in her span of days. Of course, 'twould mean the end of her days.

She crouched down, eye to eye with Artemis, and thanked her for all she'd done, telling the Human that they would ensure her safe transport to whatever destination she chose.

Knowing she'd not return, Artemis's heart broke for the Dragon she'd just met, and quietly she stated, "You are most brave, Matriarch."

Maahayyel was touched by the empathy she felt from the Human. Despite the fact that timing was crucial, she took a moment to explain. There'd be many deaths in this war, and those who remained must stand strong. "If 'tis my time, I welcome the Beyond. I only ask my ancestors to help me pass my rule successfully, afore I am gathered to them."

Artemis climbed up onto the balcony wall to face the Ancient. "If 'tis so, may your memory be a blessing."

Accepting the Human's hug, she replied regally, "And may yours, my child. In your time. Now get thee down to the Great Hall, where transportation awaits." And then the Mighty Maahayyel stepped gracefully out upon the balcony of the high tower and launched into the gray skies, her wide wings beating powerfully. Artemis watched her fade away 'cross the horizon of the Dragon's Tears afore she laboriously climbed down the massive carved stone stairs to the Great Hall, where she was met by Islyth, along with a multitude of Highlands, all staring at her. They'd Heard their beloved Matriarch give her final orders as she flew away, and they all knew 'twas the Human who'd been the last to lay eyes upon her. With intense grief registering upon their faces and in their postures, she felt numb. And then the castle trembled with the dull reverberation of thousands of tears striking the stone floor.

<center>~~~~~LESS THAN A MARK LATER~~~~~</center>

Artemis stripped and tied her clothing to her back, then climbed aboard Islyth, trying not to hold too tightly. She closed her eyes so as not to see the harrowing plunge into the well of Flight of Fire. Her destination was Evanntyr, where she planned to recover her stash. But even more important, she wanted to see her son once again. 'Twould take another few days of underwater travel, and 'twas less than a sennight afore her Vision would occur. She could only hope they'd get there in time.

Chapter Thirty-One

A Vision Fulfilled

As Mikkal writhed in pain upon the frost covered grass, Daynahmyn was drawn into the chaos of her 'Bond's mindset. She'd attempted everything she knew to prevent him from leaving, tracking him from the Lair all the way to the foothills of the Great Plains, but to no avail. Mikkal was caught in a web of evil, his soul shrouded in blackness, his mind deteriorating rapidly. The need to do what he was being told was becoming too difficult, too much for him to bear. "I have to go! If I don't, I'll do it, Day, I can't help myself any longer. I'll do something horrible! 'Tis like the worst addiction, I've grown too weak to fight it any longer. If I can't kill her, I'll end up betraying the Resistance." The desperation in his voice, the inability to even Speak with her, made her aware 'twas time to end this struggle. Even so, she could tell that he was keeping something from her, he'd not told her everything.

"Petrayyah. Send for my sisters, I Call for escort. 'Tis time." Afore helping Mikkal aboard, she handed him his favorite cloak, the one his Claim Mother gave him when he left Wyndsyr Forest so long ago. In his weakened condition the cold of flight would increase the pain by much.

Petrayyah Answered immediately and with trepidation. *"Daynahmyn! What do you mean, "'tis time'?"*

"We must go. Now. Mikkal's only chance is to kill Koryl, but if that can't be accomplished, or he's not released by her death, either way, tonight our span of days ends."

"Darque won't allow this! Killing Koryl would be an open act of war!" Immediately she realized 'twas a most ridiculous Declaration, and she would've blushed if possible.

Daynahmyn recognized her embarrassment and ignored the outburst. *"Stay away. Rakkah must not be there with Mikkal, 'twill be too difficult to control them."*

"He's already Heard. He's been Calling for days."

But Daynahmyn didn't Answer. She helped Mikkal, Blocking as much of the pain as she could, as he mounted, hugging himself tightly against the obsession to commit a vicious act. Shaking, he couldn't even tie onto the saddle.

<p style="text-align:center">~~~~~THE DEN~~~~~</p>

The Call Shared 'tween the siblings, Pelayyah came without delay, having no 'Bond. Sydrayyah walked into the Training Pits, stretched out her long wings and prepared to take flight to join her sisters. From the corner of her eye, she saw Regynn stepping out upon the sands, her saddle in his arms.

"Hunting again so soon?" They'd been topside for research along with a few others, but they'd no permission to leave the Shield. Her behavior of late was disturbing, and he thought he knew the reason.

Reluctantly, she replied, "'Tis a family matter."

"Then 'tis a matter which concerns me, as we are closer than family."

"I'd rather go alone."

"Why do you Block me, Syd? What's going on out there? What are you hiding? I know something has troubled you for many moons. In fact, since your sister took Mikkal." He stared at her, willing her to tell him the truth, to confirm his suspicions. Even though Regynn was focused upon his multiple tasks, he was more aware of his surroundings since taking the 'Bond and there'd been much going on that needed explaining.

She hung her head. "It could put you at great risk. Your position, your Oath..."

"...my life?" She was actually surprised when he finished her thoughts with such accuracy, she'd been so distracted by the Call that her ability to reason was blurred. "Syd, don't be ridiculous. If something will threaten my life, 'twill threaten yours as well. I'm coming with you. We defend each other."

"But..."

"If my span of days is to end, 'twill not be alone and without having been in the midst of the fight."

Fully armed, he tossed the saddle o'er her shoulders.

"You better double check that strap." Cathay stood just behind him, her arms crossed and brows raised. She'd been one of the few topside, helping with the gardens. The 'fertilizer' experiment was going so well they had to work hard to contain the results, and she'd been quite busy harvesting. Sighing, she should've made sure he'd changed that strap when she first noticed 'twas worn. Syd even asked her to do so, knowing Regynn was too busy and too focused upon the needs of others since the battle. The big Green and the petite Master Craftsman had become quite close of late, and Sydrayyah knew that the two held special feelings for each other from long ago and far away. But 'twas another story.

"Cathay!" His smile quickly faded and became a frown.

"You're not going hunting with her, are you." 'Twas a statement, not a question. He barely glanced her way. Her gaze flickered down and then looking back up, she said quietly, "Will you at least try to return this time? Don't make me chase you half way 'cross Kadoor again."

Now staring at her, he drank in her face, her body, her smile. He never wanted to be without her, but he had to leave. Again. He tried to commit everything to memory. With an awkward expression he stated, "I love you." 'Twas the first time he'd ever said the words aloud.

Stunned by his admission, her only response was, "I love you, too."

Then Sydrayyah was dragging him 'cross the Pits as he struggled to finish securing the saddle, mounting on the move. Cathay covered her face with her hands to protect her eyes from the cloud of sand billowing about. By the time 'twas settled, they were nowhere to be seen.

~~~~~LESS THAN A MARK LATER~~~~~

Darque didn't have time to chastise the man standing in front of her now. Mikkal's identical twin, why hadn't she seen it afore? Well, she did see it, it just hadn't registered. Priding her deductive reasoning, she'd already cast her mental vote for Rakkah as most likely the True King, although it could've been Mikkal, but she was blindsided with a third potential contender.

Maahayyel arrived less than a mark earlier, just after Regynn sent his cryptic message that they and Pelayyah were 'escorting' Mikkal and Daynahmyn to Evanntyr and 'twas a real possibility of a fight. He'd asked for backup. Now, Maahayyel brought more information, and 'twas indeed, a skirmish developing. She liked not the way this was playing out, for the True King was in their midst, but he had to go with Maahayyel. She'd made that quite clear, 'twas essential and could not be avoided. Without him, she might fail in her mission to rescue Synahmarr, yet she'd not revealed the details of how that was going to happen. And try as she might, 'twas nothing in any of the prophesies she knew, that would guide her decision. Unable to take a full Flight, she chose carefully, for 'twould not only be a declaration of open war, 'twould tell the enemy they protected one of great importance. 'Twould be Pelayyah, her and Gunnarr, Regynn with Sydrayyah already trailing Rakkah and Petrayyah who were still behind Mikkal, and Gabriel with the Mighty Maahayyel. Darque knew her health status, but she appeared strong and in high spirits now. Still, they must guard the Matriarch and the True King at all costs. This would be a duty of protection and extraction, although clueless how either was to occur, not to mention they'd be flying directly into the hornet's nest. Sending the information to Regynn, he agreed with the plan, such as 'twas, Reporting they'd been unable thus far, to Link with Rakkah, who seemed a'Flamed
~~~~~

to catch Mikkal in order to prevent him from reaching the castle. However, 'twas some indication that his Petrayyah had slowed down and was merely keeping pace a few leagues behind. And, Regynn suspected Sydrayyah was also pacing behind, although they should catch up to Rakkah afore they got to the castle. Their flight patterns led her to believe they'd all arrive close to the same timing, still behind Mikkal. 'Twas most peculiar, as if the Fates had taken control. Darque stared at the Matriarch. 'Twas obvious that Maahayyel knew more than she'd shared. The Battle Commander hoped by the 7th Egg that she had enough information to bring them all back alive.

~~~~~~~~~~

Traddya stood at alert at his left side and wrinkled her nose in contentment while Gabriel scratched behind her ears. 'Twas calming to the Beast. She wasn't happy about this journey. She was unable to fly with him, unable to protect him if 'twas needed. She was being left behind.

Gabriel listened carefully to Gheryh and Traddya's conversation, but for the life of him, he couldn't decipher the language of the Kahyah. His gaze shifted from the Beast to the woman questioningly. "She says to keep your weapons at hand, shift your weight carefully, and lead with your left."

"She always says that." Gabriel stroked the top of Traddya's head.

"Then mayhap you'd be wise to take heed." Speaking with the Kahyah again, after some elongated growls, she grimaced in disgust. "I will not, do it yourself, I have a mate." Again, the Kahyah spoke and Gheryh replied in Common. "Ryygg will understand, trust me."

Traddya turned and rested one heavy paw on Gabriel's shoulders. Staring deeply into his eyes she chuffed, and then dragged her tongue slowly 'cross his face, removing most of what was left of the paint and leaving a wet trail of slobber dripping off his chin afore she turned and sauntered away. Puzzled, his attention shift-
~~~~~~~~~~

ed back to the Word Sayer. She shrugged. "She bids her pup farewell, says she loves you, and you must return to us, if not to her."

Gabriel wiped his face on his bare arm, displaying some rather impressive muscles. "I thank you for not doing that yourself, you're like my sister. 'Twould have been a bit creepy. And I will return. To all of you."

Darque cut short any more conversation, urgency in every fiber of her being. "Enough. We ride. Mikkal is ahead of us, and we must fly hard to catch him."

Gabriel donned his cloak and mounted Maahayyel. Flanked by the Teams, they took wing to the south.

Chapter Thirty-Two

One Warrior Down

~~~~~ON THE WALLS OF EVANNTYR~~~~~

Never afore had Warrior drawn sword against Warrior. From the time of the High Races Counsel, no one had ever broken the Oath. Near extinct by the Last Holocaust, Grifynn, in his wisdom and desire to protect Kadoor, re-established the Brotherhood through the Dragon Clan in preparation for the return of the Evil One. All strong, highly skilled men and women, they were sworn to defend and keep the peace for their entire span of days, protecting society and one another against all opposing forces, bringing swift and sure justice as they awaited their true calling.

Rakkah stood with his blade at ready, facing his brother. "I cannot allow this, Mikkal. You must surrender the Eye."

Mikkal's lip quivered and he began to circle, his weapon raised. "I am but a marionette. My strings are pulled by a puppet master."

Rakkah didn't want to fight his own brother, let alone another Warrior. His eyes began to burn crimson in the Lust, as he repeated his warning. "Mikkal, give me the Eye, stop this now. You said it yourself, you don't know what you're doing. Let me help you."

Mikkal lost any semblance of control, growling, "Defend yourself, or die."

Straight away, sword rang out against sword, clashing and clanging. Sweat flew off brows as they ducked and twisted and swung, Rakkah besieged against his brother's brutal assault. Striking viciously time after time, Mikkal's anger grew as he fought, the troubles that plagued him through so many winters, pouring forth as through a failed dam. A storm began to brew high above, black clouds gathered, lightening flashed with the in-
~~~~~

tensity of the emotions and the energy thus created. Their blades sliced through the air, just missing a fatal blow against Rakkah's defensive maneuvers again and again. Mikkal's eyes matched his brother's in the Lust but 'twas a madness there that could not be denied. His face was contorted with rage and he unleashed it with a vengeance.

Rakkah felt a sharp pain in his left shoulder, Petrayyah beginning the Healing quickly, but they'd both lost a lot of blood. No longer recognizing his brother, Mikkal no longer even knew what he was doing. Only the Veil could stop him, only death could prevent death. Rakkah's anguish knew no bounds, his heart pounding. Fury boiled in his blood, but not against his brother. Such was aimed at the injustice, the hold o'er Mikkal's soul. He knew his brother for a kind, generous man, who loved children and wanted only peace for all, but who was possessed with impulsivity and rage. He was Rakkah's brother but he was also his best friend and confidant, each trusting the other to have his back in any situation. He'd never been more alive than the last few winters, sharing all with Mikkal.

As they fought along the ramparts, he was aware of Dragons above them. The blood rained down while Petrayyah attempted to defend herself and Rakkah against Daynahmyn's need to protect Mikkal. There seemed to be others as well, he could hear voices yelling and Dragon screams, but he couldn't allow himself to lose focus. 'Twas wrong. 'Twas tragic. This had to end. Realizing 'twould not change otherwise, Rakkah took advantage of his greater experience to gain control of the fight. Mikkal had always had an obvious 'tell', that only Rakkah could still recognize, giving him the upper hand through their practice winters. 'Twas something Mikkal had worked hard to lose since he'd joined the Clan. Watching his face closely, Rakkah took the offensive at last, forcefully disarming Mikkal after a particularly complicated series of strikes in which he shed more blood than his shared Healing could rapidly replace, his limbs tingling in weakness.

~~~~~BENEATH THE TOWER~~~~~

Artemis ran like the wind itself, her screams swallowed within the rising storm. 'Twas as her Vision, and her son was on that wall. The grief she felt was unbearable. She'd wanted to try to prevent such from happening but Regynn convinced her the Fates would not be shorted. She'd been in Wyndsyr Forest, having just arrived with Islyth as the action unfolded, and the Warrior fell through the limbs o'er head when his saddle strap broke, practically landing at her feet. He received only minor injuries in the fall and the Healing took care of those, but during the process his innate ability to eternally question everything, brought forth not only her identity and why she was there, but also the details of her Vision. Immediately he deduced her role, dictated within. She'd not made sense of it afore, but after the Warrior's revelation 'twas now clear. The people needed to be rallied. The voices she'd heard were of her own doing. 'Twas her responsibility to make it happen.

She'd let her hair grow and wore no paint during the time she was in the dungeons, the stains fading. No one recognized the Painted One as she walked amongst them, whispering the words they'd soon chant, seeding the truth in the background, listening to it whip through the frenzied crowd like the wind whipped up a forest fire. 'Twas easy enough with the unnatural storm brewing, fueled by the suspicious nature of the peasants and nobles. Nevertheless, once the task was accomplished with the people thronging to witness the return of the True King, she lost her resolve and ran toward the tower once again. 'Twas exactly as her Vision and she finally realized she couldn't possibly arrive in time to change what was Seen. As she came to a halt, stumbling in the leaf litter, she trembled with emotion and fatigue, choking back her tears. Hugging and rocking herself against the anguish, she whispered into the mounting storm, hoping his heart would hear what his ears would not, "I love you, my son." Regynn stepped up behind her and placed his hand upon her shoulder.
~~~~~

"I'll not leave you alone. We shall see this through together." His words and manner were so sincere, so touching, it made her breath stutter. Breaking down, she turned to him, burying her wet face in his leathers. The muscled Warrior put his arm around the weeping woman, as the rest of the Vision played forth.

~~~~~~~~~~

Rakkah held Mikkal by the throat, backed into a corner of the wall, the tip of his broadsword wedged firmly under his brother's sternum. He was fully aware that he could lose his position at any moment and if 'twas a battle to the end, hesitation could be fatal, yet he could not kill his own brother. Dragons hovered above them, and along the wall they stood with their Humans in the ensuing silence. Only their heavy breathing and the beating of wings could be heard. No one moved for several heartbeats, then Mikkal's eyes registered awareness and he implored, "Do it. Do it, Rakkah, I beg of you. I can no longer control myself. I'd rather Pass than continue this side of the Veil after what I've done. You're the only one upon whom I can depend, in my time of need. Do it. Please."

Rakkah's arms shook with fatigue, and 'twas an effort to answer. "Just give me the Eye, Mikkal. We'll work this out. We always have, 'tis not too late."

Mikkal spit blood as he replied with resignation. "The Eye is fake. I knew 'twas when I took it. I brought it to lure Koryl to her death, but she's disappeared. And you and I both know 'tis far too late. Only the Veil can release me now." His face a mask of sorrow, he whispered, "I love you, my brother."

Afore Rakkah could respond, Mikkal reached out and grabbed him by the back of his neck. With a monumental effort, he yanked his brother toward him while pushing his full body weight forward hard enough to impale himself upon the sword. Daynahmyn screamed in pain, spiraling toward the ground in an uncontrolled spin. Petrayyah dove under and slowed her descent, helping her regain her position.
~~~~~~~~~~

"I'm sorry, I'm so very sorry," Mikkal Spoke with Daynahmyn, attempting to comfort her afore their impending deaths. *"I didn't want this for you."*

"You did what was right. You are a good Warrior. Your life was never your own, 'twas all in prophesy. You've done well against such odds." With her friend's help, she was just able to catch the edge of the wall with her talons, pulling up to lay upon the sun warmed stone, gaining control of her breathing. Pelayyah and Petrayyah hovered nearby. This fight, followed by the stresses of all the events of the past several moons, had taken Day's Magic to an all time low and 'twas all she could do to keep them both from Passing right now, for the prophesy wasn't yet complete. The Fates decried that she keep Mikkal alive as long as she could, and dragging herself laboriously to within a Dragon's length of her 'Bond, in torment for his pain for she had not the strength to Block it, she struggled to help him hold on as she Reached out to him, his Life Source slowly pooling underneath his body, his beautiful cloak slashed and soaked with blood.

From her position with Gunnarr, Darque was the only actual witness to the deed. *"'Tis a crowd gathered, we need to watch them. Shock will wear off soon and actions may well run against us."* Gunnarr ordered the other Dragons to stand guard o'er the spectacle. He landed upon the wall some distance away for her to dismount and kept a wary watch o'er the crowd, who'd not moved, apparently in collective shock.

Rakkah was also in shock. He'd rarely cried in his span of days, but the tears began to roll down his sweat and blood streaked face as he tried to regain his focus. 'Twas an act for which he'd not been prepared and as soon as the sword split Mikkal's heart, his death was inevitable. If he tried to withdraw it now, 'twould cause Mikkal to Pass even quicker. What was he to do? The lightning flashed brightly and often enough that 'twas as day, the thunder was deafening, and somewhere above them another kind of battle raged, the very walls of the castle beginning to tremble.

Maahayyel landed upon the ramparts and Gabriel leaped down, running toward the pair. For a candle drip, Rakkah thought he'd crossed the line of sanity. Except for the cut of his hair he was a mirror image of the one who lay dying in his arms. Even their cloaks were the same. He was speechless. The young man knelt in the growing pool of blood beside Mikkal and took his hand. "I am Gabriel, your twin. You don't know me, but your voice saved my life. I've shared your torment, your losses, and your friendship. Trust me, had I known who you were when we were growing up, I would have been at your side. Mayhap I'd have been able to spare you this."

Holding Rakkah's arm tightly, Mikkal lifted his head to stare at the man, noting the cloak he wore, matching his own. Memories flooded in, some distressing, some joyful, then with a sad smile, his voice weak and trembling, he murmured, "No one could have spared me this. My fate was set afore my birth. But I do know you. I don't know how, but I've felt your presence as well. I remember yelling for you to reach out for that creature stuck to the side of a cliff. You would have fallen to your death. I always knew 'twas more than a dream, yet I could never explain."

"Yes, brother, 'twas me and you saved me. Now 'tis you who must reach out. Don't let go, I've just found you. Please don't let go." Gabriel turned angrily to Daynahmyn. "Why aren't you Healing him? Why are you letting him die?"

Frail and sorrowful, she spoke aloud for all to hear. "The sword has destroyed his heart. I haven't the strength, but couldn't Heal such a wound anyway. I hold him long enough for your farewells. We accepted our destinies some time ago, and we came here prepared to end his enslavement, one way or the other."

Mikkal squeezed his brothers' hands and spoke, his voice weakening by the breath. "I love you both. Take not my death as a failure, for if failure, 'twas my own and not of your doing. Fear not, for I welcome the Veil, 'twill bring me peace." He coughed and winced, then began again, blood seeping from the corners of his mouth. "I pray thee both live long and successful lives. I only wish I could tell Artemis how much I love her, how much she means to me, even now." Tears welled up in his sea green eyes, filled with pain and passion. "Long live the Dragon Clan. Long live the True King. Continue the fight in my name and honor, if you can find it in your hearts to forgive me my wrongs."

Gabriel placed his own blade in his brother's hand, holding tightly to keep it within his grasp, stuttering his farewell. "Your sword will be greatly missed."

Mikkal felt peace and forgiveness envelope him. What his brother said and did, meant much to a Passing Warrior. Staring at his best friend, his eyes began to glaze o'er. He wheezed, but Rakkah couldn't understand what he'd just said. Leaning closer, Mikkal repeated himself in his ear. "Troll." The tears fell anew as Rakkah choked back, "Piss ant."

<div align="center">~~~~~~~~~~</div>

Maahayyel was watching for just this moment. When Gabriel finally realized why he was there, she'd landed and let him go to the dying man. Now she had to act swiftly on two separate tasks. Would she be able to pull this off? She had to allow the storm of energy to peak, utilizing it at its highest and most potent moment, or she'd not be able to accomplish that which she must. She reached forth when no one was looking. 'Twas almost time. She readied herself to act.

As Mikkal exhaled his last breath and Daynahmyn sighed her own, Maahayyel struck. Her wickedly sharp talon scored Gabriel's thigh as he knelt beside his dying brother. The Blood Call spread out like a fishing net slung o'er the waters, while Maahayyel spit forth a ball of fire upon the wall. Chanting, it grew seven fold. Daynahmyn threw back her head and roared as the sparkling mist covered her, and at the very moment Mikkal Passed, Daynahmyn and Gabriel were shoved through the fire by the growing gale force winds, taking the 'Bond. Only the elder of identical twins could have done this. Only the True King would have been proven in such a manner.

At the same time, the Matriarch used the final and increased burst of energy from the incredible sequence of events to fuel her own Magical transfer. Her wings wide, she beat down upon the castle with furious strokes, the winds buffeting, the walls crumbling, anything not made of solid rock, including the slate tile roofing, was sent flying o'er the cliffs into the Ocean of Fears. The glitter of Allure fell like rain as the King's Agents scurried from the destruction, taking refuge in the other parts of the castle. The storm raged, the ground shook, and the Matriarch's Song rose. All eyes were upon the Dragon when suddenly they heard a female voice screaming o'er the winds, "'Tis working! She rises!"

Racing 'cross the ramparts toward the others was a tall, flaxen haired beauty, sword in hand, determination upon her face. As Rakkah stood up, the girl practically ran headlong into him, panting, pointing her sword toward the center of the winds' destruction. "There! You must help me!"

Stunned, yet happy to see the long lost Warrior, he grabbed her by the shoulders to keep them both on their feet, mana ing to get her attention. "How?" He stood still, listening, preparing himself for another fight, as he waited for an explanation. Abruptly baffled, she realized she had no idea how to help. Staring back at Rakkah she explained the obvious, "'Tis the Princess. 'Tis Synahmarr. She has to get out of the dungeon."

At that instant there came a roaring boom that threw them off their feet, as the entire southern section of Evanntyr exploded, dropping a quarter of the castle down the cliffs and into the Fears. Flying dust and rock hurtled 'cross Port O'Kings, and through the debris could be seen a huge Dragon, her sparkling russet scales glowing brightly with Allure, rising as a Phoenix into the sky, her Flame keeping the Agents at bay. Circling high and then plunging back down, she caught the Matriarch, whom everyone had forgotten in the spectacle of her escape, now limp and falling lifelessly toward Wyndsyr Forest. Synahmarr hovered o'er the castle that was her prison for so long. *"Goldenrod, we shall meet again very soon. You have my eternal gratitude."* Mynx nodded in acknowledgement and surreptitiously wiped the tear from the corner of her eye afore anyone saw. Gazing fondly at the girl, Syn returned her nod then gathered her aunt to her breast and departed swiftly to the northeast, and home.

Daynahmyn, weakened but still very much alive, shook her head to help orient herself, and then leaned o'er her new 'Bond. "We must leave soon. Mount and we shall fly home." Looking down from the wall, they were surrounded by residents from both King's Gate and the castle. All had been witness to the events, and from a growing number of throats could be heard mutterings about the transfer of the 'Bond from one to another as cheers began in the back, voices rising stronger and louder, "Long Live the True King!", and, "With the one's Passing, the other is proven!" Artemis had been busy indeed.

Regynn, his leathers torn and dirty, appeared from the west flying bareback, Sydrayyah's saddle dangling from a tie. He was staggered when he saw the damage to the castle where he'd spent many long winters in deployment on active duty, more from the realization that Synahmarr had been there all that time without anyone knowing, than from the destruction. Surveying the scene for the need to take further action, he noted one Warrior down. 'Twas true, then. He set his jaw resolutely, and stood ready for orders. Gabriel started to mount, then laid his hand gently upon Daynahmyn's muzzle asking for her patience, and stepped to the edge of the wall. 'Twas a sea of hopeful faces upon which he now gazed. Their passion and expectation permeated the very air. Accepting his destiny he raised his arms, weapons in hand, and the cheers grew deafening. The True King claimed his rule.

The prophesy held much hope for the people of Kadoor. To finally discover they might be freed of the oppression which began when Bryard took Koryl as his Queen, only worsening when

Shytin took the throne, would set many the will to fight and bring many more to the Resistance. But then their immediate reality became clear, and as the Agents began to pour forth from the intact portions of the castle, the people scattered and ran. "Time to leave," Gabriel shouted above the roar of the chaos below. He mounted as Rakkah carried Mikkal to Daynahmyn, who's tears fell upon his face, streaking through the grime. Then she and Rakkah shared a moment of silence afore Rakkah handed Mikkal's body to Gabriel and they took wing. Spears and arrows began to fly past them. Petrayyah grabbed Rakkah and Pelayyah grabbed Mynx in their sharp claws, flying them away from the danger, flanked by Regynn and Sydrayyah, and Darque and Gunnarr. Artemis had already left a'foot to reacquire her stash and then make good her own escape the way she'd arrived. Islyth awaited her at the river. Their destination? Drekinn. Once she delivered the Human, Islyth was going home. The Well of Evanntyr was no more. From the well of the Dragon's Den she'd easily access the Sea of Dreams and could then reunite with Myrrdin. They'd been a long time apart, and she wanted to check her treasures.

CHAPTER THIRTY-THREE

The First Born

O'ER TWO MOONS LATER
~~~~~THE LAIR OF THE RESISTANCE~~~~~

Heavy snow fell o'er King's Gate soon after the now legendary events, making travel through the Edge next to impossible for o'er a moon. 'Twas deep winter, but the weather turned relatively mild o'er the past fortnight. In the meantime, King Shytin and his new advisor, the Sorcerer, had not been idle. They'd done the unthinkable. While the Black remained unusually quiet, they'd declared war against the Resistance. Darque and Gunnarr were particularly wanted, alive if possible, but he obviously had no idea that the Dragon Clan and the Warrior Brotherhood yet lived and thrived.

The word spread throughout the land that punishment for assisting the Resistance in any way, shape, or form, was death. Additionally, Gabriel was declared an imposter, the price on his head (preferably upon a stake for all to see) rumored as the highest offer in known history. And with an impact just as heavy, all Kadoor mourned for the Last Dragon Matriarch, as her Passing meant the death of life for the Highlands. However, mayhap 'twas a tad early to predict such a catastrophe, as word was spreading just as quickly that there was a new Matriarch. With no known mate at her side, all prayed for her success.

Rakkah hadn't said more than two words to anyone since Mikkal's funeral pyre the day after their return, and then only in the line of duty. His once rakish smile and mischievous eyes, attracting every female he met, were unmistakably absent. 'Twas a pall o'er the Lair as he carried out his duties without his usual zeal, and rumors were widespread. Few knew the details of what took place upon the battlements of Evanntyr. Darque recorded a simple statement that Mikkal was impaled in the line of duty.
~~~~~

'Twas not a lie, and without naming another, neither Rakkah nor Mikkal would ever be found guilty of breaking their Oath.

All knew the True King had returned and was proven by the exchange of the 'Bond. Mikkal and his sword would be sorely missed and his memory would be a blessing, but his Passing was the only acceptable option after all that transpired. Even so, she'd heard and felt the grief, the regrets, the sorrow. Seeing his body upon the pyre freed Aalanna's memory, but she, Artemis, and Darque forgave him, for they understood he was but a pawn to the evil schemes of a wretched woman who'd pay for her treachery with her life as soon as she was captured. Darque had already sent out Teams to locate the witch, who was now hunted by both sides.

Mikkal had never wanted to hurt anyone, and now he was finally at rest. Rakkah was grateful to his Commander, even though he felt much guilt for Mikkal's death. But just now, he was confounded. After a long duty night, he'd hoped to find some solace by reading, but searching his quarters he couldn't find his mother's diary. Thinking back, he couldn't recall putting it away, and possibly left it out in the open. He'd seen one person coming from his room within the last dawn. Turning back, he walked briskly to that man's quarters.

~~~~~~~~~~

Gabriel's life had turned upside down. At just thirty winters, filled with indescribable grief, he'd been reunited with his twin brother and then lost him within mere moments. Granted, he'd known his destiny for a long time, but he wasn't prepared for the weight of the responsibility he now shouldered. One day he was a 'Gogh Hunter, and now the entire Resistance, including the Dragon Clan, the Warrior Brotherhood, the People of the Daggogh and the Gordatch, along with the Highland Dragons, had sworn him fealty. He was a King, albeit without a throne. Yet. There was no doubt that for many winters to come he'd have to rely heavily upon his rank, most important and highest amongst them being his Battle Commander. Spending several marks
~~~~~~~~~~

nightly with Darque, he didn't think he'd ever remember everything she took for granted, and he marveled at her level of expertise and maturity with only eighteen winters under her belt. Still, the most difficult change was that everyone treated him differently, even the People with whom he'd lived these past many winters. If not for Daynahmyn he'd be alone, but she'd not yet completely recovered from the trauma of the shearing of one LifeBond and the taking of another, and for now he was doing more for her than she could for him. Suddenly he didn't know to whom he could turn. Larken, Matana, Artemis, were all allies, but no one could he single out as his protector, his confidant, his advisor, his true friend. However, even with all these issues, he had other, deeper concerns with which to deal. Like what he'd just read. 'Twas an arresting revelation. Looking up at the sound of someone entering, he spoke afore Rakkah had time to open his mouth, for he knew why his brother was there. "I went to your room to talk. How long have you known your true age?"

The now too familiar sensation of dread wrenched Rakkah's gut as he glanced at the diary in Gabriel's hands. Did he know? Even with his rampant emotions, his voice was steady in response. "You don't mince words. Since reading the diary. Afore that, 'twas only a feeling."

Gabriel was not known to withhold his thoughts. He came straight to the point. "'Twould appear that I am not the First Born after all."

Rakkah was still in denial and stated firmly, "Darque may not have had time to learn the truth, but 'tis no doubt that Grifynn would have known. No word was said, despite the prophesy. And Bryard's declaration bespoke, from the date of the signing 'the first born male child from concubine or Queen' would take his throne."

Gabriel stared in absolute bewilderment. Was his brother being obtuse a'purpose? He stood up and shoved the diary into the other's hands. "Exactly. 'Twas worded exactly thus." And as the sun slowly dawned upon him, Rakkah was speechless. He'd not considered the declaration hadn't specified which mistress and therefore, after the results of Koryl's rampage, his mother the only other pregnant escapee along with the mother of the twins, and being born less than a moon afore them, not a winter as he'd always been told, made him the First Born. He could not refute the facts. Officially, he was the True King.

'Twas silent for awhile as they both considered their futures. Feeling o'erwhelmed at the enormity of the task afore him, the price on his head, the need to unite Kadoor under his leadership while still in retreat, to forcefully take his rightful throne, Gabriel quietly made his offer. "To you alone, I would swear fealty."

Rakkah sighed. He felt his brother's doubts. 'Twould take strong leadership. Gabriel had become the most prime target on all Kadoor, and although he had decent fighting skills, he was no Warrior. He would require assistance, someone he could trust, someone who couldn't be turned against him or the Resistance. Without a shred of indecision, he replied, "I'm no leader, no King. I'm a Warrior, and the Fates knew what they were doing, getting me out of King's Gate when they did. You, on the other hand, have displayed every necessary requirement, along with many desirable ones. You have the courage, commitment, passion, resourcefulness, intelligence, and common sense. You've shown the ability to garner respect and make men willing to die for you without wasting such innate influence, while proving you are just as willing to die for them." Gabriel silently watched his brother, wondering what was going through his mind. He didn't have to wonder for long, as Rakkah continued, "However, I am the one to stand at your back. Who better than I? In case you haven't noticed, the three of us could have been triplets. With little effort I could pass for you, and this gives us an enormous advantage for keeping you safe." Rakkah stroked his chin while pondering the logistics. "'Twill be difficult o'er the next few winters, 'til we get your throne secured. But I'm positive Darque would agree and encourage my choice of such a deployment situation."

Gabriel didn't miss that 'we' and 'us' language. Pleased and grateful, he silently measured the offer. Once this decision was made, it could not be unmade. If Rakkah didn't accept, he'd just lost possibly the best friend he'd ever have. He swallowed hard. "And will you also be my confidant as you were to Mikkal?"

Mention of his brother's name made it difficult to speak. He had to clear his throat twice."Although we were closer than any other in my life, and any whom I could imagine at that time, you, as his twin, would have been closer. Understand that I've let no one read my diary. Not even Mikkal. 'Twas from my mother and tells all, about many things. It speaks of mysteries I have yet to decipher. Nevertheless, seeing it in your hands did not elicit ill will. That should mean something to you." The corners of his mouth turned up slightly.

The two of them faced each other. Not quite as rugged as the buff Warrior, Gabriel was just as handsome and just as tall, his green eyes intense. Anyone would easily mistake the one for the other, with the exception of the cut of their hair. Gabriel had returned to his King's Gate upbringing. He no longer wore paint and was allowing his hair to grow, but 'twould be a few winters catching up. Since his 'crowning' held at the Lair a sennight after Mikkal's funeral, he'd not been refused a single request, however, he'd yet to make a single demand. Now, he had four in mind. The first two were critical to his rule and to garnering support, for the Resistance required cohesion. Regal character oozed forth as he began. "Know that the offer I made earlier is now null and void and shall never be mentioned again. And, I accept your offer to be my personal advisor, defender, confidant, and double. But only if you accept four conditions." Rakkah nodded for him to proceed. "One, you will share the truth with no one as long as I live, under pain of death. Everyone thinks you're a winter my elder, so be it."

Understanding his brother and King just put a death sentence upon him, he was still in full accord, although he wondered if mayhap the man wasn't quite as honorable as he'd originally thought. Crossing his thick arms o'er his chest, he replied warily, "As you say, your Highness."

Gabriel furrowed his brows in distaste for the title, afore he made his second demand. "You must swear that if ever I'm incapacitated or forced Past the Veil, you will ascend your rightful throne."

Although Rakkah truly had no desire to be King, he was secretly pleased with this proof of Gabriel's integrity, and he had to agree with his reasoning. Sighing in relief and plastering a grimace upon his face, he replied, "'Twill strengthen my resolve to keep you alive, m'Liege."

Gabriel scowled at his brother's emerging grin and the flash of mischief returning to his eyes, but was boosted by his approval of the first two conditions. Now came the more personal ones. "You must also accept my offer to be my true friend, as a blood brother."

Rakkah smirked. "We shall ever be both, my King."

In rising apprehension that this time he'd be rejected, Gabriel set forth his final and most important demand. "Lastly, you must not call me King. To you, if no one else, I shall be Gabriel. Just Gabriel."

Rakkah's grin widened as the other's fears dissolved. Clutching his brother to him in a Warrior's grasp, he tousled his hair and winked. "As protocol allows, little brother. As protocol allows."

CHAPTER THIRTY-FOUR

This Could Get Ugly

~~~~~THE KEEP OF ST SWIFTYN'S~~~~~

She'd been sifting through thousands of journals in the Hall of Life for days, and the end results were fairly enlightening. Her initial discovery was that the shelves weren't up to date. There were no new entries or new diaries since approximately thirty winters prior to what was the here and now. 'Twas apparently the time that whatever happened, happened. She started with entries of her own Passing, having little difficulty finding them, and 'twas touching for the most part. She quickly learned of the Last Holocaust and discovered they'd attempted to Call her just prior but encountered some kind of problem resulting in a prophesy telling of her reincarnation. One way or another, the First Warrior would rise again, but 'twas still disappointing. However, after finding little of interest for decades following, even centuries after, she began to see a pattern of evil once again, and focused her senses toward a particular group of journals. 'Twasn't long afore she discovered something blatantly ominous. The hair on her neck would have stood up in prickles if she was capable of such. From those of the Assembly as well as Beryl's own diaries, the woman had 'tutored' her daughter, her granddaughter, her great granddaughter and apparently a great, great granddaughter as well. Beryl and the last of her descendants were inseparable 'til her Passing, which was rumored to have been under mysterious and bloody circumstances. 'Twas described as an accidental fall, witnessed by but one, her great, great granddaughter, for whom she found no mention of death. 'Twas also the way all of the earlier ones Passed the Veil, with Beryl herself being the lone witness. Was she the only person who questioned this bizarre situation, and of Beryl's unusual length of days? But hers was the view of a Warrior, and she saw far more than most.
~~~~~

As she explored further, increasing accounts of unsettling events were recorded by various people within the last generation. According to the entries, many noted mounting mishaps, accidents, abnormal injuries, even the occasional unexplained disappearance, but no one recognized a pattern leading to a cause. There were but a handful of Mystics, with one in particular, who saw the sinister side to Beryl's relationships, who believed that evil had infiltrated the Rashei, and who had attempted unsuccessfully to get their fellow Mystics to believe as did they. She focused upon a woman by the name of Myriam, who'd been somewhat ostracized for her efforts and had withdrawn along with the few others, as their leader. As Myriam's journals became a crucial point of her attention, the reported mysteries and warning signs escalated. She'd befriended the Battle Commander of the Dragon Clan, and the last six moons of her recordings were most grievous. She'd felt strongly that the Evil One had obtained a foothold in the Keep and that something horrible was about to happen.

The wraith mouthed the words as she read the woman's last entry. 'Tis obvious we have been infiltrated and that I am one of very few who see the danger and fear for our future. Our small group have chosen to remain silent and separate from each other, in order to avoid falling to the same mysterious deaths as of some of our fellow believers. Communication is by hand written notes burned upon reading, which to our society is unheard of and therefore, our only secure option. I've been chosen to safeguard the contents of the Lost Room, but I fear I've failed in my duty, managing only thus far to secure the Dragon Sword. But when I reached for the Book, I was unable to remove it from its alcove in the vault, despite my attempt to counter the protection of the Fangs. Mayhap if I remove the Fangs first, 'twill free the Book. I can only hope 'twill not release itself to the one surely coming. I plan to make another attempt as soon as I finish this entry, but if unsuccessful, I shall at least remain vigilant. My daughter has been taken by the Commander for her own protection, fulfilling that part of his promise. I may have to trust in his skill and integrity to fulfill the other. These past few dawns have been the worst of my life and I do not delude myself that I shall ever lay eyes upon Aalanna again. I have thus far managed to conceal her absence from the others, but I think my efforts won't be required much longer. At least she is safe. Whatever is happening, will happen soon. Even the air quakes as a stifling breath in our faces and the sun in the sky appears distorted these past few dawns, yet I can get no one to listen or to see. May Legend forgive us our blind tolerances allowing this to occur, may the Fates be kind, and may we ultimately defeat those who have risen against us.'

The entries stopped there, the journal incomplete, which was odd since she would have filed it herself in such a state. After pondering this, she'd wafted about the Keep and discovered other interesting phenomena. There were unfinished journals in most of the living quarters, and she even found some scattered in various public places, as if dropped midsentence. Rashei were extremely private, and the personal journals of the living were not read by others, but regardless, they would not have been left lying about. And from this was discovered a date that was most likely the last afore the Rashei simply disappeared. She deduced that after making her entry, Myriam filed so as to safeguard her words, and mayhap then went to the Lost Room. 'Twould be her next stop. She spoke of having secured her Dragon Sword. She'd have to search for it within the Keep. But how did she expect to take the Book or the Fangs? 'Twas not as if she could simply walk about with them, she'd apparently never left home, and once they were discovered missing any Mystic could have found them in a focused search. Of course, she could have tried to use blood wax. But if her timing was correct, her final entry was within marks, if not less, of the event. And who was the person they suspected? To name something or someone gave them more control, and therefore, that none of the entries mentioned a name, revealed the depth of their fear of that one. Just like the Black himself, no one had called him by his given name since he rose to power. Yet above all, just how had a huge society of Mystics simply vanished? It had to have been something to do with the Book, something akin to what Beryl did, which caused the destruction of Rienne. So. 'Twas her great, great granddaughter. Suddenly the sun dawned upon her. She'd o'er heard Grifynn speaking to the others about the note he found in Myriam's quarters. 'Betrayed from within', confirmed in her mind that 'twas Koryl's doing. 'Works not alone', and, 'beware the bastard Fay'? Now she understood. Now she knew with whom they were dealing. This could get ugly.

<p style="text-align: center;">~~~~~THE BOOK, THE FANGS, AND THE SWORD~~~~~</p>

Everything was gone; had Myriam been successful, or had Koryl? After finding the Lost Room empty and drifting up from the bowels of the mountain, if the wraith could still spit 'twould turn to Flame, she was so angry. For generations the Rashei had kept safe the most dangerous and sought after possessions in all Kadoor, and now the three most likely to lose them the war in the wrong hands, were missing. The Book of the Conqueror, the four blades known as the Fangs of Solvyngarr, as well as her Dragon Sword. Bound in the actual skin of the Conqueror himself, the book was the keeper of his history and the entire collection of his recipes for death, disaster and destruction. 'Twas believed his eye, stitched into the center of the cover, would open willingly to the most wicked, giving the viewer the ability to read the pages as the Book revealed its secrets in the lost language of his tribe. The Conqueror was the worst of the worst in the time of chaos, coming to power through lies and sheer brutality to lead the evil forces now known as the Hoard, and 'twas even rumored his seed was used to beget the Black through a series of horrifying Spells and experiments, but she'd never believed that. Nonetheless, once the High Counsel rid themselves of his evil, they were stuck with the Book. 'Twas not a book to be allowed to lie about for any to read, but could not be destroyed, either. In the wrong hands 'twould obliterate all Kadoor and therefore, the Rashei were chosen to protect it for time immemorial. They even managed to protect it during the destruction of their ancient homeland.

Then there were the Fangs. She swallowed the pain and caught her breath. Forged in the heart of the volcanic center of Flight of Fire Keep with the actual fangs of the Ancient Highland 7th Prince and General, they had the power to free Sol from eternally wandering nowhere, bringing them back together through their LifeBond. The blades had to be used collectively in order to accomplish this and she couldn't find any one of them. She was the one who saw their potential, who realized they could truly lock the Book from those who would misuse its secrets, because the Fangs had the ability to release, restrain, reveal, or conceal, each Fang having its own special powers. Used together, they were the perfect choice to safeguard the Book. She could only hope the two were not in the same hands. And where was her Sword? It also, could not be destroyed. Where would Myriam have hidden it? She'd attempted to Call it forth, but apparently, having not a solid form, the Sword Answered her no longer. She sighed. 'Twas clear she'd not be able to wield it, so what good would it do her, anyway? 'Twould require a human body to swing the first Dragon Sword on Kadoor, and she abruptly realized who. 'Twas time to find her namesake.

<p style="text-align:center">~~~~~ALONG THE SOUTHERN SLIPPES~~~~~</p>

She needed the Fangs to open the Book, since they'd sealed it after what grandmother Beryl accomplished. But only the First Warrior realized the truth, and Beryl's deeds went unpunished. Now they were in the hands of someone who knew not their history, nor their potential. And, Koryl thought wickedly, 'twas rumored that Darque had already separated them. Thus far, Koryl had tried everything, but the Book's secrets remained a mystery. Having smuggled it from the Keep prior to vacating in order to avoid being caught in the web of the Spell, she'd been disappointed that the Fangs were no longer in their case. She thought she knew how that had happened, but hadn't had the time to confront Myriam, and of course she couldn't contact any of the Rashei now. Carefully, she re-wrapped the Book with cloth, leather, and chain, and then lowered her most valuable possession into the chasm, deep within the cave along the Southern Slippes. They'd never find her or the Book.

Beryl had given her the means to bind Mikkal and elongate her own span of days without the benefit of the LifeBond. Grandmother was so proud that she alone of her ancestors was able to duplicate her accomplishment successfully. Even her own mother had Passed in a most ugly manner, when she'd misread the Spell. Beryl had begun to think 'twas impossible to utilize the words of the Book from without. But more had proven elusive, and Beryl herself succumbed with her granddaughter's success. It seemed that the Book required blood to grant its power, and Koryl had no qualms about providing it that which it wanted. But now she'd set her sights on taking control of all Kadoor, and she had to read the book herself in order to do that.

She walked out of the deep recesses toward the entrance, and gathered her bags. Disguise was child's play. Multiple layers of bright colorful fabrics she wound loosely around her body, pulling back her long brown hair with ornate clips and combs. Then she added the gold necklaces, bells, bangles, and earrings, and left the cave with confidence. Next stop? Tupry. She'd had living quarters there for many winters, establishing herself as a traveling Oracle. The villagers didn't ask questions, everyone minded their own business and looked the other way. She'd appeared often enough to become a familiar personage and wouldn't attract undue attention if she stayed longer this time, especially with all that was happening at Evanntyr, along with the panic caused by the loss of the Dragon Clan. She couldn't appear to have her own money, and her choice of disguise allowed her to make enough coin quickly and with little effort, to pay normal living expenses in the cheap side of town, which was pretty much the entire town.

The only other thing she wanted was the official documentation of Gabriel's birth, for even though the paper could not prove the man, 'twould prove there'd been another and that 'twasn't Shytin and 'twould skew her future away from taking the throne herself, as 'twould give the peasantry hope. Such must be avoided at all costs. It had to be in Evanntyr somewhere, but she'd attempted to locate it for winters without success. Not even her scrying had revealed where 'twas hidden, but the blades could accomplish what she could not. All she had to do was bide her time and gather them. Eventually she'd be unrecognizable to those now living at the castle. Even her own son would age and Pass if not killed first, long afore she. 'Twas entirely possible she'd be able to simply walk in at some point, and search at her leisure. A cruel smile upon her painted red lips, she climbed into the small wagon, her team of horses lathered and snorting despite the chill air, anxious to be away from the cave. They could smell the evil within.

Chapter Thirty-Five

Attack at the Keep

The Sorcerer was furious. He'd lost Koryl, and without her presence 'twas evident that he could no longer use her scrying bowl. He'd also failed to obtain the Eye, failed to capture the child, and ultimately failed to conjure Grifynn, unable to drag his spirit away from Aalanna. The witch was alive and at the Keep. This much he knew, he could feel it in his bones. Leaving the last of the evening's wenches for the Agents to clean up after he'd taken out much anger on her wretched body, he was still angry. The Black hadn't returned but he was out there somewhere, and when he did, the Sorcerer had to have a very special offering to account for how he'd spent the past several moons. He needed to draw Grifynn away from Aalanna, but how?

Storming down the empty halls, as everyone knew to avoid him by now, he found himself approaching the Pits of Hades, and decided to drop in for a visit. 'Twould be calming to his nerves. But after opening the massive iron and oak door, he discovered 'twas vacant and still. Disheartened, he sat on a bench along the far wall, reached o'er head, and fingered the wrist manacles hanging from the stone. Thinking about the victims who'd been secured there in the past, he heard a very slight scratching sound coming from one of the distant cells. 'Twould have been missed if not for the silence. He got up to see who might be there. Then he remembered. His heart beat faster with growing excitement. 'Twas the Eoche. All he had to do was get a Dragon to drop the cage o'er the ward of the Keep. With no other prey available, the starving insect would find her wherever she may try to hide. She'd not be able to move a muscle that the insect couldn't feel, as her every step reverberated through the stone. 'Twould eventually find her and literally eat her paralyzed body. Then Grifynn's spirit would be vulnerable, his capture certain. The Sorcerer laughed feverishly as he ran up the stairs two at a time, to set his plan into motion. 'Twas a possibility that Darque had survived the battle and was protecting her. Therefore, he'd have to Mask the Dragon, for he'd found none loyal to the Hoard thus far, with the will or intelligence to Brew such a Spell on their own. He'd drawn much blood and caused even more fear earlier this night, his desires were well met, the immoral energy thus created giving him all he required to feed his dark Magic.

~~~~~DEEP IN BYNDYNN FOREST~~~~~

After traveling for several days he had the Dragon drop him off leagues away from the Keep, for if Darque or any of the original 'Bonds were still alive they'd feel his presence and he'd not be able to defend himself from their wrath. The danger made him tingle with excitement, but he wasn't stupid. He had no death wish. His instructions clear and simple, the Dragon flew off into a lightly falling sleet. The Sorcerer eagerly awaited his return.

~~~~~~~~~~

The Dragon was greatly fatigued, and flying through the building storm, his wings began to weigh down with the gathering ice. But the Sorcerer promised him special favors for completing this mission. Drooling in anticipation of his reward, he made haste for the Keep, taking care not to allow the tail of the insect to touch him through the tight bars of the cage, nor to be cut by the sharp jaws as the thing tried to bite its way to freedom. He'd not have to wait to see the end result as per the Sorcerer's orders, for he knew the capability of the thing he carried, and he wanted to get back as quickly as possible or he'd be stuck in the storm. He'd simply drop the cage and then return with all haste for his employer, and his reward.

~~~~~THE KEEP~~~~~

Walkyr and Fryya were visiting their friends. 'Twas a much needed rest break for them, but 'twas actually a working retreat,
~~~~~

for they were helping to map St Swiftyn's and they hadn't stopped since their arrival just two dawns prior. Spending their time exploring was fascinating and each new discovery lit up their faces like the fireworks of the Summer Faire.

Fryya had just entered another gathering area within the mountain maze. Wandering off into a separate room, she heard Walkyr's cry and came running. His face contorted in pain, he spit and shook his head to free his voice. "We have to get to the ward NOW!"

"What saw you, Walkyr?"

"I've no idea, but whatever 'tis, 'twas sent for your mother and 'twill kill everyone in its path!"

Drawing their swords, the children sprinted back the way they'd come, retracing their steps as the Seer attempted to describe the creature they'd soon face. Struck with another Vision, Walkyr grabbed Fryya's sleeve and yanked her through a detour that would take them past the Warriors' quarters and get them to the ward in half the time.

~~~~~~~~~~

Torstynn was performing his daily exercise in the ward, walking with the 'assistance' of several of the children, who all loved to spend time with him, encouraging his efforts. 'Twas humbling. Leaning heavily on the cane his brother hand carved, he winced with each step. Still very weak, he'd not be able to fight again for some time to come, although he'd already begun some easy training. Self absorbed in sobering thoughts, he became distracted by a strange whistling sound coming from far o'erhead.

~~~~~~~~~~

Aalanna was assisting the Master Educator by preparing lessons for the children. Sitting along the outer wall, soaking up the last of the sunshine breaking through the clouds in the chill morning, she knew 'twould come heavy snow very soon. Suddenly she shivered, but 'twas not from the chill air, 'twas with a sense of impending danger. Dropping the lesson plans to the ground, she jumped up and cast her sight around the ward. She noticed Torstynn as he jerked painfully, positioning himself to look upwards, and she turned her face toward the sky.

~~~~~~~~~~

Master Tyrza was below, teaching a class on artifact recognition with the rest of the children. Bynner and his little sister Kryn, two of the youngest of her charges, had snuck out to see Torstynn with the group on duty, even though 'twas not their turn. 'Twould not go without consequences but she couldn't blame them for wanting to be with the Warrior. His personal journey was an inspiration to them all. His strength, courage, and lack of complaints, served as a life lesson that every setback could be o'ercome and hard work was its own reward, an example upon which they all held tight. He was a solid pillar standing against the uncertainty and shifting sand of their existence, and could make even the most home sick smile again with his easy laughter and carefree manner.

~~~~~~~~~~

Tyrrsyn and Raynah had been working on an inventory of their supplies and were heading back up to the ward. They didn't like leaving Tor alone for long, despite no evidence of eminent attack since the relocation. But he'd insisted he was capable of at least helping them keep watch, and they did have much to accomplish. They'd only been gone for about a mark. Sauntering into the open, waving to get Tor's attention, they saw him look up just afore they heard the whistling.

~~~~~~~~~~

Something was wrong. Torstynn stared into the skies and although he couldn't tell what 'twas, he knew what 'twas not. For sure 'twas not a supply drop and therefore, 'twas an attack. He ordered the children to take cover and all did as they were told, immediately scrambling for the closest wall. All except for the little
~~~~~~~~~~

girl in the middle of the ward not far from where he stood. Stock still in the shadow of the falling box, she couldn't decide which way to run. Tor decided. He had but a few heartbeats to save her. He limped toward the terrified child while her slightly older brother (who'd been attempting to return to class) finally realized she wasn't at his side, and ran 'cross the ward as well. The box fell faster and faster, close enough now to see 'twas an iron cage of some kind. Yelling at his fellow Warriors for back up, they were already racing toward them, swords raised. Tyrrsyn watched in horror as his most recent nightmare replayed, his heart pounding out of his chest knowing that this time he'd be too late. Tor was approaching the child as the cage came closer, clearly intending to protect her with his own body. No doubt 'twould send the injured Warrior Past the Veil this time, but 'twas not his way to waver when the lives of others were at stake.

Fate had them all on a path of convergence, Bynner running toward them from the north, Tyr and Raynah from the south, Aalanna trying to get to them from the western wall, when suddenly out from the east burst Walkyr and Fryya. They were closest, and as Tor reached the child they had but a candle drip left. Diving forward, the Warrior shoved Kryn toward Fryya who grabbed her, pulling her out of harm's way at the same time that Walkyr leaped o'er them both with the Thumper he'd snatched from Raynah's quarters. Together, he and Tor ducked under it just as the cage hit, glancing off the shield to land heavily on one corner beside them, breaking open and releasing the frenzied insect within.

~~~~~~~~~~

Bynner saw that Kryn was safe, but knew something horrible had just landed upon the Warrior and the Clan Seer. Without missing a step he diverted his course to tell Master Tyrza, who'd heard the commotion and met him at the gate. All the children ran close behind, all armed. What she saw upon entering the ward was a nightmare in action. Fryya hustled Kryn to Aalanna afore returning to help protect her friends. Tor was again in-
~~~~~~~~~~

jured, his leg wound partially reopened and bleeding freely, a new one on his left side. Walkyr quickly realized his sword would be next to useless and he was valiantly protecting Tor with the Thumper as they discovered the stinger couldn't penetrate, but it could go around or under. Tyr and Raynah fought the insect with their swords but the exoskeleton could not be cracked or pierced, seemingly as hard as the scales of a Highland. The insect was the offensive player here, and for the first time in their careers they were fighting entirely defensively. The best they could manage was to avoid being stung. 'Twas incredibly fast and it took both of them to keep from being struck by that tail. Fryya couldn't find an opening, staying along the outside to try to herd them away from the entrance to the Keep proper, where the children were building a barrier as a secondary defense. After assisting Aalanna and Kryn to the rising blockade, she'd then turned her efforts to clear the way for Tor and Walkyr, as they slowly and painfully made their escape. The tail was more flexible than 'twould appear, and she discovered it could strike in any direction at any time. As the long moments turned to half a mark, Tyr, Raynah, and Fryya encircled it to keep it busy while they tried to find a weak point, but there seemed none. Each of them were well aware they couldn't keep this up forever.

<div style="text-align:center">~~~~~~~~~~</div>

Tyrza felt a sense of familiarity upon seeing the insect. Not that she'd ever seen one afore, but she'd read about it once, a very long time ago. What was it? How could it be killed? She ran to help Walkyr drag Tor out of the middle of the action. Once he was safe, Walkyr returned to the fray, while Tyrza racked her brain for the life saving information. Pulling loose the strip of fabric she used to tie back her hair, she wrapped his leg, and while Tor applied pressure she ripped another strip from the bottom of her long tunic. Folding it into a thick pad, she placed it on the rib wound and had him use his other arm to squeeze it tight. That was when Walkyr screamed.

"Fryya!" The young Seer was deathly pale, so terrified was he, as the stinger came within a handbreadth of his best friend, knocking her to the ground. 'Twas a brutal fight and they were all getting tired. 'Twas inevitable they'd begin making mistakes, their reflexes already slowing. Walkyr suddenly turned to the Master Educator, a bewildered look upon his face. His Vision made no sense. Putting his hands upon his temples, he beseeched, "Pain? 'Tween the eyes?" He stared at her, willing her to help him understand, for he was certain 'twas that which they required to kill the insect. But he just couldn't find the words, for this was truly such a foreign subject. His lack of winters might cost them their lives and he became more than frustrated as he struggled for a logical interpretation of what he'd Seen.

Tyrza's eyes lit up. His cues helped her to recall the information they needed. 'Twas an Eoche, and they had no eyes. The bumps mistaken for such were actually the two halves of its brain with a single connection 'tween them, which if cut, would cause instant death. And, there was a small soft spot the size of a coin that sat 'tween those 'eyes', which if hit directly and deeply, would sever the connection. The only problem was hitting that spot. The Eoche used its tail like a shield, and 'twas too small for their swords to pierce even if they could get close enough. Abruptly, she grabbed Tor's dagger and yelled to Walkyr, "Cover me!" Then she ran towards the fight. Walkyr realized what she was trying to do, as her revelations spilled forth to his mind. Using the Thumper, he taunted the insect to keep the tail busy. The Warriors and Fryya stepped back, so as not to distract the insect or the Master, as much as to catch their breath and prepare to continue if she failed. Tyrza came within striking distance, and if the thing should turn its attention to her, it appeared she'd have no ability to defend herself from a most horrifying death. They all held their breath as Master Tyrza, dagger ready, stood perfectly still, poised to strike. Suddenly the insect turned toward her and she threw, the blade leaving her hand with incredible speed.

CHAPTER THIRTY-SIX

From the Bog to Darkling

~~~~~O'ER A MARK PRIOR~~~~~

Bryynn was so squashed he could hardly breathe. He began to grow the instant the Egg cracked, and maintaining the internal pressure was taking all his strength. He couldn't continue for much longer. Even having withdrawn all outside efforts in order to keep out the muck, 'twas clear he'd soon lose the battle. When Gunnarr tossed him 'cross the Sea of Dreams he'd Warned him to stay put 'til he was Called forth, but very soon the choice would be taken out of his talons. Talk about dreadful timing. He could only hope by his ancestors that 'twas not a bad omen to follow his entire span of days. But those days weren't looking to be very long at the moment and he really could use a little help.

'Twas terribly frustrating to know that his brothers had actually been so close when his shell began to fail. However, then and now, if he attempted to Call, or to Push his distress into the cosmos, he'd lose pressure, the waters of the Bog would flood the Egg, and he'd drown. But if he didn't do something soon, he'd lose his ability to maintain the pressure, and the Egg would flood, and he'd drown. Same end result. Ahhh, decisions. When did he want to face the Veil? Now? Later? As 'twas apparent he was on his own, he made his choice. If he waited, he'd have no strength left to try to survive. Releasing the pressure, he pushed all four legs outward against the shell as hard and as fast as he could. The shell split in two, the water immediately surrounding him. He opened his eyes and watched an air bubble as it rose upward, giving him a direction towards which to swim, but he was so weak, so uncoordinated, he could make no progress through the thick layer that covered the surface. So close. If he didn't take a breath soon...
~~~~~

And then something completely unexpected occurred. A Dragon fell into the Bog, just missing him. He did the only thing he could. He latched onto the edge of its wing as it rolled through the muck, and held on tightly 'til the cold air of the surface kissed his face. He felt the foreign Allure covering the beast like a second skin and let it soak into his body, absorbing all he could in order to prevent his own Passing. Gasping, filling his burning lungs with his first real breath, he was flung off onto solid ground in exhaustion, watching his unlikely rescuer gather himself and launch into the sky just as a huge Green came barreling toward them, spitting Flame. Bryynn tucked his tail, and trying to see what was happening o'er his shoulder, he wrapped his wings tightly around himself and scurried away from the incoming stream of death, only to slam into a rock, knocking himself dizzy. 'Twas his brother Mystynn up there fighting the Hoard Dragon, and since he couldn't help, he didn't need to add any complications. Digging underneath the far side of the boulder, he crawled into the shallow space and ensured he was completely hidden from aerial view afore deciding enough was enough. Utterly worn out, he marveled at the fact that he'd survived his rather harrowing initiation to Kadoor, and as he lost consciousness he wondered if 'twould be his last day, or the first of many.

<center>~~~~~A FEW MARKS LATER AT THE KEEP~~~~~</center>

Everyone tried to speak at once. Torstynn's voice was the first to ring out. "I've never seen a more accurate throw on a moving target." 'Twas quickly followed by Raynah. "'Twas a thing of beauty," she stated in wonder. Aalanna replied, "She's the finest blade thrower I've ever known." With admiration in his eyes as he gazed in wonder at the Master, Tyrrsyn added, "I don't know anyone who could've made that shot, let alone under such circumstances." Tor's eyebrows raised as he gaped at his brother. He'd never seen that look on the other's face afore. Ever the loner, Tyrrsyn had hardly noticed a woman in winters, his last relationship somewhat less than satisfying and having ended on a sour note. Waggling his eyebrows and with a knowing grin, he turned his gaze to Raynah, and she winked in agreement with his thoughts.

Tyrza wasn't used to such praise, after all, she was no swordsman, she just happened to enjoy throwing blades and had been doing so all her life. After seeing the opening, she'd thrown and hit with deadly precision, the insect dropping instantly. Walkyr was fearless in his taunts, placing himself at great risk, but without him she believed they'd not have succeeded. They made a good team. Chynnar had the carcass taken to her study to dissect. They were extremely careful as even though 'twas dead, the body of the Eoche twitched occasionally and the stinger still contained exceedingly potent venom. Chynnar hoped to harvest that venom and have it ready to deliver to the Commander, whom they expected soon. Tyrza was happy to have been there at the right moment, and to have remembered about the Eoche, but from whence had it come? 'Twas obviously transported by a Dragon. Aalanna questioned Grifynn, who agreed with Walkyr's Sight that 'twas sent for her, but she still had no idea as to why. At least everyone was safe. All injuries turned out to be relatively minor, including Tor's. There was no indication that 'twas more than an isolated attack, and the Battle Commander and her Second were due any moment on a routine status check. They were actually late, and Darque would be disappointed that she missed the action.

<div align="center">~~~~~AT THE EDGE OF THE BOG~~~~~</div>

Several marks later, Bryynn awakened. Stiff, sore, and cramped, at first he thought he was still in the Egg. Once his memory sluggishly returned, he squirmed out from under the rock and peered around. 'Twas relatively safe, but he couldn't sense his brothers and had no idea where they might be now. After his earlier encounter, 'twas clear the enemy was close as well. 'Twould be wise to stay hidden and be careful. 'Twould also be wise not to try to Call in case he was in Hoard territory, 'til he could do some recognizance. Unable to put up much of a fight for at least several moons, he needed to grow and gain strength. He couldn't even fly yet.

Stretching, he wrinkled his nose. What in the name of the gods was that dreadful stench? Casting his senses this way and that, he dismissed the Bog itself as the surface was no longer disturbed. Eventually he lifted his wing to his nose. Oh. 'Tis me, he thought. He was famished, but first he'd need to find a clean source of water and take a bath. Mayhap then he might be able to secure a meal. At least his prey (or any Hoard Dragons around) wouldn't be able to smell him coming from a league distant. Waddling away on shaky legs, his head turned to and fro, his eyes taking in everything. The colors! The smells! The sounds! The... HOLE! Abruptly finding himself upside down, gaping into the cloudy skies above, his short legs pawing in thin air, 'twas clear he'd have to watch where he was going, but he couldn't have seen it under the snow even if he had been, so he forgave himself. At least there was no witness, as such clumsiness was a tad embarrassing. Climbing out and grateful he'd not injured anything, off he wobbled again, determined to get as far away from the Bog as possible afore night fell.

~~~~~SOMEWHERE DEEP WITHIN DARKLING FOREST~~~~~

Corbyn perched upon the leather clad shoulder of Caleichante as she cleaned her weapons. Stretching out his left wing, he preened in the last of the flickering firelight. He had much on his mind of late. Although the Mighty Maahayyel was successful in passing her rule and saving Synahmarr, the death of life was still a possibility given the greatest hurdle had yet to come. 'Twould take cautious and considerate handling to accomplish his ultimate goal, for there was more to the Death of Life prophesy than just the rise of the Phoenix. Ahhh, he loved a challenge.

He sensed Bryynn's hatching but wasn't close enough to go to his assistance, and was much relieved to confirm he was in-
~~~~~

deed safe after some initial difficulty. The 7th Prince showed much cleverness and common sense in his escape from the Bog. Corbyn used up a great deal of energy keeping tabs on the little hatchling 'til finally losing him. If he kept to his last route, he'd soon reach Ice Mist Falls. 'Twas good. He'd not tell anyone yet. The fewer who knew he'd hatched, the better. 'Twould be only a handful who could've sensed the event, and it seemed that none but he were currently aware. Bryynn had entered into a war torn era and would have to learn how to survive on his own. The Raven tucked his wing back in place and continued his line of thought. Personal experience was always the best teacher. Bryynn was safer alone in the deep of Byndynn than he would've been anywhere else, even with a bodyguard. No spy could betray him if none were aware of his existence. Although the region around the Bog was the warmest in the entire forest, Highlands could not freeze. They were just more comfortable, and less cranky, when warm. Gazing at his companions, 'twas but two others who knew where the 7th Egg was buried, and they'd not know of his current status, nor would they reveal the location. Per their request, he'd seen to that. All others would continue searching for it, and as 'twas still buried deep in the Bog...

He sighed. Corbyn had no problem with leaving Bryynn to his own devices as he'd be able to find him whenever he chose. However, the search would leave a trail of Allure which would compromise his safety. When the Dragon was ready, 'twould be a different story altogether. Keeping his secret would give him time to mature, and then he could gather Bryynn to the fold. Best scenario, he'd learn to fly afore he was discovered and forced to openly join the Resistance. Musing further still, he realized that the little Dragon was so filthy he'd not even been able to discern his color, and he was most curious. 'Twas a pity.

The Elven girl stepped gracefully out of the tent, distracting him from his thoughts. Anastasia was the youngest of her rather large family, a striking child with long, rich brown hair and glittering brown eyes, characteristically pale skin, and possessing wisdom above and beyond her mere dozen winters. She walked o'er to them, saying, "The Prince is still asleep." The Warriors glanced up at her words. The voices of Elves were as wind chimes amid the rustle of leaves in the breeze to Human ears, lyrical, melodic, and mesmerizing. Although they'd been in the company of adult Elves for some time, the youth's voice was still captivating. Sitting on a log beside the fire, she finger combed her hair, and then with practiced ease, swiftly braided it in multiple lengths and directions, entwining and looping 'til she had an intricate circlet with layers flowing down her back.

Calei viewed her with approval. "Good, he needs all the sleep he can get. And you may call him Kevon," she added with a wink, amused at the child's blush.

Anastasia studied their company. Although 'twas her choice to be here, she'd been concerned of her reaction to such strangeness. The father and son Warriors, the Sprite Captain, the Fay, the tall Elven girl with black hair and silver gray eyes who'd become her mentor, all sat quietly staring into the dying coals of the fire. Having never been around any but Elves afore, Ana marveled at both their differences and similarities, and it gave her much hope that they'd find her brother and succeed in their mission, of which she played a surprising part. No fears, she thought, only a feeling of rightness in her spirit. She tilted her delicately pointed ear toward the tent, her almond eyes glistening with Allure. "He wakes."

"Here, take this plate and encourage him to eat, he needs his strength to continue the journey." Calei handed her the last of the rabbit and steamed roots to share with the Prince. When she'd gone, the Captain faced their small group. "Some of us leave home, some return home, some have no home, but we each serve a purpose together, what we've found is vital, and 'tis no doubt 'twill be much needed. We must move quickly."

The Warriors nodded in agreement, then all looked to the Elf, staring quietly into the fire. Her arms wrapped tightly around herself to ward off the cold, she answered their unspoken question. "I am pulled to the Keep of St Swiftyn's. We can push through and winter there, but the weather will be a problem for Kevon and Ana."

Hearing her name, Anastasia stepped forth from the shelter where she'd just finished helping Kevon eat his meal. All eyes were now upon the child as she looked from one to the next then back to her mentor. Leaning forward with hand held out, palm upwards, the elder Elf asked her question. "What say you, Ana? What do you hear?"

Ana considered for the barest of moments, listening carefully. "'Tis as drums rolling in from Beyond. Fast, heavy, and building." The other nodded approvingly.

Calei stood up and began to rake out the coals. The others followed her lead, swiftly and efficiently breaking down their campsite. Dawn was upon them and a massive blizzard was rapidly approaching. They had to get out of Darkling.

Convergence

LATER THAT DAY
~~~~~THE KEEP OF ST SWIFTYN'S~~~~~

Huge wet flakes of snow fell heavily, making it more difficult to travel a'Dragonback and 'twas already too dangerous to travel a'horseback or a'foot. 'Twould be a hard end to winter, but with the Dragons they were no longer completely snowbound 'til the Spring Melts. Still, 'twas not safe to fly in a blizzard such as was coming. The ice would build up and weigh down their wings, making flight treacherous at best, impossible at worst. Darque stood in the tower at the southern wall, searching the skies for incoming, but she'd been so doing for marks and thus far had seen no distortions against the shimmering white curtain. Third Fighters Kydra and Ragnyrr were in Command at Drekinn, the People splitting their forces 'tween the two locations. And with Rakkah in charge at the Lair, the True King was in good hands. Nevertheless, they'd need to depart soon or be stuck for who knew how long. Still, she had an unusual sense that mayhap they had a mission here as yet undisclosed by the One.

She, Gunnarr, Mystynn and Storrm were traveling to the Keep for a status visit ahead of the blizzard when an invisible Hoard Dragon flew into them headlong o'er the Bog. His Mask bespoke 'twas the Sorcerer's doing, for the beast could not have accomplished such a feat on his own. Mysteriously, when he fell into the Bog after they tangled midair, the Mask disappeared as if something in the marsh fouled the Magic. She'd have to investigate when they returned, if the incoming weather didn't erase whatever evidence might reveal the answers. Her Second finished the intruder while she flew on to the Keep to discover an iron crate carrying an Eoche had been dropped into the ward. 'Twas most likely the creature's mission. The insects were extremely rare and she couldn't understand how 'twas obtained, but she was gratefully agitated for could have had much worse results. Aalanna, and who knew how many of the children, would have died a horrible death if not for the skill, bravery, and quick actions of all, including Tyrza, Fryya, and Walkyr. As 'twas, they suffered no casualties. She was quite proud of the children as well, for they'd mounted an immediate and collective defense.

Mystynn brought in the carcass of the Dragon for salvage, but what did it all mean? Had the Sorcerer actually known the Keep was now occupied once again, or was it truly an assassination attempt on Aalanna, as the Seer and Grifynn suggested? The Dragon obviously knew not about the Bog and 'twould have been difficult to Call during their fight, but 'twas possible he sent a Call prior, informing his master of the current occupied status of St Swiftyn's, had such been noted. There was no way to know where the Sorcerer had been, either. Was he somewhere in the forest even now, waiting for the Dragon to return to fly him back from whence they came? This notion had her Teams out in force at this very moment, searching any possible landing area where he might be hiding, the Lair on high alert, but the weather would curtail their search soon. Had he been in contact with the creature, or was he too far away to Hear? All she knew for certain was that the Sorcerer sent the Dragon and that he wanted to hide him, which showed 'twas possible he knew about the Lair. If he thought Aalanna protected, 'twould also be reason for the Mask, and the Dragon could truly have stumbled upon them by chance. But any way she looked at it, 'twould only give them two extra moons at best if he didn't know, for surely when his emissary failed to return, he'd investigate.

She'd Heard from Brannyn a dawn past but 'twas naught to do with this attack. The Sorcerer was proving himself as impulsive as was the High King, and stood always at his side. She'd learned he was furious that his ambushed contingent had not returned with Fryya or the First Born, and Brannyn had heard nothing since they'd left. Apparently the Sorcerer was contemplating his next move when he orchestrated the strike at St Swiftyn's. Regardless of the multitude of possibilities, 'twas clear that not only would the Keep soon be compromised, so might the Lair. 'Twould leave the True King exposed as well as the rest under her protection. She had to pull that rabbit out of the hat. She was the answer to the prophesy and would never surrender, but she'd not turn down a little help, either. "I'm in desperate need of a solution, m'Liege. Guide me," she pleaded, staring into the heavy snow, her arms crossed o'er her chest to keep from shivering.

Suddenly the hair on the back of her neck stood up with the sensation that someone was right behind her. Spinning around, she came face to face with a slightly elder version of herself. Darque had never been startled into slow reactions, but this time she was frozen in place, Sword in hand, mouth open. The wraith-like woman cocked her head and stared back afore she began to speak. Her voice was crystal clear, authoritative, and sounded much like her own. However, it seemed to come from a great distance, her accent was heavier, and the words she used were archaic. Darque squinted and bit her bottom lip with the effort to decipher what was as close to Ancient Tongue as she'd heard in ages, and she'd not have understood anything if not for her experiences with the Highlands o'er the past two winters. In order to their histories in the ancient manuscripts within the archives, Gunnarr was tutoring her in their 'spare time'. Thinking about how those sessions usually ended, she blushed. The spirit knew what she was thinking and raising her eyebrows, she smiled and nodded with approval. Darque sensed she faced possibly the strongest and most influential ally they'd ever have, and gathering her wits she asked the woman to repeat herself, slowly.

"I said, my name is Darque Abriya D'Rienne. I've been watching you, and I believe you are my namesake. Not only could we have been twins, you're the same age as was I, when I began the fight. Furthermore, you're the Commander of the Dragon Clan, and lifemate of Gunnarr the Mighty Blue, grandson of Solvyngarr. 'Tis as it should be." She tossed her long hair o'er her shoulder afore continuing, her voice becoming more intense. "I sense a convergence of both good and evil approaching the Keep. Come. We have much to discuss and little time to act."

THUS ENDS THE DEATH OF LIFE

Look for Further Adventures, and Answers, in:
Search for the Wyrdritch, Darque Legends Book 3

Long Live Darque and the Dragon Clan!

Author's Bio

Born in Connecticut and raised in the Midwest, Derrien Relyea grew up fascinated with mythology, Viking lore and Dragons. Her vivid imagination was kindled by her highly creative family, encouraging a love of writing and fantasy. She worked her way through Oklahoma City Community College with degrees in Occupational Therapy and Therapeutic Recreation, and later graduated from The University of Oklahoma Health Sciences Center with a degree in Physical Therapy.

Taking her cue from an exciting genealogical history and such authors as Anne McCaffrey, Edgar Rice Burroughs, and Sir Arthur Conan Doyle, she has embarked upon a new adventure in her life. Please join her at:

http://thedragonwarrior.com

Kudos and credit to my friend and accomplished artist, Lisa Dixon:

http://www.lisadixonart.com